From the author of *Fragments and The Game*
ML WISSING

Lost in Shadow

Remember to seek the Light through the Shadows!
Happy reading!
ML Wissing

THE WORLD OF HINESTRA

Copyright © 2023 ML Wissing
ISBN Paperback 978-1-961078-44-4
ISBN Hardback 978-1-961078-45-1
ISBN e-Book   978-1-961078-46-8

All rights reserved. No part of this book may be reproduced or transmitted in any form or by any means, electronic or mechanical, including photocopying, recording, or by any information storage and retrieval system without express writt en permission from the author, except in the case of brief quotations embodied in critical reviews and certain other non-commercial uses permitt ed by copyright law.

Printed in the United States of America.

Springer Literary House LLC
6260 Lavender Cloud Place
Las Vegas, Nevada 89122, USA

www.springerliteraryhouse.com

Carl, Seth, and Mike: without you, this world would have never been created and lived for so long within my mind.

David, Jacob, Chris, CJ, Logan, and Indigo: you all unknowingly grew this world through our games; I can't wait for you to read what you helped create. You've all been so supportive.

Jacob and Duke: thank you for inspiring me to write again and keeping me accountable in and out of the fantasy world.

Mama and Carl: your countless hours helping me have made this book what it is today through constant encouragement, edits, and keeping my head grounded when it gets too crazy with ideas.

To my readers, I hope that you enjoy this book as much as I enjoyed writing it. I am privileged and excited to begin sharing this world with you!

"Kruger nods."

A NOTE FROM THE AUTHOR

This book you hold started as creating a new world for a role-playing game I was running. I had no idea this world would live in my head for many years, even after the games had ended.

Now, after four table-top role-playing games in this world and almost ten years of writing and brainstorming, I present what I hope to be several books based in the world of Hinestra.

This has been a long process, with trial and error, revisions, and long periods of writer's block, but through it all, I held onto the belief that this book would become a reality.

Never give up.

— ML Wissing

ALSO BY ML WISSING

STANDALONE BOOKS
Fragments

The Game

WITH AMBER NP MAYS
To Hell and Back (The Darkness Calls: Book 1)

ANTHOLOGY
Healing Words: A Journey Through the Ladder Upp

Find these books' purchase links, as well as more information on both ML Wissing and her books on her website:

www.MLWissing.weebly.com

TIMELINE

WAR OF THE TURNING LEAVES
BYRONIAN ERA
REIGN OF SHADOW
Lost in Shadow

HASTA'KAN RANKING

One/First **hon** Hon-Hasta'kan ik' Blagdon

    Two/Second **kon** Kon-Hasta'kan ik'Halidesh

    Three/Third **kun** Kun-Hasta'kan ik'Blackmont

    Four/Fourth **kik** Kik-Hasta'kan ik'Branial

Five/Fifth **ero** Ero-Hasta'kan ik'Remhold

Six/Sixth **eri** Eri-Hasta'kan ik'Shealbri

    Seven/Seventh **eshi** Eshi-Hasta'kan ik'Armtomb

    Eight/Eighth **yako** Yako-Hasta'kan ik'Rutherrene

Nine/Ninth **tira** Tira-Hasta'kan ik'Caulmer

Ten/Tenth **takir** Takir-Hasta'kan ik'Nicholnor

Eleven/Eleventh **treya** Treya-Hasta'kan ik'Carrait

Twelve/Twelfth **tribya** Tribya-Hasta'kan ik'Livingnor

SHADESE LANGUAGE

Shadese has 6 vowel sounds: **a** |ah|, **e** |eh|, **i** |ee|, **o** |oh|, **u** |oo|, **yr** |yeer|. Shadese has contestant sounds: b, d, g, h, k, l, n, p, r, s, t, v, x, y (x is only found at the end of a word)

Some words in the Common language do not exist in the Shadese Language, as the *ro'*Shadon deem them unnecessary, such as **a**, **the**, **is**, and **are**.

Shadese has two forms, formal and informal. Formal speech is used with those of social standing, such as lords, ladies, *belvash*, and the *Kolotor'ix*.

Informal does not use the words **I** and **you**, for it is understood by whom the speaker is speaking to.

- Formal example: "*Shiresh kotu jakeitra khar,*" he said, gesturing to the other Lord he spoke with. ("I will see you tomorrow.") [lit. "tomorrow I will see you"]
- Informal example: "*Shiresh jakeitra,*" he said, gesturing to his friend. ("I will see you tomorrow.") [lit. "tomorrow will see."]

In Common, nouns have two Grammatical Numbers; Singular and Plural. In Shadese, there are Singular, Plural, and All.

- The plural of a Shadese word is denoted by taking the first vowel and turning it into an **e**.
- Example: *hasta* (house), *hesta* (houses).
- "All" are denoted with the prefix **ro'**.
- **Ro'** is always attached to the plural form of the noun.
- Example: *ro'hesta* (all of the houses).

Verbs have three tenses: Past, Present, and Future.

- Past tense is denoted with **-as** at the end of the word, which replaces the last vowel of the word.
- Example: *natshi* (attack), *natashas* (attacked)
- The future tense is denoted with **ja-** in the beginning of the word.

    Example: *ja'natshi* (will attack)

SHADESE LEXICON

This list comprises the Shadese words that appear in the book alphabetically.

-kyr "Death of", "end of." It is also used at the end of the name of someone who has passed away.

-nyta "no", "not" Also attached to a verb or noun to make it negative.

-on "People of" [Example: Nar'Shadon, "People of Nar'Shada", Shadon "People of Ash"]

'ix "leader of". This follows the noun in which the person is the leader. Example *kolotor'ix, hesta'ix, hestakan'ix, balvash'ix*.

balad "blood"

balutrae "blood foe," "rival". Plural is *belutrae*.

balvash "blood sister", females who bear the Sigil of Blood Plural is *belvash*.

balvash'ix "Leader of the blood sisters", also known as Blood Matrons, leaders of the Blood Temple. Plural is *belvash'ix*

brak'ha "Father." Plural is *brek'ha*

ero "Five," "Fifth"

hasta "House". Shadon society is based upon Houses. Plural is *hesta*.

hasta'heh "medium house", Minor House. These fall under the *Hesta'kan* and act as buffers between those lower than them and the *Hesta'kan*. Plural is *Hesta'kan*.

Hasta'kan "House large," "Major House." This is the only instance of *hasta* that is capitalized. Plural is *Hesta'kan*.

hasta'yo "small house", Lesser House. These are the lowest of nobility and answer to the higher *hesta'heh'ix* and *Hesta'kan'ix*. Plural is *hesta'yo*.

hin "Son". Plural is *hen*

hin ik'san "son of mine", "my son"

hon "one", "first"

ik' "of" Used to show possession. Example *hasta ik'Blagdon* (house of Blagdon), *ik'san* (of me/mine)

kar "you"

kava "go"

kavasta "follows," Literally "go after"

kavasha "improve", "going well". Literally "go good"

kishtu "honor"

kiv "This". Plural is *kev* (these)

kiv-kyr "This ends", "the end of this"

kolar "color"

koldraka "shadowsteel", a rare metal that few have seen, and even fewer have items created from it.

Kolosae-ro'ja'aritas "The Shadow who has eaten, eats, and will eat all things". *Ro'*Shadon reveres it as

a diety that lends them their power in the form of Sigils of Shadow.

kolotor "shadow"

Kolotor'ix "Leader of the Shadow" This is the title of the Shadon King; it is always capitalized.

kolvorvik a carnivorous horse-like creature hailing from Nar'Shada. They are used in battle as warmounts. Plural is *kelvorvik*.

kolvorkav a carnivorous horse-like creature hailing from Nar'Shada. They are bred for speed and are used as scouting or racemounts. Plural is kelvorkav.

kotu "I"

korrati "commander". Plural is *kerrati*

kreva "consort" Plural is *kreve*.

kriss'ix "soldier leader"; "captain". Plural is *kress'ix*.

nar' "from", this is used for places.

Nar'Shada "from ash", the homeland of the Shadon, also the name of the capital located there. The name refers to the legend of Thraxxis.

nar'shadon "people from ash", those born in Nar'Shada who have no Sigil upon their bodies. Like Shadon, this word has no plural form.

nogut "fool". Plural is *negut*.

nyr "lie", "false"

ro- the Shadese grammatical number for "all". It is used with the plural form of the verb.

Example: ro'Shadon "all of the Shadon"

sae- "one who", placed in front of the verb

san "me", "mine"

scrivik "fight"

scrivik'yo "little fight", "duel"

sesha "mother" Plural is *Seshe*.

shada "ash." Plural is *sheda*.

shakolar "white", a combination of "ash" and "color"

sholta're A greeting used after midday, but before twilight

sri' "old, older, elder"

sri'balvash "elder blood sister", a *belvash* of second rank. Plural is *sri-belvash*.

yok "that"

LOST IN SHADOW

PROLOGUE

Bells rang across the elvish-inspired capital of Meridiah City, growing louder as more bell towers joined in. Within the central wall that encircled the Light's District, the tolling echoed down the marble hallways of the nearby palace, interrupting the usual day-to-day lives of those working inside. Confused, the civilians stopped and listened momentarily before something more critical caught their attention: armored guards running down the halls, unsheathing their swords as they shouted for them to get out of their way.

"There's an attack! Defend the royal family!" Two groups of Byronian guards rushed past shocked and worried servants, causing them to scatter toward the nearest doors and alcoves. Shadows darkened around the hall in their wake, flowing like velvet ribbons as they gathered and formed figures adorned in black and crimson leather armor. The newcomers' boots had barely formed on the floor before the assassins fell upon the second group of guards, stabbing their quarry from behind with sharpened blades. The commotion of the armored bodies collapsing to the stone floor made the first group of guards turn as they realized, much too late, that something was dreadfully wrong.

"Shadon assassins!" The guards rushed at their adversaries with swords and shields ready, and the sounds of swords clashing rang down the hall in heated exchanges. The leather-armored figures dispersed into shadows, Byronian swords passing through the remains of darkness harmlessly as the assassins reappeared behind the guards, blades expertly slitting throats and finding vulnerable parts of the armor. As they fell, the remaining guard's last sight was the Shadon silently rushing toward the throne room.

King Byron hurried Queen Mari'anath to the space behind their thrones, opening the platform door to hidden tunnels. As soon as they were safely inside, King Byron slid the panel shut, activating the magickal lock. Together, they rushed down the tunnel that extended to various parts of the palace, including the armory, their first stop. Their guards were skilled and well-trained, but so were the royal couple, who often would spar with each other when time allowed. Once armed, they could join their guards in the fight to reclaim the palace. "Byron, our girls, do you think they are all right?"

Byron hurried with his wife, ceremonial sword in his left hand, his right arm touching her back gently as if to aid her in keeping up, though she was much faster than he. The blade he'd plucked from the display case on the wall in the throne room did not have as sharp of an edge as his actual one, which was safely in the armory, but it was better than being unarmed. Once this was over, they would have to rethink sharpening it. "Our daughters have their guards and were taught how to protect themselves. We will meet them at the armory as we had practiced."

"I am sure the Princesses are just fine... for now," a voice slithered against the stone walls around them, seeming to come from everywhere at once. Startled, the couple slid to a stop and looked around the empty hall for the source, facing each other to watch the other's back so none would sneak up upon them without being seen. The Queen gasped as a hand grabbed her arm tightly while another twisted her dagger from her grasp. A figure materialized from the shadows behind her, gripping her arm painfully, holding her dagger against her throat as he used her as a shield.

"Who are you? How did you get in here? Unhand my wife at once!"

Queen Mari'anath began to speak, and the knife pressed against her throat harder, the figure leaning in so his featureless black mask with golden lines brushed against her pointed ear. "Remain silent, dear queen; I do not wish to be on the receiving end of a spell and let you summon reinforcements to interrupt our conversation. You wouldn't want something awful to happen to your daughters." The Queen shook her head enough not to be cut; her hands curled into fists. "Good girl," the figure said dismissively before the mask tilted up to look back upon King Byron. "Now, where were we?"

King Byron's jaw tightened under his short beard, and he lowered his sword slowly to show he would not attack. "We can go upstairs and discuss any problems like civil beings. I ask that you lower the dagger from my queen."

"*Kotu nogut-nyta*; the instant I move it, she will cast a binding upon my person while you call guards to attempt to arrest me. I will keep it right where it is."

"I do not say that I think you are a fool," Byron replied to the use of the Shadese language, the little he knew of it from having a Shadon Ambassador on his Council of advisors. "You are a man desperate to have himself heard. Release my queen and explain what made you feel you must do something this irrational to gain an audience. We can work something out together."

The masked figure made a sound that almost was a laugh. "I sit in Nar'Shada and watch as your humans, dwarves, dawnwarriors, and elves all get along happily at the peace table, yet my kind is still shunned. That happens no longer." He tightened his grip on the queen, making her wince in pain. He paid her no mind other than to press the dagger a bit tighter against her, feeling the blade nick her skin, just a tiny kiss of metal on her pale neck. "Ambassador Jorrah has repeatedly asked you to bring the *ro*'Shadon into your alliance, to let us live among you beyond the Shadowgulf Mountains, yet you and your Council refused. Our lands wither and die while yours stayed lush and green, full of peace and promise of better lives for your people. How is it fair for your people to have such lives while mine suffer?"

"It was to protect ourselves! The Shadon have slaughtered thousands in the past, some who merely chose to live close to your lands; how long until--"

"Do you truly believe that we could simply wish entire races out of existence?" the figure interrupted, "If those horrible tales were true, I could see merit in your decision." The masked man leaned in slightly, dropping his tone as he continued, "But your kind is not innocent either. You did nothing as elves slaughtered each other during their War of the Turning Leaves. How many elven clans were erased from existence throughout Meridiah? How many of your wife's people, scores of men, women, and children are gone forever? Where was your righteous proclamation of protection, then?

"It was only after a famous War General of the Mun'ari Clan was named Elven Queen and then married you, a mere human noble, that there was a flicker of the promise of races living together in harmony. You created alliances with the dawnwarriors and dwarves yet shun *my* people." The figure straightened, still holding the Queen at knifepoint, the mask still watching King Byron. "I am *Kolotor'ix*, and I will not allow this insult to stand any longer. This farce ends now, with your blood running rivers across your lands. Let us speak the only language *ro'negut* seem to understand!"

The *Kolotor'ix* called upon his innate powers, moving through the shadows to appear behind Byron, his conjured sword of darkness erupting from the royal's chest. Shock and grief flashed across the human's face as life faded from his eyes, his body collapsing in a heap. Hurried footsteps made the *Kolotor'ix* look up, seeing the edge of the Queen's blue gown as she rounded a corner. He chuckled and followed at a walking pace.

A figure stepped out before the Queen, catching her as she collided with him. She gasped, shoving away at him in fear. "It is I, Jorrah; be calm." The man wore a red and black cloak over his black clothing, its clasp holding a red gem adorned with a gold chain given to him when he was made an Ambassador. The Queen stepped back slowly, tears on her cheeks. Jorrah of Nar'Shada held up his hands, showing he was unarmed, his voice gentle. "Queen Mari'anath, there is nowhere you can run where we cannot find you. If our *Kolotor'ix* wished to kill you, he would have already; he wants you to listen to reason.

"Byron was weak, growing old in his human lifespan, and had perhaps a decade as king left. Then he would die, leaving you alone and your three daughters fatherless. You need a strong king to stand beside you and rule justly, one who can match your lifespan. *Ro'Shadon* can live as long as elves." He stepped forward slowly, mirroring her steps backward, offering his hand to her. "Let the *Kolotor'ix* help you rule. For your people, your children's future. Do not be as your late husband was; *khar nogut-nyta,*" he gave a slight wince as if forgetting himself by speaking in his native Shadese, "my apologies; you are not a fool."

She slapped his hand away, her eyes filled with mixed emotions. "You want me to marry the man who has murdered my husband before my eyes? Who takes my home under siege? Threatens my daughters? How dare you suggest such a thing!" She spat at him, fresh tears streaming down her face.

A shadow tendril reached from the wall and casually flicked the spittle from Jorrah's cheek, his eyes watching her in the dim light of the lightstones. "Do not overstep yourself, Mari'anth. You are a queen, but that title only guarantees certain protections for so long."

"Protection?" She stepped toward him, using the movement to hide her hand slipping into an opening of her gown so she could retrieve her dagger from her thigh. "Where was my husband's protection? Tell me, what did we ever do to you, Jorrah, to make you betray us!"

"I acted as you grew to expect," he replied calmly, "*Ro'Shadon* do not believe in friends. Shadese does not even have a word equivalent to the concept. Instead, we have *balutrae*, those we see as equals, whose strengths and ambitions match our own yet are a constant challenge. Our *Kolotor'ix* does quite enjoy challenges.

"But to the subject at hand," Jorrah continued, "I have walked Meridiah's streets and heard your human nobles secretly plotting to assassinate Byron for his seat beside you. He was weakening, growing older, and thought they could do better. They are not worthy to rule beside you. But our *Kolotor'ix* is a--"

"Liar."

His eyes narrowed, and he stepped through the shadows, suddenly appearing inches from her. He grabbed her wrist without taking his eyes from hers, twisting it until she painfully let the dagger fall to the stone. His voice was like a threat of thunder before a storm: cold, unforgiving, and dangerous. "Do not ever name the *Kolotor'ix* a liar. He is many things, but that is not one of them. I cannot guarantee his anger will be gentle if you speak that word again. Our *Kolotor'ix* does not wish to harm you or your daughters, but he will if necessary. Say yes and offer all races, including those beyond the Shadowgulf Mountains, safety under his rule. Say yes and save your people, your daughters. Say yes and live before more innocent people die due to your delay." Jorrah moved back, and shadows brought her fallen dagger to his hand, which he offered to her hilt first.

She took the dagger slowly after a long moment, yet he made no move to stop her. "My delay is not causing people to die, Jorrah! Your King is the one doing this, not I! We gave you a home, a place to work and prosper, people to trust, and this is how you repay us by betraying us to your king?"

"People to trust." He repeated her words and rolled them around in his mouth as if tasting them. When he spoke, his voice was like hot iron. "*Ro'*Shadon are still shunned, hidden away in the northern lands while you and yours live in lush green lands! Does that sound like trust between us? Do you know what Nar'Shada is like, Mari'anath? No green plants, no blooming flowers of color, no birds singing sweetly in the air. The dirt is mixed with dragonfire ash, and plants do not grow as beautiful or lush as they do here. It is both cruel and unforgiving, and so *ro'*Shadon have become. But my people will like it here."

"Please, Jorrah, you cannot do this. Your king cannot do this!" Her tone shook as she struggled to keep her composure in the face of her world falling apart. Her husband was dead, her palace was under attack, she had no idea the whereabouts nor status of her people or daughters, and her Ambassador proposed that she marry the man behind it all.

"I tire of you telling me what I cannot do, Mari'anath. Rule under our *Kolotor'ix* as Queen or forfeit your life. He will hunt your daughters down and offer them the same choice." He turned his back at her silence and began walking down the tunnel. "I pray they are smarter than you."

With elven quickness, the Queen's hand tightened on her dagger and plunged the blade deep into Jorrah's jugular. She felt remorse as she watched Jorrah stumble forward, grabbing at his neck. She knelt beside him as he collapsed, holding his hand as he writhed painfully, gasping and choking upon his blood, eyes wide. "I'm sorry, Jorrah; I must protect my people." Slowly, the man stopped moving, letting out a long sigh. Meridiah bowed her head and folded his hands on his chest before standing slowly.

Jorrah's body began melting into ribbons of darkness flowing past her, and her eyes followed them, watching as they gathered behind her, forming the shape of a humanoid. Quickly turning to run, she was grabbed roughly and shoved against the wall, the black and gold mask of the *Kolotor'ix* forming inches from her face, filling her vision. His voice was icy steel behind it, the grip on her arm strong. "You have chosen your fate and those of your daughters. But I will let you in on a little secret," he slowly leaned in, whispering against her ear.

Slowly, horror flowed across her face, and she closed her eyes, a tear slipping down her cheek. "No… it cannot be true." She realized he had everyone beaten, that none of them genuinely knew the game's rules until it was too late. She had no choice but to concede and admit defeat to the craftier foe. "I sub--" she began, but a dark blade drew across her throat in a swift movement, cutting off her answer.

The *Kolotor'ix* lowered her gently to the ground, watching crimson soak into the light blue fabric of her gown, the purple contrasting the paleness of her skin. With her beside him or without, the endgame was the same. As much as he hated Byron's weakness, his constant need to deal with words instead of steel, he admired Mari'anath's strength and bravery. *Even in the face of defeat, she had fought until the end.* He wished she could have sat beside him, challenging him and giving him something worthwhile in the future. He could have almost counted her as *balutrae*.

But now she was nothing. He walked back down the hall where her husband's body lay cooling on the same floor and ascended the ladder to the throne room above.

His throne room.

The *Kolotor'ix* wiped his bloodied dagger on a piece of the Byronian tapestry with a silver deer leaping under a crescent moon on a blue field before yanking it down to fall in a pile. He walked around the thrones and looked at the Shadon gathered before him, who, as one dropped to a knee, right fists against their left shoulders, heads bowed, awaiting his orders. Byronian guards lay dead around the room where they had fought and fallen, their blood still wet upon the white marble floor. "Find the Princesses and bring them to me, unharmed if possible. Announce there is a new ruler; anyone loyal to the Byronian throne forfeits their lives and the lives of their families unless they pledge allegiance to me." The Shadon bowed and vanished into the shadows to fulfill their *Kolotor'ix*'s will. The *Kolotor'ix* walked up the marble stairs to the five thrones and flicked his hand, shadows wrapping around all but one, making them vanish. He turned and slowly sat upon the solitary throne, looking across the room.

My time has come.

150 YEARS LATER

APOLLO

The grass swayed in the spring wind, the air blowing ripples along the small river along the treeline as it carried the scent of the wheat fields on the other side of the woods. Apollo, a boy of twelve and six, sat with his brother on the shore with homemade fishing poles and lines in the water. Clep's hawk, Memory, flew above, enjoying the warm air. Apollo suddenly blinked and jerked at his line, excitedly jumping up from his sitting position. "I think I've got one!"

Clep rushed to help him pull in the fish wriggling on end, a homemade hook in its mouth. Once the struggling fish was in their covered basket, Clep returned to check his fishing line. "I've got no bite yet; what are you doing so differently that I have not?" Clep frowned at his empty line and threw it back into the water with a new worm. They had been fishing since early morning, and he still hadn't caught any while Apollo had gotten three.

Apollo, the elder brother by two years, smirked with a twinkle in his blue eyes. "I've been using some of the bread you baked yesterday."

"That was supposed to be for dinner tonight. I worked hard on the potions we traded for that bread," Clep scolded, slightly disappointed. Sighing, he pulled his line out of the water and set his pole beside the fish basket. "We should head back since now I must find something *other* than bread and stew for dinner."

The two gathered their things and began walking up the path toward the nearby village of Andears, where they made their home. Nestled east of the Ironfall Mountains, the Wyldwood Forest kept teagot plentiful for hunting, and the streams were full of fish. Fields of wheat stretched along the southern side of their village, and on days when the wind was just right, the smell of baking bread traveled to the farmers up to half a mile away.

Even though they were young, they still found ways to help the village however they could. Apollo continued the ways his father had taught him: hunting, fishing, or working in the fields beside the other villagers. Clep assisted those in need by using the distilling materials their mother had left him, creating salves and potions.

Clep whistled to Memory and tossed a small fish, laughing as the hawk swooped and snatched it from mid-air, flying off toward Andears. "Today wasn't that bad, Apollo," Clep spoke up, glancing over at his brother, "we got to sleep in and even had time for fishing between chores. I wish every day were like this."

Apollo chuckled. "That's because Jarrison's plow blade broke, and the blacksmith is fixing it. It'll be fixed by tomorrow, and then I'll be in the second field plowing rows." As they walked into Andears, Apollo couldn't help but look around at the people who cared for them as much as their parents had. A female walked past, winking at Apollo, who tripped on his own feet watching her. When Apollo looked back at Clep, his little brother was rolling his eyes as he set down their fishing poles beside the steps of their home. Left to them after their parents' passing, the two-bedroom home held everything they held dear to them, standing as the last home on the row beside a white tree standing nearby, painted wooden effigies hanging from its branches. Andears was one of the only villages in the territory of Cetra with an Aldarwood, and many young couples in the area had traveled here to be married under the Light's sacred tree.

He and Clep had started heading up the stairs and inside with their fish basket when they heard shouting. "Soldiers!" A boy couldn't be seen, but his voice was heard as he burst through the wheatfield. "Soldiers are coming!"

Apollo looked at Clep, taking off his belt with their father's sword and holding it out for him to take. "Your bow, quarterstaff, and my sword, take it into the woods, go!" As Clep rushed past, Apollo grabbed his arm and shoved the handle of the basket of fish into his hand. "Hurry, and get back here as soon as you can!" Clep ran back into the woods while Apollo rushed inside their home, looking for anything they'd need to hide.

Once a harvest, Leigelord Remhold would have his garrisons send soldiers into the villages to recruit more people into the Dark Army. The nearest garrison, Woodsong, was run by a Shadon who seemed dissatisfied with the people his soldiers returned with. The soldiers, in recent years, had gone from taking volunteers to picking the most able-bodied males, the best materials and goods, as well as females to take back to the garrison. Those taken were never heard from again. Apollo frantically searched his home for anything he and Clep wanted to keep safe from the soldiers, hiding some potions Clep had made behind the woodpile by their fireplace.

The horn blew, letting the farmers know it was time to come in from the fields, and Apollo left his home, stepping outside to stand on the streets with the rest of the villagers. A few looked worried, others returning from the woods as if they'd also hidden valuables. Looking around, he bit his lip nervously. *Clep, where are you?*

"I did it," Clep said, hurrying to stand beside his brother.

Apollo let out a sigh of relief and nodded. He already missed the weight of his father's sword on his hip, but he did not dare have it on him with the soldiers coming. "Where's Ma's amulet?" he asked, looking his brother's neck over for the metal chain.

"I hid it in my shoe. You don't think she'd mind, do you?"

Apollo shook his head and started to say something when hoofbeats interrupted him, and he glanced back at the road where horses were now riding in with black and red armored soldiers carrying the banner of the Dark Army. Apollo swallowed hard, trying not to let the fear show on his face. He was almost old enough to be considered a promising recruit, and having been sparring since he was younger, both with his father's sword and with sticks, he thought himself to be a good fighter. Still, he kept his head down, his shoulders hunched slightly to look smaller, meeker. *I can't let myself be separated from Clep, I'd never see him again if they took me.*

One of the soldiers dismounted, walking toward the villagers, who scrambled back away from him. "Males over there, females over here! Move!" Quickly, the group parted, the cries of scared women and children punctuating their movements.

Once among the villagers, Apollo watched the soldiers dismount and walk past the females, eyeing them before continuing in different directions, some going into the inn, others to the stables. They heard the sounds of things being tossed, metal and glass crashing to the ground. He kept his voice low to avoid the soldiers hearing him. "Why are they here so early? Aren't they supposed to come next harvest?"

Jarrison nodded, his voice carrying a thread of worry. "They were; we don't know why they are here."

Noriah, the village Elder, walked forward to the soldiers, who stopped him from reaching their commander, speaking low. Whatever was said between them, Apollo could not hear it, but Elder Noriah walked back toward the group of male villagers, his brow furrowed.

A soldier came out of a home, shoving an older man named Elias toward the others, snapping something in a language that Apollo did not know. A second soldier responded in kind, and both soldiers walked back into the home; the sounds of things clattering to the ground were heard over the soft whimpers of Elias' wife from where she stood by the other females. Clep went through the crowd of males to Elias, tending his cut arm with a piece of cloth he kept tucked in his belt for such occasions.

Their leader took a scroll from the saddlebag of his black steed, the creature walking forward, standing close enough that Apollo could see its eyes had a reddish hue and smell the scent of blood on its breath as the horse snorted, stamping. "By order of the *korrati* Kerrik ik'Remhold, every village in the territory of Cetra will be searched for the woman Dulcea, for crimes against the Dark Army, including theft and destruction of property. Anyone found harboring this fugitive will be taken to Woodsong garrison and sentenced according to *korrati ik'Remhold*'s laws."

Apollo blinked in surprise. *Dulcea was an actual person? I know of the stories of her that Nan told us, that she traveled with a great cat and stole from the Dark Army to bring villages goods in times of need, but I thought she was just a myth.* It was a tradition in Andears that villagers left tributes of homemade goods in the stables to thank her if she ever returned. Whenever soldiers were spotted near Andears, the stableboy's job was to place horse dung on top of the floorboards that hid the cache to keep it safe. Occasionally, someone would check the cache to find their tributes gone and other goods in their place in exchange. Apollo had always suspected Elder Noriah behind the trading of goods to keep hope among the villagers high.

A small whimper made Apollo's mind return to the present. The soldiers had lined up the females, forcing them to take off their head coverings and show their faces. Many females would not look at them, and a soldier would grip their chin to force them to look up, turning their faces to one side and then the other before moving on to the next female.

"In appreciation for our soldiers keeping you safe from this dangerous woman and her great cat seen beside her, we will accept tributes from your village." The soldiers' commander waved his arm, and shadows began darkening around the area, depositing baskets of food and goods taken from the homes into the wagon they'd brought. Apollo recognized one of the blankets from his bed, a handmade quilt Sophia had traded him for the meat of two teagot bucks last spring. Jarrison shook his head as if warning him against doing something that would get them in trouble. Apollo held his hands in fists at his sides, his head down. Only if one was close enough to look at his eyes behind the strands of honey-brown hair would they see the fury in their blue orbs.

"I do not see how removing goods from our homes has anything to do with searching for this woman, who isn't here," Elder Noriah said, shaking his head and gesturing to the females, some crying silently.

A soldier pulled Sophia forward, walking her toward the soldiers. "This one can work in the kitchen," he said, forcing her to climb into the wagon.

"No!" Nathan shouted, rushing forward, but two soldiers shoved him back toward the villagers. "She's my daughter, you can't take her!" The other villagers began shouting as soldiers walked another female toward the wagon, holding her arms as she tried to fight them.

A rock came flying out from the crowd, striking the commander in the head, blood spilling down the dark metal of his armor. His mount reared, nostrils flaring at the scent of blood. As the captain toppled to the ground, the soldiers drew their weapons, demanding the assaulter reveal themselves as they walked toward the villagers. Elder Noriah rushed forward to stop them advancing, his hands raised at his sides to show he was unarmed. "Please do not attack! I will find who did this, please, if you will just--" He was cut off as a soldier cracked him across the face with a gauntleted fist, making Elder Noriah fall hard to the ground, spitting blood.

The world grew silent instantly as Apollo looked at his brother with a shocked expression. The Elder was trusted to make village decisions; the villagers voted upon their position. They were the most respected of all the villagers. Apollo glanced at Clep, who had barely shaken his head at him, but it was too late; the village males rushed the soldiers around them, shouting in defiance of their actions, the females taking the distraction to run between the buildings behind them and toward the fields. Apollo caught Clep out of the corner of his eye as his brother turned and raced toward the woods. As he ran to help the other farmers, he prayed that his brother and fellow villagers would be safe. *Light, let me be strong enough to protect them.*

* * *

This is nothing like sparring with the other farmboys, Apollo realized as the first hit from a sword he blocked sent him falling back onto the ground, his arm vibrating with the force of the blow. Clep had returned in time to give Apollo their father's sword, but Apollo lost sight of him again. The soldier stood over him, readying to swing his sword down when someone tackled him, the two tumbling off out of sight before Apollo could see who it was. Elias ran forward with a pitchfork in his hands, pausing to look at Apollo and shouting to be heard over the fighting commotion. "Apollo, run! Get you and your brother to safety! May the Light--"

Apollo scrambled up and took off, running for the woods as Elias' voice cut off, frantically looking for his brother while trying to distance him and the soldiers. He raced toward the lake, hurrying to the embankment where the ground beneath an old tree had washed away in a storm years ago, making a large indentation where he and Clep would seek shelter during rainstorms and had agreed to meet if something bad had happened. He scrambled into it and crouched against the dirt wall, moving the brush back to hide himself. Apollo closed his eyes and prayed to the Light that Clep would come quickly.

* * *

Movement outside the brush before the cave startled him, and he opened his eyes quickly. *No, I'd fallen asleep!* Glancing around the cave, he noticed he was still alone. *Where is Clep?!*

"Apollo," Clep whispered his name in an announcement and crept into the hiding place. Relief and worry flooded Apollo as he moved to let Clep pass, his legs cramped with staying in one position for so long. Clep hurried past him, muttering apologies while Apollo moved the brush back into place to conceal the opening. *It will hide us if the Dark Army soldiers do not get close enough to see through the branches.* Apollo sighed in relief and handed a dagger to Clep for protection. Clep knew enough to stick people with the sharper end, but it made Apollo feel better knowing he had a way to protect himself, too. Clep liked to heal people and not hurt them if he could help it.

A twig snapped, and the brothers froze, watching through the small gaps in the leaves as one of the soldiers walked closer, his black metal boots crunching over the leaves and sticks as he walked in front of the brush that concealed the brothers. *He is close enough that I can almost reach and touch him with the end of my sword. I hope he can't hear my heart pounding.* The soldier's harsh voice made Apollo jump slightly, barely hitting his head on the dirt ceiling. "One of the villagers has to know who attacked us! *korrati* Kerrik will have our hides once he discovers that a mere villager killed *kriss'ix* Rigalo-*kyr*. We must make an example out of the villagers to ensure nothing like this happens again."

As his mind raced, Apollo bit his lip to remind himself to be quiet. *The rock killed their commander? No wonder they are so upset. All they had to do was ask for any goods; perhaps Elder Noriah would have given them some. We aren't bad people; we would help someone in need.* The thought that the soldiers could take one of the people they knew, who they grew up with, and make an example out of them was not one that he could suffer lightly. His heart and conscience wrestled within him as he debated whether they should try to defend against the soldiers or wait for them to leave. He prayed that he had made the right decision as he and Clep remained where they were.

* * *

They huddled in the cave until nightfall, long after the Dark Army had left. He hated that he did not know what was happening and that Andears may be in danger, the villagers taken or worse. He feared the Dark Army had made good on their threat and made an example of someone. *Was it Marjory, the baker's wife, who gave me a hot pie when I brought healing herbs to her for her sick infant last fall? Or was it Thomas, the stable boy who would only speak to horses and not the rest of us? Or Alexis, the girl who gave me my first kiss in the woods last season?* There were too many possibilities, each one as dreadful as the next. He finally shook his head, trying to clear out the grim thought that someone was in danger or even being tortured while he did nothing. He felt like a coward, useless. Finally, he spoke, breaking the heavy silence and making his brother jump slightly. "I think it's safe to go now." Apollo slowly climbed out of the cave and looked around before standing to ensure that no soldiers were lying in wait like hunters stalking deer. Once he was sure they were alone, he spoke. "Come out; it's clear."

Clep climbed out and stamped a few times to regain blood flow. Apollo rubbed his lower back slightly, wincing, and caught his brother worriedly looking at him, his hand reaching into his satchel for a salve or herb. "I'm fine. It should be safe to go back now." He turned and began walking up the hill, trying to sound more confident than he felt, his hand tight on the pommel of his father's sword.

The woods always grew thick with the night before any other part of the land, but as they climbed the hill quietly and carefully not to alert any soldiers, something caught his eye. In the darkness of the trees, they could see an orange glow that could only be one thing: fire. The two raced toward Andears, no longer caring if they made noise, each step taking them closer to the village, and the unknown awaited them.

LOST IN SHADOW

The Sigils were gifts from the dragons

to the lesser races,

given freely,

each one representing the dragon who gifted it.

Red for fire,

Blue for water,

Green for nature,

White for light,

Brown for earth.

Just as seasons change,

so do the nature of dragons

and so do their Sigils,

their elements and colors shifting.

Just as no two dragons are alike,

neither are two Sigils,

each having their own characteristics,

each one unique as the dragons themselves.

— Kil'lik'Draven, Bard of the Winds

RATSBAYNE

Blood. There was so much blood.

It was everywhere, stretching out into the darkness, and it was all he could see in every direction, except the blonde female floating in the middle like an island in a sea of red. He tried as hard as he could to get to her, but she kept sinking lower and lower into the crimson liquid and he feared she'd be lost forever.

The room tilted, spinning, and he suddenly was free from the liquid, the movement making him fall to his knees, looking up as the crimson sea now spanned above him, a ceiling of red. He stood, reaching up for the female still floating, still sinking into the liquid.

He tried jumping, frantically searching the darkness for anything to aid him, and found nothing.

A doorway suddenly opened in the darkness, light piercing the darkness yet revealing nothing. A young woman with brown hair stood framed by the bright light, a wooden quarterstaff in her bloodied hands, reaching out toward him.

"Help me," he pleaded, reaching for the staff in her hand. As soon as his fingers touched it, the dream changed again; the bloody ceiling with its sinking female was gone, replaced by stone, dirt, and roots. In his hands was a vial of a deep blue liquid, and he slowly took a drink as the young woman watched him.

He fell backward, the world swallowed by the darkness once more, the sounds of a horse whinnying his name echoing until it too, faded into nothingness.

Ratsbayne awoke to the sound of shouting and groaned as he rolled over in the hay, the remains of the strange dream fading. Opening his eyes, he saw sunlight coming between the barn rafters above his head and heard someone yelling outside. The hayloft was a great place to sleep; no one bothered him, no one to snore and wake him, and he had the horses below to keep him company. He grunted and looked up at the sling bed between two rafters, now twisted, his blanket hanging halfway off it. "Ah dun't remember falling out o' bed," he grumbled, rubbing his head and frowned as his hand came away with hay entangled with his dark brown hair. He sat up, groaning and cursing his aching muscles, and crawled to the window to see what Lordson Kerrik, the garrison commander, was bellyaching about this time and if it was worth getting out of the loft for.

Woodsong garrison was full of the usual noises and movement, soldiers training and working on armor or weapons. From here, he could see Lordson Kerrik coming from the gates that led to the keep and the blue-green leaves of the Aldarwood over the stone wall that separated the keep from the rest of the garrison. At night, the sound of the wind through its white branches made a soft melody, and if it was quiet enough, he could barely hear the sound of the wooden effigies hanging from its branches moving back and forth. By the time he made it downstairs and outside, Lordson Kerrik had already made it into the garrison and was somewhere among the soldiers, shouting commands at whoever would listen to him. Briar, the stableboy, was lugging two buckets of water from the river outside toward the trough. Ratsbayne went to help the lad by beginning to get hay from the hayloft for the horses.

Even though he was not a soldier, he stayed and helped with the horses, which seemed to be all he was suitable for, and he did his best to keep out of everyone's way. He lived in the confines of the loft among the smell of hay, horses, and manure. The horses didn't seem to mind him, never betraying his sneaking in at all hours, often smelling of alcohol or bloodied when he got into a brawl with the wrong soldier. Sure, shoveling manure and betting on cards wasn't a good-paying life, but he had enough coin to drink and a place to sleep. Life was simple, and that suited him just fine.

A squirrel sat on his sling bed, swaying slightly in the breeze blowing in through the window, watching him as he finished getting the last hay bale. "Shoo," Ratsbayne scolded it as he tried waving at it with his hand, "go away. Ah've got no nuts fer ye." The squirrel ran off through the rafters, headed down and out of the stables into the garrison. Ratsbayne shook out his blanket, draping it back on the sling bed, and felt something hit his boot. He glanced down, noticing a rolled parchment tied with a vine and wondering who had come to the hayloft while he had been asleep. Curious, he opened it.

Go to the fallen oak near the river.
There, you will find instructions and some coin.
Aid me, and I will help you in return.

He read it to himself, grumbling afterward, turning the parchment over to see that the back of it was blank of writing. Scoffing, he folded the parchment and shoved it away in his boot before climbing the ladder to get to work.

* * *

Walking from the Woodsong garrison was always easy; they were always willing to watch him walk away. It was coming back that they usually had issues with unless you wore either their armor or shackles. *Luckily Ah wear neither o' them,* Ratsbayne thought as he walked toward the gate as the sun descended. He was the drunk they tolerated, never doing any harm except to himself, stumbling and falling about, giving them something to laugh at. He made his way toward the east gate, where two soldiers stood guard, looking at him and chuckling. "Where you off to now, Rat Slayer?"

Ratsbayne shrugged as he walked, slightly out of balance as he turned to face the soldier, who often met with him across the card table in the tavern after guarding the gate. "Dunno, maybe to see yer mum."

The second guard began laughing as the soldier glowered and stepped toward Ratsbayne, hands in fists beside his black and leather armor. "Don't you go speaking of my mum, you drunken loon."

His partner tried to calm him down, laughter in his voice. "Easy there, Eratas; he's just a drunk. No need to get all upset."

Ratsbayne gestured to the calmer guard. "See, like Darren says, Ah'm not trouble. Besides, Ah remember, Ah saw yer mum last night, 'tis his sister Ah'm to go see now." Ratsbayne moved as a rock flew at him, and he stumbled off through the woods, laughing loudly at his joke. He walked through the woods, cursing the old leather shoes he had on as he rock-hopped across a stream and landed on the other side, shaking out his now damp foot. He made his way to the oak tree overlooking the river, and once there, he waited for someone to show up. *This was where the parchment had said to be to get some free coin, right?*

A bit of movement in the brush made him grab a large stick to defend himself, putting himself into a fighting stance while trying not to fall over rocks and into the river. A squirrel darted out of the roots of the oak, stopped and chirped at him, then took off into the brush. Ratsbayne swung at the fast critter anyway. Once he was sure it was gone, he knelt and reached into the oak tree's roots, wondering if it had stored something there and if that was what he was supposed to get. *Squirrels hide things in trees, right? Light help meh if a snake bites mah hand off.* His hand touched something soft, and he jerked in surprise, hitting his head on a low branch. Swearing, he felt again and gently pulled out a small cloth pouch and a piece of parchment. He unrolled the parchment, noting the same strange handwriting as before.

> *You cannot trust those you are with.*
>
> *Report what the soldiers are up to and what they are planning, and every time you do, I will give you coin, and will aid you in remembering who you are.*

Ratsbayne scoffed and shoved the parchment back into the roots of the tree. *Kerrik may be an idiot, but he be not dumb enough to let meh stay alive if he thinks Ah be a traitor, which was what they'd think if they found meh with that parchment.* Ratsbayne shook the pouch and once he heard the rattling of coins within it, he spilled them out into his hand, counting them quickly. He dumped them back into the pouch and tied it to his belt before heading back toward Woodsong to get a drink and forget this entire ordeal with mystery people wanting to help him. *Who would want to help meh? Ah be just a drunk, no one important. Besides, how could someone help meh remember who Ah was when* Ah *dun't even know who Ah am?*

* * *

Two hours later, Ratsbayne stumbled as he was shoved through the doorway of the wooden tavern in Woodsong's garrison, tripping over the stone steps into the mud outside for all who were watching to see. Laughter followed him with a few yells from soldiers inside as the door swung closed. "Stay out here, you swindling drunk!"

He carefully got to his feet and spat mud onto the ground, facing the tavern. He wavered a touch, shaking a fist at the closed door. "It not be mah fault that ya suck at cards!" He sighed, shaking his head to clear it, and began walking, grumbling. "Wouldn't know a winning hand if it slapped yer ugly mug."

A group of soldiers walked toward him, laughing as he tried brushing off the mud off his pants to no avail. One of the soldiers shook his head, sighing. "Ratsbayne, you *nogut*, that's our rations you're drinking. *Korrati* Kerrik doesn't just give alcohol to every garrison, so stop drinking it all up."

The drunken Ratsbayne clutched the armored man's shoulder, laughing. "Ah suppose ye be right, Eratas; after all, ya do all the fighting, and Ah do all the drinking. Ah'll tone it down; maybe tomorrow or the fortnight after that." Eratas shoved him away, and the soldiers walked off toward the tavern, muttering about the male who always was willing to enjoy a drink but did none of the work to earn it.

Once the soldiers were in the tavern, Ratsbayne opened the coin purse he'd taken off Erata's hip and slipped a few coins before dropping it into the mud. He continued down the dirt road, stumbling and mumbling to himself as he returned to the barn. If Eratas returned, he'd see his coin purse had fallen off his belt onto the dirt, pick it up, and go back inside to drink with fewer coins, but no one the wiser.

Ratsbayne went to the stables and climbed into the hayloft, settling down among the bales. Among the wood in the loft wall were little things he'd kept, small things that didn't have much meaning. He moved a wood plank from the wall, set the coin purse he'd gotten from the squirrel into it, and replaced the board, shoving hay in front of it to conceal it once more. He then plopped down onto the hay and closed his eyes, muttering his nightly prayer that he had drank enough so he wouldn't have any dreams.

He rode a horse down a hallway of white and gold, the faces of the dead among the swirling darkness outside the windows banging on it as if to be let in. His sword was ready in his hand, yet there was nothing to fight.

Blood dripped down from the ceiling, steadily growing thicker as he rode faster toward the doors at the end of the hall.

He crashed into the double doors and suddenly found himself tumbling, no longer on the horse, falling into the darkness until he landed on the ground, the blood pooling around his ankles. He kicked something as he waded through the thick liquid, reached into the redness, and pulled out a broken golden crown.

He heard someone crying and quickly waded through the blood, which steadily began getting deeper. By the time it had reached his knees, he had reached a bed where a blonde female lay, her eyes closed. A male in armor was on his knees beside her, head down. He walked over and touched the man's shoulder to comfort him. The male turned, revealing Ratsbayne's own face, eyes weeping blood and darkness.

"We failed."

APOLLO

The village looked like something out of a nightmare; no, Apollo's nightmares revolved around his parents' deaths, making him live it all over again, but not this. Never this.

Every building was ablaze, every tree and bush, every piece of clothing on clotheslines, every window pane reflecting flames inside and out. The places he knew by heart-- the stables he helped rebuild after the previous summer's storm, the shop that he bought goods from, the Aldarwood where they would gather for Sun's Day worship, the shed where he had gotten a kiss from Rosemary, the innkeeper's daughter, the home that his great-grandfather built, that he and Clep were born in, grew up in -- all of it was burning. Nothing was spared in the village, not a horse, dog, or even a stray cat. The animals lay dead in the stables or streets, livestock in the field nearby lying dead for carrion to come and feast upon.

But not even that was not the most horrible thing.

It was the people of Andears, their bodies in a morbid heap in the middle of the village square: men, women, children. Between the fall of night and blood, he was unsure where one body began and the other ended, but he caught glimpses in the firelight of the faces and figures of those he knew, those he trusted and laughed with. The children who sang songs they made up that morning, Elias, who taught him how to work a horse-drawn plow, Katherine, who had just had her baby a mere week ago, her infant lying far from his mother's protective arms. Jarrison lay beside a broken board, and Elder Noriah's head was taken from his shoulders, now stuck onto a pitchfork in the ground. *How could anyone do such evil to other people?*

Clep rushed toward the pile of bodies, grabbing for his healer's kit on his side, and Apollo let him, standing in shock and horror, unable to speak. He could not get his feet to obey him and was unsure where he would go if they did. Some of Apollo wanted to run as far away as he could and not look back. The other part was livid with rage, curling his fists at his side, one hand going to his father's sword on his hip, now the only thing he owned of his family; all their belongings were in flames.

A bloody creature looked up from the shadows of the stables, and Apollo saw it was dragging what looked like an armored torso in its mouth. He recognized it as the large horse the commander had ridden on. Apollo pulled his father's sword as the mount watched him, fire reflecting in its red eyes. "YOU DID THIS!" he screamed, advancing on it with heavy steps. The creature snorted, its ears turned toward Apollo and stamped, almost in a challenge.

"Apollo! No!" Apollo heard Clep's frantic voice, thick with tears and shock, his footsteps running closer. Clep tried to force his sword hand down toward the ground, yelling his name to get him to look at him. "Apollo! Apollo! Don't do this! Look at me!"

Apollo rounded on his brother, shoving him back, pointing his sword at the pile of dead. Fresh tears streamed down his face, and he saw similar tear marks on Clep's face that reflected slightly in the fire's glow. "Look at you? Look at THEM! They're DEAD, CLEP! Because of them! They wanted to make an example..." his voice faltered, forcing him to take a moment before continuing. "They were our friends! Our neighbors, and they killed them!" Hot tears ran down his cheek as his sword hand shook, sorrow choking him. "They destroyed everything. Clep, they burned our home!" He tried to say more, moving his mouth, but his voice seemed stuck in his throat.

Clep was able to pull his arm down, and he hugged his brother as tightly as he could, tears running down his cheeks. "I know. I know. We're still here, brother. We will be okay. I have you."

Apollo held his brother protectively, his free arm wrapped

around Clep in his moment of grief, sword arm limp at his side. But his angry gaze never left the creature, the horse now nosing the arm of the torso. *It's not the horse's fault; it didn't do anything wrong. It is just mourning its rider.* His voice trembled as it came out from behind gritted teeth. "Get out of here! GO!" The creature snorted and turned, dragging the armor into the darkness of the woods, disappearing like a specter. Apollo stepped away from his brother, walking away from the burning village. Allowing his little brother to see him cry would do him no good.

* * *

It was midday the next day, and he and Clep were still burying bodies. They had put out fires the best they could with water from the lake in the woods outside the city. The village's well had been doused with oils, making the water not only undrinkable but useless for putting out the fires, which the boys had discovered after trying to use it to extinguish the fires. During the night, he and Clep had rushed to Andears' bath house with buckets to empty the wooden tub used for easing the ache of sore muscles after working all day in the fields. Apollo started trying to put out the fire at the nearest building while Clep took his buckets and soaked the Aldarwood the best he could to preserve the tree. *Would the Light not allow the villagers' souls to enter its embrace if it burned?* So far, the flames stayed away from it, but Apollo prayed that the fire would leave the sacred tree alone while they helped douse the rest of the village. The tub only held so many bucketfuls of water, and traveling from Andears to the lake and back in the dark with full buckets of water gave the fires more time to do damage. Apollo feared that soon, there would be nothing left of the village but ashes.

Apollo said he'd get the buckets of water and left Clep to separate the dead, putting babes with mothers, children with their families. Apollo heard him saying last prayers over them like he'd seen the Priest of the Light do at his parents' funerals. Pushing back the painful memory, he went into the woods to get another two buckets of water.

The Wyldwood was much darker, the air thick with smoke and

the smell of burning wood, and Apollo found it harder and harder to keep moving forward, his arms trembling. He slipped on the leaves, falling, the water spilling all over himself. He stood carefully, trying not to slip on the now-wet leaves, and kicked the bucket as far as he could, yelling his grief to the trees around them, shouting wordlessly until his voice broke and he fell to his knees, sobbing.

He wasn't sure how long he stayed in the woods, but he came back slowly, carefully, and thoroughly disheartened. *How are we supposed to do this?* They wanted to save Andears and their friends' souls, but he was exhausted and confident that Clep was even more so. Looking around, he found Clep in the field beside the village. He had found a shovel and began digging graves in the partially burned area; the only sound was the cracking of burning wood and the shovel hitting dirt repeatedly.

Apollo kept himself busy by throwing water onto areas before him and creating a path in buildings to find anything he could salvage. *There is no point in trying to keep the village, but we should save anything we could use.* He felt selfish for bringing water into their home first. Not wanting to go into the woods and fall with the buckets again, he began using buckets of dirt to combat the fire inside instead, trying to salvage what he could. He could not get into the home as far as he wished, for the smoke drove him back out, coughing and feeling light-headed.

The rain thankfully began to move in, dousing the fires the boys could not and washing away some of the blood and ash. Apollo and Clep both found themselves slipping in the fresh mud more often than not as they tried to salvage what they could. Smoke made the air thicker, and he had to stop working, his coughing hurting enough to add more tears to his cheeks. Apollo glanced over at the field to see Clep's arms trembling, struggling as he lifted the shovelful of dirt. Apollo looked from the few graves he'd managed to dig and back at the rows of bodies still awaiting a resting place, each with rocks on their eyes with crudely painted symbols on them. *There are too many graves, and Clep must be as tired as I am.* Looking at himself, he noticed his arms were burned, with blisters beginning to form from repeated times of going in and out of the burning buildings, with so little to show. He felt hopelessness grip him.

The feeling of being watched made Apollo look up, grabbing his father's sword hilt. *Please don't be soldiers or robbers.* He looked as a figure in green stepped from the woods near where Clep sat on the ground, speaking low, but he could not hear what was said. Apollo came running with his sword out but stopped when he saw a giant black cat standing beside the woman, almost large enough to ride. He glanced at Clep, who nodded slowly to let his brother know he was unharmed, afraid to make sudden movements. *Am I imagining things? That couldn't be the Dulcea the soldiers were looking for; she's a story, nothing more.*

Apollo walked up as his brother was speaking. "It wasn't your fault. If no one here could have stopped it, you wouldn't have been able to either." The great cat chuffed and flexed his large claws in the dirt as he stretched. Apollo tried not to imagine what those claws could do to his or Clep's flesh.

"No," snapped Apollo, still dirty, tired, upset, and crankier. "It is your fault."

"Apollo?! You take that back!" Clep gasped at his brother.

"They were looking for you! That's why they did this!"

"No, someone threw the rock at their commander; they made them upset and do this."

Apollo suspected it had been Nathan in defense of Sophia being chosen for kitchen duties at the garrison, but he would never know now. They both were among the dead.

Dulcea looked at him, an eyebrow raised, then looked to her panther, who began sniffing the ground, walking toward the village ruins, seemingly bored of this conversation between them. "Both of ya are incorrect. A rock thrown may have killed their captain, and they may have been looking for mah, but they did not have to do this. No one can make anyone do anything. It is their choice that makes them do something. The soldiers chose to do this evil."

"I have heard of magicks that make people do another's bidding or make them tell the truth at all times," Clep said, speaking up about the legends Nan would tell them about at night.

The woman gave a soft smile to Clep. "Let us help so yer friends may be at rest at last." Dulcea went into the woods, brought back two long branches of fallen trees, and began weaving smaller branches between them, using pieces of long grass and wheat to bind them. Apollo watched them momentarily, shaking his head as he walked away. *I must be more tired than I thought. Imagining people from Nan's stories and now trying to make a sled out of wheat and sticks could hold anything heavier than a small animal?*

He had found a slightly burned crate earlier and now used it to bring goods to a clear spot on the ground, going back and forth between the burned buildings, many which were still smoldering after the rain. When the bottom of the crate broke and the goods spilled onto the ground, he swore and glanced at Clep, noticing that he was alone. The graves were not only all dug but covered in blooming flowers, which puzzled him considerably. There was no sign of the mysterious figure, giant cat, or grass sled, only pieces of grass and branches lying useless on the ground. *I knew I was seeing things.*

"Dulcea's gone to tell the other villages what's going on. She gave us some coin," Clep said, as he walked over, holding out a leather bag, "to start a new life in Silene."

How? She was a trick of the mind, borne from working too hard. How could she give you a coin purse? He may have found it somewhere. "Do you think they will help us?"

Clep shrugged as he handed Apollo a full waterskin, and Apollo almost drank the entire thing. "It is a week or two walks since we don't have any horses. We should get started; I don't think I can sleep here tonight."

Apollo began gathering the salvageable goods into two backpacks, preparing for the long, tiring journey south to Silene and, hopefully, to peace.

Men drink in the morning to remember,
Men drink at night to forget.
Soldiers drink to negate the horrors
Of battles they haven't fought yet.
Women drink to ease the child's birth,
Children sip to calm the cold's creep.
A long drink to the sick and the dying
Aids the journey to the Forge's keep.

-- Dwarven drinking song

RATSBAYNE

He sat on the rooftop of the stable, rubbing a hand over his face. He had drunk the previous night, but it had not been enough to have a dreamless night, and senseless nightmares had him awake long before the sun rose over the Ironfall Mountains. He groaned as he watched the garrison commander stride toward the sparring grounds, as was his habit in the morning. *Ah bet he at least got to sleep. Bastard.*

Kerrik was not a man that he would follow into battle. He ran his soldiers all over Cetra, going to villages to take volunteers for the Dark Army, who trained and lived in the encampment. *Ah think he just does it to make sure his army be larger than others, trying to make his father look good, but the fool doesn't understand that numbers do not make strength. After all, five-week weak ales will not get ya as drunk as one strong stout.*

The commander's step was heavier, Ratsbayne noticed; his shoulders had a sort of weight upon them, and he wondered if it may have to do with the parchment that Kerrik held in his fist tightly enough the parchment was crinkled. Curiosity got the better of him, and he decided to leave the barn to see what was going on, staying at a distance so he would not be a target of the anger radiating off the commander.

"What is this nonsense!" Kerrik shouted at the soldiers sitting beside the armory, washing their armor, which stank of smoke and death when they came riding an hour before sunrise. They looked up, standing as their commander came closer in his wrath, shaking the parchment with angry movements. "Do you see this wax seal? It means that this is a communication from our *Kolotor'ix*! He heard that *kriss'ix* Rigalo-*kyr* was killed while you were out at Andears! *I* wasn't even aware of that! What the hells happened out there, and why was I not informed immediately? Do you know how this makes me and my *Ero-Hasta'kan* look, that the *Kolotor'ix* in the capital heard about what happened with my own men before I did? Now he is sending someone to inspect Woodsong!"

Ratysbayne listened quietly, smirking as he leaned against a post. *It looks like ya be a piss-poor commander,* he thought, *no more than Ah would be a piss-poor soldier, which is why Ah be not one.* He managed to keep out of the Dark Army as a soldier, aiding the civilians who stayed in the garrison at times, sewing, cooking, or tending the horses, yet he was always careful not to be in the sight of Kerrik too much. When asked who Ratsbayne was, no one could give a definitive answer except that he was the drunk who often gambled and won against them.

"*Korrati*, you had requested that you not be disturbed," one of the captains said, "because you were busy with your nightly prayers." Ratsbayne tried not to snort. *Nightly prayers mah arse; he was laying with Taya.* A year ago, the Dark Army had returned from getting recruits from the villages, bringing a female recruited for cooking duties named Taya. Kerrik had taken one look at her and decided to have her for himself, taking her to bed whenever he wished. Ratsbayne felt for the girl, who could not have been more than twelve and four, and wanted to protect her; the entire situation made his stomach turn, but he decided it was better to stay directly out of it.

Lordson Kerrik was not as amused at the soldier's answer and angrily balled the parchment in his hands, throwing it at a fire pit and missing. "This has the *Kolotor'ix*'s seal upon it! I was to be interrupted and informed immediately! Now we are in real *krukshu*!" He stormed back toward the keep, muttering about how he would take his frustrations out on Taya before they had to prepare for the inspection. Ratsbayne headed to the back of the building he hid behind and whistled, imitating a bird's call three times. One of the women carrying a water basin set it down out of the way and hurried through the gate to the keep. She would help get Taya elsewhere to hide until the commander's wrath was over. *Sorry, lass, it is all Ah can do for ye.*

Since no one was paying attention, having gone back to washing and polishing armor and sparring, Ratsbayne picked up the fallen parchment from the ground, slipped it into his feed bag, and collected more water for it in the stable. Once back to the stables, he looked it over, seeing the Dark Emperor's black and red wax seal affixed to it. Curious, he unrolled the parchment, frowning, recognizing the brushed symbols of Shadese writing. Even though he had spent two years here in Woodsong under a Shadon Commander, he still did not know how to read or speak the language, only picking up a word here and there and guessing its meaning. He didn't have anyone he trusted to read it and not tell the commander that he had it, so the parchment was as useless as kindling. *Well drat. Ah wanted to know what it had said.*

A chirp made him startle, and he saw a squirrel sitting on a rock, watching him. He crumpled up the useless parchment and threw it at the creature. "Get out of here, varmint," he snapped grumpily. The squirrel dove off the rock as the parchment missed harmlessly and rolled into the grass. The squirrel grabbed it in its teeth and ran out into the woods with it. *Light, don't tell meh the damned thing can read.*

* * *

He awoke to two black beady eyes blinking at him from inches away, and he yelled, scrambling to get back away from the creature and ending up on the hayloft floor with his bed swinging above him. The barn mouse darted off as he threw his pillow at it. "*Krushku, krushku, krushku!*" he swore mightily once he could find the air to speak.

"Come on, Ratsbayne," Eratas yelled at him from outside the barn, "you're assigned to help me; the sooner we start, the sooner it can be over with," Ratsbayne grumbled a reply and began putting on his tunic.

A turn of an hourglass later, he found himself in the garrison's armory. *Inventory: whoever created it should have been tarred, feathered, drawn, and quartered. Whose bright idea was to stand around a burning wooden building and count every piece of weaponry, shield, barding, armor, and Light knew what else in Woodsong-- all by nightfall and with a hangover* to boot? Kerrik, o' course.

Ratsbayne tried keeping up with the three soldiers who were counting helms. They said he had the easy job; he just had to mark tally lines on the parchment, one for each item. *Aye, well, ya try writing with ya three banging metal around when yer head be throbbing over last night's ale.*

A girlish scream came from Eratas as he leaped onto a crate with both feet, pointing at the ground, which made Ratsbayne and the other soldiers look to see what was wrong. A squirrel darted past them, and Ratsbayne tried to kick it but missed, hitting one of the tables instead. The critter turned back, chittered somewhat angrily, and took off. The two soldiers began laughing at Eratas, but Ratsbayne swore instead; he had spilled ink onto the parchment, covering some of the tally marks. *Great, we have to count the maces again. By the Light, Ah hate squirrels.*

* * *

It was twilight two weeks later by the time the inventory was finally complete; they'd counted every piece of armor, weapon, food, hay, blankets, and whatever else was in Woodsong. Ratsbayne had tried volunteering to inventory the tavern but was quickly shot down before he got the entire question out of his mouth. But it was finally over, and he was heading to the tavern for a well-deserved drink.

"Rat Slayer, the *korrati* wants a word with you." A soldier stepped in his way, the tavern just in sight over his shoulder.

Korrati? Ratsbayne had to think for a moment before remembering that it was what the Shadon captains called Kerrik. *Why can't they use the common tongue like everyone else?* "That be nice, and he can have more than one word with meh after Ah've gotten mah drinking started," Ratsbayne said as he sidestepped to go around the captain, his eyes fixed upon the divine light coming from the tavern window.

"He said now."

Ratsbayne almost stamped his foot in frustration. "Damnit, Lukras, Ah just want my drink, mah hand be cramping from the *krushku* tally marks."

The captain gestured toward the opposite way of the tavern, toward the keep. "I'm supposed to escort you to the *korrati*'s office. It shouldn't take long, and then you can return to drinking and losing at cards."

Ratsbayne grumbled, turning and walking back away from the welcoming light and laughter coming from the tavern, the footsteps of Captain Lukras behind him as he led him toward the keep.

Lordson Kerrik was standing behind a long table, pointing a map of the territory of Cetra, when Ratsbayne was let inside. Ratsbayne nodded to the three soldiers who stood around the table, who didn't acknowledge him but were listening to their *korrati*. *All captains,* he observed, seeing their ranking upon their uniform shoulders, *and Captain Lukras not among them. No wonder he be upset, he not be invited to the important meeting.* He gave a crooked smile and crossed his arms but ended up losing his balance and half-stumbling against the table, the pieces on the map wobbling fiercely, making Kerrik and the captains stop talking and look at him. "They said ya wanted to see meh, so here Ah am. Can Ah go now?"

Kerrik sighed and gestured back at the map. "As I was saying," he continued, glancing at the captains around the table, "you three are going to take your assigned soldiers and head out to deliver the extra supplies listed, as well as the inventory we took over the last two weeks to Redwood garrison's *korrati*. Rat Slayer, you are going with them."

"Ah'm Ratsbayne. Ah'm the bane of rats; ya want mah twin brother Ratslayer. Ah'll go get him," He turned and immediately approached the door to escape.

"Ratsbayne, get back here." Sighing, he turned back and went to the table. *According to the map, there be one village from here to the other garrison we be heading to. Maybe we could stop, and Ah can get some new pants.* "By any chance, are some of the extra supplies ale?"

One of the captains reviewed the list. "Two barrels."

"Hot damn, count meh in. Now if ya excuse me, Ah've got some drinking to do." He began walking back toward the door to get to the tavern. *If Ah hurry, Ah may be able to drink enough to forget this entire two-week ordeal.*

Kerrik spoke up as he reached for the door handle. "You leave as soon as this meeting is over."

Wait, what?

Aldarwood, Light's wood,
Knowing wrong-and-right wood,
Standing firm, standing tall
Light's effigies held above us all.
Alarfruit hanging on branches abound
Ripe to eat after they hit the ground,
Aldarfruit to close the wound
Gifts from our old Aldarwood.

-- Children's song

APOLLO

"Apollo, Apollo, please, can't we slow down?"

Apollo glanced over his shoulder at his brother, startling slightly at the first sound other than their feet on the dirt road and birds chirping in hours. Clep had stopped walking, his face contorted in pain and sorrow. Tear streaks had created paths on his dirty cheeks as he dropped his bag to the dirt beside his leather boots. Apollo went to his brother, took up his bag, and added it to the two others over his shoulders, grunting slightly as his back protested with a shooting pain that seemed to end at his right ankle. "No, we need to keep moving." He turned and began walking, wishing to put as much distance between them and the horrors in Andears as possible.

"Apollo, we need to stop. It's late; I'm hungry, and I know you must be tired and hungry too."

Apollo shook his head, though his stomach growled loud enough he was sure his younger brother heard it. "Fine, we can stop for the night, just away from the road." He walked quickly into the woods beside them, looking for a flat spot in the trees where they could stop and Apollo could get the rock out of his shoe.

Clep sat down on a log, groaning in pain, and began pressing his hands into his lower back to stretch his muscles, looking around as he did so. "We can camp here for the night, maybe make a fi--" he began.

"No, no fires." *I've had enough of fires to last a lifetime and then some.* At Clep's wince, he softened his tone. "I'll look for some water nearby. Maybe you can find some berries?" He dropped the three bags of belongings they had, the only things left of Andears, and walked into the woods, hoping a stream or lake would be nearby. Twilight was settling in fast, and soon, darkness would become so thick they couldn't see their hands in front of their faces. Having a fire to keep away predators would be wise, but Apollo and Clep couldn't bring themselves to make one when they camped a few nights prior. Since then, they'd only stopped to rest, taking short naps. It was only the Light's blessing that they hadn't found themselves as a snack for a local werg pack.

Once away from his brother's watchful eyes, Apollo allowed himself to attempt to relax and not carry the weight of their fates on his shoulders for just a moment. He ached everywhere and was sure his feet were blistered from walking so much over the past week. *Once we get to Silene, we can relax*, he promised himself half-heartedly, fully knowing that there was a possibility that the Dark Army had already headed south toward Silene after putting Andears to the torch. *For all we know, Silene is just like Andears, and all this traveling is for nothing.* He thought of his brother, sitting in the woods, waiting for him to return. *If that happens, where do we go? Who knows if the Dark Army had already swept through the other five villages in the territory?*

He breathed, trying to stop his spiraling thoughts from getting too out of control. Tightening his hand on a short bow he'd found in the woods outside Andears, he pulled an arrow from his quiver and kept walking through the woods, hoping to see some teagot to kill before the darkness swept in. The deer-like creatures were plentiful in the woods, feeding on the younger plants that grew between trees and in clearings. Apollo had been hunting them since he was eight seasons old with his father, who would sell the skins to the women of Andears to make goods with. *When I killed my first teagot, Father was so proud of me and had its fangs made into arrowheads for my next hunt and its horn made into a dagger. It was twilight, too, and we were heading back to Andears, tired and empty-handed. But we saw a teagot and got lucky.* Looking at his hands, he saw they were trembling just as hard as when he'd first pulled back the bowstring ten seasons prior.

The sound of rustling in the woods made him freeze, dropping low. His eyes widened as he looked all around, panicked, his mind back in the woods outside Andears when the Dark Army soldiers were looking for any of the villagers to answer to the arrow hitting their commander in the throat. *I need to hide, where do I hide? Where's Clep?! I need to find Clep!* He raced toward the small area where he'd left his brother as fast as possible. *If something happens to him, I will never forgive myself.* He burst into the clearing, his voice low but rushed. "We have to go; they're going to find us!" Looking around, he saw their bags, but his brother was nowhere to be seen. "Clep?! Clep, where are you?"

"Right here," came the reply, and Apollo turned to see his brother holding a wooden bowl full of berries, "I found some berries we could eat in case you didn't find a rabbit or teagot, though if you did, how we'd cook it without a fire is a problem."

Apollo rushed to his brother and hugged him so tight his brother made small sounds of protest and hit his back with his hand to get him to lessen his hold. Apologizing, he let go, stepping away to look around and listen to the woods around them. He could hear the sounds of Clep unstoppering a waterskin, pouring some liquid into a wooden cup, and taking something from his bag. "Here," Clep said, offering him the cup, "you need to sit down and drink, Apollo. I added some berries to make it sweet."

Apollo nodded as he sat and sipped the water, downing it and coughing. "It's a little bitter," he added as Clep drank from the waterskin, "I couldn't find a stream or any animals to hunt."

Clep looked around the darkening woods. "We won't be able to see anything besides ourselves soon anyway without a fire. Will we be safe?"

"We are far enough from the road that no one will see us."

"What about animals? Doesn't fire keep them away while we camp?"

Apollo blinked heavily; keeping his eyelids open was suddenly harder. *I've been pushing us, but we still have days to walk to Silene.* He looked at the cup, noting the herbs at the bottom, then looked at Clep in surprise. *He drugged me with herbs?!* The last thing he remembered was falling over to the ground.

* * *

It was bright when he opened his eyes, feeling more rested than in days, though his back was aching. Rolling over, he found he had been sleeping on the ground with a light blanket over him. A small fire pit had been dug in the ground, and a rabbit was stuck on a stick, roasting over it. Clep was sitting beside the fire, his eyes closed. Apollo dug out the stick from under his back and tossed it aside before standing and going to his brother, who didn't notice that he was awake. Glancing around, Apollo saw Clep's bow and arrows sitting beside a pair of rabbit skins, and a mound of fresh dirt was off to the side. *It's probably where Clep buried the bones.*

Apollo adjusted his tunic and his belt with his father's sword on it, glad to see it was still with them. He frowned as he heard Clep begin snoring softly. The sunlight was high in the sky, coming straight down through some branches in the tree's canopy, telling Apollo that he'd slept much longer than he'd realized. He went to his little brother and wrapped the blanket around his shoulders, helping him lie down and straighten his legs before going to the rabbit and began eating hungrily. *I should have been watching over us and getting food, not you.* Apollo said a prayer of thanks to the Light for providing them with food, as he'd been taught to by his mother, before eating hungrily. He then sat and began sharpening his father's sword with the whetstone in his belt pouch and tried thinking of what they would do once they got to Silene.

Clep crying out in his sleep startled Apollo, making him drop the whetstone on the ground in his haste to stand and get ready to defend them. When he realized nothing was attacking them, he went to Clep and shook his shoulder to wake him. "Clep, Clep! Wake up!"

Clep sat up, screaming something wordlessly, his hand out as if to reach out for something or stop something from happening. Fresh tears lined his cheeks, and he gasped, looking around wide-eyed before recognizing Apollo. He quickly wiped at his face, stammering. "I-I'm sorry, I fell asleep, I-I smell burning!"

Apollo bit his lip, his heart aching for his brother's pain and panic.

"My rabbit was a little burned, that's all, Clep. We are far from Andears, on our way to Silene, remember? We stopped in the woods to rest."

"I must have fallen asleep."

"It's okay, Clep. You are tired, too. You can rest, and I can take watch. I feel much better now that I've eaten."

Clep rummaged through his bag, taking out a vial and dumping some of the leaves into a cup, pouring the last water from his waterskin into it and taking a long drink before lying back down, turning over so he didn't have to face the fire. After a long moment of silence, he spoke. "I've been having nightmares."

"Yeah," Apollo admitted, "me too."

"Why did they attack us? The soldiers were supposed to keep up safe from bandits and wergs, not be monsters poising as humans."

Apollo wasn't sure what to say, so he told the truth. "I don't know."

"Did the people the Dark Army took over the years to become soldiers, do you think they do these things too now?"

He thought about the of-age boys and men who were taken over the years as volunteers to become soldiers, who were supposed to become soldiers who would fight and defend the people. *They were people we knew, and even though I don't think I saw any of them in Andears ever again, I still wonder, are they cruel men now? Would I have become one of them if the Dark Army also took me?* Apollo was glad he didn't have to answer Clep's question because his little brother was fast asleep, and he didn't have an answer.

***

Four nights later, the two brothers arrived in Silene after a farmer took pity upon the two boys and let them ride in his wagon. Clep apologized profusely, saying they had nothing for payment for the kind deed, but the farmer would not hear his words, saying there was no need to repay him. Clep and Apollo fell asleep in the hay as the wagon bounced down the dirt road. When they awoke, they rode beside fields of golden wheat, the familiar scent blowing gently in the morning breeze. Silene was larger than Andears and had more farmland around it than their village, but it also had a blacksmith shop, where Apollo's father had gone a few times south to get better tools, but neither Apollo nor Clep had gone with him. *This is the furthest south we've ever gone.*

The first place they went was the inn, which had a sign that had a bed and tankard engraved upon it. Like many villagers, Apollo and Clep could not read nor write, and pictures were standard on signs to direct travelers. In farming villages like Silene and Andears, villagers wrote numbers in Common to keep up with an inventory of farming equipment, crop yields, and counting rows of plants. Their mother had been a skilled artist and had drawn images of plants in her notebooks so Clep could follow the instructions even though he could not read her writing. When asked if she could read, their mother had said she could, that her grandmother had taught her and she would teach them one day, but unfortunately, the Lingering Rot took her before she could fulfill the promise.

A brown-haired woman with a slightly crooked smile looked up from washing a cup as Apollo followed Clep into the inn and came around the bar, wiping her hands on her apron. "Hello, are you two all right?" *I'm sure we look and smell worse for wear,* Apollo realized as the woman's eyes filled with worry; *at least I know Clep could use a bath, and Light knows what I look like.* Without finding more than a stream along the way, Apollo hadn't had much of an opportunity to see what he looked like, but glancing at a mirror behind the bar, he saw his startled and pale expression, the soot all over his body from the flames and the still-healing burns on his arms. It had rained twice, but it seemed not even the rain could wash Andears from them.

"Could we have a place to stay? Our… our village…" Clep started, and his voice broke.

The woman immediately went into action, going to the bar and pulling out plates and cups for them, waiving off any explanation. "No need to explain, dears, come sit and get food in you." She set down some bread on the plates, and Apollo was already eating before he'd fully sat in his chair. The woman left to speak with someone in the other room and came out with the innkeeper, who set down two bowls of stew for them. "There's a bathhouse out back, and you two will have a room set up when you're done," he said, warm and welcoming, "Let me know what you need from the store next door; I'll tell the clerk in the morning."

Apollo nodded, his mouth full of stew and bread, reaching for his cup of water to drink with one hand and putting a coin purse down with the other. The man nodded, taking out a few coins and slipping them into his pouch. "Keep the rest; it seems you've gone through hells."

"More than you know," Clep said, finally swallowing enough to breathe, "Andears was burned to the ground by soldiers."

The woman paled, looking at the innkeeper with worry. "Certainly you are--" she began, but Apollo couldn't bear the thought that she may call them liars.

"I swear upon the Light, they slaughtered everyone; we managed to escape after we had returned to bury them all." His stomach lurched at the thought of the pile of bodies, and he had to take a long breath, or he would lose what he'd just eaten. "Please don't ask us any more questions." *I don't think I can handle it.*

"Of course," the male said, refilling their bowls. "Here, you deserve this." He set small wooden cups in front of each of them. Apollo tasted it, blinking in surprise as he discovered they held a little bit of ale. *We deserve this? What did he mean by that?* He half-wondered if the male thought they had become men now, as if witnessing such a horrific ordeal was a macabre rite of passage. He was thankful when the woman gave them their key, saying they just had to ask if they needed anything.

The bathhouse was similar to the one in Andears, with a single tub that would be emptied at night and then filled with water from a nearby source. A firepit stood nearby with large rocks and tongs for dropping hot rocks into the water to warm it. He glanced at the boy sitting outside in a chair; his duty was to ensure the fire didn't catch the village ablaze during the night. Apollo turned and looked at Clep, who looked more tired than he felt now. "Why don't you get a bath? I will see to our rooms and get new supplies." Clep nodded, heading into the bathhouse with his broken walking stick and clothing Apollo had managed to salvage from a clothing line.

Apollo did not head for the inn, instead heading to the forge, where the assistant looked up at him from beside the fire, resting while he filed a nail. "Can I help you?"

"I was wondering if I could get my sword and dagger sharpened," he answered, handing over his father's sword and teagot-horn dagger. The assistant looked it over and nodded, naming a couple of coins as his price, which Apollo paid, and then headed back to the inn. He told the innkeeper what he'd like from the store, and the innkeeper said he'd see that they were taken to his room. Apollo waited outside, sitting on a bench as he listened to the blacksmith humming as he worked on the weaponry. *It feels so wrong to have people humming around me. You would think the world would be mourning Andears as well.*

Once Apollo had gathered his weapons from the blacksmith, he returned to the inn and into their assigned room, finding a sack with goods beside their door. Taking it into the room, Apollo took a moment to around. It resembled their room back in Andears, with two beds and a dresser between them, blankets upon straw-filled blankets. He touched the pillow and was surprised to realize it was filled with feathers instead of cotton, as they had had. *I wonder if the feathers came from chickens in the coop we heard about earlier from the farmer when we came into town. He did seem rather proud of his neighbor's chickens.* He opened the sack, finding the items he'd asked the innkeeper for, as well as a scrap of parchment with the number of coins he owed.

A noise at the door made him startle and grab for his father's sword, his hands shaking. The door opened, and Clep blinked at him, his brown hair darker with wetness. "It's just me, Apollo," he said, slowly coming in and closing the door behind him, "You can take your bath now."

Apollo slipped his father's sword into the sheath and nodded shakily. He gathered a tunic and breeches from the sack, and headed down to the bathhouse to take his turn cleaning up.

Once he climbed into the water, he realized just how filthy he and Clep had been during their journey and began scrubbing at his skin as hard as he could, as if to wash away everything that had happened over the two weeks. His hair took multiple washings before he finally felt clean enough to put on the new clothing, though they were a bit big for him. He glanced back at the water, seeing it was almost black with soot and dirt. After replacing the rocks into the firepit to warm and muttering apologies for the next bather, he returned to the inn.

In their room, Apollo found Clep was already sound asleep, an empty vial beside the bed on the stand. *He must have taken something not to have any nightmares.* Apollo set down his bag on the other bed, taking out some meat wrapped in paper for Memory, Clep's hawk, and put the package on the table beside the vial. He noticed a second vial sitting beside the second bed, presumably for him to take. Apollo picked up the vial and downed it without a second thought, and before his head hit the pillow, he was asleep.

***

The next afternoon, Apollo finally awoke, having slept in longer than he could remember doing in his life. Clep was absent, which immediately worried him, and he rushed downstairs, tripping on two stairs and almost falling down the rest of them before he realized the inn downstairs was packed with people, all looking and listening to Clep, who stood at the bar, speaking.

"I don't know," Clep was saying, "but I do know from hearing the lengthy and rather loud discussion here that some feel that it is too dangerous to stay here, and there are those who want to stay. So why can't those of us who wish to leave the search for the dawnwarriors and see if they will help those find shelter while the rest of you stay here?" *What is happening, why is everyone looking at Clep, and what are they talking about?* Apollo tried making his way through the crowd, and few of the people moved aside for him as if he were cursed and would infect all the village if he made contact with them.

A male laughed at Clep's suggestion, followed by a few others. An older female frowned at the ones who laughed, speaking up from the back of the room, leaning heavily on her wooden cane. "Stop laughing; at least he has a sound idea, rather than the ones I've heard thus far. The boy is talking sense, and everyone knows where Exonesis Mountain is," she said, gesturing to the east with her cane. "We already know which way to travel for the dawnwarriors; may the Light bless us with their aid. If our Liegelord's army decides to come south toward Silene with hostile intentions, those who wish to go can be away from it and safe. I am too old to make the journey myself, but our children and perhaps our children's children may live their lives peacefully."

Apollo made his way to Clep and leaned in, speaking low. "What is going on?"

Clep handed Apollo half of the bread on the plate beside him on the bar. "Some people want to leave now that they know what happened in Andears. They sent two people to see if it was true as if our presence wasn't enough to convince them of the truth."

Apollo frowned. *Do they really think that someone would lie about something so horrible?*

The village Elder finally stood, shouting to be heard over the many discussing people. "We will hear no more of this right now from Clep and his brother; let their minds have some peace. For now, everyone goes about your days, and will the eldest of Silene stay here so we may speak among ourselves and weigh the options presented." With the Elder's words, the people of Silene filed outside, going to talk to those who had gathered outside.

The innkeeper's wife set down a bowl of porridge for Apollo, and he thanked her, giving her a coin. "It's a shame you boys are in the middle of such a discussion, I do hope you slept well, at least."

"Yes, ma'am, we did," Apollo said, glad to have something warm to wake up to. His and Clep's strawberry patch they had tried tending behind their home never did have such plump strawberries as was sitting on the porridge, and he opened his mouth to ask her what they could do differently to their patch before he remembered the fire had destroyed their garden. *How long would this happen, remembering and forgetting?* It had been three years, and he was still doing it with his parents, forgetting they weren't at home, like when he'd shot and killed his first teagot buck on his own last summer. He'd rushed home excitedly to tell his father, but when he burst through the door, it was Clep who was baking bread, chiding him for the mud on his shoes. He blinked, realizing the woman had been talking to him still and he hadn't heard a thing, but luckily Clep was keeping her occupied with small conversation.

After he ate, Apollo followed Clep to the outskirts of Silene where he whistled for Memory, who ate some meat from his gloved hand. "Thanks for the meat, Apollo," he said, "Memory appreciates it. She's the one who brought back rabbits the other day for us."

"What were they saying about the dawnwarriors and Exonesis Mountain? I was still waking up and came in the middle of it all."

"They heard what happened and began asking questions. I answered them, but they are really scared."

"So am I," Apollo admitted, "if it wasn't for your potion, I don't know what I would have dreamed." Clep nodded and pulled out his satchel, beginning to busy himself with measuring dried herbs and putting them into vials that he had purchased to create droughts, which would have different effects. He kept his mother's book open and glanced from his vials to it, carefully counting the leaves he put in. *I could never do that, I have the patience of a flea.* Clep continued after he finished counting and began carefully adding water from a waterskin. "I think the dawnwarriors can help like they did in the stories Nan told us."

"Those were mostly of the Scourge War and probably made up," Apollo sighed, "After all, I never saw any flying creatures around besides birds, and definitely not winged humans."

"Nan told us about Sigilbearers, and they were true," Clep

answered with such conviction that Apollo wasn't sure what to say to argue. "I think we can have some people head to Exonesis Mountain and ask for help before the Dark Army comes here and repeats what happened in Andears."

"What makes you think they are going to come here?"

Clep finally stopped to look at him. "What if the soldiers find out that we survived? They think they killed everyone, and we are witnesses."

That thought did not sit well with Apollo, but he had no counterargument. Glancing back at the village, Apollo saw that the farmers had gone to their fields, but some men lingered nearby, awaiting the decisions of those who had the say in the village, trusting them to choose the right path for their future. "For all we know, the Elders could deny the idea and make everyone stay here. Then what do we do, Apollo?"

Apollo wasn't sure what he'd say to that because a door opened, and the elderly woman came out and leaned on her cane, looking at those who came over to hear what she would say.

"A decision has been made."

* * *

The village of Silene had been in a state of chaos ever since the Elders had announced that a group of thirty-one would be heading toward Exonesis Mountain before the end of the day two days. Those who wished to go with them were allowed, and those who wished to stay behind in Silene could do so. Few people could leave, for too many missing people would be evident if the Dark Army came to Silene. With what happened in Andears, no one wanted to risk having the soldiers angry with the villagers. Clep spent the next few days creating salves and potions for those leaving, aiding those packing and preparing for the long Exonesis Mountain trip.

Clep will be safe here in Silene, but I can't stay here, knowing those who attacked and slaughtered would escape justice. During the night, he could take the thought no longer. He dressed, careful not to wake Memory in her burned metal cage, and gathered some vials from Clep's satchel. *He won't like that I am taking them, but knowing Clep, he'll have them refilled in less than a day's work.*

He slipped empty vials he'd bought in their place, and once he was ready, picked up his father's sword and put it on his hip. Looking at his sleeping brother one last time, Apollo slipped out, heading to the stables. He'd used the last half of the coin to purchase an old horse, a mare who could no longer pull a plow but could allow a boy to ride upon her. Apollo climbed onto the mare, wishing he had enough coin to get a saddle. *The Dark Army must have headed north after they burned Andears since they had not come south to Silene yet. If I hurry, I may be able to catch them while they are on their way here and kill them while they are camping.* He glanced back at the inn, the darkened window which was his and Clep's. "I don't care what it takes, I will kill them and keep us safe, I promise." He flicked the reins and took off down the dirt road back toward the Dark Army.

LOST IN SHADOW

Mother, nurture us and keep sickness at bay,
Father, protect and guide us through the day
Brother, see to it our crops grow tall
Sister, watch and help our livestock to live and feed us all
Grandfather, lead us and show us the way
Grandmother, grant us wisdom and protect our babes,
Aspects of the Light, all of us save.

-- Prayer to the Light

RATSBAYNE

Whoever had said that ya couldn't walk in the woods and stay in a bad mood had been a lying piece of shite, Ratsbayne thought grumpily as he walked behind the Dark Army wagon along the dirt road, *and hadn't had any ale to drink, and a rock in their shoe.* The group had left Woodsong before he'd been able to get his drink at the tavern; when Kerrik had said they were going right then, he'd meant it. So here Ratsbayne was, with a rock in his shoe and feeling his world start to fade further into clarity. *By the Light, Ah hate being sober.*

Like the other lower-ranking soldiers, he walked on foot while the three captains rode horses. They did not want to risk Ratsbayne in the wagon; they didn't trust that the two barrels of ale would remain untouched with the rest of the inventory they had to deliver. One of the soldiers began singing a tune, and the soldiers started picking it up, their voices filling the area. Ratsbayne muttered to himself, wishing for some cotton to stuff into his ears.

"O'er ale I heard the tale

Of a maiden fair

Her lips were red, and her head

Had brown hair to her rear.

Oh what a sight late at night

Pointing to the sky

"Please," she'd say, "take me away

To where the shadows lie."

I did as she said and lay her bed

Upon a quilt of night

Well, I guess I'm not the best,

But she said I did all right."

"Ratsbayne," one of the soldiers spoke up after the song ended, "why aren't you singing?"

"Ya don't want meh singing," Ratsbayne answered, "it'd be sounding like a cat being strangled." The soldiers began laughing at that and kept singing old bard's tunes to keep themselves occupied while they made their way to the other garrison. *There'd better be a tavern there because Ah'm going to need a drink to get these screeching sounds out of mah ears.*

The day passed uneventfully, and a clearing in the woods by the dirt road seemed good enough of a place to stop for the night, and they began making camp in the dwindling light of the day. Being denied the opportunity to help get supplies out of the wagon, Ratsbayne was tasked with gathering firewood. He picked up the sticks, grumbling about the soldiers and their singing while keeping an eye out for squirrels.

After dropping off the firewood, he tied his sling bed between two trees, hanging feet above the ground. One of the soldiers began laughing at him. "What are you doing, Ratsbayne? You don't have a tent?" A few others glanced over from their tents, snickering at the drunk with the bare minimum of anything.

"You couldn't buy one with all the coin you won at cards last week, or did you drink it all away?" Another soldier chimed in, sharpening his sword.

Ratsbayne looked at him from over the sling bed, smirking slightly crookedly. "Well, it's got mah blanket, mah gear in it, so why do Ah need a tent? Besides, the stars be nice tonight."

The soldiers laughed, shaking their heads and making jokes about him as they relaxed beside their tents around the fire pit, the wagon and horses off at the opposite end of the camp. Ratsbayne paid them no mind, removing his shoes and the damned rock before getting stew to eat. He then climbed into his sling bed and reclined, listening to the others grumble and swear about their thin bedrolls in their tents not being as comfortable as their beds in Woodsong. *May a thousand small rocks abuse yer backs,* he thought quietly as he closed his eyes.

Horses. Horses ran on the clouds above the ground, over mountains, lakes, and villages.

The ground below cracked, and tendrils made of skeletons rose from it, whipping about like a great beast, destroying villages. Darkness crept toward the capital like a slow wave of water, and it crashed into the white and gold walls of the city, lapping at its sides, growing higher and higher.

He stood on the ground with a sword in his hands, watching the mighty wave of black gather, racing toward him.

He readied his sword and swung.

* * *

Ratsbayne woke, the sling bed swinging as he sat upright too quickly, almost falling out onto the ground. Looking around, he saw no horses running in the air or mighty waves of darkness crashing around him. The only sounds were soldiers snoring in their tents and the footfalls of the soldiers walking their patrol as he watched the camp. *What in the world was Ah dreaming about?* He looked at his empty hand, flexing it slowly, feeling as if he had been holding that longsword in reality instead of a dream. *It felt too real.*

He reached into his pocket and felt the parchment he had written the previous day while gathering firewood, informing his mysterious benefactor where he was and where they were heading. He was sure he could find a squirrel somewhere, or if the same one was following him, get it to deliver it to its master. *Wait, am Ah seriously thinking that the squirrels Ah see be delivery creatures? Ah can't even train mah hair to sit right, and Ah think a squirrel can be taught? Sobriety be messing with mah head worse than the ale did.* He looked the folded parchment over, frowning. It wasn't that he was an enemy of the Dark Army; after all, they did supply him with a place to sleep and ale to drink, but he did not agree with everything they did, especially Kerrik. He had no idea what his benefactor could do about it, but a part of him hoped that somehow it would help in getting Kerrik removed from Woodsong and someone smart be put in his place. *See, Ah be not a spy or a traitor, just someone trying to get his commander removed from duty by leaving messages of what we're doing and when we're going.*

Wait, he realized, *that is precisely what a spy be. Ah be going to get mahself killed.* He quietly walked into the woods to relieve himself and wash his face in the nearby creek. He then left the folded parchment in the crook of a tree before heading back to his slingbed, lying down once more. *Ah am entertaining the idea of a squirrel delivering missives. By the Light, Ah really do need a drink.*

APOLLO

He had come upon a fire burning in the night and started toward it, wondering who it was camping there and if they had seen which way the Dark Army's garrison was. He hoped he'd catch up to the Dark Army before they returned to their garrison, where there would surely be more soldiers than he could take on alone.

He had tried making camp for himself a few nights before, and once the fire reflected in the grass and the smell hit his nose, his stomach rolled, forcing him to put out the fire immediately, shaking. It had taken him a while to stop trembling and steady himself again. *I should have taken some herbs with me for an upset stomach. I wish I had paid attention to Clep's herbal lessons.*

His mind wandered to Clep, hoping that his brother had been doing all right since his departure, and the time away from him seemed longer than three days. Still, the rising and falling of the sun said otherwise. Apollo dismounted his horse, tying it further in the woods, and set an apple down for the mare to eat while he went forward alone to quietly see who was around the fire built up ahead, in case that it was the Dark Army instead of a friendly party. *If it is thieves in a small group, I can easily fight them off with my father's sword. If it's the soldiers, I'll try to take out a few if I can. If there are too many, I'm not sure what I can do; maybe take them out one by one on guard duty or when they head off to the woods to use the restroom or get water. It's not quite the best of plans, but it is at least a plan,* he admitted, trying to avoid thinking of his plan failing. *I have to succeed in this, for Andears, for Clep.*

He moved cautiously as he saw several tents around the fire, at least enough to guess at least two dozen men. The symbols on the side of the fabric told him that, yes, these were Dark Army soldiers, and he crouched by a tree, trying to figure out the best way to approach this. His eyes fell upon the wagon, and he looked at it for a long time. *If I can get the wagon by hooking the horses up quietly, I'll be able to deprive the Dark Army of valuables and possibly use them to help Silene survive the coming months or even fight back, depending on what was inside.* But the idea of keeping two horses quiet long enough to hook up the wagon and take control of it without waking or alerting the soldiers, who no doubt had someone on guard watching for any thieves, greatly made him doubt that idea.

Apollo moved around the camp carefully, using his knowledge from hunting to be as quiet as possible. He looked around until he saw a soldier seated against a tree, whittling a stick with a knife, his sword on the ground beside him. He looked bored in his black and red armor, now and then glancing around the camp before going back to his stick, apparently just doing something to keep him occupied until his watch was over. Apollo approached the male, staying in the shadows as much as he could, dagger in hand. *I can slit his throat so he can't shout out a warning, then have a better chance to kill the Dark Army soldiers as they sleep. After that, it won't matter if the horses make noise. I can get the wagon to Silene and back to Clep.* He crept closer to the tree the soldier was leaning against when a gloved hand pressed over his mouth, a knife to his throat from behind.

"Shh," a voice hissed in his ear, "don't make a sound," and he was pulled into the darkness of the woods.

RATSBAYNE

The lad be either the bravest Ah'd ever seen or the dumbest. Ratsbayne was sure that if he had been drunk, he wouldn't have been able to control the boy as he pulled him further from the camp. The boy kept fighting him, elbowing him in the abdomen and biting down on his leather-gloved hand, which made Ratsbayne bite back the swearing forming in his mouth. Finally, they were far enough down a hill that the firelight was barely seen in the distance before he shook the lad, speaking low.

"Ya dumb lad, why ya bite mah? Peace, and Ah'll let you speak. Don't run off; we don't need the Dark Army's attention on us." He wasn't far from where he'd just gotten done stashing the parchment with the Dark Army's plans for his benefactor; if it was found, he would surely be in danger. He lowered his gloved hand from the boy's mouth and turned the lad to look at him properly, taking in his dirty clothing, stinking of smoke and blood. *He looks as if he's barely outgrown being a boy. Oh by the Light, please let this not be mah benefactor.* The look in the lad's eyes, the determination, anger, and hurt, struck him the most, reminded him of the look he'd seen before in the faces of Dark Army recruits brought to Woodsong to become full-fledged soldiers, assholes, and killers.

Ratsbayne realized suddenly that he did not want this boy among the ranks of the Dark Army, though he could not think of a good reason why not. "What the hells do ya think yer doing!" Ratsbayne fought to keep his voice down when he wanted to yell at the lad, box his ears, and shake sense into him. "Ya don't go--" The lad grabbed his sword and readied himself to fight. Ratsbayne blinked and looked at him flatly. "What are ya doing?"

"Your men killed my village, everyone I know!" The boy struck out at Ratsbayne with his sword, swinging it widely.

Ratsbayne sidestepped the blow without thinking about it. *The lad has no technique whatsoever, whoever trained him was a bigger fool than Ah am.* "One, they aren't mah men. Ah not be part o' the Dark Army. Ah had nothing to do with that village, or any other villages fer that matter."

"Liar," the kid hissed, swinging again.

His form be sloppy, Ratsbayne noticed, *but the kid had a beginning o' control.* He guessed the boy probably practiced a lot on his own but had no formal teachings. Ratsbayne had seen many young boys brought to Woodsong in the last few years who were similar and after being trained, could easily cut a man down with a sword. Ratsbayne waited, watching the boy telegraph his subsequent action and moved into the swing, shoving the boy's arms upward and leg-swept the lad, grabbing the sword on the way down by twisting it out of his hands and pointing the blade at the lad's throat. He watched the boy's eyes widen in surprise and fear. The lad had enough sense to know he was beaten, but a fire in his eyes said he'd fight as soon as Ratsbayne turned his back.

Ratsbayne glanced around to make sure no one else was watching, and he looked down at the boy. "Ah'm not with the Dark Army, lad. Ah'm a drunkard." He couldn't think of another word for what he was. "Ya can't… Ah can't let ya attack them because ya'll die, plain and simple." He lowered the sword and held his hand up for the boy to take to help him up. "Yer fighting style is sloppy, too telegraphed. If ya be serious about wanting to fight against those men up on that hill eventually, ya be going to have to do hells of a lot better than this."

Ratsbayne sighed, looking back at the direction of the Dark Army's camp. He opened his mouth to tell the boy to take his sword and go home, wherever that was, and stay far away from the Dark Army. However, that was not what came out of his mouth. "Ah can teach ya how to fight." He blinked as he realized what he had said, and wondered how in the world those words came out when he was just a drunkard.

What do Ah know about actual fighting besides watching soldiers train outside through the loft window?

The boy ignored the hand and stood on his own, glaring at him as he reached for his sword from Ratsbayne's other hand. Ratsbayne absently spun the sword and switched hands, keeping it out of reach with a muscle memory movement he couldn't explain with anything other than dumb luck. "Ah be Ratsbayne, the drunk who went to take a piss and found ya in the woods. Ah captured ya, and ya be a prisoner--" He paused, hooking his leg behind the boy's and shoving him backward as he tried swinging at him and held him by the collar, keeping him suspended.

"Listen, lad, Ah be trying to save your life. Ya'll be a prisoner, aye, but ya'll be alive. Ya'll walk beside me, ya'll eat beside me if they'll let ya, which they may because Ah be just a drunk and not a threat to anything but their coinpurses. Ya'll learn about the Dark Army; ya'll listen to what they say, what they do, how they do it. In return, they'll teach ya how to swordfight properly, so that when the time comes - if- the time comes, ya can fight and maybe not get yerself killed."

The boy looked at him, his eyes narrowing. "You're a long away from camp for a piss." *Fantastic, not only did Ah find Ah poor fighter who was trying to kill every soldier in the camp without a lick of sense, but he has to be smart too. Did the lad see meh planting the parchment? If so, he's more of a danger to meh than not. By the Light, please let him not know about the parchment and just be asking an innocent question.*

"Ah be a drunk, and Ah had to take a piss and a shite if ya had to know, so Ah went deeper into the woods fer privacy. Ah can't let ya leave now, lad, so ya be a prisoner or a corpse; which is it?" *Ah can't let the lad leave mah sight until Ah know if he saw meh plant the parchment or not. If he tells them and they find it, Ah be as good as dead.* But it was not something he could openly ask the lad; he'd have to observe him.

The boy looked at him, ready with a remark on his lips, but Ratsbayne could see it as the boy realized he was being serious; that he would stop the kid from running off by any means available. The idea that he may have to harm or even kill him to keep this secret was tearing him up inside. *By the Light, who am Ah to even think about this? Ah be no hero, but Ah am not a villain. What am Ah becoming?*

The lad licked his dry lips and slowly nodded. "All right. I'll be your prisoner."

They made their way up the hill toward the Dark Army's camp, the boy's wrists tied in front of him with twine that Ratsbayne wore around his waist as a makeshift belt. Ratsbayne spoke quietly as they walked, moving slower as he shuffled along, holding the boy's sword in one hand, his arm in the other. "What be yer name, lad?"

"Apollo," the lad stated, and Ratsbayne could feel the tension singing through the muscles in the boy's arm. He wanted to tell the boy it would be all right, but he couldn't bring himself to lie. After all, the Dark Army had a reputation for stealing men and boys of fighting age, corrupting their minds, and turning them into their *Kolotor'ix*'s soldiers, which, from what Ratsbayne had seen over the last two years, was nothing particularly good. It was a serious possibility that this lad would become another pawn in the game, but watching the determination in the lad's eyes, a part of him had hope.

Hope. Great, he chided himself at the word, *Ah be as bad as the damned squirrel scribe now.* "Don't fight them, Apollo. Don't look them in the eyes; let them think ya are cowed and obedient, and maybe, just maybe, we will both survive this." He took one last breath before half-stumbling into the camp, pulling the boy along. "Lookie what Ah found while taking a piss."

The lad tensed greatly as the soldier on watch came over, looking down at him. The lad dropped his eyes, looking at his feet as he shook slightly. It might have looked like fear to the soldier but Ratsbayne knew better. *It not be fear but holding back the urge to strike.* He had those feelings, often when he saw the Lordson walk around with Taya under his arm. The soldier went to a tent, pulled some rope from a backpack, and headed back toward them. Ratsbayne tightened his grip a touch on the lad's arm in warning before letting the soldier tie the boy's hands securely, then kept the lead rope in his hand as he took the sword from Ratsbayne and looked it over.

"Pretty pathetic sword you got, boy. What did you plan to do with this, hmm? Gut you some Dark Army soldiers? It's hardly fit for cutting frogs."

"Yes," came Apollo's reply, and Ratsbayne wanted to plant his face into his hand. *Perhaps the lad wasn't as bright as he looked after all.* The soldier began laughing as if it was the funniest thing he'd heard in a while and shoved the boy toward a tree and tied him to it before walking off, still laughing. Ratsbayne lay back in his sling bed, shaking his head to himself. *This Apollo was going to be a handful, Ah can tell.* But simultaneously, the lad intrigued and stirred something in him that he hadn't felt before.

Now Ah know Ah be crazy.

APOLLO

Ratsbayne. What kind of stupid name was that? Apollo walked behind the Dark Army's wagon, the lead rope from his tied hands attached to its back. Try as he might, the binds had proven impossible to untie, and he wished he had hidden his dagger better. Not that it would have helped any; they searched him for any weapons already once that morning and again when they began moving out. *The soldiers,* he admitted grumpily, *if anything, were thorough in everything they did, from searching for daggers to murdering entire villages.*

He glanced at Ratsbayne, who was stumbling along behind the wagon humming to himself. He seemed nothing like the man he'd met last night who had said he'd train him. Apollo did notice, however, that Ratsbayne seemed aware of everything going on around him, stepping over rocks and moving to not stumble into things while at the same time being utterly oblivious to the looks that other soldiers gave him. *The soldiers didn't seem to think of him as one of their own; they didn't even provide him with armor or any weapon. Perhaps he had been a prisoner who had been turned to their side. They're never going to get me into that armor,* Apollo promised himself, *I'll die before I become murderers like them.*

Apollo counted well over two dozen soldiers, not including Ratsbayne and himself. Seeing their black and red armor in the growing light of day did nothing to settle his nerves or anger, but try as he might, he was unable to get out of his binds. Even when they allowed him to make water behind a bush, a soldier held the other end of the rope that held his wrists. It concerned him how they were much more professional than he would have thought them to be, and for the first time, he began doubting that he was going to be able to get his revenge. *No,* he thought, shaking his head to clear it of such thoughts, *I must find a way.*

From what he'd gathered from listening to the soldiers speaking as they walked, Lordson Kerrik, the son of Liegelord Remhold, was their commander at Woodsong and had sent them on an errand to deliver supplies to another garrison. Now Apollo would have to come along with them on the journey. It was clear that they were not pleased with the mission other than that they got away from Woodsong for a while. *Was Lordson Kerrik as cruel to his army as he was to the people of his lands?* Apollo almost started to feel sorry for the soldiers, but then the faces of the dead people of Andears reawakened his anger and shoved aside the temporary feeling of sympathy.

Ratsbayne looked over at him, grinning wildly. "So, yer ready to have an adventure, lad? We're going... er... somewhere else, but Ah can't remember where. Oi, shorty," the drunkard yelled to a soldier shorter than some of his comrades, "where we be heading again?" The drunkard had a thick accent, and Apollo guessed he wasn't from the area.

"Just keep walking behind the wagon, Rat Slayer," the soldier replied, rolling his eyes before joining the men walking alongside the wagon, "keep your new friend company." With soldiers around him and the wagon he was tied to, there was no running off for him now, and soon, Apollo would be far away from everything he knew without knowing how to get back. *Clep, I will find a way back after I get our revenge, I promise.*

* * *

His body ached up from his feet to his neck. He'd lost count of the steps and unique trees or turns in the dirt road that could be used as landmarks to help find his way back to Silene once he escaped. There was no way of knowing how far they had walked, and the woods had only grown denser. The shade was welcome, but without sighting Exonesis Mountain, he could not determine which way they had been walking. Nothing seemed familiar to him, and he began to fear that he'd be unable to find his way back to Silene or Clep.

Thankfully, Ratsbayne stopped humming long ago and limped slightly on his leg, wincing with every step. It almost pleased him when Apollo glanced over his shoulder to see some of the soldiers had slowed down, grumbling and bickering about why they had to walk while the officer and sergeants rode horses at the front of the caravan. Apollo could hear his stomach growling as he did not get much to eat from the soldiers, who were probably reluctant to feed a prisoner who had intended to kill them in their sleep. *I suppose that I would feel the same if the roles were reversed.*

A rustling in the woods made one of the soldiers stop and look around, hand on the hilt of his sword, eyes narrowed. The wagon and other soldiers stopped, and some soldiers passed up the word that something was in the woods. Apollo followed his gaze and listened for the birds. He heard them off in the far distance, but none near them. *I hope they stopped chirping because they are afraid of us, and it is nothing else.* Apollo peeked around the side of the wagon, looking up at the officers on horseback, who were steadying their mounts and murmuring as they glanced around before shouting the order to go once more.

The soldiers began walking again, muttering about teagot when the first black beast raced out through the brush, colliding with a soldier's horse hard enough to send his horse stumbling, the soldier fighting for control as the horse began screaming. Suddenly, the soldiers began drawing their swords and shouting. Ratsbayne immediately moved closer to the wagon for protection, and Apollo decided to follow his lead, crouching beside him, staying low.

Three more black creatures rushed from the one side of the woods where the first one had come from, and Apollo could hear shouting and screams of pain from both men and horses alike. He huddled against the wagon, his breath and heartbeat fast, hoping that whatever attacked them would not come for him. He tried not to imagine that this was what Andears had to have sounded like while he was cowering like a coward in the cave with his brother and the archer. *No,* he thought, standing up, hands in fists at his side, *I'm not going to be a coward, I'll fight back this time!* He started forward, hands in fists, and he was yanked back hard into the wagon.

Ratsbayne looked at him with serious eyes. "Don't be an idiot. Run." Ratsbayne began running away from the wagon, pulling Apollo along before he could realize that his bindings were free; Ratsbayne held their ropes in one hand and Apollo's sheathed sword in the other. *When did he get those?*

Ratsbayne pointed at an old tree up ahead as they ran, tossing Apollo's rope to him. "Up there! Ah'll give ya a boost, climb!" Apollo opened his mouth to ask what good climbing a tree would do when the soldiers had bows and could shoot them down when they were collided into by something vast and black, knocking both he and Ratsbayne away from each other and onto the ground hard.

Blinking his eyes to clear his head, he looked up to see a giant horse with a coat as black as night and almost glowing red eyes, turning from running into them. Apollo couldn't tell if the horse had a rider because he was focused on the blood dripping over its lower snout. The horse's breath smelled of old and fresh death as it stepped closer to Apollo, leaning its head down toward his face, its lips pulling back to reveal not the flat teeth but bloodied, sharp teeth that had remains of fabric in between them.

A whistle and clicking of a tongue cut through the air, making the horse's ears turn toward the sound, creating a low growling that Apollo had never heard a horse make in his life. Out of the corner of his eye, he saw Ratsbayne standing feet apart, manipulating a rope in his hands like a whip. "Look'a mah, ya big brute," Ratsbayne said, his accented voice having a gentle tone, "not the lad, come look'a mah."

The horse turned its head to look at Ratsbayne, but its body still faced Apollo, giving him a view of the blood fresh on its dark coat, legs, chest, and stomach. The horse was the tallest and widest that Apollo had ever seen, even larger than the farm horses that had lived in Andears. Blood and saliva dripped from its chin and landed on the ground before

Apollo, who swallowed hard and fought not to move yet. The fact that the horse was bare of saddle and rider did not ease his fear. *What kind of beast would ride down armored soldiers independently, without prodding from a rider?*

"Lad, whatever ya do, do not run." Ratsbayne kept his eyes on the horse, his voice still low and gentle. "Just walk to the tree behind mah slowly and climb up. Keep your attention on mah, ya big ol' horse." The drunkard moved carefully and smoothly, and the horse watched him. Apollo slowly started to stand but froze as the ears of the beast turned toward him at the movement. "Lad, get moving some; it not be angry yet, but Ah don't think it has to be to run us down."

The horse snorted, stamping the ground.

Apollo made his way to Ratsbayne and tried to stay behind him as he tried getting his father's sword out of Ratsbayne's other hand, but Ratsbayne wouldn't let go of it, his eyes on the creature before them. "Lad, Ah ain't letting ya have the sword right now 'cause if Ah take mah attention off it, it's gonna charge us."

Apollo wrapped his hand around the hilt of his father's sword and the horse's ears flattened. It let out a high-pitched whinny that ended like a growl, making Apollo's hair on his neck stand on end, and he pulled his hand away from the sword quickly.

Other whinnies answered it as six more of the black creatures galloped toward them, one of them having the head of a soldier's horse in its mouth by its throat, the body was torn off, the reins flapping uselessly from the harness. *They look like the creatures I saw in Andears, I thought it was nuzzling its rider, but could it had been eating him?* Apollo suddenly wasn't sure he felt too well.

A smaller, greyish horse came running through the woods, and Apollo wanted to shout at the horse to run, run away as fast as it could before it was torn apart by the black creatures. The pale creature slowed to a trot and found some grass to begin grazing on, flicking its tail, and looked around at the strange horses, nickering. Apollo looked away, knowing he would watch a beautiful creature die before his eyes.

Ratsbayne flicked his wrist, the end of the rope snapping like a whip, and he shouted to get the horses' attention. Seven sets of red eyes in black fur turned toward him, the white horse seemingly not noticing. Ratsbayne snapped the rope again. "Back! Back! Hiya!" His voice was no longer gentle or low but louder and sharper. *That man is going to get himself killed,* Apollo thought as he watched the drunkard walk toward the horses instead of away like any sane person would be doing. Apollo slowly started toward the large tree, trying and failing to get a good grip on its bark.

Ratsbayne kept his eyes on the first blood-covered horse as he slowly moved but kept the rope whipping the ground in purpose-filled motions as if trying to keep them from rushing him. None of the black beasts had moved more than a few steps toward Ratsbayne, growling or gnashing their sharp teeth and stamping the ground, their eyes on him. Ratsbayne made it to the grey mount and threw the rope around its neck, climbing onto its back. He took a long breath and suddenly spurred the horse with his heels, racing Apollo as fast as he could. *Is he insane?*

Ratsbayne tossed Apollo the sword and he caught it, holding out his opposite hand. They clasped hands and Apollo jumped at the same time, Ratsbayne pulling him up behind him, racing through the woods. Apollo glanced behind them, paling. "Faster! They're chasing us!"

RATSBAYNE

The beasts chasing them were faster and larger than he'd ever seen any horses around Woodsong be. He'd seen many creatures in his dreams, but nothing compared to these nightmarish horses gaining on them. They had to be at least sixteen to eighteen hands high. *Not that Ah be going to stop to measure it.*

Glancing behind him, he could see all seven of the beasts weren't slowing but gaining on them as the poor mare under them ran as fast as she could safely through the woods, leaping over logs and through brush that stung at his legs through his pants. "As soon as we can get to an open area, ya can run," he promised the mare.

He felt Apollo behind him, holding onto his tunic with a death grip with one hand, the pressing of the pommel of the lad's sword into his back beginning to hurt. *When I don't feel that, Ah be worrying the lad fell off.* "Are you sure this was a good idea?" the lad yelled at him.

"Ya had a better idea? Why the hells didn't ya say so? Please, Ah be all ears!" He swore as he ducked a branch that would have taken his head off if he'd been drunker. *Two nights of sobriety, and Ah get a tagalong child, and chased by killer horses. What are the odds?* At Apollo's silence, he urged the horse faster, apologizing to it and promising that he'd get apples if they lived through this.

"Do you think the soldiers back there are dead?"

Ratsbayne thought about that for the first time. "Dunno, dun't care right now. Ah only know that we need to be moving faster!" He glanced to the side to see two horses had begun pacing them, trees between them. "How many are behind us?"

"Four… five! But one's breaking away; I think it was the one that saw us first." He felt Apollo's shift in weight as the lad turned back and forth to look on either side of them but was careful enough not to fall off.

Ratsbayne gave a bitter laugh. "Have ya ever seen a pack o' wergs hunt?"

"No… why?"

Poor lad. If they lived through this, he would have to tell the kid some lessons about the world that the lad's parents never taught him. "No reason, ya may just find out in a bit, Ah think."

"You mean they are *hunting* us? Horses don't eat meat!" Apollo kept his weight behind Ratsbayne as they ducked another low branch. *At least the kid knows how to ride behind someone somewhat.*

"Ya be going and tell them that!" Ratsbayne breathed a sigh of relief as the woods gave way to the dirt road, and he felt the mare open her stride and start to run. *Good girl*, he prompted silently, patting her neck, the rope loose against her neck and chest, he holding onto that instead of her mane. He'd not tried steering her the entirety through the woods, letting her instincts take her to safety. It was safer this way for all of them.

The mare began to slow her run, and Ratsbayne looked further down the road, swearing. He glanced to either side to see the two beasts still pacing them in the woods beside the road and looked over his shoulder, noticing that the four creatures behind them had slowed to a gallop, letting them get further away. *Something's not right; why aren't they chasing anymore?* Ratsbayne turned his attention back to the road ahead of them. "*Krushku*, Ah know where we be."

At the fork in the dirt road up ahead, a massive black stallion stood sideways in front of them, looking at them with those unnatural red eyes, tail flicking. Upon his back was a black saddle, with large saddlebags decorated with silver adornments. No bridle sat on his head, no reins to aid the male who sat astride the beast, his black leather armor covering his form, a cloak over his shoulders. Four Dark Army soldiers stood with him, two on either side of the large stallion, which made them look tiny and insignificant. The other beasts who had given chase walked closer, snorting as they came from the woods on either side and behind the mare Ratsbayne and Apollo rode. The rider of the large beast watched them with dark grey eyes as the mare stopped before the stallion, who sniffed her and licked her nose. *Traitor.*

Behind the soldiers, the wall and gate of Woodsong stood open and welcoming. *Kerrik was going to love this,* he thought, as the soldiers from beside the mounted man stepped forward to unseat them. Apollo tried struggling but was easily grabbed and forcibly walked toward the gate. Ratsbayne dismounted and patted the mare's neck, telling her that she did a good job trying to outrun the beasts, and if he had oats and apples, he'd give her them. He began walking toward Woodsong, a sway in his step, and humming to himself to mask his real feelings. He felt the eyes of the soldiers and rider on him as he made his way through the gate. *So much for running to safety.*

MYKEL

He stood at the desk in his new office in the keep, sighing as he looked at the map of Cetra. He would have to get to know it better in the coming days if he were here as *korrati*. Woodsong was the first garrison he had been to that did not belong to *Hon-Hasta'kan ik'Blagdon*, but to *Ero-Hasta'kan ik'Remhold*, which was much different than what he was used to. For one, he'd never seen a garrison that allowed civilians to live among the soldiers.

Mykel agreed with his father that the civilians would be moved into the keep, away from the garrison, where they could do their duties safely. Idle soldiers were not the most intelligent of men, and Mykel had seen reports of misconduct, including coupling between the soldiers and civilian women there. Having babies born in a military garrison would reflect poorly upon Woodsong and himself, making the *Hasta'kan* look bad. The keep and stables had a wall separating it from the garrison, and Mykel would now ensure that the gates would be closed to keep soldiers away from the keep and *kelvorvik* stables at night for protection.

Woodsong was the site of the largest Aldarwood in Cetra, and according to records, residents of the territory would come to be married in front of it or ask for blessings of the Light in the past. A Liegelord had the idea to build his keep beside it, surrounding it and the Aldarwood with a stone wall to protect it, the gates left open for the people to see their Liegelord as well as receive blessings from the Priests of the Light who lived in the keep, only closing at night for protection. When the trade routes were updated, two intersected nearby, one dirt road heading toward Meridiah City to the northwest and the other heading toward the harbors by Exonesis Mountain to the east. The Liegelord had taken the land in front of their keep and turned it into the largest trading market in the territory, taking in part of the coin made there and ensuring the keep's guards protected it.

During the Scourge War, the Liegelord had extended the keep's walls to enclose the market to keep it safer from the undead who had poured through the Shadowgulf Pass to the far north, invading Meridiah. Soon after, as the Scourge War grew closer to the area, Woodsong became a garrison, for it was already the walled fortress that Mykel would call home for the foreseeable future. He looked out the window at the soldiers and *belvash* carrying items to and from wagons to the keep and felt a tinge of nervousness grow within him. He should have felt at home surrounded by the men and women who served *Hasta'kan ik'Blagdon*, those he knew and trusted with his life; he could not help but feel the pressure upon his shoulders. *Brak'ha will be watching me, as will be the other Hesta'kan'ix, waiting for any mistakes or missteps that could send me tumbling down into failure, making our Hon-Hasta'kan look bad. I cannot afford to make a single mistake.*

The thundering sounds of hooves and growls brought him out of his troubled thoughts, and he looked to the gate, seeing that the *kelvorvik* had returned from their gory duty his father had sent them on. Watching the black beasts run through the garrison toward their paddock near the keep made him feel a little more at home, and he could not help but smile.

After glancing at himself in the mirror to ensure his leather armor had not shifted enough to make him look unsuitable, he slightly adjusted his blonde-brown hair. His hair had been darker when he was born but began taking on his mother's summery hues as the time outside in the sun training dyed it. His skin was also darker, lightly tanned by human standards, but to a Shadon, his skin was dark. Nar'Shada did not get a lot of direct sunlight; the cloud cover kept the lands dark, and the plants grew in brown or black hues, at least from what he'd seen in the few times he had visited his people's homeland.

Stepping outside the keep, Woodsong was already looking better than when Lordson Kerrik-*kyr* was in command. A little over two weeks had passed since his *brak'ha* had first received word from the *Kolotor'ix* that a *kriss'ix* had been slain in a village not far from here and was to see what transpired. Blagdon had left and returned with the news; the *Kolotor'ix* had given *Hasta'kan ik'Blagdon* the territory where Woodsong was located, stripping it and the surrounding lands from *Hasta'kan ik'Remhold* completely. Now his *brak'ha*, Wilhiem Blagdon, would be Liegelord of Cetra and in charge of all who lived within it. But the most surprising news was that he would grant Mykel, his only living Lordson, the title of *korrati*. It was a great honor and one he accepted gladly but with nervousness. His father reassured him that the ones beside him would be well-trained and trusted by him to make sure everything ran smoothly. As easy as it sounded, Mykel knew that the eyes of many were upon him, waiting for him to fail and Cetra to be taken from his *Hasta'kan*.

The *kelvorvik* had slowed to trot, heading into the paddock without any help from the soldiers around, who were doing their part to stay out of their way. They were Mykel's favorite animals; native to Nar'Shada, they were tough creatures his great-grandfather had learned to harness and breed to ensure their survival and bring his *Hasta'kan* honor by providing them to the Shadon cavalry as mounts. With these mounts, they rode south into Meridiah and defeated the Scourge, ending the Scourge War once and for all and securing a new place to live for the ro'Shadon. Due to the *Hasta'kan*'s service to the *Kolotor'ix*, they were elevated to the rank of *Hon-Hasta'kan*, and they planned to remain there.

Mykel glanced at the gate, watching as his father rode Ruin toward him, beside him walking the grey mare, which looked almost tiny beside the great *kolvorvik*. Several soldiers walked behind them, escorting a boy and a staggering male. Mykel frowned, seeing the boy's hands tied with ropes. *A prisoner? From where and what did he do?* His father rarely took prisoners when wronged by someone; the matter was generally settled with a duel or coin. *Brak'ha believes in swift and fair justice, not prolonged punishment, nor does he believe in dealing with punishments that outweigh the crimes. I wonder what it was that he had done.* Too many times, they had witnessed others who had done a petty offense and received an unfair punishment. His father had told him that this led to nothing being taught or learned and was a waste on both the punisher and the punished.

Blagdon dismounted Ruin, who waited as his rider removed the saddle and set it on the stand beside the stables before walking toward the paddock with the other *kelvorvik*. A soldier ran ahead, opened the gate, and quickly stepped out of the way. Ruin stopped, letting out a growling grunt, and walked inside. A soldier started toward the grey mare, a rope in hand to slip around her neck to guide her into the paddock. Blagdon held up a hand to stop him. "*Belvash* will attend her." After closing the paddock, the soldier saluted a fist to his opposite shoulder and returned to his duties. Blagdon turned his attention to Mykel, gesturing to the two newcomers. "These were the only survivors of the culling. Lordson Kerrik-*kyr* had tried to send his worst men and faulty supplies away on a so-called mission in hopes that he would look better and I could report back to the *Kolotor'ix* that all was better than it truly was. It instead only served to weed out the chattel and provide meat for my *kelvorvik*."

Blagdon then turned to his soldiers. "See to the survivors."

RATSBAYNE

There was no mistaking the aura of command that radiated off the male who stood before them, wearing worn black leather armor that moved with him like a second skin, though no adornments signified ranking sat upon it. The side of his neck had a mask drawn in bluish-red ink upon his skin. A carved emblem of the rearing horse's head dominated the upper right part of the chest of his leather armor, his gloved hand rested near the sheathed rapier at his side, and his braided leather belt had more miniature emblems hanging along it. They each held a different design, from an upside-down sword to what seemed to be newer looking and more familiar to Ratsbayne, the raven inside a skull's mouth, the emblem of Kerrik's banner. *Ah wonder what that means.* Pouches sat secured to the man's other hip, and one appeared to have been dipped in red dye so the bottom was layered with uneven dark crimson color. It was odd that someone with such a pristine appearance could allow himself to wear something imperfect. For that reason, it bothered Ratsbayne.

The man's sharp eyes seemed to take in every detail, and his left eyebrow held a scar that had faded in time but left a mark that ran to his upper lip. His skin was tanned with slight wrinkling along the eyes and forehead. The man's voice was exactly what you would have imagined a commander's voice to be and what an actual commander wished his voice sounded like. *There be no mistaking that this man, whoever he be, be in charge of something. Where be Kerrik?*

When the soldiers came toward them with purpose, Apollo tried fighting as much as he could with tied hands, perhaps thinking, as

Ratsbayne did, that they would be put to death for surviving the attack of the beasts. *Maybe we were all supposed to die out there, and now he be trying to finish the job.* Ratsbayne clasped his fingers with both hands and prepared to use elbows, knees, and teeth to stay alive.

A soldier took out a knife. "Let us cut your binds, then you can clean up. The bath house is this way." Ratsbayne blinked stupidly at him and noticed the soldier had gestured toward a cabin with smoke coming from its chimney. He glanced at Apollo, who rubbed his newly freed wrists, frowning in confusion. *Well, in Ironfalls, do as they do,* he thought and began walking, hearing Apollo and the soldier walking behind him.

Taking the time to look around, he noticed that Kerrik's banner, which generally hung either under or beside the larger Dark Army banner, had been changed from the previous red and green command to a flag of blue with a silver rearing horse's head, its mane sweeping down into a braid and back up again to create a circle, enclosing the image. It was the same emblem the male who had ridden the giant beast wore on his black leather armor. D*id that mean Lordson Kerrik was removed? By the Light, Ah hope so, the man was a piece of shite.*

Inside the cabin sat four large metal tubs of water, each with a hearth under them to heat the water to a constant temperature, with trays of soaps and oils sitting along their edges. Ratsbayne blinked, wondering where the tub of hot rocks to heat the water had gone. Standing frames with curtains lined the wall, and Ratsbayne wondered if they could be moved to provide privacy if someone wished for it. Apollo and he were left inside, the soldiers shutting the door behind them. Ratsbayne undressed and cautiously stepped into the water, preparing himself to be made into soup. Apollo slowly did the same into his tub, hissing with the heat. "This not be here three days ago," Ratsbayne remarked, the water to his abdomen, tickling his slight chest hair as he leaned back against the tub.

Looking around, Apollo glanced in his direction as he began splashing water on himself. "The water tubs?"

"Aye," Ratsbayne said, just letting the heat of the water soak into his muscles, "Ah mean, sure, the keep's gotta have one like this, but one fer the garrison side? Hells' bells, who brings a bathhouse this nice to soldiers?" *Lordson Kerrik might have washed the stick out o' his arse if this had been here before.*

The door opened, and two women came in carrying clothing and towels, wearing half-masks over their lower faces that were engraved with an image of something, but it was not the masks Ratsbayne paid attention to. Their leather armor was black with crimson trim and form-fitting, with pieces of metal armor that made each woman's outfit protective yet flexible. Ratsbayne appreciated the view as they set the clothing near their two tubs. The raven-haired female went to Ratsbayne, dipping the ladle into the water and pouring it over his chest and shoulders before gathering a cloth over the soap and washing his chest with sure motions. A moan escaped him before he could stop it. *Ah've died and gone to the Light.*

A startled sound and the quick water movement made him open his eyes lazily. Apollo was trying to scramble out of the tub, a shocked expression on his face. The blonde, who had one hand full of a soapy cloth, reached her other hand quickly and grabbed Apollo's ear, squeezing. "Ow, ow, ow!" Apollo's surprised and pained voice came out shakily.

Her tone was gentle yet commanding. "We have been told to see to your cleaning, and you will remain in the tub while I do so. Either I can twist your ear to keep you here, or I can use another part of you. It is your choice, so choose now."

She could hold a part of me, and Ah'd stay here until Ah shriveled like a raisin. Ratsbayne sat back, closed his eyes, and gave himself to the female washing him. He bit back a laugh. "Relax, lad. Yer mother washed ya as a babe, so it be not the first time a woman touched ya."

Apollo grumbled and sank back into the water. "I can wash myself," he said sullenly.

The blonde female did not seem bothered, letting go of Apollo and going to Ratsbayne instead. She began washing the other side of his chest, mirroring the actions of the raven-haired female. Ratsbayne sighed as he relaxed more than he had in a very long time. *This be how a man was supposed to live, attended by two lovely females, not a care in the world. Now all ah need is a drink and a bed.* He heard the sounds of Apollo washing, and when he peeked his eyes open to check, the lad had turned his back to the room and was washing himself. *Suit yerself, lad.*

Ratsbayne sighed and focused on the feeling of the females washing him, not giving Apollo any more thought until he heard the lad get out of the water, dress, and leave the bathhouse. *Ah will have to stay by that boy before we both get into trouble, or worse. That lad will be mah death, and Ah thought that job went to that damned squirrel.*

* * *

When he came to the dining hall a bit later, Apollo was halfway into his stew and bread. Ratsbayne took a seat beside him, his bowl and cup in hand. "Slow down, ya be going to choke. How long has it been since ya last ate? Besides the gruel in the camp this morning?"

Apollo looked at him, swallowing. "Sorry, it's really good."

Ratsbayne snorted and took a bite of the stew, blinking in surprise. *This not be the usual stew made of leftovers and no spices, but a rich and flavorful one with fresh meat and vegetables. Even the bread tastes recently baked.* The entire time he had stayed at Woodsong, the soldiers had the same tasteless meals, as if the spices that were delivered went to the keep and Lordson Kerrik instead. Shaking his head, he began eating, genuinely enjoying the sensation for once.

"I haven't eaten since..." Apollo's quiet voice trailed off, making Ratsbayne look up at him, the euphoria of eating such good food fading him. Apollo's face held the look of someone who had everything ripped away from them suddenly and bloodily. *He has the look of someone who had nothing to live for, and everything to die for. Ah know that one all too well.*

Glancing around the dining hall, he noticed three women in the same crimson and black leather with metal embellishments similar to the women in the bathhouse standing, talking. Like the other women, their hair was pulled back in intrigue up-dos, leaving their faces unadorned except for crimson leather masks covering their noses and lower faces. Gone were the flirty body language from before; instead, sharp eyes watched dangerously over their masks. *Mmmm, a little danger never hurts anyone.*

Taya, the young lass Lordson Kerrik had as his nightly maiden, walked to the leather-clad females cautiously, whispering. The women's eyes softened enough to let Ratsbayne know that Taya was not in danger from them. Taya was nodding, her eyes red, a touch with tears that must have been shed earlier, but a slight twitch of her lip when she saw Ratsbayne. It gave him hope that she wasn't completely broken and now had companions to help her heal, maybe even keep her safe. *Ah couldn't do much more fer her, but perhaps they could save her. That should count for something, right?*

The Shadon way of life is unforgiving and cruel; strive and make it your own.
There are a great many number of rituals, rites, rules, and laws,
but the rule of the Hasta is one of the most important:
Always obey your Hasta'ix.
Treat those under you respectfully and protect them as you would your own.
You owe them protection and safety; they owe you their existence.
Do nothing that would dishonor your Hasta, whether with words or actions.
Let no insult to your Hasta stand without resolution.
Do not cross those of higher Hasta unless you plan to move upon them,
and even then, do not reveal your intentions to anyone other than yourself.
Without the Hasta, you are nothing.

-- Wilihem Blagdon, a letter to his unborn son

APOLLO

As soon as he was finished eating dinner, Apollo was taken to the sleeping cabin, where the soldiers had cots and chests for their items. Apollo didn't pay much attention; he was exhausted and overwhelmed and just wanted to get some real sleep. He put his bag into the chest at the end of the cot, set his father's sword under the blanket beside him, and fell asleep before his head had fully hit the pillow.

* * *

The sounds of nearby cheering, shouting, and fighting awoke him. Grabbing his father's sword, Apollo looked around frantically for signs of fire, his heart pounding with fear. *Clep?!* He blinked, not recognizing where he was, before he calmed, slowly rubbing his hand over his face. *Clep is safe in Silene.* Apollo pulled on his boots and headed to see what was happening outside.

Cheering and laughing soldiers crowded around an area, and Apollo saw two men fighting with swords and shields in the middle of a fenced area. *Are they sparring in a goat pen?* "Don't worry, lad," a soldier quipped, seeing the concern on Apollo's face, "they are dulled and made for practicing. They are the same weight as the real ones, so you get your arms worked, though."

Apollo nodded wordlessly, watching the soldiers spar against each other with metal that made clashing ringing sounds so loud that he could feel it. He watched the spar, which finished and two others took their places, squaring up in the pen. Apollo felt his heart sinking. *There are more soldiers here than I expected.*

The soldiers grew quiet as a lythe figure stepped into the ring from between the ropes. Instead of black and red metal like the rest of the soldiers, he wore black leather, his movements making no noise as he straightened, a shortsword on his hip. He glanced around, and his gaze landed on Apollo. *He looks to be my age.* "You," the boy said, pointing his shortsword at Apollo, "You have your own sword, so I assume you can handle yourself decently enough. I want to see you fight. Bring your sword if it makes you more comfortable than a practice one."

Being singled out, Apollo glanced around uneasily, feeling the soldiers now looking at him, and slowly slipped between the ropes into the ring nervously. As he walked toward the center of the ring, he heard a few soldiers whispering to each other excitedly.

"It is only appropriate that I introduce myself since you are my opponent," the boy said, looking at him, "One should always know their opponent's name. I am Mykel Blagdon, Lordson of *Hon-hasta'kan ik'Blagdon* and *korrati* of Woodsong."

Apollo blinked at him, surprised at the formality and the strange words. *What did he say?* "I'm Apollo." His mother would have scolded him for not using manners and saying it was nice to meet him. *It's not nice to meet you; you are one of the people who slaughtered my friends. Forgive me, Ma, I cannot greet him with manners.*

Mykel stood a respectable distance away and saluted him with his shortsword, waiting. Apollo copied the movement after a moment, ensuring his grip was confident on his father's sword. Mykel gave one slow nod and suddenly was moving toward him. Apollo managed to get his father's sword up in time to block, but the shortsword was already moving for another blow and Apollo was still registering the vibrations in his arms. As metal hit metal, Apollo forgot about the soldiers watching them and began fighting back, shoving to move Mykel away and stabbing at him with the sword, aiming to kill the other boy who represented everything he hated, every soldier in black and red armor who took his old life from him.

Mykel turned, deflecting the stab with his sword, and his wrist twisted, the side of his blade touching Apollo's neck. "Dead," Mykel announced and stepped back, giving Apollo a chance to regain himself and try again. Apollo blinked, having forgotten that they were supposed to be sparring and not actually trying to harm the other.

The other boy waved Apollo forward, and Apollo rushed, stabbing at his hip, but Mykel moved to the side and turned, blocking his sword again. They began trading short parries, metal clashing against metal. Apollo had to push himself to try to be there to stop Mykel's blade from striking him. The boy was faster with his shorter blade, and Apollo struggled to keep up, constantly backing up around the pen. Apollo aimed a stab at the boy's stomach and Mykel used his sword to deflect it to the side harmlessly. Twisting his wrist, he pointed his shortsword at Apollo's open side. "Dead. You should use the side of your blade, not just the end. Slash, do not just stab." He stepped back to allow Apollo another moment to recollect himself. Apollo's jaw tightened hard enough that his head started to hurt. *He's the same age as he was; how dare he act like he knows everything and that I know nothing!* He started forward, slashing instead of stabbing as often, and Mykel had to maneuver more to block. "Good, you are learning," Mykel said, and Apollo wished he'd stay silent.

The two made their way around the sparring ring, their grunts of effort and the ringing of their swords filling the air. Mykel ducked under a swing, stepped into Apollo, who had no way to block him now and put the point of his sword on Apollo's throat. Apollo's heart was pounding so hard, he could hear it in his ears. *Was this how I die? To a boy who is my age?*

"Dead." Mykel stepped back, saluting with his sword once more. "You need to train more, but you are not bad. I look forward to seeing your fighting improve," he said, making his way out of the sparring ring.

The laughing of soldiers slowly faded into sound, and his fists curled in anger and humiliation. He grabbed the other boy's shoulder, turning him back toward Apollo. Apollo barely registered the confusion on the other boy's face when his fist cracked him across his jaw.

MYKEL

Mykel's jaw ached, his world rocking a moment as he stumbled. The laughing and talking from the gathered soldiers and *belvash* gave way to sudden silence. *How dare a human attack a lordson of a Hasta! Does he not know it can be punishable by death?* Mykel's eyes rose to see the figure watching from beside the sparring ring, and a chill ran down his back. The *Hon-Hasta'kan'ix* stood silently, a gloved hand raised in the air, the fingers open and relaxed.

That hand was the same one which, with a single motion, had sent Shadon cavalry riders to meet their foes on the battlefield, sent *kelvorvik* to feast upon the still-living bodies of their enemies, and brought down swords to take heads off condemned men. *That hand was the only thing preventing any action of the soldiers and belvash present, the only thing keeping Apollo's blood in his veins. I wonder if he knows how lucky he is right now.* Blagdon's eyes watched his son, much like how a curious predator would watch prey; wondering what it would do next and giving no indication of what he expected him to do. *I am on my own.*

Mykel turned back to the farmboy, who raised his sword and rested the tip on the middle of Mykel's chest. "Dead." The blade trembled slightly with effort or even perhaps rage with being humiliated during the spar.

Mykel could hear the sound of a few of the soldiers snickering, though on whose behalf he could not tell. He looked at Apollo's fiery blue eyes and made his decision, his hand tightening around the pommel of his sword angrily.

*Ro'*Shadon used the shadows as their way of life, from moving things, teleporting, and defending themselves. They were taught to properly incorporate them into their daily lives from a young age and sometimes created their own ways of accomplishing tasks, which could grow enough to become part of their Sigils' images. His father had often said how one uses the shadows was a trademark of Shadon's control and mindfulness. Controlling one's emotions was just as crucial as controlling one's power.

Mykel forgot all his lessons as he stepped back from the tip of Apollo's sword, calling the shadows from the soldiers and surrounding posts to gather around and wrap around him. He stepped through the shadows and appeared behind Apollo, flicking his wrist so his shortsword appeared beside the fence and out of reach.

Apollo turned quickly, his face confused. "How did you--" he began, but Mykel was already leaping upon the boy before he could react, the two of them falling onto the ground. The sounds of the drunkard laughing were barely heard over the sounds of shouting and flesh hitting flesh and leather.

BLAGDON

"*Kiv-kyr.*" Blagdon's voice cut through the sound of the boys' foolishness like a rock in a lake, echoing slightly without the use of power to do so. Mykel shadowed from under Apollo, who slammed his fist into the ground instead of his son's cheek. *If Mykel had been human, I'd allow this to continue, but as Lordson ik'Hon-Hastakan, he cannot be part of such a ridiculous display of immaturity and loss of control. This is beneath him.*

Mykel reappeared from the shadows, away from Apollo, pointing at him with furious motions. "I accept!" He shouted angrily, his lip bleeding and already beginning to swell.

Before anyone could make the situation worse than this already was, Blagdon spoke, his tone holding no room for discussion. "*Belvash* will look at your injuries. Everyone else, back to your duties." The soldiers walked off, talking amongst themselves in quiet excitement. Mykel shadowed his shortsword to his hand and stormed off toward the infirmary cabin, *balvash* Desira walking beside him. Apollo picked up his sword, dusted it off, and limped after him. A second *balvash* followed him closely, ready to interfere if the farmboy tried attacking again. The drunkard finished collecting coins from soldiers and then hurried away quickly when Blagdon looked at him.

Blagdon walked to the keep silently, noting human soldiers stealing nervous glances his way, but the Shadon soldiers watched and spoke low amongst themselves. Blagdon need not listen via shadows to know what they discussed; Mykel had created a problem for *Hasta'kan ik'Blagdon*, one that could alter his plans for remaining *Hon-Hasta'kan*. *I will have to remedy this before heading home.*

A human punching a Shadon, especially one of a *Hasta'kan*, though both foolish and dangerous for the human, was an experience that he'd not seen personally in many years. *Either the boy had no wits in his head, or he was utterly ignorant of how dangerous an action he performed.* He refused to believe the boy wanted to throw his life away carelessly. The boy showed smarts, adapting to Mykel's sparring tactics and instruction, but showed no signs of formal training.

Blagdon sat at his desk and began writing a letter for his wife, *Sri'balvash* Narisa *ik'Blagdon*, informing her of what had transpired. Once he had finished his letter and affixed the wax seal of *Hasta'kan ik'Blagdon* upon it, he sent it to be delivered to Stormhold immediately. *It has not been a week, and already Mykel has done things worthy of the Kolotor'ix's ears. He has great things to come in the long road ahead if he can stop himself from stumbling upon its path first.*

* * *

Going through the parchments of reports that Lordson Kerrik-*kyr* had kept took his mind from the sparring ground and only served to cement further the thought that the fifth Lordson of *Hasta'kan ik'Remhold* was a complete and utter fool. *Lordson of a Hasta'kan or not, the Lordson-kyr should have known better and not treated those under him as chattel.* After hearing what Blagdon would send the *Kolotor'ix* in his report, Lordson Kerrik-*kyr* had angrily and arrogantly challenged him to a duel, which Blagdon accepted after ensuring that was what the Lordson-*kyr* truly wished. Blagdon did not want to kill him unless he had to and had offered to send him home to his father, *Hasta'kan'ix ik'Remhold*, alive. Not wishing to return home a failure, the Lordson-*kyr* had demanded retribution in the form of a duel, and Blagdon held it in front of the entire garrison to see.

For the first time, Blagdon kept his dueling rapier from delivering the killing blow. He instead gave Taya, the girl whom the Lordson-*kyr* had kept as an unwilling bedmate, the option of castrating Kerrik-*kyr* before Blagdon gave him his death. The poor girl had cut him three times before a *balvash* aided her in the act, but both the member and head of the fool were on their way to *Hasta'kan ik'Remhold* in a box affixed with the seal of *Hasta'kan ik'Blagdon*. A large bag of the coin was sent to the girl's family in a nearby village, explaining that Taya was safe under a new Leigelord.

Taya herself was given a choice to either leave or remain at the garrison if she wished, safe in the company of the *belvash* who would be here serving under Mykel as healers and protectors. *No one would dare harm her again, especially now that the Lordson-kyr was dead and she was protected. It would not surprise me if Taya were taken to the Blood Temple for training to become a belvash. I hope she survives it.*

But in reading the other reports, Blagdon found nothing that spoke of a farm boy with a sword in any capacity or even where he'd come from. *This Apollo certainly did not have the training nor discipline of a soldier. It is possible that the first time he stepped foot in Woodsong was when he arrived with the drunkard.*

Ratsbayne was mentioned many times, going out and about, leaving the garrison at night, and returning in the mornings, presumably to drink, but other than that, he was harmless. However, it bothered Blagdon why the two civilians were with the soldiers in the woods. *He could be trying to get rid of Ratsbayne, but the boy showed promise if he had training. It simply does not make sense.*

A knock at his door made Blagdon glance through the shadows to see who it was, not stopping from reading the report or writing his notes. "Come in." The *balvash* walked in, her lower face covered in a mask with a snakelike fang engraved, blonde hair pulled into a long braid that brushed her hip as she walked. "Tell me, *balvash* Alandra, how is my Lordson?"

"Cuts and bruises, *Hasta'kan'ix* Blagdon, the same with the farmboy. I felt no internal bleeding in either of them. It would have been worse if Lordson Mykel had pulled the knife he keeps in his boot."

Blagdon nodded. "Mykel would have automatically lost the fight, for such an action would not have been honorable." He turned a few pages, frowning, and changed the subject from his son's foolishness. "Have you spoken to Taya?"

Alandra's eyes narrowed over her mask. "Yes."

Blagdon ignored the icy tone. *Belvash* took crimes against females personally, and he could not blame them; he looked upon such subjects with as much disdain. "How was she not with child?" He flipped through a few pages before looking at Alandra, who blinked in surprise at him. "I have reviewed all the notes, reports, and entries I can find upon her. In his journals, any mention of her is… disturbing, to say the least." He gestured to the fireplace, where said journals were already ablaze, pages curling and handwritten notes slowly fading to ash. " I cannot find any reports of her being with child or giving birth."

"She told us that someone had given her herbs to steep and drink to ensure she would not, and others to knock Lord Kerrik-*kyr* out so he would not be able to perform most nights. No one would know he'd be unconscious in his bed while she escaped unharmed to her room."

"Who gave her these things?"

"She won't say. She does not wish they would get into trouble for saving her."

"Saving her would have been killing him or sending her away under cover of night," Blagdon remarked bitterly, "whoever thinks they were helping her only prolonged her misery."

"Lordson Kerrik-*kyr* would have just picked another girl as a bedmate, my Lord; we'd seen it happen enough times in other places." *Balvash* Alandra took a moment to get her anger in her voice under control before speaking again, which Blagdon appreciated, understanding it was the situation that enraged the *balvash*, not the person she spoke with. *It is wise for her to realize that as well.* "Whoever gave her the herbs was, she's grateful to them. The other women in Woodsong were given herbs to ensure they were safe from bearing children as well; they merely showed up in a leather pouch tucked inside a cooking pot on the shelf or in a laundry basket. No children have been born in Woodsong for the last three years."

Blagdon nodded. "Ensure that no females can grow with children, at least for now. If any male takes advantage of a female, make him limp for as long as Mykel controls the garrison." Wording the order carefully would serve two-fold; it would ensure that the females of Woodsong were safe from assault and unwanted pregnancy. But more importantly, *belvash* now had their reasons to ensure that Mykel would be in command of the garrison for as long as possible and more willing to aid his goal of keeping his son safe. Keeping the balance between Mykel's protection and the *belvash*'s agendas was delicate, but he had learned to manage it over time.

It helped that Blagdon's current wife was *sri'belvash*, though there was only so much she could share with him about their ways, rites, and rituals. Over the years, Blagdon had worked hard to guide those around him toward his goals. Like training *kelvorvik*, patience, proper wording, and the right motivation were vital to success. Now that he ensured his son's protection with some of the deadliest assassins, Blagdon turned and walked to the window, looking at the paddock where the *kelvorvik* walked alongside the grey mare. "Tell me, how is our mare?"

"She is doing well, my Lord," Alandra said, joining him at the window. "The blood going to her womb is rich and illnesses-free." It was the primary duty of any *balvash* attached to *Hasta'kan ik'Blagdon* to ensure that babies, Shadon, humans, and *kelvorvik* were healthy, tending to injuries and illnesses. Many *Hasta'kan'ix* did not care if the human children born under their territories were as healthy as *ro'*Shadon babes, often leaving nature to take its course. Still, Blagdon managed his territory differently, earning loyalty from many humans. It was one of the reasons that the territories of *Hasta'kan ik'Blagdon* had a large population of humans and Shadon.

Though probably seen as beneath them, the *Belvash'ix* allowed the tending to the *kelvorvik*'s blood because it elevated the status of *ro'belvash* to more than mere spies, assassins, or mistresses. Blagdon ensured that any *belvash* attached to his House was cared for, protected, and given credit for aiding the Shadon cavalry to grow stronger with every generation. Blagdon nodded, pleased to hear that the developing foal was doing well. *Soon, we will have a new breed of kelvorvik under Hasta'kan ik'Blagdon, which would ensure that we remain Hon-Hasta'kan for many years to come, and when Mykel becomes Hasta'kan'ix, he will be well protected.*

APOLLO

"Ow!" Apollo shook out his hand after he was in the safety of the infirmary cabin, safe from the eyes of the soldiers who whispered around him. He looked over his bloodied and bruised knuckles, frowning. *Why does it hurt now when it didn't earlier?*

A black-leathered woman walked into the cabin with another woman who wore crimson leathers, the former carrying a tome and quill. "Well," she said, slightly amused, "that was quite a spar."

"That wasn't a spar," Apollo grumbled, dropping his hand into his lap.

"No, it was rather personal for a spar. Why did you fight Lordson Mykel?"

"I hate him. I hate them all." He winced as the woman looked at his bleeding lip, touching it with her gloved hands.

"You are too young to know true hate." The pain in his mouth stopped throbbing, lessening.

"If you'd known what they did to Andears, you'd hate them too."

"Hating *ro'*Shadon is like hating the moonlight. It accomplishes nothing. Beating them at their own game, however, is another story." She stepped back from him. "Remove your tunic; you have bruises on your chest that need to be healed or you will be too sore to move tomorrow."

How does she know that if she hasn't seen it? He slowly removed his tunic and set it aside, wincing as he looked himself over, feeling the bruise where Mykel's elbow had caught him in the side. He tensed as the woman touched his skin, her leather gloves warm and gentle, though the sword on her hip suggested she could be anything but.

"He accepted you as *balutrae*, and you didn't offer it. A mistake that could cost him dearly."

"What's that?"

"*Balutrae* means blood rival in Shadese, from the word *balad*, meaning blood." Apollo could hear the slight smile in her voice, though, with her mask, he couldn't see it. "It means that you are his rival, and as such, he is the only one who can claim your life, and you his." Her blue eyes raised to look at Apollo's. "You are safe from everyone as long as you are his *balutrae*, and one day you two will go into combat, and one of you will lose dearly."

"What do you mean; that it's to the death?"

The *balvash* laughed, shaking her head as she touched his ribs. "No, sweet human, it's worse than death, especially for *ro*'Shadon. You truly are ignorant of our ways."

Apollo narrowed his eyes. "I'm not stupid."

"I never said you were. Ignorance suggests the lack of knowledge of a subject, not the lack of brains in a person."

"Oh."

"If a *ro*'Shadon were to lose the combat with their *balutrae*, they would gain their possessions, their positions, their powers."

Apollo blinked at her.

"If you were to defeat Lordson Mykel *ik'Blagdon*, you'd become *ik'Blagdon*, *korrati* of Woodsong, protector of all the villages in Cetra. You'd gain his mount, titles, and his Sigil of Shadow would be absorbed into yours."

"I don't have a Sigil of Shadow."

The *balvash* thought about that for a moment. "A *balutrae* has never been named by a human, so it is possible you would gain his Sigil."

"I'd become a Shadon?" Apollo revolted at the thought.

"What is a Shadon but a human with power? What makes him any better than you?" The *balvash* ran her gloved hand over his arms slowly, making Apollo's skin heat up slightly. "Before your combat, you'd learn everything about *ro'*Shadon society and, of course, how to fight and kill, much better than you know now. You'd be trained by the best to make Lordson Mykel train harder for himself. None could touch you while you are *balutrae*; *Hon-Hasta'kan ik'Blagdon* protects you while you wear the mark of *balutrae*."

Apollo watched her fingers trace over his knuckles each time the bruising was lessened. Apollo found it slightly distracting. "Mark of *balutrae*?"

"Each *balutrae* has the other's mark put onto them by a ritual, so all who see them know they are protected. You could travel through *Hon-Hasta'kan ik'Blagdon*'s territories untouched and seek their aid if you wish. Their doors would be open to you for shelter. Being that they have the best duelist in the realm as their *Hasta'kan'ix*, you'd be taught by the best."

"Their what?"

The *balvash* looked at him, blinking. "You never learned Shadese as a child in your village? What has Lordson Kerrik-*kyr* been doing here?"

"Burning villages to the ground."

"Was your home burned to the ground? Is that why you hate *ro'*Shadon?"

"The soldiers did it too. They killed everyone…" his voice broke slightly.

The *balvash* didn't look at him, just at his hand, which was clean of blood and bruising. Apollo used it to wipe his face when she turned to hand him a waterskin.

"I will talk to *sri'balvash* Desira about that and see if we can help you. But to continue, *hasta* means house, *and kan* means large or major. So a *Hasta'kan*…"

"Is a large house?"

"Very good. Now, *ix* means leader. So a *Hasta'kan'ix* is a leader of a Major Shadon House. See? It is quite simple."

That wasn't as complicated as it sounded, Apollo realized.

"You will be taught everything if you accept Lordson Mykel's *balutrae*. After all, he said he accepted you naming him *balutrae*."

"But I didn't, I just hit him."

"Yes, that is his mistake; now you can make him pay for it."

Apollo leaned in slightly, listening.

"Name him *balutrae*, and say that you accept his mark. Make him train you, teach you. Make him elevate you while protecting you and yours from harm. Do you have a family? You can ask *Hasta'kan ik'Blagdon* for their protection. The more you better yourself, the more he has to work to better himself. Your enemies become his enemies, and vice versa. You defeat him in your combat, the *scivik'yo ik'balutrae*, which takes place years from now, and everything he has to gain is yours. Until then, you are protected; no one can come after you without risking the wrath of *Hon-Hasta'kan ik'Blagdon*. You will be safe."

Clep and I would be safe for the rest of our lives, and no one would ever suffer how Andears suffered if I became commander here. This balutrae thing doesn't sound so bad. Apollo turned his gaze upon her, his eyes and tone eager. "What do I have to do?"

For every dreamer,

There is a time

Which one can never tell

What is real

And what is not.

It is there

Where we truly exist.

--Kil'lik'Draven, Bard of the Winds

RATSBAYNE

He plopped onto the hay beside Apollo, who was sharpening his sword with quick, angry motions. "What a way to draw attention to yerself, lad. What part of 'lay low' did ya not get through that thick head of yers?" He kept grinning, though his tone didn't quite match it. "It looks like the commander's ring cut yer cheek. That's going to hurt for a bit." He opened a coinpurse and began counting the coin he'd won during the brawl. "Let mah give ye a piece of advice."

"Please don't."

Ratsbayne ignored him."Don't walk in somewhere and pick a fight with the second most dangerous person in the place, especially if you don't know what you are doing."

"Speaking from experience?" Apollo snapped back. Ratsbayne couldn't argue that, and the two of them sat in silence for a while, Apollo angrily sharpening his sword and Ratsbayne slipping his coinpurse away for safekeeping once he had finished counting his earnings.

A shadow fell over them, and Ratsbayne glanced up to see the elder Lord Blagdon in the barn doorway, watching them. "Er, hello, your lordship. Yer lad's a fine fighter."

Blagdon stepped into the barn, seemingly not bothered at the stench of old hay, manure, and fur. "My son has been training for fourteen years; he is quite better than a 'fine' fighter, as you so put it. It has not escaped my notice that you made some coin betting with my men."

"Yes sir, ten gold worth," Ratsbayne said proudly, grinning. *Why deny it?*

Apollo glanced at him, frowning. "You bet against me?"

"No," answered Blagdon before Ratsbayne could answer, "he bet my men a gold coin that you'd land a blow on my son." *And two silver for every blow after that,* Ratsbayne added silently. Blagdon's attention, however, was on Apollo. "Can you read and write, boy?"

"My name is Apollo, not boy," snapped Apollo, and Ratsbayne fought every instinct to either facepalm or hit the boy upside the head. *The lad has a death wish as large as the sun in the sky.*

"I am to be addressed as Lord Blagdon, *Hasta'kan'ix*, or Sir. My son is My Lordson, Mi'lordson, or Lordson Mykel. You may also use My Lord, Mi'lord, Commander, or *korrati* for either of us. Now, can you read and write, Apollo?"

"No, sir."

Blagdon nodded once as if making up his mind about something. *Oh boy, ya be in fer it now, lad.* "You will be given a tutor. You will learn to read and write, as well as how to fight properly. Since you do not know *ro*'Shadon etiquette, you will also learn that starting tomorrow morning." He turned and walked off.

"Great," muttered Ratsbayne to Apollo, "yer gonna be the smartest stupid boy Ah know." He left the barn before the new lord or commander thought of something for him.

* * *

Standing at the second paddock on the far side of the keep, Ratsbayne was sure he'd never seen creatures like these before. *Ah can't remember before waking up in a cave with the mother of all hangovers two years ago, but Ah'd surely remember killer carnivorous horses.* Though he hesitated to call them horses; they sure as the hells below were not donkeys. He watched them from safely outside the fence, frowning.

"Beautiful, aren't they?" There was no mistaking the air of command in the voice, and he didn't turn to see if his guess was accurate.

Ratsbayne wasn't sure if the beings were beautiful, still remembering how they looked chasing him and Apollo down. "Well, if ya call murderous, flesh-eating, faster-than-ya-can-ride, smart beings beautiful… then yeah; they got a well-cared fer mane, tails, and coats, trimmed hooves, and no signs of bad teeth, at least from what Ah saw while they were chasing meh like a leg o' lamb."

"Is that all you see when you look at them? Somehow, I doubt that is the case." Lord Blagdon watched the paddock as he spoke, his eyes following one of the creatures as it ran, kicking up dirt as it did so. "They are called *kelvorvik*."

Ratsbayne shrugged, glancing at the Lord, then back at the giant murder ponies walking around the paddock, instincts telling him that the creatures in the fence were more dangerous than the man beside him, but only slightly. The only animal out of place in the paddock was a mottled grey, the mare he rode earlier to what he thought was safety. *It not be yer fault,* Ratsbayne silently thought to her, *ya were doing what ya do instinctually, and that was to run to what ya know. Ya know these creatures, apparently, and feel safe with them. It wasn't safe in those woods, that's fer sure.* The normal horses were kept in a paddock on the other side of the garrison near the barn where he slept. Why was this horse given the unlucky honor of being here? Was it to be lunch, and the murderous ones hadn't decided to pounce upon it yet? Ah hope not; it is a magnificent creature. "They be intelligent, frightfully so," Ratsbayne admitted, "but they be kept from the other horses except fer that grey one there."

Lord Blagdon set his gloved hand on the fence quietly, his voice slightly amused at the observation. "Why do you think that is?"

Ratsbayne thought about that and came up with a better-sounding reason than lunch. "She doesn't have a white coat or red eyes, so she not be one o' them with missing color. Would they still have red eyes then?" he wondered aloud, "Ah be guessing that she be either a part of their blood or with their foal and she doesn't smell like prey to them."

"I am impressed, not many would make such observations after such a short time seeing them." Blagdon stepped back from the fence, removing his hand from the wood that separated them from hooves and teeth. *Perhaps he understands that even he be not safe among the predatory animals.*

"Well, ah be running for my life, not studying them."

"Not studying them, *sir*." The tone was not as light now and emphasized the last word. It made Ratsbayne glance at him slightly to see the man a little clearer than just from the corner of his vision.

Lord Blagdon was looking fully at him. "You have no idea who I am, do you?"

A little honesty never hurt anyone. "Not particularly, no." Something screamed at him not to smart off to this man, and he took a moment to think before speaking. He had the strange urge to stand straighter under the man's gaze, but he shoved the thought away.

"Lordson Kerrik-*kyr*-" the tone held disdain at the man's name, "-did not inform many here about my coming here."

"Kerrik didn't tell anyone about anything unless it benefited him immediately. He be a poor excuse for a commander, and yer murder ponies could shit out a better man."

Lord Blagdon's lip visibly twitched. Whether in amusement or disgust, Ratsbayne could not tell. It took a long time for the man to speak. "I am Wilhem Blagdon, *Hon-Hasta'han'ix*."

"That be one hells o' a last name."

Blagdon gave a sort of sigh. "It is my title. Titles are essential in *ro*'Shadon society. Considering that your Legielord Remhold, Commander Lordson Kerrik-*kyr*, and his captains here were Shadon, you should have known that."

"Oh." That was an explanation for nothing that meant anything to Ratsbayne. Kerrik had always mentioned something about an '*Ero-Hasta'kan*,' but Ratsbayne never knew what it meant and didn't care to learn everything he needed to know about the man he'd learned via observation.

The simple response made the Lord's jaw tighten, and his eyes narrowed as they searched Ratsbayne's face. *Apparently, Ah'd disappointed him, but Ah am not sure if Ah care enough to be worried.* " Oh? Is that all you have to say to a *Hasta'kan'ix*?"

"Er... congratulations? Ah'm not sure what you want meh to say, sir." He remembered the 'sir' this time, just in case it bought him a few more minutes of breathing. "Ah dunno anything about Shadon except they are sneaky bastards who'd sooner stab ya in the back than slit yer throat." *Maybe it was sooner stab ya in the back,* then *slit yer throat?*

"I see. Your accent is unfamiliar to me, and I have traveled to many of the territories in Meridiah, during the last one hundred and fifty years. Where are you from that you don't even know the dynamics of living under a Shadon's rule? How do you claim to know nothing of basic knowledge even children know?" Neither Blagdon's stance nor composure changed, but Ratsbayne's mind was shouting at him to tread carefully and be ready for violence.

When all else fails, use the truth, someone had once told him. He wished he could remember what happened to them to decide if that was good or bad advice. "Ah dunno; Ah stumbled mah way to a village where they nursed meh back to health and gave meh a job tending the horses there. Then Ah was 'volunteered' for the Dark Army when they came looking for males. Well, volunteering be a strong word... let's say Ah punched one of the soldiers who grabbed at a maiden inappropriately during the visit and got taken instead o' her."

"I see. Did your people teach you nothing in childhood? Surely your land's Leigelord would have insisted everyone in the territory knew--"

"Oh no, sir. Ah woke up in a cave two years ago. Ah dunna remember anything about mah life before then. Ah don't even know mah own name; Ah just got called Ratsbayne on the account of Ah being good at keeping rats out of the village, and the name stuck."

Blagdon's jaw tightened. Apparently, this was not going in the direction the man had intended. *Ah know the feeling all too well.* "I see. What exactly is it that you do here at the Woodsong? You are not a soldier; you must have been useful to Lordson Kerrik-*kyr,* or why else would he have you here?"

"Ah tend the horses, clean the barn, fetch water, sleep, eat, drink. Sometimes Ah hit on the female help, and they hit back. Most of the time, they take the hitting part literally," he said, rubbing his cheek in remembrance.

Blagdon just looked at him flatly. Ratsbayne wondered if he was mentally counting. "Lordson Kerrik-*kyr* had written reports and observations while he was in command. I've asked around about you as well. The stableboy, Briar, said that you are extremely good with the horses, though, with people, you need drastic improvements."

Ratsbayne blinked at that. "Ah'm surprised you know Briar's name; Kerrik never learned the names o' the people under him. He only knew mine because his men kept complaining that Ah was beating his men at cards too much."

"Lordson Kerrik-*kyr,*" Blagdon corrected, his voice steely.

Ratsbayne finally turned and looked the slightly taller man in the eyes. "Ah'd call him a Lordson if he deserved it. Ah dunna be believing in being born a title making a man worthy of it. A man has to be worthy of the title before he be called by it. That man 'Lordson' Kerrik wasn't worthy of any title other than *krushku,*" he said because he could not think of a worse thing to use as a title than a swear word that meant to fornicate without honorable intentions.

Blagdon was silent for a long moment as if either pondering what Ratsbayne was saying or debating what punishment to give him. "*Kyr* means death, or an end, in Shadese. It is added to the name of one who has passed away. The Lordson Kerrik-*kyr* is no longer among the living, so use it. You have an interesting state of mind and a bold tongue, especially of someone who says that they cannot remember more than two years ago."

"Ah blame the lack of ale, sir. Ah'll be back to my normal state of mind once Ah go to the tavern." He gave a shaky bow and headed off before he used up the rest of his good luck and got himself thrown into the murder pony pen as punishment. He could still feel Lord Blagdon's eyes on him as he walked away.

BLAGDON

Ratsbayne, what an interesting person. It wasn't that Blagdon was impressed or struck with some emotion at him, but was interested in him the same way one would find a new creature, wanting to know everything there was to know about him so he would know how to squash it or use it if he proved advantageous. The drunkard had been correct about a few things, including that most *kerrati*, or even some *Hesta'ix*, would not know Ratsbayne's name nor care about the Woodsong drunk except to give him tasks that others did not want, such as scrubbing the bathhouse tubs or cleaning manure out of the barn. That was exactly how the third Lordson of the *Ero-Hasta'kan ik'Remhold* had used the man, and Blagdon cursed the nogut for not seeing the potential he had wasted. *Kerrik-kyr should have never had a command, as there were as many inconsistencies as stars in the sky.* Then, the Lordson-*kyr* had tried sending his worst men and broken supplies away when Blagdon had come to the garrison for an inspection ordered by the *Kolotor'ix* to make him look better. *It was a nonsense mission from a nonsense male.*

Blagdon's thoughts turned to Ratsbayne, the only being stupid enough to run through a pack of *kelvorvik* to rescue an ordinary horse and then attempt to outrun them to safety. Ratsbayne had not chided the mare for taking them back to the garrison nor held a tight rein but let her run via her instincts, trusting her more than his own, even though he'd never seen this mare before Blagdon had brought her down with him to Woodsong. The conservation outside at the paddock only cemented his thoughts of the drunkard, though tinged with annoyance at the same time. But even he had to be both pleased and impressed by the drunkard's knowledge of horses and observations of *kelvorvik*.

Hasta'kan ik'Blagdon prided itself on their equine training, raising, and breeding, as well as partially being responsible for the creation of what the *ro'kelvorvik* were today, which gave Shadon an incredible edge during the Scourge War, creating a cavalry unlike any ever seen south of the Shadowgulf Mountains. It was due to this that their *Kolotor'ix* had named them *Hon-Hasta'kan*.

Blagdon knew precisely what kind of job he would give Ratsbayne if he were *korrati* here: his head stableman, caregiver to the mounts on the Woodsong, and eventually, to the grey mare he'd brought with him from his land. The foal she'd birth would be Mykel's mount, and with it came the promise of a new kind of *ro'kelvorvik*. *Perhaps Ratsbayne could be an asset in ensuring the foal reached adulthood.*

Blagdon sent word via the shadows that he'd like to speak with his son and waited for him to come to the *korrati*'s office. He would have to ensure that there was limited alcohol at Woodsong, for Ratsbayne would be no good to them as a drunkard, and he wanted to see the man sober. *What type of man are you really under the drunken mask, Ratsbayne? What are you hiding from?*

* * *

Word of Apollo accepting becoming Mykel's *balutrae* soon spread like wildfire among the garrison, and Blagdon could not be more disappointed. Now, instead of tending to the garrison and getting it ready for Mykel to take control over, Blagdon had to write to the Blood Temple and request a ritual of *balutrae* to be performed as soon as possible. He requested that *sri'balvash* Desira write to them, for she could contact the Temple faster than his ravens would through means known only by the *ro'belvash*.

Blagdon looked from where he stood beside the window as Mykel walked into the *korrati*'s office, looking embarrassed and newly cleaned. He had changed into a simple blue tunic with leather pants, and Blagdon could only surmise he was having his leather armor cleaned. Mykel said nothing, sitting behind the desk, sighing as he saw the piles of reports

Blagdon had written while he was being tended to.

Blagdon spoke after a long silence, returning to the window. "You've accepted a *balutrae* where none was offered by a human who doesn't even know what the word means." He did not need to peek through the shadows to know Mykel flinched slightly. "I thought we had taught you better than this."

"Yes, *brak'ha*," Mykel said quietly.

Blagdon turned to look at him. "Do not mumble; you are a *korrati*. Whatever decision you make, you stand beside it. If you must delay making a decision, do so because you are gathering information from sources more informed than you, not because you are scared to do so. You chose to believe that the human was challenging you to be his *balutrae*, in front of others. Do you understand what you've offered, and he has now accepted?"

"Of course I do," Mykel said, sounding offended. Blagdon raised his eyebrow at his son, who quickly added, "Sir."

"If you truly did, you would have chosen someone worthy to be your *balutrae*, someone who will better our *Hasta'kan* when you gain what they have. We gain *nothing* from this! You allowed a human to strike you before your *kress*, which you then took as a personal challenge for *balutrae* when none was offered! You lost control of your actions and, in doing so, made our *Hasta'kan* look foolish. We cannot afford such embarrassment or weakness."

Blagdon watched his only living Lordson, the youngest of his children. *We must remedy this situation before the other Hesta hear about it.* "You've accepted the status of *balutrae*, and it cannot be undone until your duel. Our *Hasta'kan* will have to protect him. He will be trained and taught in our ways. He will know our culture, history, and language because if you lose this duel, he will gain your Sigil, your power. He will gain your possessions. He will have to learn how to ride *kelvorvik*, in case he defeats you and takes your mount as his own." His jaw tightened at the thought of a human possibly riding the grey mare's offspring, the future of the *kelvorvik* bloodline. "Then, you will no longer be considered

Lordson *ik'Blagdon*. You will no longer be heir of the *Hasta'kan*, nor *korrati* of Woodsong. If the *scrivik'yo ik'balutrae* goes wrong, your Sigil could be absorbed into him, making him a Shadon. You will be known as my human blood-son, and only thus. You will have lost everything you've ever gained because of a foolish, prideful mistake of youth!"

Mykel's eyes widened as if realizing what he'd done. *You learned this lesson too late, and now we must reap the consequences of your actions.* "Brak'ha, I--" he began, but Blagdon walked toward the door.

"You both will go through the ritual. The soldiers are already writing to their *Hesta*. Judgment will be upon not only yourself but also our *Hasta'kan*. This will forever change the way others see us. The only hope we have now is that you make him worthy of the title. You beat him in such a way that a human never thinks to challenge a Shadon as a *balutrae* because if not, we will have humans challenging us at every turn for a chance to steal what is rightfully ours. If you lose, the heir of *Hasta'kan ik'Blagdon* will be dead, and if something happens to me, everything we worked so hard for will be lost, and it will be your fault." Blagdon stormed out, slamming the door behind him.

RATSBAYNE

Anyone worth his salt would have noticed something was not right, and he stopped brushing a horse to step outside the barn, looking up to see if something was in the sky before looking around to see if something was amiss. He headed to where he could see the murder pony paddock and frowned. Horses, when spooked, made a stir and pitched a fit until they could run off to safety. These creatures were silent, sniffing the air as if waiting for a treat. *No, these murder ponies not be natural at all.*

Lord Blagdon stepped out of the keep, his steps measured and heavy, as if bearing the weight of more than just the man. Ratsbayne knew of severe thoughts and troubling dreams that made no sense. *Ah usually just drink them away, and that was the end o' it.*

Lord Blagdon walked to the paddock, and the largest of the creatures came to him immediately. Blagdon carefully touched the nose of the beast with slow movements as if not to spook the creature into biting him, speaking low to it for a long time. When Blagdon patted his mount and began walking back toward the garrison proper, Ratsbayne almost ducked back into the barn, for he felt his instincts screaming that danger was coming, to hide and pretend he wasn't around.

The commander seemed to pay him no mind as he moved down the main path of the garrison, nor even acknowledging those soldiers who hurried to get out of his way. Ratsbayne watched him head toward the sparring areas and the fool that he was, followed at a distance. *Perhaps Ah can learn something or ensure that Apollo doesn't become the target of someone's wrath and get himself killed with his mouth.*

Watching the sparring rings was always interesting, no matter who owned Woodsong, and he seemed to be familiar with the soldiers' styles. They rarely had him spar, for a drunkard with a sharpened stick was indeed a danger to himself more than his opponent, and he would end up dead instead of learning or better for the experience. *Perhaps death would be better, he thought bitterly, for what life do Ah have if Ah cannot correctly remember the one Ah had before?*

Two men were already in the sparring ring, using dulled swords and shields to swing at each other, the sounds of laughter and cheering. They immediately stopped, fists going across their chests in a salute and quickly vacated the ring as Blagdon stepped into it. A brave soldier stepped into the ring, saluting the Lord with his sword, and the sounds of metal ringing were lost as Ratsbayne's mind wandered.

The sound of clashing metal shook him to the core, and he opened his eyes quickly to see an armored man swinging a great axe at him again. "Keep your eyes open; how else are you going to see what you are blocking?"

The great axe came back down, and he blocked with his shield this time, the strike vibrating down his arm. "That's it, Lad! Keep your shield between your opponent and you!" The weight pressing on the shield lessened quickly, and he stumbled under the lack of it, but looked around and saw the head of the great axe coming toward him again.

He sidestepped, using the shield to deflect the deadly edge to the side, and struck out with his longsword at the armored male, who was grinning beneath his black beard. "There you go!"

They repeatedly clashed for what felt like hours until he was trembling with the effort to stand under the weight of his armor, barely able to lift his sword and shield. The male smiled at him and put his great axe's handle in the straps attached to the saddle of a griffin who had watched the entire thing stoically.

He turned to him, placing a sizeable armored hand on his shoulder. "You did great; you'll be one of us soon, lad."

The sound of moaning snapped his mind back to where he was now.

Blagdon stood in the middle of the sparring ring, five armored soldiers in different states of injury or consciousness, groaning. Soldiers entered the ring to aid their companions to be healed by belvash, who were watching silently, humor in their eyes above their masks. Blagdon slowly opened his eyes and lowered his rapier to his side. *Krushku, Ah missed it.*

"See to the injuries, and those who sparred will be given the rest of their shift off to recover," Commander Mykel spoke up from outside the sparring ring. *When did he get here?* Lord Blagdon glanced at the young commander before walking off silently. *He didn't even look like he'd broken a sweat.* Ratsbayne quickly went to find someone who could tell him what in the world had happened.

APOLLO

Few things frightened him; his father had taught him that fear was something to respect but not shy of because it would ruin you once you allowed it to hold you back. Letting fear get in the way of something important could ruin others, too, especially in their time of need. But watching Blagdon was one of the things he truly hoped would never see aimed at him because if that was just a spar, he was terrified of what the man fighting in anger would look like. The man betrayed nothing in his movements, even with five soldiers as opponents, moving and striking with a calm surety that Apollo could only dream of achieving. Blagdon had had a rapier against longswords and shields and still managed to get past defenses, landing fatal blows swiftly and directly as if swords and shields meant nothing to him. There was nothing showy about the fighting, nothing like how he'd seen the soldiers sparring before or how he and the other farmboys would practice with their wooden swords in Andears. No one tried fancy spinning, kicking, or flourishes. There was no banter, and nothing said to bait the others, no taunts; it was silent, strong, calculated, and deadly.

His father once had said to see a man fight was to see a man's true self. Apollo had never understood that until now. Blagdon was a man he had never seen before, cold and calculating, yet he was warm and caring at the same time toward his horses and his son, the commander. This man would demand loyalty and gain it. He'd leave everyone alive to see his example of what would happen if he were angered, and all would be alive to pass the word along as a warning to all nearby, bringing the land to its knees. This wasn't the type of man to go into a village and slaughter everyone in it, then burn it to the ground.

Blagdon terrified Apollo, and he had no idea what to do now. *If he's trained Mykel to fight, I cannot win our balutrae combat. What do I do now? Do I stay here? Can I even leave?* He wasn't a prisoner that he knew of; after all, his hands were not tied, nor was he kept in a cell, but was he free to leave the garrison and go home? *Home. Where was home now that Andears was gone?*

He started to walk away when he realized that he still needed to find those responsible for the slaughter of Andears and make them pay dearly for it. *I can't return to Clep without ensuring justice has been done. Suppose Commander Blagdon planned on expanding and taking over the land as Legielord Kerrik had, going to villages and collecting people for his army, gathering supplies and taxes. Shouldn't I get the word out to Clep to warn him?* It had been so long since they'd spoken that he was sure his brother was worried sick.

"You seem deep in thought," a voice said beside him, making him jump. He turned to see Mykel watching him curiously.

"I'm thinking," he snapped without meaning to.

Mykel frowned at the tone but didn't demand an apology or flinch. "I gathered that. I am just curious as to what your thoughts were to make such emotions cross your face. It must be sad and serious."

"It's private." Apollo went to turn to walk away from him.

"It is a good idea to know one's *balultrae*, Apollo, for knowing them often reveals things about yourself that you may not have known until that moment. You cannot read or write. I would have you taught, for all our soldiers can do so, so why would my *balutrae* be any less?"

That surprised Apollo, and it showed on his face. "Your soldiers can read and write?"

"Of course. Why would we want an army of uneducated fools? *Hasta'kan ik'Blagdon* believes in the betterment of others and ourselves. *Balutrae* and *ro'Shadon* push themselves to be better than the other. Besides, it says a great deal to have educated soldiers intelligent enough to know right from wrong, don't you agree?"

Apollo had to stop and think about that for a moment. If the soldiers were educated and knew right from wrong, why did they burn Andears to the ground and murder everyone?

"As my *balutrae*, I require you to be better than mere soldiers. You will know how to read and write, not just in the common language, but Shadese as well. You will be taught how to duel and its rules, as well as how to fight with a sword and fists, if you wish," Mykel touched his jaw in remembrance, "which I will learn as well to better myself and become a better *balutrae* to you. *Ro'belvash* are experts in such things and will enjoy teaching it to us, I believe."

When Apollo just looked at him, Mykel continued. "You will also learn to ride a *kelvorvik*, for if there is a chance that I lose our *balutrae* duel and perish by your hand, my mount will become yours to claim and ride as a trophy. Not that I intend to lose, for my *sesha* will be very upset with me." Apollo looked at Mykel, unsure if he was jesting or not at the last statement. It was hard to read the other boy, who seemed as serious as his father.

"What exactly are the *belvash*?"

"*Ro'belvash* are females who are deadly assassins of rogue Shadon, from what my *sesha* has said. She would know; she is s*ri'balvash*." Mykel seemed to notice that the new words confused Apollo because he added, "In your common tongue, I suppose it would translate to 'Elder Blood Sister,' if that helps, they are in charge of the lesser *belvash*. *Ro'belvash* have the Sigil of Blood, which gives them magick over blood, which is incredibly deadly yet can be used for healing purposes, which is why they are here. They will be our healers in Woodsong, as well as charged with protecting me."

Now that makes sense, Apollo thought, nodding quietly. He had wondered how his bruises had healed so quickly. Sigilbearers were only spoken of in Nan's stories, and knowing they existed was quite surprising. *I wish I could tell Clep about them. Right now, he'd be asking many questions about healing if he were here.* Apollo felt a pang of guilt for leaving his brother behind, but he pushed it aside. *I can't return until I find out who was behind the attack on Andears and avenge our fallen brethren.*

Mykel turned, walking to one of the soldiers and speaking to him, pointing and instructing him before walking off. *As korrati, he has duties besides seeing to our balutrae bond,* Apollo remembered. But if the spar between him and Mykel had taught him anything, he would have to get stronger before he did so. *Maybe this balutrae thing wasn't so bad after all.*

* * *

Apollo sat in the grass under a tree beside some other soldiers, frowning slightly as he looked around. So far, he'd seen none of the males taken from Andears in the past, nor their healer. He'd been hoping to speak with them, to let them know what had happened to their beloved village and families, but so far, he'd not seen anyone he recognized from his life before Woodsong.

A boy a few years older than him sat beside him, taking a blade of grass and holding it between his thumbs before blowing on it, making it buzz loudly. A few soldiers glanced his way but turned back to their quiet conversations. Shrugging, the boy continued playing with grass blades as if seeing if different lengths produced different sounds.

Apollo was tired of sitting silently and wishing for someone to talk to besides the drunkard lying in the grass, eyes closed. Apollo suspected he was asleep, but he was still too irritated with him to find out. "You're the stableboy working with Ratsbayne, right?"

"That's me," Briar said, blowing on a longer piece of grass between his thumbs, "you're Apollo, the boy brought in with Ratsbayne last week."

Apollo frowned. "Do you know if any of the others from Andears are here? I need to talk to them."

"You won't find anyone from Andears here," a soldier spoke up, using his dagger to clean his nails, "Lordson Kerrik-*kyr* never kept people from the western villages in Woodsong; they were sent to the garrisons in the east. The people from eastern villages were brought to

Woodsong to train."

"Why is that? It would be faster to take people here since we are closer, wouldn't it be?" Apollo asked, remembering the map of Cetra from the previous day's lesson.

"He sent soldiers further away from their homes so they wouldn't be tempted to desert and return to their villages. You won't find anyone from Andears, Thraesh, or Silene here."

Apollo opened his mouth to ask another question, but a female's sharp voice spoke up, and he turned his head to see their instructor, a *balvash* named Inara, with parchments in her hands settling onto the grass. "Today, you will learn about the *hesta* since, apparently, Lordson Kerrikkyr never taught anyone about them." She rolled the parchment before them, and the soldiers leaned in to look at the drawings. Apollo glanced, worried that he'd not be able to understand anything, but instead saw a variety of small drawings and lines connecting them. "As we are aware, many of you do not know how to read and write under your previous leigelord, and I have brought this to aid in teaching you today. However, under *Hasta'kan'ix ik'Blagdon*, you will be taught to read and write in Common and Shadese."

She pointed to the top drawing, an image of a black mask. "This represents our *Kolotor'ix*. He is the leader of the *ro'*Shadon. He has two palaces, one in Nar'Shada, and one in Meridiah City." She traced a line down that branched out from the central line into twelve smaller drawings. Apollo recognized one of them as the rearing *kolvorvik*-head from the banners around Woodsong.

"*Hesta*, or Houses, in your tongue, are all the smaller crests you see here. The Lords of these *Hesta* are called *Hesta'ix*. Each one is called a *Hasta*, and its Lord is a *Hasta'ix*. *Hesta* are separated into three groups. These twelve are called *Hesta'kan*, or Major Houses. They were created when the *Hon-Kolotor'ix* rose from the dragonfire ash of Nar'Shada, and they answered his call. There have only been twelve and there will forever be only twelve. Their Lords are called *Hasta'kan'ix*, so *Hasta'kan'ix ik'Blagdon*."

Apollo nodded slowly, looking at the drawings. Under the crest of *Hasta'kan ik'Blagdon* were even more lines and emblems. *I hope that I don't have to remember all of them.*

"Under the *Hasta'kan* is *Hesta'heh*, or Medium Houses, and *Hesta'yo*, or Minor Houses. They belong to their *Hasta'kan*, and obey their *Hasta'kan'ix*. Human villages also fall under the *Hasta'kan* and its Lord. They are often referred to as Leigelords by humans."

The *balvash* moved the parchment, showing a single listing of the flowing vertical script of Shadese; alongside each line were the *Hasta'kan* sigils. "This is a record of the current *Hasta'kan* ranking. Since the *Kun-Kolotor'ix*, the *Hasta'kan* have competed for higher rankings. These give them prestige and special honors, such as audiences with the *Kolotor'ix*, more lands, better supplies, and other privileges. A *Hesta* can lose or gain rankings, depending upon what happened. Some *Hasta'kan* has been lost and replaced with a *hasta'yo*, which became elevated to *Hasta'kan*. *Hasta'kan ik'Blagdon* is known as *Hon-Hasta'kan*, which means they are in the first ranking."

"What makes them go down in rank?" A soldier asked, listening intently.

"Assassination of the *Hasta'kan'ix* or Lordsons could affect it if they cannot recover from their loss, acting inappropriately toward another *Hasta'kan*, dishonoring the *Kolotor'ix*, for some examples. Rankings are decided by the *Kolotor'ix* once a year, though some movements can be used as a reward or punishment at any given time."

"So Lordson Mykel's actions, choosing Apollo to be a *balutrae*, will they make *Hasta'kan ik'Blagdon* go down in ranking?"

Apollo flinched, glancing at the soldier who was glaring at him. *Don't be mad at me, I didn't start it.*

"Only time will tell."

He thought for a moment and spoke up, wanting the subject to be off him and the whole balutrae subject."What about *belvash*?" Apollo spoke up, puzzled.

The *balvash* blinked at him, and Apollo wondered if he'd surprised her. "*Belvash* live alongside *ro'*Shadon society but do not belong to any *Hesta*. We follow our own religion and have our rules and customs set down by the *Belvash'ix*. Many of us stay with *Hesta* as healers, informants, and scribes, recording important events and ensuring laws are upheld."

One of the soldiers muttered to the one beside him, "I heard they were mistresses; I can't blame them with their tight leathers."

As the other soldier chuckled, the *balvash* looked at them. "Some are mistresses, yes, you are correct. We are taught various skills which allow us to do our jobs properly. Now, moving on to the emblems of the *Hesta'kan*. Know them; it may save your life one day." As she taught how to identify the *Hesta'kan* by their emblems and colors correctly, Apollo realized that the *ro'*Shadon life was much more complex than he'd ever imagined.

Be careful who you trust,

Be careful who you follow

For in the hearts inside their chest

Shadows may soon swallow.

-- Kil'lik'Draven, Bard of the Winds

MYKEL

The soldiers gathered around Woodsong the next morning, talking amongst themselves as they waited for their honored guests to arrive. Now, after a day of scrubbing the garrison and making sure all was acceptable, the gates opened, and three pairs of *sri'belvash* rode horses beside a black carriage with red curtains drawn over the windows, keeping those inside from view. A lone figure in black with a blue-lined cloak rode a *kolvorkav* behind the wagon, their hood up and shortsword clear to see on their hip.

Mykel waited beside Blagdon, looking as if he were fighting the urge to fidget slightly. Wearing his newly cleaned armor, Blagdon had ensured he'd sharpened his sword and looked presentable. Blagdon himself wore his best leather armor, his cloak fastened so it lay behind him, leaving his arms free to pull his rapier from his hip, though he'd not need it. Mykel may not know a lot about them, but if the individuals inside the wagon wished them dead, they could stop their hearts with a flick of their wrists; blades would be useless against them.

The carriage stopped behind the mounted *sri'belvash*, and Blagdon stepped forward. "I am *Hon-Hasta'kan'ix ik'Blagdon*, and I welcome you, honored guests, to our garrison and keep. Enter and be safe under guest rights."

Mykel stepped forward, clearing his throat slightly. "I am *korrati* Mykel *ik'Blagdon*, Lordson *ik'Hon-Hasta'kan ik'Blagdon*, and I welcome you, honored guests, to our garrison and our keep. Enter and be safe under guest rights."

He stepped back, Blagdon mirroring him on the opposite side of the gate to the keep.

The *sri'belvash* said nothing, riding onward through the gate, the carriage following. Only the rider in the rear stayed back further as they rode, to prevent their mount from hungrily eyeing the horses of those before them. They rode forward after a moment, stopping to nod their thanks to Blagdon, which he returned.

Blagdon glanced to Mykel, who spoke to his soldiers watching. "*Kress'ix*, you are in charge while I attend to matters inside the keep. You will continue training your *kress*, and ensure they are ready for whatever missions we will be assigned. *Kriss'ix* Lukras, see that Apollo is sent to the keep immediately."

The *kriss'ix* saluted, bowing his head at the same time. "Yes, *korrati*," he said, then turned to do as he was bid.

Blagdon said nothing, walking through the gates with Mykel, which shut behind them. "Now, the reality of your actions begins."

The *sri'belvash* dismounted their horses, walking them to the paddock Blagdon instructed them to, keeping them safe from the *kelvorvik* and *kelvorkav* hungrily watching the newcomers. The cloaked figure dismounted their *kelvorkav*, walking it to the other paddock, stopping to allow Ruin, the alpha, to smell it. Mykel released a small breath of relief when Ruin snorted and walked off. At least the person will have a living mount to ride back to the Temple. The figure then walked toward Mykel and Blagdon, taking off their hood to reveal a young woman with white hair pulled into a braid, which fell over one shoulder, the tip ending where the emblem of *Hasta'kan ik'Blagdon* was embossed upon her chest.

"Senka, I didn't know you were coming," Mykel fought the urge to hug the daughter of his *brak'ha*, not wanting to embarrass himself for their *Hasta'kan* in front of the *belvash* watching them.

"My brother is gaining his first *balutrae*, I did not wish to miss it." Senka smiled, then looked to Blagdon. "*Brak'ha*."

Blagdon nodded, his face softening slightly. "I will see our guests inside to get ready for the ritual. Do not delay in joining us." He walked off toward the carriage.

Mykel turned his attention back to Senka. "I didn't think you'd be here; after all, you aren't a *belvash*."

Senka shrugged as she walked with him toward the paddocks. "I trained at the Temple, so I know how to do the ritual, but without the Sigil *ik'balad*, I can't participate. I am allowed to watch, however. Lady Narisa wishes she would be here to assist but has duties to attend to and asked me to come in her stead."

Mykel nodded, watching the *kelvorvik* walk around the paddock, making threatening growls at any horse that got too close to the grey mare. "I'm nervous," he admitted quietly.

"That you are about to have your first *balutrae*, or you are about to have a human *balutrae*?"

"I don't want to disappoint *brak'ha*, and I'm afraid I already have."

Senka shrugged. "I'm the first female with a Sigil of Shadow in two thousand years; you're the first with a human *balutrae* in recorded history. We don't follow tradition, we make it." Her lip twitched as Mykel felt himself relax a touch at the comment. "You won't let him down."

"You don't have a *balutrae*, Senka; I do. I can stand to lose my Sigil, my standing, everything."

"I can't accept any *balutrae* because a male Shadon will beat me easily in a fair fight, no matter the weapon. I don't have the physical strength that men possess nor the manipulation of shadows like *ro'*Shadon, so I am forbidden from participating in a *scrivik'yo ik'balutrae*. Besides, losing the status of having a female Shadon would cost the *Hasta'kan,* and *brak'ha* is counting on me to marry in order to secure an alliance with another *Hasta'kan*."

"I have more to lose than you do."

Senka was quiet for a long time, and Mykel wondered if he'd insulted her. "I didn't mean—"

"It's fine. Males always have more to lose in our society." Senka pushed away from the fence and headed toward the keep. "They are ready for us." Mykel followed, unsure what to say.

APOLLO

He had finished washing in the washroom of the keep when a *belvash* came to escort him to the room where the ritual would take place. Wearing a fresh set of white linen clothing, he followed the crimson-clad female, listening to the metal of her outfit click against the leather armor. Viewing her from the back, he noticed this *balvash* had metal covering her back in segmented parts, reminding him of a spine of a teagot he'd butchered two summers ago. Not every *balvash* had metal adornments like this, and some had more than others. He wondered if the amount of metal on their armor had something to do with their rank or achievements, but was unsure he could ask and get an answer if he did.

Before he could open his mouth, deciding to claim ignorance and ask anyway, the *balvash* stopped, gesturing him into the room, before walking away. Apollo pushed open the door and stepped inside, the door closing behind solidly. He suddenly felt trapped and wished for his father's sword to be on his hip, or better, in his hand. He looked around the room, trying to get a better look at his surroundings.

The dining table had been removed from the room, leaving it long and empty, and candles of red and black surrounded the area, standing on iron stands or settled on the floor, casting thick shadows that covered everywhere the flickering light missed. The *sri'belvash* who had come with the carriage were there, one in each corner and two outside the door as if guarding to ensure they were not interrupted. They did not indicate that they saw him, staring ahead as they continued to chant softly under their masks. Apollo wasn't sure what they were saying, but it made the hairs on his neck stand up slightly.

The air was heavy, with scented herbs coming from the cauldron in the middle of the room. A table stood beside the cauldron with a dagger upon it, its blade a glinting metal of deep blue in the firelight.

But those were not the most spectacular sights in the room.

Three figures in crimson stood on the other side of the cauldron, wearing headdresses of varying heights and shapes, long red linens hanging over them, concealing their faces completely. Each wore outfits created with layered leather, linen, and metal, creating three different silhouettes that made them inhuman. Their hands were clasped in front of them, and Apollo could not see their fingers clearly, for each had many rings or gauntlets with claws upon them that glinted in the light. He did not see any weapons on them, but he wasn't sure if their many layers of hanging cloth did not hide some, and he decided he was better off standing across the room and not coming closer unless he had to. *Are these beings even human?* He couldn't remember any of Nan's stories having creatures such as these.

The door opened behind him, and Mykel entered the room, followed by Blagdon and a white-haired woman. Like him, Mykel wore a white tunic and tan pants with simple sandals. *Without his armor and weapon, he looks more of my age than ever.* The door closed behind them, and the female stepped to one side while Blagdon stepped to the opposite side of the door, leaving Mykel in the middle beside him. *He looks as white as his linens,* Apollo remarked silently before suddenly wondering if he looked just as pale.

"Come before the *Balvash'ix*," three voices said in unison, and Apollo jumped slightly, looking around for the source before deciding that the voices had come from the three strange beings before them.

Apollo glanced at Mykel as if willing him to go first, the other boy seeming to be doing the same, before they looked at each other, then stepped forward.

"Closer… come closer," the eerie voices said, rising over the chanting to echo around the stone walls of the room. Apollo and Mykel came closer slowly and stopped before the cauldron. Apollo glanced down, expecting to see things of nightmares inside it, but found it was empty. *What was making the smells of herbs then?* He glanced at Mykel, who gave him the barest of shrugs.

Apollo looked up and was startled, realizing the three beings had come closer, and he hadn't heard them move. *With their metal trinkets and chains, you'd think they'd make more noise.* He glanced at their feet to see if they floated but couldn't see them.

"You are here to be bound as *balutrae*," the three voices spoke as one. Apollo could pick up a slightly raspy voice and a younger, higher voice among them. "As *balutrae*, your lives will be intertwined until the bond is broken by *scrivik* or death. One will gain everything, and one will lose all."

"Your *hasta* will be demanded to protect your *balutrae* as long as your signet rests upon their skin," one of the voices spoke, and Apollo looked to the speaker. Now that he was close enough, he could see individuality between them, their outfits differing slightly from the style to the adornments upon the metal they wore. This one moved her head, turning to look at Blagdon; he saw metal snakes curled around her upper arm, holding the crimson linen tight to her until the elbow, where the cloth flowed like blood to the floor. "*Hasta'kan ik'Blagdon* is expected to fulfill its demand of *balutrae* by the *Belvash'ix* and the *Kolosae-ro'jo'aritas*."

Blagdon spoke calmly. "*Hasta'kan ik'Blagdon* accepts this demand."

The second figure looked to Apollo, and he saw that her pauldrons had metal roses on them and a quill hung from a chain from one of them. "You are *ro'Shadon-nyta*, you are human. Your family will be expected to fulfill this demand of *balutrae*, to protect your *balutrae* and have his enemies as your own. Where is your sire to speak to accept this demand?"

"I have no father," Apollo spoke up quietly, speaking the words he was prompted to by a balvash who told him very little of what to expect.

"Then do you accept this demand in his absence?"

"I accept," Apollo looked at Mykel as he said it. *I will accept and become better than you and become the protector of the villages of Cetra so what happened in Andears won't happen to anyone else.*

The second figure continued. "You have no *Hasta* of your own. You were asked to choose an image that represents you, something important to you, so all who see it know it is Lordson Mykel *ik'Blagdon* who is *balutrae* to you. Throw the parchment with the image into the cauldron."

Apollo took out the rolled parchment scrap he drew on with a charcoal stick he had been given earlier and dropped it into the cauldron. He wasn't a good artist, but he hoped it would suffice.

The third being spoke up, their voice raspy. "Lay the sigil of *Hasta'kan ik'Blagdon* into the cauldron, for it will be put upon your *balutrae* so all who know it is Apollo who is *balutrae* to you."

Mykel removed a medallion with the signet of *Hasta'kan ik'Blagdon* and placed it into the cauldron beside the parchment.

The three began chanting, their voices joining those of the *sri'belvash* who still had been chanting the entire time, and now the shadows grew darker, the air thicker. Apollo felt fear rush through him and, glancing at Mykel, saw he felt the same. Apollo felt as if someone was whispering in his ear, translating the words into Common, but when he turned, no one was there.

"Come to us, all shadows, one

Weave between thee what cannot be undone

Feast upon the pride of sin

Fueled with the blood within

Create with words that those cannot say

Name these til blood or death balutrae."

One of the beings held the dagger to Mykel, who took it and

sliced his palm, wincing as he let the blood flow into the cauldron. The being turned with the dagger toward Apollo, offering it hilt-first. He took it shakily and ran the blade over his palm, the pain sharp and immediate. The being took back the dagger, and Apollo flinched, feeling the blood run faster into the cauldron. *Did I make the cut too deep?*

The blood mingled in the cauldron as Apollo watched the parchment and signet disappear under the red liquid. Apollo started to pull his hand back, and a hand of darkness shot out of the cauldron, wrapping its fingers around his own, his palm touching the one of shadows. Apollo gasped, trying to fight its grip, which only made it seem to tighten. He glanced at Mykel, who was struggling with a shadowy grip around his hand as well, his eyes wide, and he looked at Blagdon, who was stone-faced as he watched.

Pain tore into Apollo's hand as if the palm of the black hand was tearing into his own, making his cut wider and trying to climb inside his hand. His blood poured steadily into the cauldron, and he grabbed the side of it, feeling light-headed. His neck burned as if white-hot metal was being pressed against it, and he squeezed his eyes tightly. *Light, make it stop!* He heard Mykel cry out and bit his lip so as not to do the same. He could feel his heart pounding harder, and now it had an echo as if he had two hearts instead of one inside his chest.

As suddenly as it had started, the pain lessened, and his heartbeat returned to normal. The shadowy hand released him, sinking back into the cauldron. Apollo yanked his hand back to his chest, gasping, his other hand keeping him steady, gripping the side of the cauldron so hard his hand was turning white. The room was silent, and Apollo realized that the three beings had stopped chanting during the ordeal, as did the *sri'belvash*, but he was unsure when they had stopped. He glanced at his hand, gasping as he looked at his palm. There was a scar there, but nothing else. The cauldron was now empty and clean of any blood.

Apollo caught movement out of the corner of his eye as the white-haired female hurried toward Mykel, helping him sit, but couldn't think any more of it before he collapsed, unconscious.

* * *

It was still light when he awoke in the soldier's cabin, alone on his cot. Sitting up slowly, he realized he didn't know how he'd gotten there. Memories of the ritual came flooding back, and he raced to the bath house, losing his breakfast in the chamber pot.

He walked to the water basin and washed his face, looking at himself in the mirror that hung above it. The mirror told him he looked almost the same as before, but he felt different, though he couldn't explain how. He did notice one difference, though. Now, he had the rearing *kelvorvik*-head of *Hasta'kan ik'Blagdon* on his neck, a bluish-purple marking that reminded him of the coloration of a bruise. *Leigelord Blagdon has a mark similar to this but of a mask. I wonder if he is balutrae to someone as well.*

He changed into his leather armor and headed to the tavern, his stomach growling. As he walked, he noticed there were soldiers staring, some whispering as they looked at him. *I wonder if it is because of the balutrae mark on my neck. I know what it is supposed to mean for me and Mykel, but what does it mean to them?*

He spotted Mykel in the tavern as well, eating hungrily. Apollo watched him for a moment, then realized that Mykel had a marking on the side of his neck as well now. It was just as Apollo had drawn it, and he made him slightly embarrassed to know Mykel was wearing something he drew upon his skin.

Before his bath, a *belvash* had told him to draw something important to Apollo that he would want to represent him. Apollo wasn't sure what to draw but finally came up with something that made him think of Andears whenever he thought about it. Taking the charcoal pen, he drew a tree, thinking of the Aldarwood that stood for so long by his home. Now, Mykel had that image on his skin for all to see, even if he wore armor. He'd forever have the mark of Andears upon him until Apollo took revenge on the men Mykel commanded. *This will be our justice.*

Be not afraid of the blinding light,
Be not fearful of the dark,
For the Shadow watches you,
Upon your skin, he left his mark.

-- Shadon nursery rhyme

BLAGDON

Nothing quite ended a frustrating day like a good glass of wine and the arms of the woman who loves you, Blagdon thought, but alas, Lady Narisa *ik'Blagdon* was in Stormhold, the home of *Hon-Hasta'kan ik'Blagdon.* He settled in the *koratti's* office in the keep with a glass of wine while looking over reports brought to him by messenger, informing him of things happening in his lands outside of Stormhold. He insisted on the information be sent to Woodsong while here, for he did not wish to leave until the garrison was adequately set up, but being Leigelord meant that he always had duties to attend to. It would not be an easy task, nor a perfect transition, but having people he trusted already in place would be smoother. Mykel sat across the room from him in a chair, sipping his watered wine and watching the fire in the fireplace, lost in thought. His new *balutrae* mark was easily seen in the firelight, and it frustrated Blagdon when he saw it, but there was nothing he could do about it now but to ensure his Lordson grew stronger.

Blagdon set down his wine, clearing his throat. "If you can inspire your men out of love, then do so; care for them, treat them accordingly. Earn their trust and give them yours. Loyalty requires loyalty in return. But if you cannot inspire out of love, fear works just as well. But remember, once you turn from love to fear, they will never fully trust the love again, for they know what lies beneath."

Mykel seemed to think about this for a long moment, and Blagdon approved. *You should have learned to think before speaking before this, but at least you are showing you are capable of it now.* "Brak'ha, how do you know when to use love and when to use fear?"

"A wise question. That is the task of the leader to find out, and unfortunately, it is not something you can learn by listening to anyone else but yourself. However, I will tell you this: always show respect, even when using fear. Show you have the strength to hold yourself in check and not cast aside all thoughts, and you will earn respect, even from your enemies. Because once you lose that control, you will completely and utterly destroy whoever is standing in your way."

Mykel swallowed slightly as he thought, and Blagdon kept the frown off his face. Showing nervousness or fear could signify weakness, and Mykel could not afford such luxuries. "You did not say your enemies, but whoever is standing in your way. Does that include allies? *Hasta*? Family?"

His son did not disappoint, reading outside of the spoken words and finding something that bothered him and immediately going to remedy it rather than let it fester. "I said it as I meant it. Rage and love are two sides to the same coin and are born of passion. You rage as deeply as you can love, and vice versa. If you love fully and without end, then so will be your rage whenever it is unleashed at whoever is unlucky enough to see it." It was a lesson he had not learned until he lost his first wife and second son on the same day to assassins. It was then he truly understood where his rage came from, even now, so many years later.

"Is that why you were so upset with me earlier?"

"Yes. I do not wish to lose you." *I have lost too much already.*

Mykel turned from the fire and looked at him. "Have you ever lost control, *Brak'ha*?" It was an innocent enough question, but the shadows darkened around Woodsong. The *kelvorvik* he could see outside the window grew still and quiet, sniffing the air and looking around with their red eyes. Mykel glanced around the room, then at his father, who hadn't moved nor changed expression.

Five seconds that seemed to last an eternity passed before Blagdon spoke again, breaking the heavy silence. "Yes. Pray you never see it." With that, Blagdon got up and walked out, the dark shadows fading as the door closed behind him.

Blagdon stood in the *kelvorvik* paddock, brushing down Ruin. Even though the patriarch of the pack had been his mount since he was a colt, Ruin was just as dangerous as any other *kolvorvik,* and Blagdon treated him with the same caution and respect deserving of such creatures. Brushing Ruin's coat with sure, quick strokes to get rid of dirt, debris, and loose hair, Blagdon listened quietly through shadows to the sounds around Woodsong. *Lordson Kerrik-kyr's and my son's soldiers are getting along so far, making things easier for Mykel's command.*

"Hasta'kan'ix ik'Blagdon," a female voice greeted him from behind him, further away from the fence, "I've returned from the culling site." Blagdon glanced through the shadows to see who was speaking, for turning one's back on a *kolvorvik* was deadly and foolish, even if seemingly tamed. Desira wore crimson-trimmed black leather with metal pauldrons and a red cape over one shoulder, signifying her rank of *sri'belvash*. Her black hair was pulled back with a bun with hanging braids down her back, decorated with silver beads, and her lower face was covered with a crimson mask, an engraving of a crossed quill and dagger upon one side. A whip stayed coiled on her hip, and a short sword rested in a sheath attached to her thigh. She carried a parchment in one hand and a leather bag in another.

Ro'belvash did not fall under any command of a male except the *Kolotor'ix* himself, and there were rumors that *ro'belvash* only followed his orders if they ran parallel to the *Belvash'ix*'s interests. Ran by the *Belvash'ix*, *ro'belvash* was a culture of secrets. Blagdon's current wife would shed light about her culture if the *Belvash'ix* allowed it, annoying him not to have information instantly available. He was glad to have *belvash* attached to his House, coexisting in a mutually beneficial relationship.

"All of the Dark Army soldiers whom Lordson Kerrik-*kyr* had sent away have been accounted for, identified by their armor and belongings."

Blagdon's lip twitched at that, nodding. If hungry enough, *kelvorvik* could eat and digest any organic matter and reduce the human body to a bloody stain in less than two hours. The seven *kelvorvik* who had gone out to hunt had done well. Blagdon glanced around the paddock and found them walking around, satisfied and with full bellies. The other five *kelvorvik* kept an ear turned toward Blagdon in case he whistled and pulled out a treat from his pouch on his hip. Years ago, *sri'balvash* Desira had gifted Blagdon with the enchanted leather pouch that would keep any meat and blood inside it fresh and would not smell and ensure his leather armor stayed unstained.

It greatly aided in the survival of the movement south during the Scourge War, for undead meat did not satisfy *ro'kelvorvik* and made pregnant mares give birth to ill foals, many of whom did not live to adulthood. In appreciation of such a rare gift, Blagdon had rewarded her with books he'd recovered during the Scourge War. *Sri'balvash* Desira had so greatly appreciated the books of the southern lands that she later introduced him to her sister and fellow *sri'belvash* Narisa, whom he later married.

Blagdon continued brushing Ruin as *sri'balvash* Desira told him about what she had discovered while ensuring that all soldiers on the inventory mission had been accounted for and killed. Bloody scroll cases held sealed orders for the *korrati* of the next garrison, which was to keep the men who accompanied the scroll. *If the Lordson-kyr had been intelligent, he would have left the failed soldiers here so I could have killed them immediately upon doing something stupid instead of hiding them in the woods. Lordson Kerrik-kyr did not have an abundance of intelligence, which became his downfall.*

"There was a mention of another village, my lord," Desira continued, opening a scroll. *Ro'belvash* had been taught to read and write by their teachers at their temple, which Blagdon also demanded of all his troops and servants. A *koratti*'s reputation and standing were only as good as the soldiers under him, and if the soldiers were educated, it said much about their *korrati*. Also, as Blagdon knew, uneducated soldiers made idle hands and got into more trouble than needed. He had a strong suspicion it was one reason that Lordson Kerrik-*kyr* had problems in Cetra. "Soldiers had gone to one of their villages named Andears to find any sign of a woman stealing from soldiers and destroying Dark Army property. While there, the villagers killed the *kriss'ix* of the soldiers. The soldiers defended themselves, but the villagers were killed, and a fire got out of control, burning it entirely to the ground."

That got Blagdon's attention. A human could not often kill a Shadon, though it was possible. *Ro'*Shadon could easily use the shadows as shields and weaponry or shadow step out of the way. Either way, what happened in this village should never have happened. "If someone killed a *kriss'ix*, Shadon or not, you punish the one responsible, not the entire village." He stood, brushing off his pants, setting his brush and hoof picks down, and shadowed back outside the fence to stand beside *sri'balvash* Desira. As he spoke, he began buckling his rapier to his side and putting his cloak on his shoulders again. "How many were lost?"

"An estimated fifty-seven souls, many of them children," she answered, "judging by the number and size of the graves in the field beside the village ruins. It does not look like a mere fire had gotten out of control, either, sir. I believe it was intentional."

"Villagers would not burn their village to the ground. You said that you went to Andears?" Blagdon looked at her. "Did you go alone?"

Desira gave him a flat look. "I am *sri'belvash*, not a maiden who requires--"

Blagdon cut her off, his voice holding no room for argument. "While in my territory, everyone will have an escort of at least three soldiers of my or my son's command, which includes *belvash*. You are fully aware of this; it is not a new decree."

Desira's eyes glared at him. "You cannot command a *be--*"

"Someone has killed a *kriss'ix-kyr*, not a young Shadon first learning his powers. This is not to be taken lightly, *sri'belvash* Desira," he interrupted her with a voice like cold steel, "Your presence is valuable, and I wish not to replace you. If I must, I will have *sri'belvash* Narisa write to the Blood Temple to make your having escorts an order from the *Belvash'ix*." Blagdon was confident he could convince his wife to write to their Temple to create such an order, considering that he protected those considered his people fiercely. Blagdon returned to the paddock, assuming *sri'balvash* Desira would follow the ordered suggestion. "Tell me, have you heard of the whereabouts of the *kolvorvik ik'kriss'ix-kyr*? I'd be remiss to think what would happen to the first few humans who tried capturing it, thinking it to be a regular horse and finding the truth quite the opposite."

Desira sighed, shaking her head. "I think you are the only Shadon who would think to ask about it; most would just let the poor humans live without knowing the beast's true nature. I can return to the area to look if you wish."

"No," said Blagdon after a moment, "let *korrati* Mykel deal with it. He should go and see the damaged village for himself and see firsthand what happens to innocent people under bad leadership. It will be a good lesson of what not to become. While in the area, perhaps he may find our wayward *kolvorvik* and bring it to its rightful home."

"I will see Lordson Mykel gains this information," she said, walking toward the keep.

Blagdon watched the grey mare grazing on the grass in the middle of the paddock while the dangerous *kelvorvik* walked beside her harmlessly. *Soon, the next generation will lead, but will they repeat the mistakes of the past? That is another matter entirely.*

RATSBAYNE

Ratsbayne groaned, lying in his slingbed in the hayloft. He threw a blanket over his face and muttered a prayer to the Light that his stomach would stop twisting in his body. Two months had passed since returning to Woodsong, and he'd kept his head down and Apollo's on his shoulders. He counted it as an achievement; Commander Mykel Blagdon stayed closer to Apollo, who had begun training beside the garrison soldiers, whether or not the lad wanted to. He wasn't sure what this new infatuation the young commander had with the lad, but the word *ball-u-tray* kept being said, and try as he might to understand it, he still wasn't sure what it meant.

Unfortunately, Leigelord Blagdon aided in overseeing the garrison and inventory. Once the tavern reopened after the inventory was reported, it would limit the number of drinks to two instead of letting the men be grownups and drink until they felt they were finished, as Kerrik had done. *Ah never thought that Ah'd be missing anything that idiot had done.* Said tavern was closed until the commander had gone through the tavern, inventoried everything himself, and had the establishment appropriately cleaned. Even without the distraction of alcohol to take up his time, Ratsbayne had discovered was he had less opportunity to sneak off the garrison and into the woods to see if the squirrel had any messages or another coinpurse for him. *Ah wonder if Ah can convince it to leave a bottle of ale in the oak tree for meh, instead of a parchment.* Watching Lord Blagdon, he wondered if the man would kill him if he found out Ratsbayne had been communicating with the squirrel. The thought of it made Ratsbayne decide that he'd have to keep his secret correspondence to a minimum.

Ratsbayne flinched, looking out from under the safety of his blanket, seeing that the sun had already risen and was shining in between the barn boards, a sliver of light directly into his eyes. Cursing, he sat up and looked at his shaking hands, his stomach rolling. *Krushku, Ah need a drink, and then Ah will stop shaking.* He dressed and descended the ladder into the stables, almost falling as someone shouted his name.

"Ratsbayne!"

"Ah be here, what ya want, Briar?" He snapped at the stablehand, who set down an empty bucket, picking up a pitchfork.

Briar didn't seem to take offense to the tone, shrugging. "Oh, you're awake. The *korrati* said you're to report to the sparring ring right away."

Ratsbayne looked back up the ladder to the loft longingly, wondering if he had a wineskin hidden somewhere under the hay that he could find. He was tempted to go back to look but decided it would be too much work and begrudgingly headed toward the sparring arena. *Great, just the perfect way Ah want to start mah mornings; sober and in pain.*

***

Soldiers were already sparring when Ratsbayne finally made his way to the rings. Apollo was sitting on a log bench, already rubbing his arm, a frown on his face. Lord Blagdon looked over as he walked up. "Good, get in the ring, I want to see what you can do."

"Ya don't want to see that," Ratsbayne said, "Ah'll just make a fool of us all and probably end up hurting mahself." Some of the soldiers laughed, agreeing.

"The better place to make a fool of oneself is here among your peers rather than the public," Lord Blagdon gestured. "Get in the ring."

Ratsbayne made his way to the ring slowly, grumbling. He'd found a wineskin hidden in the hay loft the previous night, but unfortunately, it was empty. Cursing his luck, he'd snuck out to the hollow tree and tried to see if the squirrel had left a wineskin or coin to bribe someone to give him some ale, but it was also empty. *Even the damned squirrel be plotting against meh.*

The commander stood near the fence, stretching, looking as if he'd already sparred that morning. He gestured to a soldier. "Get him a sword," he said, "and accompany him in the ring."

"Yes, *Hasta'kan'ix ik'Blagdon*," the soldier said, and he walked into the ring. Ratsbayne looked around, trying to think of a way out of sparring, and was so lost in thought he didn't notice the hilt of the sword being held out to him until it nudged him in the chest. He looked it over, testing the balance as if he knew what he was doing. "Go slow on me, Ah haven't drunk this morning,"

"Begin."

APOLLO

The morning was nothing but drills for him. Instead of learning to swordfight, as he'd thought he'd be doing, he was getting buckets of water and holding them out at arm's length in front of him for a time, then adding squats to it, then holding bundles of sticks out to the sides with his arms extended for as long as he could stand. *Who knew that stakes could become so heavy? I wanted to learn how to fight; not be too sore to lift my father's sword.* The only good thing about it was the commander was right beside him, doing the exercises, wincing. It made Apollo feel a little better. His arms were aching, as well as his shoulders, and it was not even time for breakfast.

Watching Ratsbayne in the sparring ring, he thought he'd still be able to do better than the drunkard, who was swaying so mightily Apollo figured he'd fall over at any moment. He winced as Ratsbayne fell to the ground under a hit for the fifth time in that many spars. His opponent shook his head and scoffed with every win, looking around as if waiting for his commander to relieve him of this simple duty of beating a drunk in a spar. *I almost feel bad for Ratsbayne.* A particularly hard hit with a shield sent the drunkard back hard, falling over his feet onto his back. Ratsbayne scrambled to his feet and swung his sword as the soldier descended upon him again. Apollo glanced at the ground, noticing Ratsbayne had dropped a coin purse, and he used his father's sword to pull it closer to pick it up. It was a small but well-worn leather pouch with some weight. Curious, he opened it and poured the contents into his hand.

A metal chain poured into his palm, attached to a flat circular medallion. It was of a creature with the head and wings of an eagle but a lion's body in flight in front of a sun with the beams of light carved above it, and below were hills and a valley. Around the edges were carvings in strange writing. Turning it over, he saw the back had an image of something, but it was so worn down that he could hardly make out the crescent moon with a leaping deer under it. Apollo felt his stomach tighten as he curled his hand around the amulet, his hand shaking with anger. *Clep has worn this pendant every day since Ma passed, never taking it off.* According to her, it had been in the family for generations. *Clep cherishes this almost as much as I cherish our father's sword. When did Ratsbayne steal it? Was Clep alright, or was he injured in trying to fight back to keep his most prized possession safe? Perhaps Ratsbayne was one of the evil soldiers and had played the fool this entire time. But if that were true, why would he never don their armor or do drills with them? Why was he so bad at fighting, or was this all an act? If so, for what purpose?* There were too many questions and insufficient answers, and Apollo was unsure what to do. He returned the pendant to the pouch and slipped it into his pocket. *I'll confront him later about this.*

"That is enough for the moment," Lord Blagdon said, finally speaking something other than the word 'again.' Apollo wondered if the Lord had something against Ratsbayne, for he hadn't made anyone else spar repeatedly. Commander Mykel stood beside his father, speaking low to him, using his hand to block anyone from reading his lips. Lord Blagdon listened, then nodded after a long moment.

Commander Mykel took a step forward and pointed at a group of soldiers watching the spars after participating in them earlier. "Come with me; I have an idea for your next spar, which will require some setup," he said with authority. The six soldiers saluted with fists over their hearts and head bowed, then hurried off to do the young commander's bidding. Lord Blagdon watched passively for a moment before walking toward the soldier's area of the garrison, speaking to soldiers as he passed. From the soldier's reactions, it was encouragement, but Blagdon's expression never changed. *That is one scary man, but at least I know what he truly is.*

But watching Ratsbayne, who was using a ladle to drink rainwater out of an open barrel and pour some over his head, he was not sure what to think about the drunkard who had first captured him at the camp, saved him from the creatures in the woods, befriended him, and now had his brother's pendant hidden on his person. *Who are you?*

* * *

When Apollo went to the area under a tree to report for training, he was surprised to see that Mykel was there as well, waiting, his eyes closed as he rested with his back against the trunk, his sheathed sword across his lap. Apollo slowed, not wanting to disturb him, but Mykel spoke, not moving. "Sit. Our *balvash* instructor is coming; she's heading from the keep now."

Apollo frowned, sitting not far from Mykel. "How do you do that?"

"How do I do what?"

"How do you know what is going on around you? Your eyes aren't open, and we can't hear to the keep." Apollo glanced at the wall around the keep, which obscured most of the building from view, but he could see a *balvash* in crimson and metal armor begin heading toward them in the distance.

Mykel opened his eyes, looking at him as if wondering if Apollo was serious. After a moment, he spoke. "*Ro'*Shadon are given the ability to manipulate shadows through our Sigils of Shadow. Surely, you know about Sigils."

Apollo shrugged. "Our Nan told us about Sigils and Sigilbearers through stories, but I thought they were just stories to make us sleep at night."

"They are not just stories. What did your... Nan, you called it? What did she say about them?"

"They were magick users, that they could manipulate the different elements of the world, fire, earth, water, air, and others. But no one's seen a Sigilbearer, at least no one I'd ever spoken with."

"Sigilbearers exist, especially those of Sigils of Blood and Shadow. That is what *ro'*belvash and *ro'*Shadon are."

"I guess I had never thought of Shadon as Sigilbearers," Apollo admitted, turning a stick in his fingers after a moment.

"*Ro'*Shadon have black Sigils on their skins, *belvash* have crimson ones, the colors of shadow and blood. I cannot believe you did not know that, nor how to read or write. Did you not have any education in Andears?"

Apollo looked at him, eyes narrowed. "We live and work on farmland; we didn't need fancy things or knowledge that was useless outside of our work," he snapped, "not everyone has the same thing you do, just because you're a Leigelord's son."

Mykel started to stand, and a female's voice stopped him. "Perhaps it is a good thing your Leigelord is allowing you to obtain said education now, so you may teach your children when you have some, and it is good that you are teaching Lordson Mykel about the villages around Cetra and how to improve them better." *Balvash* Inara said as she walked up, looking the two boys over with an almost amused look over her mask.

Mykel straightened slightly, frowning. "Yes, it is, *balvash*."

She nodded, gesturing to the grass, and sat before them. Apollo sat, casting looks at Mykel now and then in irritation.

"You two are *balutrae*, and *Hasta'kan'ix ik'Blagdon* wishes you both to review and learn the rules so that you understand what this status means."

I don't know them, thought Apollo, *and I suppose it is a way for me to learn them without looking any more foolish than I do already in front of Mykel.*

"Of course, *balvash*," Mykel said, as if he'd expected this lesson. It irritated Apollo, knowing that Mykel was more educated than he, and the other boy seemed to like rubbing it in his face with little insults.

"*Balutrae* comes from the Shadese word of *balad*, meaning blood, and rival, *utrae*. The former term was *balad ik'utrae*, but over centuries, the word became shortened into the term we use now. *Ro'*Shadon can only have one *balutrae* at a time, and they last for as long as the other lives."

Balvash Inara has a soothing voice, Apollo noted as he leaned in slightly, becoming more interested and less irritated. "The function of the *balutrae* is now for *ro'*Shadon to better themselves by competition with another who has wronged them without resorting to revenge. *Balutrae* spend years trying to become more than their counterparts. In the long run, this betters our society by having those lessons and behaviors learned through the generations."

"There's been talk about a *balutrae* duel; what is that about?" Apollo asked, feeling slightly confused.

"To end our *balutrae* with each other, we can duel. Many of these end in the death of the weaker opponent," Mykel stated, "so many do not duel to keep their *balutrae* alive. If you manage to win, you will gain my mount, any personal belongings I own, and be able to wear *Hasta'kan ik'Blagdon*'s emblem on your belt to show all you have bested me. *Hasta'kan ik'Blagdon* can never come after you in revenge for my death."

"What if you win? I don't have anything for you to gain."

Mykel was quiet for a moment. "I don't know."

Apollo blinked. *I am not sure I had heard him say he didn't know anything before now.* "What do you mean, isn't this your society's rules?"

"Humans have never been considered as a *ro'*Shadon's *balutrae* before," Balvash Inara spoke up, "they are considered too low in society to be worthy of such status."

Apollo was puzzled, and it showed on his face. "I don't understand. If I am 'too low' to be considered a *balutrae*, why am I Mykel's *balutrae*?"

"Lordson Mykel or *korrati* Mykel," the *balvash* corrected automatically, the warmth leaving her voice.

Apollo ducked his head. "My apologies. Why am I Lordson Mykel's *balutrae*?"

Mykel didn't look at him, shuffling slightly. It reminded Apollo of how Clep looked after he swung Pa's sword around the main room of their home and knocked over Ma's bowl, breaking it. Ma had confronted them, asking who did it, and Apollo had said he had, but Clep looked guiltily on as Apollo took the punishment.

"This is a lesson to remember: actions and words have good and bad consequences. Perhaps this *balutrae* between you will teach you both lessons you were not expecting." The *balvash* stood, bowed her head, and walked off, leaving the two boys to think about the actions that brought them to this path and where it would lead.

The truth sometimes
Is harder to keep than the lies.

-- Kil'lik'Draven, Bard of the Winds

MYKEL

It was after midday the next day by the time the setup in the sparring area was complete. Two large barrels were suspended parallel to each other using ropes, able to swing freely, with reins fastened to an end. A long rope was attached to the barrel so a soldier could pull on it to simulate the movement of a horse while the two 'riders' could train in mounted combat safely.

"I need a volunteer," Mykel said, raising his voice to be heard. He could have used the shadows to speak through, to make his voice heard all over the garrison if he wished, but he was taught not to rely upon his ability for simple things. His *brak'ha* had said it would allow the soldiers to respect him more as one of them and not someone who flaunted his abilities that others did not possess.

One of the soldiers stepped forward, saluting. "I volunteer, *korrati*. Your word shall be done." Three others also stepped forward, but the volunteer had already spoken before they could. I suppose that is a good sign, Mykel thought, glancing at his father to see him give a slight nod of approval.

Mykel spoke up once more. "As you know, *Hasta'kan ik'Blagdon* is the supplier of our *kelvorvik* and *kelvorkav*, our mounts for the cavalry of our *Kolotorix*. We live with the knowledge that our cavalry was a large reason why the undead army did not spread as far and was finally beaten during the War of the Scourge. We were instrumental in saving thousands of lives and will continue to do so." The soldiers cheered at that, which made Mykel feel a touch of pride break through his nervousness. "As such, I want you to train for sparring on horseback as well. Since I do not trust some of you not to break your backs trying to fight mounted or accidentally kill your mount," he fought to not glance at Ratsbayne, "you will first sit astride this log and spar with sword and shield until one of you is knocked onto the ground."

The volunteer laughed and headed to the barrel stand-ins, climbing up and sitting astride one. He tested the balance of it before being handed his sword and shield by another soldier. "Who is to be my opponent, *korrati*?" asked the mounted soldier, laughter in his voice.

Mykel glanced around before his eyes landed on the person he'd created this exercise for. "Ratsbayne, you are his opponent. Get up there."

"Mah? Oh no, ya got the wrong drunkard. Ah'd fall off before Ah sat down. Ah can't even beat someone standing on two feet. Now you want meh to stand on none? Ya be crazier than Ah be, lad."

"Commander or *korrati*," corrected Mykel, trying to add more authority into his voice, "I am your *korrati*, and I order you to mount this log."

"Ah'd rather mount a female, if ya don't mind, commander. The barrel isn't mah type." Some of the soldiers chuckled beside Ratsbayne, but he headed toward the barrel and tried three times before he finally could pull himself up and sit up. A soldier handed him the sword and shield he'd been sparring with earlier.

"The first one to unseat the other wins," Mykel said, crossing his arms and settling in to watch. Glancing through the shadows quickly, he saw soldiers whispering to each other, making bets on how long it would be before Ratsbayne was on his back in the dirt. Apollo frowned, running his fingers over the pommel of the old sword he had at his side. His father stayed in the back, watching with interest.

"You may begin."

BLAGDON

When his son had suggested his idea for the sparring area, Blagdon initially thought it a foolish plot for the drunkard to fall off and break something to get him out of sparring. But Mykel had a theory about Ratsbayne, and Blagdon was curious to see if it was true, so he allowed it.

Ratsbayne had been forced to sober up in the past few days, thanks to the tavern being closed and having the *kriss'ix* Lukras use shadows to find and destroy every hidden bottle of alcohol in the garrison. Blagdon also had the *belvash* force all the alcohol out of his blood, which unfortunately meant that Ratsbayne was often too sore or too ill to move, or when he did, it was almost as if he were drunk once more. From the exaggerated movements that Ratsbayne had made on the ground while sparring, Blagdon knew there was no way that he could ever be helpful in combat; Ratsbayne leaned too far when he tried dodging blades and stumbled instead of moving smoothly, so regaining his balance took more time. *In a real fight, Ratsbayne would have been killed many times.*

But this was different. Mounted combat was nothing like fighting on one's two feet on the ground, and often, one was much better at one style of fighting than the other. While many men could claim to be born to fight, there was no being born to do mounted combat. It had to be learned. Ratsbayne held onto the barrel with his legs, but not too tight, using different muscles to maneuver himself forward to backward, side to side, to use his fluid positioning to advantage, whether counterbalancing a blow to his shield or a swing with his sword. In contrast, the other soldier held on tightly with his legs, using brute strength to stay onto the barrel under swings and parries. It made his movements not as fluid, and he'd fight against the momentum of the barrels moving. *It is the difference between a tree swaying in a windstorm and one gripping hard into the soil,* Blagdon thought, *eventually, the one that does not sway will be uprooted and fall.* He understood this concept, for he'd been trained in mounted combat; as the *Hasta'kan'ix* who provided *kelvorvik* to the Cavalry and Shadon, he'd insisted upon it. After all, one could not provide what was needed if one did not know what was required firsthand.

Staying behind his shield in his left hand, his right holding the longsword, which he used in various thrusts and slashing motions, Ratsbayne showed a much different fighting style than his opponent while also keeping mindful of where his sword was, not swinging it wide to the front of him. The other soldier did not, trying to dislodge Ratsbayne from his seat with heavy blows from all angles. Lord Blagdon observed bitterly if the barrel had been an actual mount, the soldier would have decapitated his mount several times already. *Ratsbayne lacks the imagination to pretend the barrel has the head and neck of a horse, so why is he doing this now?* The only mounted soldiers now made up the Shadon cavalry, and if Ratsbayne were a Shadon, Blagdon would eat his leather boots.

The soldiers cheered and shouted as the two swung at each other, each trying to dismount the other with blows. Finally, the soldier leaned too far to dodge a swing from Ratbayne and fell off the barrel onto the dirt, much to the laughter of his peers. He got up, brushing dust off his armor, grumbling, but saluted the *korrati* and walked off to stand with his peers as other soldiers shouted to volunteer.

After three soldiers had volunteered, yet Ratsbayne still sat unseated upon the barrel, Blagdon stepped forward. "I will have a turn. Bring us saddles." *If the barrels were to stand in as mounts, they should have a little more authenticity and difficulty. If one did not fasten the saddles around the log, it could spin around, leaving the rider underneath his mount rather than upon it.* Two soldiers grabbed saddles and brought them over, settling them upon the logs, and went to fasten the girth straps. "No," interrupted Blagdon, "let us put on our own." He glanced at Ratsbayne. "If you do them too tight, your mount will be unable to breathe, and you will be bucked off. Be grateful these cannot do that." Anticipation filled the air, soldiers betting with each other quietly, and even the *belvash* looked on with rapt attention.

Blagdon mounted and settled quickly into the saddle after removing his cloak and setting it down upon the sparring ring's fence. It was narrower than a *Ruin*'s back, but he could adjust easily. He would dispatch the drunkard quickly. Blagdon kept his rapier in his right hand, his left hand settled upon the saddle's horn, waiting.

Ratsbayne frowned slightly, finishing strapping his saddle onto the barrel. He clumsily swung himself up as if unsure about his weight, leaning too far at first but finally adjusted in the saddle. A soldier handed him his shield and sword before stepping back to watch. Ratsbayne looked over, confused. "Aren't ya going to use a shield?"

"No," answered Blagdon as *sri'balvash* Desira brought him a lance with a blade as black as night, lighter-colored flecks of metals twinkling like pale stars captured within the metal. *Koldraka* was a scarce metal that had been discovered during the Scourge War. Blagdon was gifted the lance by the *Kolotor'ix* when his *Hasta'kan* was named *Hon-Hasta'kan*. Not a fan of mounted combat, Blagdon preferred duels and fought with a *koldraka* rapier that had cost him a lot of money and three *kelvorkav*. But as he had never been beaten in a proper duel, Blagdon felt he deserved such an extravagance as a treat to himself and a warning to all others who dared cross him.

Blagdon tested his lance with his left hand, frowning slightly to himself. Years ago, Ruin had bitten off the last two fingers of his left hand and now wore a glove with stuffed fingers to hide the weakness. He practiced left-handed swordplay with Lady *ik'Blagdon* privately within the safety of their home but still was not as proficient as he'd like to be. *This will be different,* he thought as he decided not to wrap shadows around his hand to keep the lance in a better grip. To *ro'*Shadon, it wouldn't be considered cheating if he had, but he felt it would be dishonest. If this were actual combat on horseback, he'd take advantage. But against the drunkard, he'd suffice to work on his left-handed lancing. *My Narisa would be proud.*

Mykel waited until both of them nodded that they were ready. "Begin the spar."

Ratsbayne seems more at home in the saddle than on the ground, Blagdon noted as the other man kept his body behind his shield, blocking on one side, the other side using his sword to parry and thrust at him. The soldiers held the ropes attached to the barrels and began moving them, making them pitch and sway as lifelike mounts would in combat. Blagdon used his lance purely for parrying and deflecting blows, the stuffed fingers of his glove keeping the hilt against something so he did not hold the lance as loosely in his hand. Not having a shield, he was at a disadvantage defense-wise, but his wife had taught him to train with both hands in swordplay, for you never knew if one's sword arm would be injured and have to resort to the non-dominant hand. Blagdon had thought it was folly, but she began sparring with him using her lefthanded swordplay. Being beaten by a female hit his pride, and he soon began training every day for hours just so he could beat her, and she began training for hours to keep him beaten. *I see now where this is truly an advantage; thank you, my love, and I shall repay your wisdom when I return home.*

Ratsbayne, he had to admit, surprised him. The too-long thrusts Ratsbayne used while sparring on the ground now were blows that could reach past an opponent's shield to hit them; the swaying he had while walking or standing now helped him maintain his balance as he moved out of the way of Blagdon's lance and rapier, as well as adjusting for the moving barrel beneath him. *He has had training before in mounted combat; I would almost bet a kolvorvik upon it.*

Blagdon braced himself as Ratsbayne gave his left arm a workout, the longsword and lance repeatedly clashing as swing and thrust met parry and deflection. Ratsbayne kept his shield up by resting upon the top of his boot to take the pressure off his arm and shoulder, for holding the metal shield for three earlier spars took a toll on his strength. But when Blagdon's rapier and lance kept stabbing toward him, he'd move the shield just enough to deflect the blade. It was beginning to irritate Blagdon, and he enjoyed the challenge.

A feint on Ratsbayne's part had Blagdon committed to blocking with his lance, and Ratsbayne's wrist twisted, the blade knocking the lance to the outside. Blagdon could not keep his grip upon the shaft, and it fell to the dirt harmlessly. Ratsbayne's lip twitched, and Blagdon moved his arm, settling his left hand to the small of his back, his favored dueling stance, and adjusted his rapier, never keeping his eyes off Ratsbayne.

Sword met rapier repeatedly, Blagdon leaning or twisting in the saddle, causing Ratsbayne's sword to miss him by mere inches. Ratsbayne kept up his defense, but the Leigelord had been patient, waiting for the right time. Blagdon struck like a snake, his rapier skirting the shield's edge and stabbing at Ratsbayne's shoulder. Without being prompted, Ratsbayne dropped his shield, keeping his sword up and ready, surprising Blagdon. *Many would keep the shield and continue, but he seems to understand that such an injury would make him drop it. He is practicing as if he has seen actual combat.* Blagdon tested a few thrusts of his rapier, seeing how Ratsbayne would react now that he had to adjust his fighting style. Dueling was Blagdon's forte; no matter his opponent's weapon, he had yet to lose a duel. Ratsbayne thrust the sword at Blagdon, who, with a practiced flick of his wrist, sent the sword falling to the ground. Without hesitation, Ratsbayne grabbed a dagger from his boot and threw it.

Shadows stopped the dagger an inch from his forehead, hovering close enough that Blagdon could see every detail of the blade's grip. Instantly, the excited sounds from the soldiers died out. Once Blagdon was sure the knife was not moving, his eyes looked past it to settle upon Ratsbayne, who was watching him, his hands in fists at his side. Mykel stepped close enough to be seen by his father, a gloved hand held out toward them. *Mykel's shadows stopped the dagger just in time.*

"That's enough for today," Mykel said, the dagger vanishing in shadows and appearing in his palm. Ratsbayne dismounted, almost falling as his right leg swept over the saddle, which shifted a touch under his weight, but managed to stand on the ground again. He sat heavily on a log, holding and rotating his sore shoulder. A soldier came over with a ladle of water, which Ratsbayne began downing immediately as another picked up the fallen sword and shield, replacing them on their racks.

Blagdon dismounted, feeling heavy gazes upon him. He did not react but sheathed his rapier and refastened his cloak around his shoulders, his back to them. *Sri'belvash* Desira went to him with his lance and a ladle of water in the other. As he took the ladle, her fingers gently brushed his hand, and he felt her power flow over him, taking blood from bruises and healing them, and his left hand's cramping lessened. He nodded his thanks to her, and to anyone else, it would be seen as acknowledging her giving him water, not thanking her for soothing his aches.

Ratsbayne then walked toward Mykel and stopped and put his hand out. "My dagger."

Mykel opened his mouth to snap at the drunkard, but Blagdon spoke instead. "That is a well-kept dagger, sharp and balanced. A good soldier knows how to care for his weaponry." Mykel stayed silent and held it to Ratsbayne, hilt first.

"Ah ain't a soldier," Ratsbayne muttered, taking his dagger and walking back toward the barn.

Mykel went to say something, but Blagdon shook his head. "Let him go." Blagdon wanted nothing more to do with the drunkard at the moment. He nodded once to Mykel and headed toward the keep as he heard *kriss'ix* Lukras instructing other soldiers to continue the sparring practice. Once Blagdon was away from the sparring area, he spoke through the shadows in Desira's ear. "I want to know everything about that man right now."

APOLLO

That man has a death wish. That was the only way that Apollo could comprehend what Ratsbayne had done. Besides somehow surviving three spars with seasoned Dark Army soldiers and then with the scariest person he'd ever met, Ratsbayne had shown he was the most prominent idiot in the world by attacking the Liegelord of Woodsong. *This was the person who wanted to teach me how to sword fight?*

"So," Ratsbayne spoke as Apollo walked into the barn, "whose sword was that?"

"My father's," Apollo simply replied, sitting on a hay bale and pulling out the blade to sit across his lap.

"Ah see. How'd he die?"

Apollo narrowed his eyes at him. "I never said he died." *I've never spoken about him.*

Ratsbayne tossed a few hay bales in the corner beside the door, dusting off his hands. "It be an older sword, has good balance, is in decent condition, though it has some pits and scratches from age, the leather grip has been redone at least once. Ya don't let a good sword like that go without reason. Death is a good reason, Ah suppose."

Apollo wasn't sure what to say about the observations about the sword, so he told him about his father. "He and Ma got sick four years ago. Ma got sick; she began coughing up badly, and her skin grew hot to the touch with a fever. Dark veins started growing on her skin, and she started losing feeling in her hands and feet. After she started coughing up blood, Pa began getting sick as well. They died about a month after each other. That was three years ago. From what my brother had researched through our temple's records, it was something left over from the Scourge War called Lingering Rot."

Ratsbayne scratched his head like he had an itch. "Why didn't ya go to a healer? Ya said Andears had an Aldarwood, right? Ain't nearby a priest stays to tend it?"

Apollo's movements became angrier, sharper. "Our healer was taken by the Dark Army a season before. He was supposed to help heal some soldiers at Woodsong and return to Andears. We never saw him again, and my parents died." His voice shook with anger and grief. "Then I got here and went to find that he and all the people taken from Andears are at another garrison on the other side of Cetra."

"Aye, lad, Kerrik thought it would narrow down desertions. The soldiers here are from the other side of the territory."

"I hate them all."

"Well, that sucks because ya be one of them now," came the reply from the drunkard.

Apollo looked up at him with hate in his eyes. "They'll never get me to be one of them. I'll never wear their armor; I'll die first."

"Good luck with that, lad."

"Well, what about you? You're here, and you don't wear their armor. You're not a soldier either."

"Yeah, but they don't like mah any," Ratsbayne replied, "ya be young and moldable. They'd rather see meh go than ya."

"Then why don't you go away then?"

Ratsbayne went quiet for so long Apollo wasn't sure that he would answer. When he finally did, his voice was quiet, smaller than usual. "Ah've got nowhere else to go."

"You don't have family somewhere? You've got to have some kids running around; you're twice my age."

"Lad, Ah woke up two years ago in a cave without memory of

mah life. Ah don't know how old Ah be, if Ah have a family, or even know mah own name." Ratsbayne began shoveling manure, dumping shovelfuls into a bucket to take out of the barn.

"Maybe you'd remember if you didn't drink so much."

Ratsbayne shrugged, dumping another shovelful into the bucket. "Maybe, maybe not. All Ah ever get are weird dreams that are pointless to have; they aren't even good entertainment at night. All Ah ever see in them is blood and death again and again, so why not drink to forget it and at least have a good night's sleep for once?"

"Does it work?" He'd had more than a few sleepless nights because he dreamed of his friends and fellow villagers calling out to him from the pile of burning bodies, calling for him to help them. *Maybe I should drink a little to help, too. It seems to work for Ratsbayne.*

When he looked back up, Ratsbayne was looking at him with concern in his eyes. "Ya need to breathe shallow breaths, lad; ya be looking a touch green. Don't be like meh, don't drink to escape, but push through it to be a better man."

Apollo shrugged off the fatherly advice. "I'm going to be a better fighter; one day, I will kill them all. All of those who burned Andears killed my friends. I left my brother behind to hunt them down, and I can't return until I finish what I swore to do."

Ratsbayne started counting off on his fingers. "A drunkard has so far captured ya; ya be in their garrison after being chased here by murder ponies and pissed off the Liegelords' son by punching him in front of everyone, making you public enemy number one. Great job, ya be doing great, keep it up."

Apollo glared at him but could not find room to argue, so he changed the subject. "You dropped this while you were rolling around on the ground earlier," he said, pouring the necklace from the pouch it was in, the chain around one finger. The sunlight caught the pendant, which spun slowly at the end of the chain.

Ratsbayne froze and then glared at Apollo, coming toward him.

"That's mine, ya little thief."

Apollo snatched the pendant away from him, holding it at arm's length. "I'm the thief? You stole this from my brother! It was my ma's!"

"No, it's not," Ratsbayne snapped, grabbing for it. "That be mine."

"Liar! When did you see my brother? Did you go off to Silene and take this off him? I swear if you harmed him--"

"Shut up 'fore someone hears where yer brother is, ya idjit," Ratsbayne hissed, "Ah thought ya be smarter than this. Ah ain't seen yer brother, Ah don't know anything about him except 'or his name, and now Ah, and probably whoever be listening outside the stables, know where he be, thanks to yer big mouth."

Apollo glanced around at that, looking out the window to see if anyone was outside the stables. Ratsbayne took the opportunity to snatch the pendant from his grip and put the chain over his head to hang upon his chest. "Hey! Give that back!"

"It's mine, and Ah'll prove it to you," Ratsbayne snapped, "not that Ah need to. But ya see these markings around the edges of the circle? It says, 'Strength o' the storm, heart o' the griffin.' See, it's mine." He stuck it into his tunic, out of sight. "Next time, lad, keep yer hands off mah stuff," Ratsbayne snapped and walked out of the stables, a bucket of shit in one hand, the shovel in the other, slamming the barn door behind him.

Was he telling the truth? The markings are in another language, but I don't know it. Could there be two exact pendants? But why would Ratsbayne have one and his mother have the other? Had they known each other? Every time I think I figured him out, he leaves me with more questions than answers.

RATSBAYNE

He dumped the manure from the bucket outside Woodsong's gate and returned inside. Instead of heading straight for the stables, he walked around aimlessly, wanting to avoid any more confrontation with Apollo today. He finally found himself at the *kelvorvik* paddock near the keep and watched the murder ponies walk around, ears turned toward him as if waiting for him to do something stupid like a step too close to the fence so they could eat him for a snack.

"Ratsbayne, what a stupid name you've stuck yourself with."

He turned at the sound of the female speaking to him, expecting to see a *balvash*, but no one was in the immediate area. "Who said that?"

"*I did,*" came the voice from inside his head, "*Are you telling me that you have forgotten me? After all we had gone through?*"

What in the world? Have Ah finally gone crazy? Maybe the knocks to the head during sparring had done more damage than he'd thought.

"*I hope not, but I am disappointed in what you've become. I expected you to be more than this.*"

He looked around for the squirrel. This is something that the squirrel would do. After all, it apparently could write demands and pay him for reports, so why was it so far-fetched that the animal could speak? Animals are speaking; what nonsense. Ah really be going crazy, or maybe Ah just hit mah head too hard in sparring today.

As he frowned, turning back toward the barn, Commander Blagdon approached him. "Ratsbayne, come with me," and the *korrati* began to head toward the *kelvorvik* stable, not glancing back to see if he was following. Begrudgingly, he followed him, wondering what was going on.

Mykel began speaking once Ratsbayne started walking with him. "My father and I have observed your horse handiwork and wish to see if such work extends toward other mounts. You will begin as stablemaster of the *kelvorvik* stables, and if you are found suitable, you will be placed in charge of both garrison stables."

"Ya be kidding, right? Meh, working with the murder ponies? Is this just a set-up to get meh eaten?"

"No, this is punishment for throwing a dagger at my father's face during a spar." The young commander snapped as he opened a door in the stable and stepped back, letting Ratsbayne look inside. "This will be your living quarters during your time as stablemaster." Built onto the side of the stables, the stablemaster's room had a bed, dresser, armor stand, and weapon stand. Ratsbayne stepped inside, looking around. *Ah'd not slept in anything but the hayloft for quite some time now; who knew that a stable could have such accommodations? The Blagdons are certainly different from Kerrik.* "What be the catch?" Ratsbayne asked finally. *This be too good, and nothing came without some price.*

"There is a chance if you do not pay attention or they don't like you, the *kelvorvik* will eat you. After all, you did throw a dagger at their master's face." Mykel gestured to the dresser, the lightstone lantern upon it. "There is new clothing for you to wear in there."

"Ah be not part of your Dark Army, Ah won't wear your armor."

"Simple jerkins, tunics. You will be covered in hay, dirt, and manure; I would not sully our armor with such filth."

"Ya be a strange lad, ya know that, commander? No wonder you and Apollo butt heads so much, ya too much alike."

Mykel looked at him and set down a jar of salve on the dresser. "Rest tonight. You will be sore tomorrow but will grow into your new role. This should aid in your sore muscles so you can get proper sleep. Perhaps do not get beaten so often in spars?" Mykel turned and walked out of the stables.

"Well, that was rude," Ratsbayne said to the empty room, though he walked to the jar and opened it, smelling the salve's herbs. It tickled his memory slightly, and he looked through the drawers to see what was in them, finding clothing, as the commander had said. At least now Ah have new clothing, he admitted and shut the drawers. Two rows of shelves were built into the wall, and upon one of them was a mirror, shaving kit, and comb. The other one was empty, presumably for his belongings.

Ratsbayne wasn't sure what to put on it since he had few possessions. He set his knife upon it with his coin purse but then changed his mind and decided to keep that with him instead. He pulled the amulet out of his tunic and looked at it, turning it over in his fingers. *Strength o' the storm, heart o' the griffin.* It was pretty, but he was not sure where it was from. Was it a motto of some sort? Perhaps it was an award, but of what? What would he ever have an award from when all he could remember was screwing up? He lay down on the bed, looking at the pendant with more questions than answers.

* * *

The garrison bathhouse was empty when he got to it after spending the rest of the day cleaning the *kelvorvik* stables, and he changed out of his clothing and sank into the herb and flower-scented hot water slowly, sighing with relief. The crackling of the fires under the tubs and in the lanterns made a nice atmosphere, he had to admit, as did the sheer dividing screens that separated the tubs now, so he didn't have to see another male bathing. All the irritation and confusion of the day, along with the aches from sparring and cleaning stables, seemed not to bother him as much as the water warmed him, and he leaned back against the side of the tub, closing his eyes.

The door opened quietly, and he heard the footsteps of someone walking toward the other tub. A soft female humming made him glance at the sound, surprised. The females of the garrison were to use the bathhouse inside the keep, per the commander's orders, and the males were to use this one. The dark silhouette of a rather attractive female shape moved along the dividing screen, backlit by the flickering lanterns. The female let down waist-length hair from an updo, shaking it out and removing something from her face. *Ah, he thought, one of the masked leather-clad females, belvash, Ah remember the commander calling them.* She propped a leg up on the side of the tub on the other side, untying her boots before setting them aside and undoing the fastenings on her leather armor before slowly peeling it off. Ratsbayne stayed as still as he could, not wanting to make any noise to indicate that he was watching her, trying to breathe as shallowly as he could. *Ah could watch this all day long and into the night.* The female silhouette stepped into her tub, bending to gather the soap and cloth, rubbing it over her body slowly while humming softly, oblivious to the male watching her as if he'd be tested on every curve and movement.

Ratsbayne's hand twitched, hitting the tray of oils and bars of soap, knocking a bottle off onto the ground before he could catch it, and the humming stopped abruptly. "Shite, damnit, *krushu*!" Ratsbayne muttered under his breath as he fought to keep the tray from falling entirely into the water, grabbing it quickly and putting the items back onto the tray and the tray back on its stand on the side of the tub. The female sank into her tub, so now her shoulders were all he saw, and Ratsbayne just wanted to bang his head against the wall in frustration.

The female chuckled, standing once more, and walked to the screen, staying on her side of it. "You were watching; tell me, did you like what you saw?" Her voice was soft, silky, and held amusement.

"Ah... er...." Ratsbayne swore to himself. Ah had my eyes closed; Ah didn't see much," he lied.

"Oh? Too bad," came the reply, "I was hoping you were watching. After all, I came in here just for you, Ratsbayne." The silhouette ran her hands over her body, and he followed the movement with his eyes.

"Ya did? Ah mean, o' course ya did. Ah mean..." *Why the hells am Ah rubbish with words today?*

She laughed at that, pulling up her hair in both hands and letting it fall back down her back slowly.

"Perhaps I should join you, and you could wash my back, and we can talk." She stepped around the screen just a touch, so one long leg and arm were showing as she peeked around the edge, one blue eye looking at him, the rest hidden behind the screen, revealed only in shadow. "That is if you wish me to."

Ratsbayne cleared his throat several times. "Yes, please. The more, the merrier. Ah mean... that's not what Ah mean unless ya be into more females being in here." He watched her step around the divider, her blonde hair brushing her lower back, covering her breasts, and framing her stomach, bringing his eyes lower, then quickly back up. *By the Light, there are no words for how beautiful she is.* He stood immediately, holding out a hand to steady her as she stepped into the tub as if escorting a lady of the court into a carriage.

She smiled at that, her eyes roaming over his form. "You'd never think you were muscular under those tunics," she said as she sat upon her knees in the tub, the water around her abdomen, hair floating gently back and forth, teasing glimpses of the breasts behind the golden strands. Ratsbayne had to feel for the tub as he sat back in the water, his eyes watching her.

"Well, when ya be working the stables, ya have to be strong enough to carry the heavy things around, like hay and feed," he explained. "So, ya know mah name, but Ah dunno yers."

"Alandra," she said, smiling softly, "*belvash* Alandra." She slowly picked up a soap bar and rubbed it with the cloth before pouring oil onto it.

Ah'd never thought of myself as jealous of a soap bar before. "Alandra, what a beautiful name for a beautiful lady." *Finally, I can think enough to speak.*

Alandra ran the cloth over her arm, leaving a soapy trail behind it. "So is Ratsbayne truly your name? Or is it a nickname?"

Ratsbayne watched the bubbles on her pale skin and followed the cloth with his eyes as she washed her other arm. "Ah dun't remember my real name, and the nickname stuck with meh, which Ah don't mind, after all, I be pretty good at killing rats."

Alandra's eyes flicked to him, framed with long lashes. "You don't remember your name?"

Ratsbayne shrugged in reply, watching her wash her palm in slow, bubbly circles. "Ah woke up in a cave without memory of before ah got there."

Alandra soaped the cloth and took his hand, washing it as she slowly moved toward his shoulder. "Tell me more, Ratsbayne," she asked him, looking at his arm as she washed him.

"After the cave, Ah went to a village named Thraesh and began living in a room above the inn. Everyone was nice to meh, considering that Ah had little coin and no memory. The innkeeper's wife was an amazing cook and soon had meh back to the proper weight, and the innkeeper put meh to work in the carpenter's shop as an assistant. One night the roof was leaking and Ah kept getting wet in my sleep, so Ah climbed up and fixed the hole in the roof the next morning. Ah became Thraesh's gopher."

"Gopher?"

Ah hope she doesn't think Ah mean that Ah was turned into an animal. "Yeah, ya know, go-fer this, go-fer that.. Ah thought it was funny. But anyway..." He held out his other hand for her to continue cleaning since she had finished on his left arm. "Ah did odd jobs, like clean their stables, fix the roof, chase out the rats from the tavern's basement."

Alandra listened to him talk, the cloth never stopping as it covered him in suds. She washed his chest, watching the suds play along his dark brown chest hair. "So why did you leave Thraesh?"

"Ah didn't want to. It was mah home, but then Kerrik's people-- Ah'm not calling him 'Lordson'; the man didn't deserve that honor-- his soldiers came, trying to get volunteers for the Dark Army. Ah was told in Thraesh, the Dark Army yearly took fifteen men o' fighting age as tributes for the Liegelord's army. They had their fifteen volunteers and were leaving when one of the soldiers decided to try grabbing at a tavern wench on his last night there. No one was doing anything, so Ah punched him."

She stopped running the cloth over him to look at him, her eyes holding his with close attention. "You punched a Dark Army soldier?"

"Ah sure did. Three soldiers separated us after he got off the ground, bleeding. Ah may have been holding a metal cup in mah hand when Ah hit him; the details be fuzzy."

Alandra chuckled softly. "Somehow, I doubt that."

He shrugged as she continued washing his chest and abdomen, and he adjusted in the water to let her reach more of him, enjoying the attention and touch. "Yeah, well, Ah be hauled outside, and they threatened to chop off mah hand for hitting a soldier. Ah told them fine, as long as they never touched another maiden without her consent again."

Alandra's eyebrows raised in surprise. "You are serious. You'd allow them to cut off your hand for a female to be safe from unwanted advances."

Ratsbayne shrugged again. "Of course. That's why Ah brought herbs to the females here, so Kerrik's men couldn't get them pregnant and gave Taya vials o' stuff to pour in his drink so he'd pass out at night and she'd be left alone. Ah couldn't stand that piece of shite." He was quiet for a moment. "Is Taya all right? Now that she has ya and yer friends, now? She be safe now, correct?"

Alandra looked at him briefly before nodding as if she'd decided something, then resumed washing. "We are called *ro'belvash*; in your tongue, the closest thing would be Blood Sisters. We all have Sigils of Blood upon our skin." She brushed one side of her hair back over her shoulder, and a red Sigil adorned the space under her left breast, looking like a flowing serpent. His eyes fell upon her Sigil after lingering upon her newly exposed chest.

"May Ah?"

Alandra looked at him, a small amount of surprise in her eyes. "Yes, you may."

He touched the Sigil with his hand, hot and rough with calluses built up from hard work in the barn. Her breath caught a bit with his touch, his thumb running over the marking, his fingers lying along her side. He never tried to touch her breast or anything other than the Sigil. "It's beautiful. Did it hurt when it was inked onto ya?"

She shook her head, her hair brushing his fingers along her side gently. "It is not inked but given by the *Balsesha*, our Blood Mother. She is our patron, whose teachings we follow and obey. It is she who guides us, mentors us, through the B*elvash'ix* who run our Temple. When we graduate to *belvash*, we participate in a ceremony where we dedicate our lives to the *Balsesha*. Then the Sigil appears upon us, and our journey truly begins. But enough about me, Ratsbayne, I am curious about you." She stood, giving him a close view of her lower half, and sat behind him, moving him so she could wash his back with the same slow circles as before.

It took Ratsbayne a few moments to figure out what they had been speaking about because he was busy watching water drip down her skin and her lower blonde hair. "There is not much more to say; the innkeeper spoke up, asking they spare mah hands and instead take meh with them to learn how to fight, that Ah be a strong and a good man, how it would be a shame to waste such things. So they took meh."

"I see," Alandra said softly, running a hand over his shoulder gently. She took a wooden cup off the tray beside the tub and ran water over his head before pouring soap into his brown hair, massaging his scalp. A moan escaped his lips, and he leaned back to let her have better access to his head. After she'd rinsed out the soap and had him lean back against her chest, she gently wrapped her arms around his waist, holding him. "Why do you drink?" She asked softly against his ear, kissing his shoulder, her hands playing along his abdomen.

He thought about that for a long moment, distracted by the rise and fall of her breathing against his back. "Ah began having these nightmares that don't make any sense," he finally admitted. *Ah want to tell her everything about mah, she be so easy to speak with.* "It has only become more and more frequent, and there are many nights Ah wake up in cold sweats, but Ah can't remember when Ah awaken. Ah don't know what caused them, but the only way Ah can get them to go away so Ah can have a good night's sleep is to drink."

Alandra nodded behind him, and he felt her moving her hands over his skin as she did so. "I can help with that," she said, kissing his neck, "I can give you sleepless nights for as long as you wish me to."

He turned his head toward her. "Why would you offer meh this? Ah be Woodsong's screw-up, the drunkard. The one who threw a dagger at yer Liegelord. Why on Hinestra would you help meh when you should hate meh?"

Alandra turned him fully to look at her. "Because you risked your hand for a maiden in the village of Thraesh. You risked your life for Taya and the other women here, for all those women to be safe." She raised to her knees, pushing her hair back over her shoulders, giving him a full view of her body above the water, her hand gently on his neck. "Because of this, I wish to be with you, as much as you need for these nightmares to cease, for your mind to be still once again, for you to speak to be heard and not laughed at." She kissed him gently, and after a moment, his arms wrapped around her, pulling her in, deepening the kiss until it was no longer chaste but a thing of need and want, hands gripping and massaging, fingers touching and exploring.

At the end of the hour, Alandra and Ratsbayne left the bathhouse and wemt their separate ways, she toward the keep where the other *belvash* stayed and he to the stables. He had a profound sleep that night that no dreams could rouse.

BLAGDON

He had retired to his room when there was a knock at the door. His armor stood on its stand, the leather freshly clean of any dirt and treated with oils to prevent cracking and scent of sweat. Blagdon checked himself in the mirror, ensuring his black vest with blue embroidery sat unwrinkled over his white tunic. After glancing through the shadows, he allowed his guest inside. "I assume you have information for me, *balvash* Alandra," he said, walking to a decanter and pouring watered wine into a glass. It was the last barrel of alcohol in Woodsong until the soldiers learned to act like proper servants of the Dark Army, so he might as well enjoy what little luxuries he could.

"I do, Lord Blagdon; I have just come from interrogating Ratsbayne." That caught his attention, and he went to her, offering her a glass of watered wine. Of course, she could not drink with her mask on, but the gesture of hospitality was there. Many *balvash* did not remove their masks, making it easier for them to move throughout the lands if no one knew their true faces, making them the perfect spies. Blagdon was not even sure if the *ro'belvash* used their given names or if they created aliases for when they were out of their leathers. *I will have to ask Narisa when I see her again. Perhaps she may even be able to tell me.* He gestured to a chair and sat near the armor stand, facing her and the door. "What did you learn of our drunkard?"

"He truly has no memory of his life before two years ago. He woke up in a cave and traveled to a village called Thraesh, where he lived for six months doing odd jobs and working as an assistant to their carpenter. When the soldiers came to collect their volunteers for their numbers, one harassed a female, and Ratsbayne punched him. They threatened to take his hand for the assault but were convinced to take him back instead." Blagdon noted a touch of pride in her voice but did not comment upon it. A male standing up to a group of soldiers over such a matter was brave but foolish. *It seemed that Ratsbayne was at least consistent.*

"I see," he replied. *I can only imagine what the belvash will think of him now. I need him to be useful to me, not a lord of a harem of female assassins.* He gestured for her to continue, taking a sip of his wine.

"He drinks to avoid nightmares that make no sense," she continued, "I used oils to loosen his tongue and make it easier for him to speak truths without realizing it, as well as hard interrogation. He told me a bit about the nightmares, and I must confess that even I am unsure of their meaning." Hard interrogation was a polite way of saying she'd slept with Ratsbayne to gain information. It was a common technique of *ro'belvash* and quite effective, for men were known to have loose tongues when their blood ran to other body parts rather than their minds. The use of oils during such felt vaguely like cheating and pricked his sense of honor slightly, but not enough to wish to challenge it. *The poor man didn't stand a chance.*

"What else did you discover? How did he learn how to fight mounted? Who did he train under to have such instincts?" She raised an eyebrow, and Blagdon was sure the *balvash* was smirking under her mask. *She thinks the dagger incident bothers me, which it does, but I will not have her think it is my weakness.* "His acting irrationally is deadly for my son, and I will not put him in unnecessary danger. If Ratsbayne cannot be controlled, he will have to be dealt with before I leave."

"We will be able to control him, *Hasta'kan'ix ik'Blagdon*," *balvash* Alandra stated, "do not worry about that. Lordson Mykel will be safe; he has Shadon soldiers here to protect him, and *sri'balvash* Desira will not allow her sister's son to be harmed."

"Did you at least find out his real name?"

"He truly does not know it," she said, absently running her

gloved hand over the arm of her chair. "He was given the nickname, and it has stuck with him. However, I can tell you that he was responsible for the herbs and potions given to Taya and the other women to ensure they were not with a child under Lordson Kerrik-*kyr*'s command of the garrison, though how he acquired them was... troublesome."

"Troublesome? What do you mean?"

"He said a squirrel delivered them to him at the barn in a bag."

Blagdon blinked, knowing he had to have misheard. "Did you say..."

"A squirrel, yes. Ratsbayne said that a squirrel often follows him and he has no idea why."

"Is he a Sigilbearer?" The most common Sigils were Sigils of Shadow, only formed upon males with few exceptions, as with his daughter, Senka, and Sigils of Blood, which he knew were only seen on *ro'belvash*. *I haven't seen many Sigils of another type since the Scourge War.* The appearance of another Sigil showed promise; if Ratsbayne were a Sigilbearer and were brought under his heel, *Hasta'kan ik'Blagdon* would have yet another achievement that would elevate them in the eyes of the *Kolotor'ix*.

"No, he is not." He knew not to doubt her statement, for he was quite sure she checked every inch of him for such Sigil.

"Is it possible it was a hallucination brought on by drinking, or perhaps you misjudged the oil dosage, and he began speaking nonsense?"

Balvash Alandra's eyes looked at him flatly, and her gloved hand raised to tap her index finger once on the side of her mask, pointing to the embossed image of a crossed fang and dagger. "I am certain."

Blagdon knew little of what happened inside the Blood Temple or the hierarchy of *ro'belvash*, but he knew that *ro'belvash* had different emblems embossed onto their masks. *Sri'belvash* Desira and Narisa both had crossed swords and quills, and he'd noticed that the two women often wrote in notebooks and kept journals of what was going on around them, though the few times he'd gone to see what they were writing, they closed their journals to keep their secrets. *Balvash* Alandra, he knew, had poisoned vials built into the hilts of her blades to unstopper during an attack. He wondered if they were emblems of groupings that were similar to *Hesta*. His wife said it was something she was not permitted to speak about, no matter how creatively he'd tried discovering the answers from her.

"He's not spoken of any training of any type, and the few times he has sparred under Lordson Kerrik-*kyr* had been drunken disasters. Being seen as a danger to himself and others, he was not permitted in the rings and could only watch. I do not know where he honed the instincts to perform how he had today during the spar."

Blagdon nodded, thinking back at the close call on the barrel and what had been discovered. "He speaks with a slightly familiar accent, and I cannot place it as one I have heard recently. Do you think he is from land outside Merdiah and has returned from being abroad? If so, then why has he returned? But if he had awoken in a cave, then who put him there, and for what purpose?"

"He's never spoken of any travels before waking in the cave, *Hasta'kan'ix*; he has no memory of such."

Thraesh. I will have to go there before I head back to Stormhold and see what I can discover myself; I may find this nearby cave and see it for myself; it may hold answers to secrets. "Very well. I appreciate your quickness and thoroughness of your duties. Do you have anything else for me this evening?"

She stood, shaking her head once. "Thank you, *Hasta'kan'ix ik'Blagdon*. I will continue to see what I can discover." She walked out of the office, closing the door behind her.

Blagdon sipped his wine thoughtfully, looking at the empty chair. It was hardly possible that Ratsbayne would have gotten through a skilled *balvash* soft and hard interrogation without giving up almost everything he knew, especially when drugged by oils. Blagdon thought himself a strong man, but he'd asked his wife to interrogate him once to see if he could withstand it. That night, he had told Narisa about a rather embarrassing story which he made her swear not to tell or write anyone else about. Blagdon got up and walked to the map on the table, looking for Thraesh, locating the village northwest of Woodsong. *There is where I will find my answers, and then I will find out who you truly are, Ratsbayne.*

***

The following day he had his men ready to leave Woodsong before the sun had risen too far over the trees. He was confident in the Shadon and *belvash* that he chose to leave behind to guide Mykel through his time as *korrati*. Though Mykel was young and would make mistakes, he would learn from those mistakes and improve upon himself and those around him.

After bidding him farewell, Blagdon rode Ruin out of the gates, heading northwest toward Thraesh, with some of his soldiers and *belvash* alongside him with a wagon of goods. Cetra was far from perfect, but it held the promise of being a good investment for his *Hasta'kan*, as long as they could begin righting the wrongs of *Hasta'kan ik'Remhold* and get the villagers to trust *Hasta'kan ik'Blagdon*. That would start with Thraesh, where he would introduce himself to the villagers as their new Leigelord and provide them with goods that would be needed. Lordson Kerrik-*kyr* had taxed the people so much that they were in dire need of good tools and resources. Correcting this would be a promising step in the right direction, and the villages could begin providing *Hasta'kan ik'Blagdon* with supplies. He would see to the village of Thraesh, but the other six villages would have to be visited by Mykel as one of his duties as *korrati*. He had impressed upon his son the importance of this task to win over the villagers. *After all, the people of a territory are the tools of their Hasta'kan, and good tools must be well-maintained to work properly.*

Only after they had traveled a good distance away did Blagdon take a moment to look around the surrounding area to ensure no one was following them. With the slightest glance toward the direction of the garrison, now far away and barely seen along the side of the dirt road, hidden by the surrounding woods, he allowed himself to feel the absence of his living Lordson in his heart. *Kolosae-ro'jo'aritas watch over you, hin ik'san.*

* * *

The trip to Thraesh was quick and uneventful, thanks to the uses of Sigils of Shadow to teleport those with him, taking five Shadon with their *kelvorvik, balvash* Alandra on a borrowed horse, and his mount, Ruin. The rest of the soldiers and *belvash* he'd brought to the garrison would remain where they were, serving and protecting Mykel while Blagdon returned to Stormhold. But first, he wanted to see the village of Thraesh and its surrounding area for himself and see if he could glean any insights on Ratsbayne, for his curiosity would not be satisfied until he'd learned something about the human who'd thrown a dagger at his face and come closest to killing him where many had tried and failed.

The villagers were terrified to see the Dark Army's red and black banner, shouting warnings to each other as they ran to get inside the nearest building, closing the wooden shutters over the windows as if that were to stop the soldiers from knowing they were there. The villagers did not seem to notice that the yellow and black emblem of *Hasta'kan ik'Remhold* had been replaced with the blue and silver emblem of *Hasta'kan ik'Blagdon*, and Blagdon wondered if they'd even know what it meant. Lordson Kerrik-*kyr* must have inspired such fear that even the soldiers meant to protect the people terrified them instead. *How foolish*, Blagdon thought, dismounting Ruin, his men following suit behind him; *fear was not how to win the respect of those under you, nor was it a successful way to get the villagers to work appropriately to supply the territory with goods needed.*

Blagdon walked to the first building he came to, an inn with a sign with a tankard carved into it, and frowned, noting no writing in either Shadese or Common. *Another village where no one knows how to read or write wastes potential.* Knocking on the door, he waited for it to open and noticed movement as a child ducked behind the corner of the building.

He walked from the stoop, going to the child and kneeling to be at eye level with her. He held out his gloved hand, shadows twisted in his palm, flowing upward and growing until the darkness gave way to a small bunch of flowers he picked with shadows from the field nearby, and he grasped them gently, holding them out. "Hello, little one. I am Leigelord Blagdon, your new Liegelord. I have a gift for you, beautiful little flowers for a beautiful little girl." He smiled, imagining the young girl as his own Senka in her youth. After a moment, the girl took the flowers, a touch quickly in fear, but smelled them, giggling. The door opened, and Blagdon stood, looking at the woman who opened it. Her eyes were wide with fear that gave way to relief before she could hide her face by looking at her daughter instead of him. "What do we say?"

The girl curtseyed awkwardly. "Thank you, Weigeword Bwag don."

Blagdon nodded, not bothering to correct the child's pronunciation of his name for the moment. *The child will learn in time.* He glanced around, looking at the fearful faces of the women and the cautious eyes of the males behind the woman. He used shadows to speak, his voice carrying throughout the buildings to speak to the hidden villagers simultaneously. "I am not here to conscript your men to the Dark Army, for your people have given more than enough this season. I come to introduce myself, for I am your new Liegelord, and Lordson Mykel Blagdon is the new commander of Woodsong. Lordson Kerrik-*kyr* will never bother you or yours again, for his head has been cleanly separated from his shoulders."

He held up his hand, and he heard the women exclaim in fear slightly as if he were signaling archers to rain arrows upon the crowd of villagers. *If I could slay the Lordson-kyr again, I would, for this is no way to rule a people properly. At this rate, the people would be too frightened to do their duties, which, I assume by seeing a sawmill set up by the stack of wood, was carpentry.* He gestured and lowered his arm slowly, not wanting to spook the people more than they already were.

Two of his *kress'ix* came forward with bags, setting them on the ground beside their Lord and opening them slightly so the people could see the contents. *Lordson Kerrik-kyr had done what he could to deny the people goods to gain information and provoke fear; I now will use it to my advantage.* "Come out; there is nothing to fear from me now."

Slowly, villagers came out of the inn and other buildings, coming closer carefully. Others stayed back, near doorways and places to take cover should his soldiers attack. Blagdon pretended not to notice, holding the bag with his left hand, using the bags to hide the stuffed fingers of his glove, his right hand lifting blankets, dried meat, and fresh fruits, distributing them to those who looked as if they needed them most, as well as newly sharpened tools and bags of wheat. It was not well known about his missing fingers, even among his people, and although the glove's stuffed fingers hid the missing appendages, he would rather not chance anyone knowing what could be seen as a weakness. "I promise that as long as you obey my land's common law, *Hasta'kan ik'Blagdon* will protect you and yours."

He took a bag of coin to Thraesh's Elder, who bowed his head as he accepted it. "Thank you, my Liegelord. Your words and actions honor us and say much about you and your *Hasta'kan*. We serve at your will."

Blagdon gave a nod in reply. "I am looking for information about a man named Ratsbayne."

The Elder nodded, looking at a couple who came over, bowing their heads in greeting to him and the Elder. "This is Axis and Eva, our innkeepers. They knew Ratsbayne better than others, our Liegelord."

Blagdon rested his left hand upon the pommel of his rapier absently and noticed the slight flinches of the three nearest him when he did so. "Speak in peace, for my rapier hilt is simply a place to rest my hand, nothing more at the moment." Two *kress'ix* walked forward and began speaking to the villagers, asking questions about the woodworking that Thraesh was known for. Meanwhile, *balvash* Alandra went with a third soldier to see the sick and injured, using her abilities to aid where she could. The other soldiers remained beside the *kelvorvik* to keep the humans away from them and remained beside Blagdon if he needed protection.

"My Liegelord," Axis began, "we allowed Ratsbayne to remain in our inn for about six months or so last year, for he'd come from the woods in that direction," he turned, pointing in the west toward the Ironfall Mountains, "and he had no belongings but a bag on his back, and no memories. We let him eat for free, and he could work for his room, and often did, with no complaints about hard work, even when the rain poured, and he was on the roof attaching wooden shingles to stop leaking."

"He is a very good man, my Leigelord Blagdon," Eva added softly.

"You said he came from the west," Blagdon replied, ignoring the comment about the type of man Ratsbayne was, for it mattered little.

"Yes, he said there was a cave he'd woken up in with no memory of how he got there."

Blagdon nodded. "I appreciate your honesty." He turned and headed to Ruin, petting his muzzle and waiting for his *kress'ix* and *balvash* Alandra to finish. Once they came over, Blagdon switched to Shadese, the smile in his voice fading. "What have you learned?"

The captains spoke in the same language quietly. "Ratsbayne wasn't as much of a drinker until about six months after he arrived, sir. He arrived with no belongings and never spoke of a family. He stayed away from people, unsure who to trust, and did not seem to like squirrels."

"Let us see this cave so we can head to Stormhold."

One of his *krss'ix* opened his eyes after a moment, having been silent. "I have located a cave outside of the town deep in the woods via shadows; it could be the one he came from. Forgive me, my *Hasta'kan'ix*, but it has been two years. Do you believe there could be anything useful to learn in it?"

"We will not know unless we look." He mounted Ruin and began riding down the dirt road, the *kess'ix* following with *balvash* Alandra between them. Once they were out of sight of Thraesh, Blagdon ordered his soldiers to wait for them and nodded to his *kriss'ix*, who wrapped them in shadows.

They appeared in the middle of the woods, and it took a moment for Blagdon to notice the cave obscured by brush and trees. *If it were not for the ability to feel the depths of the shadows within it, I would not have known a cave was here.* Blagdon dismounted and peeked into the cave via shadows to look for any predators before walking toward it, pulling out a lightstone and holding it up in his left hand, his right hand resting on the pommel of his rapier.

They found the cave was thankfully empty of large predators and full of old bones and leaves, but no signs of any humans staying in it for any time. *There has to be some sort of clue that Ratsbayne has been here.* Looking through the shadows, Blagdon found a crack in the stone wall large enough that a human could squeeze through, but small enough that a large predator such as a werg could not, nor would someone easily find it unless they were deep enough inside the cave. Feeling the shadows on the other side, he brought the lightstone close enough to cast shadows into the cavern beyond. Blagdon wrapped *balvash* Alandra and a *kriss'ix* in shadows and stepped into the shadows of the room, the lightstone illuminating the small area.

"Interesting," Blagdon noted as he knelt beside a straw mattress covered with a threadbare blanket and dust, "I believe we have found where Ratsbayne had been living."

"*Hasta'kan'ix*," spoke up balvash Alandra, picking up a vial beside the cave wall. She closed her eyes, smelling it before replacing the stopper, "you will want to see this." She held out the vial. "The wax seal was broken already."

"What is it?" Blagdon turned the vial over in his hand, frowning that there was no label or tag affixed to it to say what it had once contained.

"It is a drought," she said, frowning, "an extremely strong one. Nyf'er elves once used rare herbs to take out large predatory animals. However, there are other herbs mixed with it which can be used to knock out someone instead of killing them."

"You can tell that just by smelling it?" asked the *kriss'ix*, curious.

"I am trained in such things. Whoever did this has access to materials that are no longer available and are extremely skilled. Handling venoms can be deadly if one does not know what they are doing."

Blagdon frowned as he thought about the drought and what its presence meant. In the few times he had run into bands of the Nyf'er elves, he had lost *kelvorvik* and good soldiers to their poisoned-tipped arrows. Of all the elven clans, the Nyf'er Clan was one he'd rather avoid, for their combative nature made reasoning with them almost impossible. "Nyf'er elves were not native to this territory but further south near the plains or the ocean. They would not have willingly given the herbs or drought to someone unfamiliar with their ways." Not finding any solutions to how Ratsbayne had gotten a hold of such herbs, he decided to look at the problem from a different angle. "How long would such a potion knock out such a creature?"

"Weeks at a time with the smallest doses, such as an arrowhead, at least from what I have heard. I've never seen it used personally; we've never gotten our hands on it. Most of the Ny'fer clan of elves were wiped out in the War of the Turning Leaves; then, whatever survivors were there were further dwindled by the Scourge War. I've yet to hear them being spotted anywhere near this area."

Blagdon searched through the shadows, hoping there was another vial he could use to gain favor from the Blood Temple in exchange for such a rare item, but he did not find any more and hid his disappointment.

Balvash Alandra looked over the empty vial in her hand. "There were most likely ingredients added to the solution to stabilize the venom, so it did not kill Ratsbayne but possibly knock him out, though for how long, I cannot tell you. It may explain why he had no memory before he took it; it could be a side effect."

"I am curious as to why he took it," Blagdon said quietly. "Why would someone take something like this knowingly? This is not a tomb," he said, gesturing around him, "but a place to wake up in. He did not mean to kill himself by taking it but knew he would be unconscious for a time. The cave is very well hidden, with a place for a predator to stay in the cave as its den and protect him unknowingly. What was he hiding from?"

"Perhaps he was not hiding but rather lying in wait for someone or something," the *kriss'ix* spoke up, "Ratsbayne does not have a shortage of enemies at Woodsong, it seems, so perhaps he made some out here as well." Blagdon glanced at him, gesturing for him to continue his thought, but the *kriss'ix* shrugged. "I cannot think what he'd be waiting for, my *Hasta'kan'ix*, for you cannot wait for something if you are unconscious while it happens."

"What if he was drugged?"

"I can imagine a thousand reasons someone would want to drug Ratsbayne."

Blagdon chuckled; he could not help it. "I believe we have found all we can here, but take the vial to your *Belvash'ix*, and perhaps they can glean something from it that can be useful. After that, I would appreciate it if you would return to Woodsong and further find out more from Ratsbayne."

Balvash Alandra bowed her head gracefully. "You are too kind, *Hasta'kan'ix ik'Blagdon*."

Checking once more and finding nothing more of use, Blagdon finally wrapped them in shadows and returned them to the rest of his waiting soldiers so they could continue their journey toward Stormhold and home.

I sometimes mourn the passing of time,
I never know what moments are important
Until it is too late.

-- Kil'lik'Draven, Bard of the Winds

APOLLO

The months passed, feeling like another lifetime. The days blended until Apollo could no longer recall easily a day that he did not have the same routine: waking up with the sun to train with the soldiers in running, exercising, and hand-to-hand combat, learning to read and write Shadese with *belvash* Inara until lunch and studying *ro'*Shadon culture until it was time to spar until dinner. Most nights, he was so tired he fell asleep immediately after, too sore and exhausted to do anything else.

Apollo began to see differences in himself as he looked at his body while bathing; gone was the lithe young farm boy he once was. He noticed larger muscles along his arms and legs, his back was straighter, and he'd found it easier to keep up with the grown soldiers as they ran down the game trails in the woods around Woodsong. His father's sword was becoming easier to swing, which made him move faster while sparring, and he soon learned how to use a wooden shield in his left hand, knowing that he would move up to steel when he was strong enough. His body was not the only thing changing, but his attitude as well; the anger that had once kept him going was slowly being tempered, honed, and given direction and purpose rather than a burning fire threatening to engulf him.

As Mykel's *balutrae*, the Shadon *kress'ix* treated him respectfully, though they were quick to correct him if he made a mistake. The other soldiers seemed to give him a slight berth as if afraid to harm him in sparring or risk the *korrati*'s wrath, but Mykel ensured that if Apollo were harmed within reason during a spar, he'd seek no retribution.

Apollo began to feel that he was fortunate to receive training from *Hon-Hasta'kan ik'Blagdon*'s men and *belvash*.

Now that Apollo was beginning to train harder, Mykel also was pushing himself, training alongside the soldiers, running through the woods with them down the trails, or sparring with them in the rings. Between training, eating, and sleeping, Mykel often sought Apollo out to speak with or sometimes sit in silence. It at first unnerved Apollo, but then he realized he and Mykel were among the youngest at Woodsong. *Am I the only one he feels a kinship to, that he is uncomfortable around the others?* Apollo was sharpening his father's sword when he felt Mykel watching him, and he gestured to a second haybale with a whetstone sitting upon it for him. Mykel took the invitation and removed his sword, sharpening it quietly.

"I've been thinking," Apollo said between strokes, "the leader of the *ro'*Shadon is the *Kolotor'ix*, but is there a queen?"

Mykel was quiet for a long time, debating how to answer the question. Finally, he spoke. "There is no Shadese word for queen or Empress. There is a word for consort, *kreva*, used for the title of women who carry the *Kolotor'ix*'s children, *kreve ik'Kolotor'ix*."

"There's more than one woman who carries his children?"

"There can be, but the *Kolotor'ix* had not had a *krava* since I have been alive, nor is there an heir currently."

Apollo frowned. "What about Princess Mari'ana?"

Apollo swore that Mykel's cheeks reddened just a touch. "It is not a *ro'*Shadon title. The *Kolotor'ix* adopted her when her mother, Li'ana, was chosen by him to aid in securing peace among the lesser races." Apollo was used to humans being called lesser by the *ro'*Shadon and *belvash* by now, having many conversations with those around Woodsong over the past months. It didn't bother him as much as before, and he shrugged it off. Mykel looked at him, continuing. "Remember that *ro'*Shadon society, heirs can only be male. A female cannot take over as *Hasta'ix*, nor sit as *Kolotor'ix*; she must bear a son or marry the male who will become the leader. When Princess Mari'ana and I have children, our Lordsons will become heirs to *Hasta'kan ik'Blagdon.*"

Apollo blinked at him. "Wait, you are..." He blushed, unsure how to word his question.

"I am betrothed to the princess, yes, though that is not the topic we speak of right now."

"But won't your heirs be the next *Kolotor'ix*, since she is his adopted daughter?"

Mykel frowned. "The *Kolotor'ix*'s heir will be next. The more *kreva* a *Hasta'ix* or *Kolotor'ix* has, the more chances he has for an heir and the more chances he has to have in-fighting. My *brak'ha* has had two wives; his first wife was assassinated along with his second Lordson, and his first Lordson died in battle. I am the heir to *Hon-Hasta'kan ik'Blagdon,* as well as my heir will be."

"There's never been a queen in the entirety of *ro'*Shadon society?"

"There was one, once, though not serving with the title. She sat beside the *Kolotor'ix* and helped attempt to ease the suffering after the Scourge War."

"What happened?" *He must be speaking about Princess Mari'ana's mother, since the Scourge War ended over a hundred years ago.*

"It is forbidden to speak about, but she has gone missing and is still being searched for. I insist we speak about another subject."

Apollo opened his mouth to push on the subject but instead asked about something that had bothered him since he had begun learning to write Shadese. "I have noticed a difference between the plural forms of many words; at least three, but there are only two for the word Shadon, *the people of ash,* and Nar'Shadon, *the people from ash.* Why is that?" Mykel nodded, seeming to understand the question, but asked Apollo to elaborate to understand exactly what he wanted to know. Apollo felt that he was being tested somehow but allowed it if it would give him an answer to the frustrating question. "There is *kolvorkav*, which means one of the creatures, *kelvorkav*, which is more than one of the creatures, and *ro'kelvorkav*, which means all of them. The same is true with *balvash, belvash*, and *ro'belvash*. But there is only Shadon and *ro'*Shadon. Why doesn't the word *Shedon* mean multiple Shadon?"

Mykel nodded and looked almost proud of Apollo as he sharpened his sword. "Very observant, my *balutrae*. You are beginning to understand Shadese nicely with your studies, and it was once a question I had asked my *brak'ha* as well."

At least, I am not the only one confused by the language's lack of logic. "What did he tell you?"

Mykel sat back quietly as if remembering. "He said that *ro'*Shadon are all connected by the *Kolosae-ro'ja'aritas*."

Apollo nodded, listening. The term meant *the Shadow who has eaten, eats, and will eat all,* and was the closest thing that the *ro'*Shadon had as a deity. According to their religion, it gave them their Sigils in exchange for their devotion and loyalty, but would destroy them if a Shadon made a vow to it and broke it. *I am sure how much I believe in that.*

"*Brak'ha* said that being we *ro'*Shadon are all one being, so there is no plural of Shadon, except *ro'*Shadon, which means all of the Shadon as a whole."

That makes sense. "Are *belvash* considered Shadon?"

"No, but they are a part of *ro'*Shadon society. Only those with Sigils of Shadow are considered Shadon."

"Are other Sigilbearers considered in *ro'*Shadon society?"

Mykel shook his head as he inspected his sword and continued sharpening. Apollo was sure his weapon was plenty sharp, but perhaps Mykel was enjoying the conversation, having someone to speak with who didn't seem to question his knowledge due to his age. *Maybe he thinks the soldiers listen to him only because of his rank, not his intelligence. He is smart, but they may not see it as I do.* Apollo could understand the sentiment. "But *ro'belvash* are included in *ro'*Shadon society, but other Sigilbearers are not? That doesn't make sense. Why aren't they?"

"It is the way it has always been, and so it is the way it will always be."

"Well, that's stupid," Apollo grumbled.

Mykel stood, wiping his sword and sheathing it, before bowing his head and walking away. Apollo wasn't sure if he was imagining things, but he could have sworn he'd spotted a ghost of a smile on Mykel's lips.

MYKEL

"You seem to be in good spirits," *sri'balvash* Desira spoke up as Mykel sat in his chair in the keep's dining room. He nodded, reaching for the decanter and pouring water into his cup. Now that the watered wine was gone, there was no more alcohol in Woodsong. As both *korrati* and a Shadon Lordson, he could have held himself to a higher standard and kept alcohol in his room while the garrison had none, but he did not trust that Ratsbayne would not find and drink it. Besides, holding himself to the same standard as his soldiers may earn him some respect, and soldiers who respected their *korrati* followed orders better and quicker. *Brak'ha would be proud.* "Let us begin, *sri'balvash* Desira. What is today's lesson?"

"Tell me about the villages in Cetra, Lordson Mykel."

Mykel played with his cup in his hand as he began reciting, staring at the map on the wall of Meridiah and the territory map beside it, the writing too small to read at this distance. "Neppa village's Elder is Frenka, and their main export is Fishing, as well as Epine Village, whose Elder is Arami. Silene Village has an Elder named Ida, and they are known for Farming. Andears village is known for Farming and their small Aldarwood, in which people travel to ask for blessings for smaller yet serious matters instead of smaller shrines in other villages. Its Elder is--"

"Dead," *sri'balvash* Desira answered for him.

Mykel looked at her. "What do you mean he is dead? When did this happen?"

"Andears village no longer exists, for it was completely burned to the ground and its people slaughtered a mere two months ago when Lordson Kerrik-*kyr* was *korrati*."

"Why was I not informed of the people being killed? I was only told it had burned, so I assumed the people had escaped and were rebuilding."

"*Hasta'kan'ix ik'Blagdon* was informed; I reported to him directly after visiting the ruins and seeing the graves of the villagers."

"You said the people were slaughtered. Was it bandits who slew them?" *If there is a bandit problem, I'll have to address it sooner than later, especially if they were murdering dezitens.*

"Your *balutrae* was from Andears, Lordson Mykel. You could ask him and receive a more direct and accurate answer to your question."

He frowned, not liking the diversion of the question. "I will, but I am asking you."

"I did not disturb the graves to inspect the dead, no matter what rumors have of the *ro'belvash*." She sounded insulted.

Mykel gave her silent eye contact as he set down his cup and smoothed his tunic with his right hand, the silver ring on his finger bearing the signet of *Hasta'kan ik'Blagdon* glinting in the light. His brak'ha sometimes used this trick when silently warning someone not to do or say something foolish, though Lord Blagdon's hand would have smoothed his tunic and ended on his rapier hilt as punctuation to said the statement. Mykel was not arrogant enough to make the gesture, knowing that he could not back it up with the chance he could attack her and win, so he folded his hands upon the desk. "I did not mean that you did so, *sri'balvash* Desira; that was your assumption. The *ro'belvash* ability to sense and read blood patterns is unparalleled, even if one without a Sigil of Blood were to study for as long as they lived. I had hoped you had gathered some idea of what had transpired and would speak upon that."

Sri'balvash Desira nodded approvingly. "Whatever blood was shed during the event had been burned away, so it was hard to tell what transpired, but I could feel the blood on the bodies beneath the field of flowers, and the patternings showed they had been attacked and killed with blades of different sizes; swords, daggers, arrows were the most common."

Mykel blinked in surprise. "You could feel their wounds?"

She shook her head. "I killed a rabbit and used its blood to sink into the ground and feel along the bodies, filling wounds as I felt them to determine size and depth. Those killed with bladed weapons were made by those who knew what they were doing and what strikes would kill fastest. Some had broken necks, and there were burned bodies as well; it is possible some villagers were killed by fire and smoke."

"But you could not determine any proof of who had committed such acts?" He was sure of the answer but wanted to hear her say it aloud.

"No, Lordson, I found no definitive proof of who, only what killed most of them." Her tone was slightly defensive, as if ready to defend her abilities to him.

"Thank you, *sri'balvash* Desira. Our lesson is done now; I'd like time to process this information and determine my next action plan. You are a credit to the *ro'belvash*, and I will never forget your aid to myself and my *Hasta'kan*." The woman bowed her head and walked out, shutting the door softly behind her.

As soon as the *sri'balvash* shut the door, Mykel took a long breath and pulled out a series of parchments from the shelves on the wall, looking over the reports his father had collected. Still, he found he could not concentrate upon the familiar symbols of Shadese writing, his thoughts going to his *balutrae*. *If this was true, and Apollo's village had been slaughtered and burned to the ground, no wonder he had so much anger.* Mykel could only imagine that he'd feel the same way if someone had destroyed *Hon-Hasta'kan ik'Blagdon*. He knew there would come a time when the *Hasta'kan* could be knocked down from *Hon-Hasta'kan*, but it was unimaginable if it were one day wiped out entirely with everyone killed.

He walked to the window and looked out at the garrison, watching across the grounds to the sparring area on the other side, at Apollo, who was swinging a sword as *kriss'ix* Lukras stopped him, adjusting his arm before making him try again to swing the sword properly. *My balutrae, your enemies are my enemies, and those injustices against you are also against me. I will discover the truth, and if the kolosae-ro'jo'aritas wills it, I will find a way to correct this wrong.*

RATSBAYNE

Ratsbayne grew more accustomed to working as the stablemaster of the *kelvorvik* paddock, in charge of keeping them supplied with clean hay and fresh meat and brushing their black fur out so it did not become matted with dirt. He'd stopped calling them murder ponies; it wasn't as amusing now that Leigelord Blagdon had left for Stormhold. Sobriety weighed heavily on Ratsbayne's mind, plaguing him with dreams that made a little more sense than the nightmares but not by much. While he worked in the stables, he would often hear a female's voice in his head, whispering to him. *Ah wish Ah be having a drink again to make it all go away*, he complained. The Light was silent in its glory every time he lay down, praying to have another dreamless night and voiceless day once more.

The grey mare's swollen belly was much more noticeable now, and the *kelvorvik* around her would slow and sniff her carefully. *They better not be waiting for a meal to come from her belly fer them*, Ratsbayne thought every time they sniffed at her stomach, but so far, the *kelvorvik* did no harm toward the expecting mare, much to his relief. A figure stepped up beside him at the fence, watching silently.

Ratsbayne turned to see a *balvash*, looking at the gathered creatures around the paddock. "Did the commander need to see mah, lady *balvash*?"

The *balvash*'s eyes flicked to him over her mask and back at the paddock. "*Ro'belvash* are not ladies," came the short reply.

"Ah beg ya pardon, but the House Blagdon Lady wife is a *balvash*, and so she be a lady, but besides, ya be a female, and it is rude not to call a female a lady, balvash or not, so until ya bring a male to ya ranks, then lady *balvash* ya shall be."

"Lady ik'Blagdon is a *sri'balvash*, not a *balvash*. Follow me." The *balvash* turned and walked toward the stables without looking back to see if he was following.

Ratsbayne was halfway to the stables before realizing he had begun following her, so fixated on the leather-clad backside of the female, her blonde hair braided and swinging back and forth with her movements. Once he was in the stables, he was pinned against the stone wall, and the female was taking off her mask, dropping it to the haybale beside her. He smiled once he recognized her face.

"Alandra, Ah be thinking ya weren't returning, Ah missed ye…" He couldn't get more out as she kissed him deeply, making him moan as his arms caressed her as if making sure she was there with him.

She slowly stepped back, a playful smile on her unadorned face; she grabbed her mask and pulled him into the stablemaster's room, his room, where she continued kissing him, undoing the laces of his tunic. "I have missed you, my Ratsbayne," she said in between kissing, taking a moment to pull his tunic over his head, "I could not wait to return to Woodsong, to you." She gave a slight wanting sound as he undid the fastenings on her leather armor, opening the front to kiss down her neck and cleavage. "Tell me what happened while I was gone, my Ratsbayne; tell me."

He pulled her leathers down her arms and legs, then picked her up, holding her as if he could not believe she had returned. *Ah'd thought Ah'd dreamed her up; after all, what gorgeous female would ever want a man who cannot remember his past?* But the woman in his arms was no dream but was real and there for him to hold, kiss, and taste. For the next hour, he did that and more, their soft cries echoing off the stone of the stablemaster's room, their clothing lying across the floor, and the desk moved away from the wall by a foot or two. He lay in the bed, covered in sweat, his breathing finally calming, holding the *balvash* to his side, watching her play a hand over his chest, tickling his chest hair gently as she did so.

"Where did ya go, Alandra?"

"I had some training and business I had to attend to elsewhere, but you've remained in my thoughts; after all, it is quite a feat you have accomplished, Ratsbayne," she replied, looking at him, "you've sobered up, and you started proving yourself as a man who can handle himself. Have you started remembering more about your past?" She raised slightly on her arms, leaning down to kiss him, licking his lip before climbing over him and gathering her clothing, dressing once more.

Ratsbayne rolled to one side, watching her. "Did ya say something? Ah wasn't listening."

Balvash Alandra laughed, pausing to pull up her leather armor to reach into her bag and pour some oil into her palm, rubbing her hands together and rubbing the oil on her arms before pulling the leather sleeves up her arms and over her shoulders. "It makes it easier to put on the leathers," she explained, fastening her armor over her chest.

"Ah," replied Ratsbayne, "that explains how ya *belvash* get into such tight leather armor."

"And it helps with sweating, to keep it from chafing. It also smells nice, at least, I think so," she said, holding out her hand for Ratsbayne to take in the smell of the oil.

"Aye," Ratsbayne said, inhaling the scent, "it smells like pine trees, flowers, and something else, like ash or dirt." He closed his eyes, trying to remember the smell, and shook his head after a moment, his eyes unfocused slightly when he opened them. "What were we talking about?"

Alandra knelt, looking at him. "You were telling me if you remember anything else about your past while I was gone."

"Ah, that... no, Ah haven't, but Ah be hearing a female's voice at times now, when Ah be awake, but Ah dunno if it's mah imagination, or wishing it be ya, or if it's the damned squirrel that's talking in mah head."

Alandra listened, nodding as she began putting on her boots and lacing them. "What does the voice tell you?"

"Different things, that mah name be stupid, that Ah'm not who Ah used to be, but the voice dunno seems to know who Ah am either, so it ain't much help to me."

"Have you been having more nightmares?" She leaned over him, kissing his chest, hitching his breath slightly.

"Ah haven't had nightmares as much, but Ah keep dreaming that Ah'm a knight, and Ah trying to save a beautiful woman, but Ah can't, every time Ah try, she dies, and there be so much blood. Once she drowned in a lake o' the stuff. Ah even rode a horse across the skies; how weird is that? It didn't even have wings." He laughed at the mental image of it.

Alandra stood, pulling on her gloves. "Sleep, my Ratsbayne, I will return to you later; for now, I must meet with my sister belvash and let them know I have returned from training." She kissed him deeply, put on her mask, and left the room.

Ratsbayne felt his world spin slightly and closed his eyes, falling asleep.

I am not sure what I am more fearful of;

The past,

Or the future.

-- Kil'lik'Draven, Bard of the Winds

APOLLO

The garrison tavern was open finally, but no alcohol was allowed. The tables were soldiers sipping fruited water from mugs, discussing the spars of the day excitedly. Apollo sat quietly at a table by himself, looking over a parchment, trying to study the *Hesta*, but could not help but overhear some of the conversations nearby.

"We were looking for the woman who had destroyed some of our wagons last season," a soldier named Eratas was complaining to his companions a few tables over, "but then one of the villagers throws a rock at *kriss'ix* Rigalo-*kyr*, killing him before he hits the ground. The Elder comes forward quickly, trying to tell some lie that it wasn't them, but then the villagers all rushed us. We had no choice but to defend ourselves; they out-numbered us three to one."

Apollo froze, his blood cold, his mug trembling in his hand. He stood and started toward the table where the soldiers were sitting, his hands slowly curling into fists at his side. He was so focused on the soldier speaking that he did not realize someone had stepped before him until the man's tunic was all he could see.

"Easy lad," Ratsbayne's voice came low, soothing as if he were talking to the *kelvorvik* instead of people, "don't be causing a scene."

"Move out of my way," hissed Apollo angrily. Nothing mattered right now except punching Eratas in his smug, smiling face. He tried stepping around Ratsbayne, but the man moved with him, staying between him and the soldiers. *Fine, be like that.* Apollo raised his voice. "Are you speaking of the village of Andears?" The soldiers glanced over to see who was speaking but could not get a good look at the smaller

Apollo behind Ratsbayne's larger frame. "You know, the village you burned to the ground, killed every animal, put oil in the well, and then slaughtered every man, woman, and child, leaving them in a bloody heap in the middle of the square for all to see?" His voice shook with rage, but only Ratsbayne was close enough to see Apollo's eyes shine with unshed tears and his hand on his father's sword hilt so tightly that his knuckles were white.

The tavern grew quiet, and Apollo wondered if everyone could hear his heart beating through his chest. He glared at Ratsbayne's tunic so he didn't have to see Eratas because he wasn't sure what he'd do if he did. "Did you laugh as you did it? You and your buddies, did you joke about it? You stole a newborn babe from his mother's arms; it was Katherine's first child. WAS IT FUNNY?" His voice rose to a choked yell, tears streaming down his cheeks. "That was my home! My brother and I buried each of them by hand, all of them!"

"There's a lot more of us than you, boy," the soldier snapped, looking at his mug, "so don't think you'll get any revenge. They shouldn't have attacked--"

Apollo stepped around Ratsbayne before the man could move to get in his way, but Ratsbayne grabbed his sword arm in warning and to keep him back. "You were taking away girls to work in the kitchen; there's more than enough people here! You didn't need them! You were taking our things, ransacking our homes!"

"We were gathering things we needed for our garrison, not that you'd understand that; you aren't a soldier, neither of you are."

"You didn't need quilts, carved wooden spoons, or a wooden box of handmade goods!"

"Are you calling my men liars, boy?" Eratas stood, his companions standing with him. "We were there; we saw the rock hit *kriss'ix* Rigalo-*kyr* and knock him to the ground where he broke his neck.. You want to do something about it, get from behind Ratsbayne's apron strings, and come take your action."

The shadows flickered around the room slightly. "Challenge

him," Lordson Mykel's voice came from behind Apollo, "Challenge him to combat to settle the matter once and for all. Challenge him for your people, for your village. But know that his companions and neither will yours be able to aid him, and I will not be able to step in either unless the challenge begins to look as if it will cause your disablement, maiming, or death. Make your accusations and responses wisely, my *balutrae*, but do what you feel must be done to ease your conscious."

Apollo stepped around Ratsbayne and looked at Eratas fully in the face. "I challenge you."

RATSBAYNE

He'd be facepalming if he wasn't so intrigued by the suddenness of the commander who had appeared out of nowhere. The Blagdons did not flaunt their powers like Lordson Kerrik-*kyr had done, and sometimes Ratsbayne forgot that they were not ordinary men.* The Lordson had a conscience, which was refreshing since the conversation about the horrible things in Apollo's village had bothered the Lordson enough to step in. *He be young, but he'll grow up to be a good commander and an even better man. However, Apollo be not in the right mindset nor strong enough to challenge Eratas, and encouraging him to do so would get the lad hurt.*

"Well?" said the commander, his voice not harsh like his father's but still had a touch of youth under the air of authority, "Are you going to accept the challenge and be a man, or not and be a coward?"

It took Ratsbayne a moment to realize that the commander was looking at the soldier, Eratas. *He is baiting him, he realized, possibly hoping that Eratas would lose control in the middle of combat and actively try harming Apollo, just so he could beat the man himself.* Ratsbayne had to admit, it was refreshing to know there were limits to what the Lordson would accept, but this wasn't the way to do it, and he worried for Apollo's well-being if Eratas beat him in this challenge. *He'd regain all that anger and rage that he'd worked so hard to temper.*

"What does this say of you, Lordson?" Eratas snapped, his eyes raising to look past Apollo to Mykel. *Oh boy*, thought Ratsbayne, *are ya asking to get yer arse kicked or what?*

"Excuse me?" The commander sounded surprised, as if not expecting the question.

"What does it say about you to have such a human child as what you stated publicly as your *balutrae*? Isn't a Shadon *balutrae* something to be proud of, that the stronger he is, the stronger you become by beating him?" That's what the talk has been, that this is supposed to make you and your *Hasta'kan* better. How will you be stronger if you've picked someone so weak and childish?" The soldiers in the tavern looked at their commander at that, awaiting his response, the Shadon gathered in the room particularly paying closer attention now.

Ratsbayne could not stay silent any longer. As much grief as he gave Kerrik-*kyr*, the man deserved it and more. But this commander was doing the best he could with what he had been given, and Eratas calling Apollo weak and childish awoke a protectiveness in him. He turned back to the soldiers, looking around the tavern. "Since when is grieving for yer murdered village, family, and friends weak? Since when is wanting retribution for crimes childish? The standards for men must have fallen while Ah be hanging out with the *kelvorvik* on the other side of the wall if ya call yerself one, Eratas."

Eratas glared at him as a few soldiers began snickering and whispering. "Stay out of this, Rat Slayer. This does not concern you."

Well, Ah've never been one to listen to good advice anyway. Ratsbayne raised his voice a touch, continuing, taking the attention from both Apollo and the commander and placing it entirely onto him. Apollo sat in a nearby chair and Ratsbayne set his tankard down beside him, pushing it to him slightly. "How manly is it to go around murdering, raping, and pillaging? When did soldiers become the monsters they were supposed to defend the people against instead of their protectors? When did they allow shite like ya to wear armor and call themselves a man?" Out of the corner of his eye, he could see the black and red leathers of *belvash* turning toward them in interest from their table, watching.

Darren at Eratas' table started to get up and walk toward him at the accusation, but Ratsbayne kept his eyes on Eratas, ignoring the advancing soldier. "Here's an idea; don't accept the lad's challenge; he be grieving, and grieving people be impulsive and make stupid decisions. Accept mine, or are ya a spineless piece of shite who hides behind attacking and killing those who ya know cannot fight back?"

He walked to Eratas' table and stepped in to be nose-to-nose with him. Ratsbayne dropped his voice so only the soldiers at the immediate table heard him, though he was sure the Shadon were listening through shadows. "Ah almost killed your Leigelord once in a spar, remember, lad? Take a moment to imagine what Ah be going to do to you because it not be a spar when we cross blades. Ah gonna beat the breaks off ya, and then ya gonna apologize to Apollo. Ah be waiting outside." With that, he turned and walked out, leaving the tavern in stunned silence.

MYKEL

I'd never seen a human who was as confusing as Ratsbayne. He wasn't even sure what to do as the drunkard walked outside, but as *korrati*, he'd have to say something. "Settle down, everyone. Go back to your drinks."

A soldier scoffed. "You mean our fruited waters, commander?"

Mykel glanced at the soldier who spoke. "After this display, do you think I would allow you to drink alcohol and further impair your judgments? You're lucky I do not remove the fruit from the tavern as well." He looked around at the soldiers and *belvash* around the room. "You are supposed to be soldiers, protectors of the realm and her people. Act like it."

He glanced at the Eratas' table, where the soldiers gathered their things and headed outside swiftly. *There may be bloodshed tonight after all,* he thought as he walked toward the door. He turned and looked at Apollo. "My *balutrae*, you have my condolences for the actions toward your village and people. Such acts will never happen while *Hasta'kan ik'Blagdon* owns Cetra, and anyone who thinks otherwise will be shown the truth very quickly." He turned and walked outside, hoping to stop any fighting before it started. He could hear movement behind him as soldiers and *belvash* hurried to the windows.

Eratas was walking after Ratsbayne, who walked to the rain barrel and helped himself to a ladle of water. "Rat Slayer, you dare try to embarrass us? Try to teach us; you, of all people?" When Ratsbayne didn't reply but to take another sip of water, Eratas slapped the ladle from his hand. "Are you going to answer me, drunkard?"

Ratsbayne looked at the ladle and bent to pick it up slowly, taking time to look it over for damage. "Ya've dented it, look," he said, curling his hand around the ladle's spoon, punching Eratas across the face, and turning his body with the blow. Before the man could straighten up enough to fight back, Ratsbayne was already hitting him again and, this time, followed him down, raining blows upon the man's face, first from the right, then from the left, his fist still curled around the metal ladle.

The other soldiers grabbed Ratsbayne, holding him as Eratas punched him in the stomach, forcing the air out of Ratsbayne's lungs, one, two, three times. He was readying for a fourth time when shadows wrapped around his arm, keeping it held backward. Shadows wrapped around the other two soldiers, throwing them bodily aside, far from Ratsbayne.

From the shadows outside the tavern stepped the Shadon soldiers of the garrison, their eyes filled with black as they used their shadows to pin the soldiers down to the ground and wrapped around their throats in warning to stay silent. The Shadon stood around Ratsbayne, making a physical barrier with their backs to him, facing the other soldiers who had rushed outside to either help or spectate. The *belvash* walked outside and stood in line between the soldiers and the Shadon, facing the soldiers as if to say they'd have to go through them to get to Ratsbayne. Mykel blinked in surprise at the solidarity of the two most dangerous groups in Woodsong with the former drunkard. *This is a most unexpected development.*

"We may not agree with Ratsbayne often," *kriss'ix* Lukras said, his eyes dark with his use of his Sigil of Shadow, "but a challenge was given and accepted, and there is no honor in what you were doing."

Eratas spat blood on the floor. "It's my challenge; I can do what I want to. I'm not a Shadon, so you can't hold me to your rules."

Mykel flicked his wrist, the shadows twisting Eratas' arm up and behind his back painfully. "That is enough talking from you," he commanded. He looked at Ratsbayne, who had fallen to his knees as soon as he was released, coughing in the middle of the Shadon protecting him. "Are you all right?"

Ratsbayne gave a thumbs up, nodding.

"Commander, I--" Eratas began.

"I will hear no words of this matter tonight. You four are dismissed for the evening, and tomorrow we will go out to Andears. If what was said is true, if you were part of a massacre of innocent people in--"

"You weren't the korrati then, sir," Eratas snapped, "Lordson Kerrik-*kyr* was, and he--"

"Kerrik-*kyr* be a pissant, and ya know it," gasped Ratsbayne, who slowly stood, holding his ribs, "ya followed someone who be a bully and murderer, who took young females to his bed against their wishes, and allowed murderers to wear his armor and call what they did justice."

"I said, that is enough," Mykel snapped, twisting Eratas' arm higher behind his back. "Ratsbayne, go back to the stables and rest. As for you four, get to your rooms as well. That is an order." There were mumblings of "yes, *korrati*." The soldiers walked off toward the sleeping cabins while Ratsbayne went opposite toward the *kelvorvik* stables, *balutrae* Alandra beside him, her hand on his shoulder as she tended his wounds. The others walked inside or back toward the cabins, talking in hushed tones about what happened, a few giving Apollo a sympathetic look as they passed.

This is the beginning of future problems. Humans did not solve issues between them as *ro*'Shadon did, with honorable duels and *belutrae*, but often with underhanded means. *I will have to keep them apart for a time. It is only luck that Ratsbayne is kept in the kelvorvik stables on the keep's side of Windsong, and the soldiers are on the other side of the wall separating the keep from the garrison. Perhaps I can ask the belvash for assistance in keeping an eye on them all until this all blows over.* He nodded his thanks to the Shadon soldiers, who all saluted him and went back to their nights.

* * *

Once Mykel returned to the *korrati*'s office, he sighed heavily as he shut the door.

"Care to share your thoughts?" a female voice spoke up from the dim light of the lightstone on the desk. Mykel turned, jumping, his sword shadowing to his hand, having not seen someone else in the office when he walked in. Fear that Eratas had sent someone to kill him raced through him, making his heart quicken. *That's not good; what if an assassin came to kill me, and I was too much into my thoughts to notice?*

Lady Narisa Blagdon stood, wearing black leather armor with crimson trimmings, a red cape down the front and back over one shoulder under her metal paldron, signifying her status as *sri'balvash*. She had braided her blonde hair with the *Hasta'kan ik'Blagdon* colors of black and blue ribbon woven into it and twisted into a bun. She watched him with sharp green eyes over her half-face mask, which depicted a quill and sword engraving on one side, the rearing horse emblem of *Hasta'kan ik'Blagdon* on the other. Her shortsword was sheathed on her hip, and a dagger on her opposite side in a thigh sheath. She stood her arms to him in greeting. *"Hin ik'san."*

My son. No matter how old he was or who or what he became later in life, he was always her son, not a *korrati*. At that moment, that was what he needed more than anything. He closed the door behind him and hurried into her arms. *"Sesha,* what are you doing here? How did you arrive, and when? I wasn't informed of it. Is *Brak'ha* here as well?" A small bit of fear ran through him on the last question. *Had they seen the display outside at the tavern tonight?*

"Sri'balvash Desira has been keeping me updated upon affairs here, and I missed you." Mykel heard a soft smile in her voice. "Senka sends her love."

She must have used her Sigil to bring Sesha here in secret. I'll have to write to her and thank her later. He let go of his mother and went to the decanter, pouring two glasses of water and taking one to her. "How is she doing?"

"A story for another time, but she is doing well. Your *brak'ha* told me how your idea of mounted combat had shown great merit with the soldiers. He also has said he is quite impressed and proud of your grasp of using shadows." Mykel had never known his father to lie or mince words, so what his mother said of his father's impression of him meant a great deal.

Sri'belvash Narisa set down her drink on the desk and looked at her son, slightly leaning forward in her chair. "Tell me, *hin ik'san*, what is bothering you? I could tell something was wrong when you walked through the door." Realizing he needed someone to talk to who was not his father but still trusted with these thoughts, for he did not want to show weakness to the man he looked up to most, he began speaking, first about the sparring and Ratsbayne throwing a dagger at his father, and ending with the incident in the tavern that night. His mother listened quietly, nodding but never saying a word until he was finished. *Ro'belvash* were trained to be everything a male desired, in and out of the bedroom, and knew best when to listen and when to use their tongues.

"*Brak'ha* would have stopped the dagger, even if I hadn't," Mykel replied, "but I cannot be sure if it was an assassination attempt on his life or just a man reacting out of instinct."

"I see," his mother said, nodding, running a finger over the rim of her glass absently, "what do you think it was?"

Mykel frowned, pacing. "Ratsbayne is too smart to try to kill *korrati* in front of the entire garrison. But if it was pure instinct, then what triggered it? From what Lordson Kerrik-*kyr* had written about him, he's been drunk for as long as he has been on the garrison, and Ratsbayne has never shown any aptitude in fighting, yet his instincts made him react so? First his throwing of the dagger, and now this sudden standing up for Apollo after hearing of his village?"

His mother was silent, letting him talk out loud, thinking the problem over in his mind. *Sometimes, all one needs is to speak out loud to the darkness*, Mykel remembered her saying and was glad for her assistance of just listening. "He is good, great even, fighting with simulated mounted combat. I cannot wait to see if he can defeat others in mounted sparring. He might have been trained as cavalry, but *brak'ha* has had *belvash* look through the written records of the cavalry and has found nothing so far about any soldier, squire, or trainee who disappeared two years ago or more. Ratsbayne is a fake name, obviously, but he says he cannot remember his name. There have been no serious injuries to his head or body that would result in such memory loss, either."

He could see from her eyes that his mother was smiling proudly at that behind her mask. "You've had *belvash* look to see if he had any bleeding on the brain that caused his memory loss? I am impressed, many Shadon would not even think of doing such; it shows what a creative *korrati* and future *Hasta'kan'ix* you will become."

Mykel felt his cheeks redden with the praise. "I have *sri'belvash* as both a mother and aunt. Senka started to train as *balvash* before she was removed from the Blood Temple, but why wouldn't I use all the resources available to me, female or not?" *The females often perceive things that males do not, yet in a male-dominated society, ro'Shadon forget to use their better halves.*

"You will make a fine husband one day, Mykel," his mother said approvingly.

Mykel scoffed and fought not to roll his eyes. "I'm *korrati*; I don't have time for love. Or lust," he added quickly, which made his mother laugh harder. *Not that some of the belvash and other ladies of Hesta have not offered their services to me, I have just politely turned them down. Those who lie are good spies, Brak'ha says, so even though the belvash assigned to us are trusted by Sesha, they could just as quickly be reporting back to the Temple about our Hasta'kan. I do not want to be a font of information for a spy.*

Sri'balvash Narisa nodded, smiling. "I understand you are busy with your *korrati* duties, but sending more than one message to your betrothed per week would be wise. Mari'aida misses you and will be pleased to hear you have not had a mistress here, even though it is acceptable in our society." She set down some folded parchments with black and blue wax seals on the desk. *Has Mar'aida written all of them for me?*

Mykel took another sip of his water and turned the conversation from his love life, or lack thereof, to the issue worrying on his mind heavily. "Do you think I am weaker for taking Apollo as my first *balutrae*?"

"Why do you ask that?"

"He's human, brash, doesn't know his sword from a stick in the ground, and couldn't fight worth a wrightwing's spit."

"Yet he punched you in front of the entire garrison and your *brak'ha*. Yes, Wilihem told me about that. You could not have let something like that stand, Mykel." Mykel grumbled under his breath, embarrassed.

His mother was silent for a moment, thinking. "These soldiers you complain of in the tavern, Eratas, and Ratsbayne, are either of them Shadon?"

"No, Sesha, Eratas is a human, a good soldier, and he has those who follow his lead. One day he will make a great *kriss'ix*, if he so wishes. Ratsbayne... well, something about him is different, almost honorable, strangely. I cannot put my finger on it, but there is more to him than he shows everyone."

"So they are both a male and human. Who cares what they think is weak or strong? You are a Shadon and his *korrati*, both stronger and smarter than they. At times when you are not, that is when you rely on those around you, correct?"

"Yes, but they will not follow me if they think I am weak. I cannot be *korrati* of an empty garrison. What would the other *Hesta'kan* think of me?"

"You mean to ask what would *brak'ha* think of you?" Narisa commented as she came around the desk and sat upon it, taking his hand in hers. "Look upon me, *hin ik'san*, and hear my words. Nothing in this world would make *brak'ha* or I love you any less. As for our *Hasta*, we have risen from lower ranks to *Hon-Hasta'kan*, named so by the *Kolotor'ix*. We have endured the deaths of our *Hasta'kan'ix*'s first Lady *ik'Blagdon*, their first two Lordsons, and the birth of the first female Shadon. How you have the first human *balutrae*. Whatever the other *Hesta* think of us, let them as long as we remain true to ourselves and hold onto our honor.

Remember our *Hasta* words."

"Power from honor."

"If this Eratas wants to think you are weak, let him. Feed him to the *kelvorvik* for all I care," she said, and Mykel laughed in surprise. "Send him to another garrison if you wish, but do not allow him to plant seeds of doubt within you. If he and his soldiers attacked that village and slaughtered those innocents, you stand beside your *balutrae* and see that justice is brought to their memory and his. Remember, your *balutrae* drives you to grow stronger, and you will do the same for him until the time comes for your duel, where only one of you will walk away victorious. There have been *belutrae* who never dueled for years because they were using each other in their ways to become better, including rising against their common enemies together."

Mykel nodded, thinking about that. "Like the *Kolotor'ix* and *brak'ha?*"

Lady Blagdon nodded. "Just so."

Mykel sighed. "Watching Ratsbayne fight, there is so much rage in him; I do not know where it comes from. He is aloof and acts the fool the rest of the time, until something seems to trigger this protectiveness within him."

"Perhaps he does not remember it, but his body does. As long as he does not turn that rage toward you and yours, do not think too hard upon it. You have a great many other things to worry about, *korrati*." She smiled and stood, letting go of his hand. "Now, think upon our conversation and rest for tomorrow's training of *negut*, drunkards, and *belutrae*, so I suggest you sleep. I will speak with *sri'balvash* Desira before heading home once more. Do not worry about these small things; the *belvash* are here to aid you."

"Thank you, *sesha*." He hugged her gently and headed to his room.

"Always, *hin ik'san*, always."

Running is not the sign of a defeated man,

But a wise one.

-- Elvish proverb

RATSBAYNE

Toy soldiers stood in a row, blue and silver armor shining in the sun. A horse with a white coat and blue eyes blinked at him. Awards lined a velvet board, colors of blue and silver thread neatly hanging with a silver griffin in metal.

A soft, pale hand picked up one of the medals and placed it upon his chest. He looked into the beautiful blue-green eyes behind blonde strands of hair and felt his heart quicken.

Red lips curled into a soft smile; then blood began running between them. They parted in pain, a rattling breath fading away, leaving silence and blackness behind.

"Wake up! You need to wake up right now!"

A different and frantic feminine voice in his head shattered his dream as he opened his eyes, trying to figure out what was happening. He awoke in time to see a dagger coming down at his chest, and Ratsbayne instinctively threw up his arms and shoved it away, the blade stabbing into his pillow beside his head instead. Now that the attacker was leaning over him, Ratsbayne curled, slamming his knees into the attacker's side as he pushed away, rolling off the opposite side of the bed. The air moved above him as the attacker slashed at him with the knife, barely missing him. Ratsbayne blindly felt under the bed, his left hand closing around the lip of his chamberpot, and he swung before he was fully standing, the iron pot connecting with the side of the male's head with a dull clang. From this close, he recognized the attacker, Darren, one of the soldiers, wearing a simple tunic and breeches instead of armor. Darren staggered, half-falling, and Ratsbayne ran out the door and into the stables.

A second soldier stood in the open area before the stalls as Ratsbayne ran out of his room. "You're alive?" He blinked at Ratsbayne in surprise, his sword in his hand.

"So Ah am, why are ya doing this? What did Ah do to ya and Darren?" Ratsbayne asked, moving to put more distance between the soldiers and himself.

The soldier began walking toward him, spinning his sword in his hand. "You thought you could humiliate us before the entire garrison and go unpunished? You and that brat think you are better than us? Time to teach you a lesson, Rat Slayer."

Glancing over his shoulder, Ratsbayne saw Darren rising from the floor and heading toward the door, dagger ready.

Ratsbayne feigned as if to throw the chamberpot at the soldier in the barn, instead making the contents splash out at him, causing him to recoil as he tried to block it. Ratsbayne ran to the nearest pitchfork by the window across from his room, grabbing it to defend himself. Keeping the chamberpot in his left hand and holding it at the lip, he held the pitchfork near the middle; the reach would be shorter, but he'd have better control of it. As Darren advanced, Ratsbayne jabbed the pitchfork at him, forcing him to back up and keeping him out of his blade's reach.

The second soldier wiped at his soiled armor and started swinging at Ratsbayne, who began using the chamberpot to deflect the sword, moving closer to the soldier as he did so, forcing the man to back up. As Darren grew closer, Ratsbayne turned his body slightly, using the pitchfork in short jabs to keep him distanced while he maneuvered along the wall to get out from the corner to the open, where he could fight them properly. He thought to call for aid but was unsure who would come to his aid or who would join his assailants. *Ah be on mah own fer now until Ah can get to Apollo and ensure he is all right.*

Ratsbayne threw the chamberpot at Darren and adjusted his hands on the pitchfork, holding the shaft with two hands. When Darren rushed at him with his dagger, Ratsbayne saw the second soldier moving, both charging to attack him simultaneously. Ratsbayne struck out with the pitchfork, aiming for the first soldier's chest, the soldier leaping backward to avoid being stabbed by the tines. Darren slashed him with the dagger, and Ratsbayne swore, feeling a burning sensation across his side. Ratsbayne maneuvered to try to keep a wooden beam holding up the rafters between the one soldier and himself as he thrust the pitchfork at Darren but found that fighting two soldiers at once was going to get him killed. *Something has got to change, or we'll be playing ring around the beam until Ah be a pincushion.*

A stinging sensation in his back made him hiss in pain as the soldier with the sword got lucky, stabbing him from around the pillar. Ratsbayne turned and ran, diving out the window into the *kelvorvik* paddock, landing hard onto the ground below and rolling to a crouch. When the second soldier rushed to the window to look for him, Ratsbayne took the opportunity without hesitation, stabbing the pitchfork up and into the soldier's throat, yanking him into the paddock, the scent of fresh blood in the air. Ratsbayne stood with his foot on Darren's sword arm, keeping him there, the tine still in the man's throat. Seven sets of red eyes were now watching him, the sound of growling growing slowly.

"Good murder ponies...." Ratsbayne glanced down at the soldier, then at the now-advancing *kelvorvik*. "Ah brought ya a treat, ya can eat him if ya don't eat meh."

The black creatures began running across the paddock toward him.

"*KRUSHKU*! Bad murder ponies, bad murder ponies!" He lept back from the soldier, leaving the pitchfork in the man's throat, not wanting the *kelvorvik* to think he would attack them. His foot hit the soldier's sword on the ground, and he brought it with him with his foot as he made his way back toward the barn as slowly as he could. *Kelvorvik*, he knew from experience, chased things that ran.

A greyish blur of movement slammed into the closest *kelvorvik*, making it stumble slightly. It immediately turned, snarling, and Ratsbayne looked in horror as the pregnant grey mare snorted right back at it, snorting and huffing, ears flat. The other *kelvorvik* slowed, watching the display as the grey mare stomped, snapping her teeth, staying between them and their wounded prey.

"You idiot, get out of the paddock!"

"Ya don't have to tell meh twice!" He yelled to no one as he grabbed the sword at his foot and heaved himself through the window and into the stables, hitting a knee as he fell back inside, looking around for the soldier with the dagger.

The other soldier started coming closer, waiting for him, the dagger's blade dripping with Ratsbayne's blood. Still, they both hesitated as the sounds of bones breaking and the strange growls the *kelvorvik* made as a wet gurgling sound ended suddenly. Ratsbayne cringed, knowing he'd gotten the mare and its unborn foal killed by letting it protect him. *Ah'm sorry, Ah'm so sorry.*

Using the distraction to his advantage, Ratsbayne pushed off the floor and rushed Darren, dropping his shoulder at the last minute, connecting with the male's midsection, and sending them both into an open stall. Ratsbayne repeatedly drove the sword pommel into Darren's face until it was bloody and unrecognizable. Ratsbayne fell back onto the hay beside him, listening to his heart pounding, his breathing ragged and harsh. His aching body was bleeding from various wounds, but he did not care at the moment; only one thing mattered. He slowly stood, his legs still shaking with adrenaline, and he wiped his face off with the back of his sleeve, which was just as bloody as the sword's pommel.

"Ah've got to get to Apollo."

APOLLO

He awoke in the middle of the night when a gloved hand pressed over his mouth, a voice warm and low against his ear. "Wake up; we have to go."

Clep? He opened his eyes, not recognizing where he was for a moment; he had been dreaming that he was back in Andears, and Clep wanted to pick herbs that were best if picked at sunrise. Seeing Ratsbayne's face come into focus made his memories return, and he slowly sat up. Ratsbayne let his hand fall away from his mouth and looked around at the sleeping soldiers in the cabin. "What is going on?" he whispered, noting it was still dark outside the windows.

"We need to leave right now," said Ratsbayne, handing Apollo his boots before glancing around as if someone was following him. Apollo set his father's sword beside him on the bed before putting on his boots. Ratsbayne grabbed Apollo's bag of belongings and was practically pulling Apollo toward the door before he'd gotten his boots laced.

"Ratsbayne, slow down; what's wrong?"

Ratsbayne shrugged. "Not sure, but the voice in mah head said we have to go."

Apollo yanked his arm back and turned, heading to his cot. "I'm going back to bed, and you're drunk. Go away."

"Where would Ah get a drink? Ah've not had a drink in so long Ah've nearly forgotten the taste, lad. Two soldiers just tried to kill meh in mah sleep."

"How's that different from any other time you play cards

with them?" Apollo looked at him and blinked, seeing the blood on Ratsbayne's clothing and face by the torch's light outside the cabin. "By the Light, are you okay? What happened?"

"Keep your voice down, Apollo. Ah just told you, Darren and another soldier tried to kill meh fer the incident in the tavern. Weren't ya listening? We need to go." Ratsbayne grabbed his arm and hurried him out the door, heading toward the garrison wall, keeping to the shadows as he did so. He stopped, looking back at the keep.

"What's wrong?" Apollo looked around, wondering if someone had spotted them.

"Should Ah tell her we be leaving?"

"Tell who?"

"Nevermind, let's hurry." Ratsbayne rushed between the buildings, careful not to be spotted by soldiers roaming around the garrison as guards, even though the front gate was locked at night and only opened for emergencies. Once they got to the stone wall, Ratsbayne looked at it, muttering to himself, before finally moving some stones aside to let them slip under. "Hurry, through here."

"Shouldn't we just tell Lordson Mykel? I'm sure he--"

"Apollo, lad, shut up and get through. We're in bigger trouble than ya think, and Ah dunna want to wake up dead, do ya?"

"Who do you think were the ones that attacked you?"

"Darren and another soldier. They probably would have attacked ya after a shift or poisoned yer food."

Apollo frowned at him, turning his neck, showing the sigil of *Hasta'kan ik'Blagdon*, formed in blood under his skin, the coloration a faint bluish-red, much like the veins in his arm and wrist. "This shows I am *balutrae* to Mykel, or at least his *Hasta'kan*. If they attack me, it is the same as attacking Mykel. Attacking a Lordson of a *Hasta* can be punishable by death."

"Yer alive, and ya punched him when ya first sparred."

"*Hasta'kan'ix* Blagdon prevented them from killing me," Apollo shrugged, "Mykel thinks he saw potential in me, and my death would have been a waste."

"So what, they attack meh instead? Because Ah be yer friend or such?"

Apollo thought about that. "Maybe? It's not like we can question them now. But we need to tell Mykel what happened."

Ratsbayne blinked at him. "The lad Ah met months ago would have killed ta leave this place, the soldiers, and run to find his brother. Now ya wanna stay?"

Apollo looked around at the garrison. *I have a place to sleep and food to eat. I'm learning how to speak, read, and write Shadese and am even learning about their culture. They aren't the enemies I thought they were before. I've accomplished more than I had ever dreamed.* "Yeah, Ratsbayne, I'm sure. If you want to leave, I won't stop you. But…"

Ratsbayne blinked at him. "Yer serious."

"I'm sorry, Ratsbayne."

"Ah can't believe ya. Ya wanted so badly ta get out o' here, and now, ya all friends with the commander and wanting ta stay."

"He can help us, Ratsbayne; he's the *korrati*. They are his men; he won't allow something like this to stand. *Ro'*Shadon are all about honor. There is nothing honorable in what the soldiers are doing to you. I'll go with you if you want."

Ratsbayne looked at the wall and gave a long sigh. "Fine, we'll go see the *korrati*."

If someone gifts you a kolvorvik,

Never check its teeth.

-- Shadon proverb

MYKEL

The shadows grew darker as they approached the *kelvorvik* stables, moving like living beings. Those inside Woodsong suddenly found duties to take care of on the other side of the garrison, speaking in hushed whispers, trying to figure out who or what had angered the *korrati*. Mykel stalked toward the stables, his cloak flaring behind him, his hands in fists at his sides, the shadows whipping throughout the barn, hay strewn everywhere even before he had entered. "Do you have any news?"

Sri'balvash Desira stood beside the bloody hay in a stall as if the Lordson wasn't furiously glaring at her. "The *belvash* are working on finding out the reasoning behind the attack, Lordson, but it will take time to question everyone in Woodsong."

Mykel flicked his wrist, shadows sending a hay bale flying angrily into the wall. "It isn't a mystery why they attacked Ratsbayne, *sri'balvash*!" *Of course, Eratas and his fellow soldiers were upset with Ratsbayne, especially when he broke Eratas' nose and knocked out a tooth, but also because Shadon and belvash stood up for him. But I never thought that they would stoop so low as to retaliate in such a cowardly manner.*

Balvash Alandra stepped into the barn, and Mykel's gaze settled on her like a weight. "Well?" he snapped, taking a moment to let a long breath out. When he spoke again, his voice was a touch calmer. As angry as he was, he knew not to provoke the wrath of *ro'belvash*, who were trained in killing Shadon and sometimes used by the *Kolotor'ix* to hunt down rogue Shadon who crossed him. "What have you discovered in your investigation, *balvash* Alandra?"

The *balvash* took a long breath, flicking her wrist, blood from her clothing flying off in a crimson stream to the *kelvorvik* stables to land outside for them to drink later. "The first squads of soldiers we have questioned do not know anything about the attack nor who ordered it, Lordson."

Mykel blinked at that in surprise. The body they found in the stall was wearing simple clothing and had black hair, and his face was smashed in so severely that they could not identify who it was. The other body had been eaten by *kelvorvik*. "How do you know?"

Sri'balvash Desira spoke up. "*Ro'belvash* are adept in knowing blood, Lordson Mykel, and if *balvash* Alandra says she is certain they were not lying, then I believe her." Mykel frowned, not liking the explanation. He caught the movements of *balvash* Alandra using her hands to sign in a secret language to the *sri'balvash* out of the corner of his eye, and he rubbed the bridge of his nose as the beginnings of a headache threatened him. *So they communicate with each other, but not everything to me. Do they do this with brak'ha as well? What secrets do they keep to each other but not to their lords?* He took a few steps and adjusted so he was watching them both. *Balvash* Alandra's eyebrows raised a touch in surprise, and Mykel would have smirked had he not felt upset and slightly betrayed. *You are not the only one who can play games.* Now that they could not pass along information secretly without him seeing, Mykel felt himself a touch clever for figuring it out, yet an idiot for not figuring it out sooner.

"Write a missive to the Temple of Justice in Meridiah City and request a Truthspeaker to come to Woodsong," Mykel said, and he did not miss the slight raise of eyebrows in surprise, followed by slight stiffening of soldiers from the two *belvash*. Mykel felt as if he was missing something important, but at the moment, he was upset and not caring. *Because they are communicating outside of me, I feel slighted, but I need to discover who is behind this sooner rather than later. Whoever attacked Ratsbayne will surely try again and with deadlier means.*

"Lordson Mykel," *sri'belvash* Desira spoke up, "you do not need to call for a Truthspeaker to find who is behind this attack, for *ro'belvash* can--"

"Why would I trust the *ro'belvash* to get to the truth of the matter when the ones before me, who I am to trust with my life, are keeping secrets from me? *Yok-kyr*, enough with the looks and secret signs. Tell me what you know; I am the Lordson *ik'Hon-Hasta'kan ik'Blagdon*, not a mere child pretending at the role," Mykel snapped angrily, "Should I inform my *sri'balvash* mother what is happening, and perhaps she can give me the counsel you are sharing amongst yourself? Perhaps she can write the Blood Temple and inform the *Belvash'ix* of your games." He'd generally ask his *brak'ha* what to do and say first before saying such, but he was frustrated, tired, and now had to worry about his soldiers possibly attacking each other.

Both *belvash* were silent for a moment, blinking in surprise. "Lordson Mykel," *sri'balvash* Desira began, but Mykel spoke first.

"Do not baffle me with words of flattery and attempt to dissuade me from my mission to seek what is truly going on here. You may be my mother's blood-sister, but I expected you to respect her and me better than this."

"It is not Ratsbayne's fault in the attack."

"How do you know that for certain?" Mykel asked, turning to her.

"After the incident on the barrel sparring where Ratsbayne almost killed Liegelord Blagdon, he'd ordered us to find out what we could about him. I used hard interrogation on him multiple times to see what I could uncover."

"Hard interrogation? What is that?"

"This is something I must show you, for mere words will not get the point across. May I?" When Mykel nodded his permission, the *balvash* walked to him, put a gloved hand on his shoulder, and ran up to his neck and cheek softly. He was not sure if it was the *balvash* using her powers or not, but when she leaned in and whispered against his ear, he had to clear his throat, for his blood headed to southern places that had him adjusting his stance a touch and folding his hands in front of his pants.

"Hard interrogation, Lordson, is when I sleep with the man or woman I need to get information on, that when they are under me, moaning my name, they forget what secrets they guard so tightly, and they flow freely like wine from a bottle. I have learned Ratsbayne's body well and any secrets he held." Her finger played along his earlobe gently. "Perhaps one day you also will ask for such times, not to keep secrets, but to find a release you've denied yourself for so long." She stepped back, standing where she had been earlier, watching him.

Mykel had to try three times before speaking, his face red with blush. "So… you… what did you discover?" He swore at himself for being so flustered. *I'm a Lordson; I am supposed to be better than this, not a mere boy to manipulate so easily.*

"She knows his body more than others here do and knows if he is lying. But she will go and see him again," *sri'balvash* Desira said pointedly, and *balvash* Alandra bowed her head, turning and walking out.

Mykel watched her walk, her form-fitting leather over her and her blonde hair in multiple braids hanging from a bun, moving back and forth as she walked.

"Lordson? Lordson Mykel."

Mykel turned to look at *sri'balvash* Desira, embarrassed that he'd been caught staring. The woman didn't seem to mind, though her tone had a touch of amusement in it. "Lordson Mykel," *sri'balvash* Desira said as she went to Mykel, placing a hand on his shoulder, "There is no shame in giving in to your desires. B*alvash* Alandra is a talented lover, and she'd be honored to aid you if you need release." She gave him a nod and walked out the barn door, leaving Mykel to search through the shadows to find cold water to soak in.

* * *

Mykel sat in the *korrati*'s office, sighing heavily, his hair wet from his bath in the keep's bathhouse. He had *sri'balvash* Desira write to his *sesha*, informing *Hasta'kan'ix ik'Blagdon* of what had transpired and that he was working to remedy the issue. He waited for *sri'balvash* Desira to return with his father's reply. His s*esha* and *sri'balvash* Desira had a way of communicating over a great distance that took less time than a messenger by horse or raven. Some Shadon could send messages over shorter distances via shadows, but how the *ro'belvash* completed this was still a mystery. What once was a frustrating mystery to him was now one of his greatest assets as *korrati*, for the speed of communication in times of trouble was paramount to success, as his *brak'ha* had once said.

Perhaps I may ask while the Truthspeaker is here and gain more insight into the ro'belvash, he thought, though he knew he would not do it. Truthspeakers were rare, even before the Scourge War, having a Sigil that allowed them to force the truth from anyone standing near them. They had been used in Meridiah before the Shadon had migrated here and now were housed in the Temple in Meridiah City under the protection of the *belvash*. As tempting as learning some of the most guarded secrets in the empire was, eventually, the Truthspeaker would leave Woodsong, and he'd be here, dealing with the aftermath of furious *belvash*. *No, I'd rather not die by the Blood Temple's command.*

A knock on the door made him focus on the here and now. "Come in."

Sri'balvash Desira walked in, shutting the door behind her, parchments in her hand. "Korrati, we are done interrogating the men about who may have attacked Ratsbayne."

"How?"

"Various ways."

Mykel waited for her to elaborate, but when she stayed silent, he nodded. *I am not going to learn any ro'belvash secrets today.* "What have you learned?"

The *sri'balvash* walked over, setting the testimonials on his desk. "Darren, the soldier who we found in the barn, had a newer soldier aid him in the attack on Ratsbayne, and a few of the other soldiers were aware of it. They were planning on threatening Apollo as well but not harming him since he is your *balutrae*, and it would bring the might of the Shadon present in the garrison upon them."

I am glad Ratsbayne killed the two soldiers, so I did not have to come up with a way to set an example with them. He'd never killed anyone before, and if he could help it, he wouldn't for a long time. *Even though brak'ha is well-known for dueling to the death, he said that you never forget the first life taken by your hand.*

"Were there others involved?"

"In this, no."

Mykel felt irritated at the lack of answers. *Do they do this with brak'ha?* "Is there anything else you wish to tell me?"

Sri'balvash Desira seemed to think about it for a moment. "The *belvash* are keeping our eyes on some individuals. When we are certain there is information to give you, we shall, Lordson."

"Why not give it to me now?"

"Because you have enough on your plate and need not worry about it now. Do not be concerned; the *belvash* are here to ensure any plots are uncovered and will be brought to your attention when appropriate. You must trust us."

"Very well, thank you."

The *sri'balvash* nodded and left the office, leaving Mykel frustrated and wondering what the *belvash* were doing. *I will have to keep an eye on them, nonetheless.*

After a moment, he sat behind the desk, pulling out a fresh piece of parchment, reaching for his brush, dipping it into the inkwell, and writing in his journal. He tried to set aside his feeling of betrayal at the fact that someone near him was trying to attack his men, and the *belvash* were less than forthcoming with information. *With a blending of Shadon and humans, there is bound to be some in-fighting, but I cannot look over my and my people's shoulders and simultaneously fulfill my duties. I need to adjust how Woodsong is organized.* Mykel pulled out a parchment and began to write.

APOLLO

Sitting at the table in the Woodsong keep, Apollo opened his bag, took out a wooden box, and looked it over before setting it down. He could appreciate the black engravings in the wood more now that he'd learned a bit more about the *ro'*Shadon. Made from a tree in Nar'Shada, the wood was greyish white, much like ashes after a fire had died down, and had black engravings of *kelvorvik* on the smaller ends. Along the two long sides were carved Shadese symbols that Apollo could read now, and he ran his hand along the engravings, which had been filled in with a black substance so the entire surface was flush and smooth. "*Nar'shada ro'kebat.*" he read aloud. *From the Ashes, all rise.*

In his history lessons, he had learned that Nar'Shada, once as lush and plentiful as Meridiah, had been burned to ash when the Elder dragons fought across its skies thousands of years ago. From what Mykel had said of his few visits to his people's homeland, the plant life in Nar'Shada grew in shades of dull colors since the ground was full of dragonfire ash. Apollo knew that farmers would burn fields after the harvest so the future crops would become more robust and healthier. That the same did not happen in Nar'Shada made him ask what the difference was in the ash, but Mykel did not know. Apollo ran his hand across the inscription, thinking upon words. *It is fitting since I've risen from the ashes of Andears.*

Dark blue silk lined the inside of the box, with silver-handled brushes of different sizes and an ink pot for writing. Given as a gift, Mykel had explained that blue and silver were *Hasta'kan ik'Blagdon*'s colors, and if he learned how to write Shadese, he'd scribe it properly with the correct tools. Apollo had never had a gift like this, beautiful and exotic, and he was unsure if he should even accept it. But now, looking the gift over, he was unsure what to feel. Training and living among the Dark Army for months had taught him many things, but he had not expected compassion to be one of them. Now he understood that not all of the Dark Army was the enemy, for not every soldier in Woodsong was like the ones who slaughtered and burned Andears to the ground. Even as he was named Mykel's *balutrae*, he'd learned that Mykel, like himself, was still just a boy in a world of men, trying to find his place and fit in. He looked over the *kelvorvik* outside the window overlooking the paddock, standing side by side as the pregnant grey mare grazed on grass, the *kelvorvik* nuzzling her and sniffing her swollen belly gently, their strange red eyes watching for danger. *If those creatures, prey and predator, can get along in harmony, why can't we all?*

He was practicing his letters when Mykel came into the room, parchment in hand. Mykel took a moment to watch his brush make the markings of Shadese upon the parchment before pointing slightly. "It needs to be smoother here, one motion. You can tell that you have done it in two." Mykel picked up a brush, dipped it into the ink, and copied the letter, drawing it effortlessly and making it look too easy. *Shadese is a beautiful language*, Apollo admitted as he copied the letters, this time trying to keep with the stroke-making in one motion.

"Shadese is not just making the motion; it is a balance of how much ink is on the brush, how many bristles touch the parchment. You rise and lower your brush, adjusting the pressure to make thicker and thinner strokes, which is why we practice our basic strokes repeatedly. You are doing quite well, but remember, you must be balanced and fluid simultaneously."

"I thought I was practicing inkwork, not swordplay."

"Is there that much of a difference? Each can be just as devastating." Mykel straightened, setting the brush on a stand beside the parchment to keep the bristles off the table so they kept their shape. He was quiet for a moment, watching as Apollo continued his copying of the basic upstrokes followed by a downstroke, focusing on making it in a fluid motion and adjusting pressure to make the ink thicken and thin in the right areas. "Leigelord Blagdon has said it is time for tax collections."

Apollo concentrated on the brushwork as he spoke, not looking at Mykel. "Tax and tribute collection was never a good time. A lot of the villagers hated it. You may see some issues, such as refusals. I loathe thinking what the soldiers will do to them."

"Why is that?"

"*Hasta'kan'ix ik'Remhold* taxed the villagers so much; more than half of what we harvested and made in trade went to Woodsong for his soldiers. If we didn't give them what we had, more people were taken for refusing." Apollo frowned. "Andears had almost a hundred people once, but last year we were to a fifty-nine." *Of those, the soldiers killed all but two.* Apollo pushed the thought aside. "If it was not for the fact that we are in a long summer season, we could have starved. At least, that is what it was like for Andears, I'm not sure how it was for the other villages. Lordson Kerrik-*kyr* kept raising the taxes and tribute amounts every year."

Mykel was quiet, and Apollo glanced to see that the *korrati* was frowning. "I do not understand why he would raise the taxes and tributes, especially that high. The Scourge War ended over a hundred years ago, so *Hesta'kan* do not need the funds to build walls around keeps and protect the villagers from the Scourge, nor do we need to pay soldiers in the numbers we had back then."

Apollo frowned, listening. Thanks to his lessons, he knew about the Scourge War: the rising dead had marched south into Meridiah through the Shadowgulf Pass from Nar'Shada. Many Shadon had left because they had been assaulted by the Scourge and needed a new, safer place to live, but the king and queen of Meridiah had refused to give them harbor. *Why would they not wish to help those refugees from a war? The Kolotor'ix only took over after someone killed the royals, then created an alliance so the humans, Nar'Shadon, belvash, and Shadon could unite to defeat the Scourge, bringing peace and safety to the people.*

Mykel drummed his fingers on the table in thought. "I suppose with the war, combined with the Lingering Rot, the number of those lost was too much for the *Hesta'kan* not to tax in high amounts to offset the costs of supplies and resources. But I do not see why *Hasta'kan'ix ik'Remhold* would allow *korrati* Kerrik-*kyr* to continue raising it unless it was simply a way to try to get more coin to make themselves look better. Petty, but a truth among many Shadon, is that appearances are better than reality."

Apollo quietly looked down, swallowing hard. "*Balvash* Inara says it had no cure."

"She is correct. From what my studies have shown, in the past, many *belvash* had tried stopping the blood flow to affected areas or amputating the infected limbs, but the sickness often spread too quickly for them to get to those who were ill in time."

Apollo nodded quietly. Clep had studied under Andears' healer for two years and tried to make healing salves to aid their parents, but none had lasting effects. In the end, the boys became orphans. That did not deter Clep, who continued improving his potions and salves enough that he would trade them for coins or goods from the other villagers or travelers. *I wonder how he is doing; I hope he is all right. He probably is busy making salves and potions for everyone in Silene now.*

"Tomorrow," Mykel was saying when Apollo blinked, coming out of his thoughts, "We will begin to travel to the seven villages of Cetra and collect our taxes and tributes, as mandated by the *Kolotor'ix*'s law, but not in the same quantities that *Hasta'kan ik'Remhold* had demanded. Also, I have decided that I will be sending many soldiers back to their villages."

Apollo blinked at that. "To gain more recruits?"

Mykel shook his head. "No, I want those who wish to return to their villages to do so and live their lives. I want them to farm, do woodwork, fish, and have families. I want them to protect their homes because they want to, not because they have to. Those who wish to stay may remain here, of course. Only when the Law of Protection demands it or they volunteer will I bring any Cetran new soldiers here."

"What if everyone wants to leave and go home?"

Mykel gave a small smile. "As my *balutrae*, you cannot leave, for you have to learn our ways more than mere soldiers. You will be expected to know the *ro*'Shadon society inside and out. Besides, where would you go? Your village is burned to the ground, and you have no home other than here." Apollo frowned but said nothing. "But if enough soldiers wish to leave, I can allow it; Stormhold is sending cavalry-trained soldiers to aid in patrolling the territory."

"The Law of Protection states that every time the soldiers come to a village, the Dark Army can choose any one of twelve and six years to join their ranks?"

Mykel blinked at him, frowning. "Was that what was happening here? No wonder the villagers hated the Dark Army so, as well as *Hasta'kan ik'Remhold*. I now fully appreciate why the *Kolotor'ix* gave Cetra to *Hasta'kan ik'Blagdon*. No, the *Kolotor'ix* had brought many of our laws down with us from Nar'Shada, and many humans and *ro'Nar'Shadon* follow them."

Apollo thought about that. Nar'Shadon were the most similar to humans born in Nar'Shada; they did not have Sigils of either blood or shadow, and they did not fall under Shadon hierarchy, such as being a *Hesta'ix*. They ranked lower than the *belvash* yet higher than the orcish population in the mountains in Nar'Shada, which framed the northmost part of the continent of Andora. Apollo had never seen a map of anything larger than Cetra before, and the first time he had seen a map of Andora, he had audibly gasped. *I had no idea that the world was so big, and Mykel had said that there was even more of it outside the borders of the parchment.*

"The Law of Protection," Mykel explained, "is that one male every two generations in a family must enlist into the Dark Army to maintain protection of their territory. For example, if a grandfather has served in the Dark Army, the father may see his family furthering while his son enters the Dark Army as a recruit. None of that generation of the immediate family needs to serve further in the Dark Army unless they wish it or the *Kolotor'ix* enacts wartime recruitment."

"Oh."

"Lordson Kerrik-*kyr* had insisted that the Dark Army checked for eligible males over twelve and six years to take as recruits every year? Woodsong does not have the room or resources to support that amount of people. No wonder it caused animosity; there were problems from unwilling recruits and overcrowding."

"While serving as a soldier, males are educated to read, write, count, and basic Shadese or Common, depending on the soldier's native language. This way, no matter what, the soldier can understand orders of the *korrati* of humans, *Nar'Shadon*, or Shadon descent. At the garrisons, they have housing, food, and livable wages, which, if they wish, they can send back to their families via visits once a season if they can."

Apollo blinked at that. *No wonder the Hasta'kan ik'Blagdon soldiers were more relaxed and loyal. Perhaps if it had been like that, I might not have grown up hearing the horrors of the Dark Army and their evil soldiers, nor would Andears have been destroyed.*

Mykel held up the parchment that he had brought in with him. "I have written to Stormhold, asking for soldiers from our cavalry. Any soldiers at Woodsong who wish to protect their villages from within or even retire may do so. Perhaps they will father children and teach them to read, write, and count, furthering the territory's education and bringing them higher. There are Shadon who feel that keeping the people ignorant and simple would make better simpletons to command, but *Hasta'kan ik'Blagdon* does not believe in that."

"I've seen that first-hand," Apollo replied, setting down his brush to shake his cramping hand. *Not many months ago, I would have never dreamed that I would learn to write Shadese or see an image of the entirety of Andora.*

"I also wanted you to know, Apollo, that after midday's meal, we are riding out to Andears. I wish to know the events spoken about in the tavern and see it myself."

Apollo froze, looking up at him, torn between shock and panic. "I don't know if I can go back out there," he admitted.

"I will not allow you to be kept back by the ghosts of the past, my *balutrae*, and seeing this will aid in your healing. This furthers my understanding of Cetra, the people, and you. We will ride out together, and I will not allow you to mourn alone." Mykel began walking toward the door, heading out of the room into the keep's hall. "I plan on you learning many great things, Apollo, and I look forward to watching you grow further." *So am I, Mykel, but I am not sure I can ever grow strong enough to face the past.*

* * *

He'd never thought heading back down a dirt road would make his stomach turn into knots, but it was churning so severely that he'd thought he'd become sick before they even reached the farm fields. Apollo rode a horse beside Mykel, surrounded by soldiers who carried both the red and black banners of the Dark Army as well as the blue and silver banner of *Hasta'kan ik'Blagdon*, with a golden ring at the top of the pole signifying that it was the rank of *Hon-Hasta'kan*. There was a small two-wheeled cart of supplies with them, just in case they ran across anyone needing assistance. *I doubt anyone around here would ask for help from anyone carrying the Dark Army banner. I knew that I wouldn't have.*

Mykel had attempted to carry on a conversation, but Apollo couldn't seem to get words out of his throat the closer they got toward Andears. Soon, the two just rode in silence, the only sound coming from the soldiers singing a few songs to pass the time and the birds flying overhead in the blue sky. *It feels wrong to have the sun shining and the sky blue, the birds chirping happily. The world should have ended that day with Andears.*

There was no mistaking the area, acres of farmland surrounded by woods. With no one to tend it, the farmland was full of weeds where once there had been wheat crops. It saddened Apollo; he missed the smell of cut grass and fresh-turned soil. As Mykel slowed his *kolvorvik*, Apollo reined his horse to a stop and dismounted, walking to the familiar black ruins of timber that stood like the skeletal hand of a giant creature with blackened fingers, pointing up at the sky where buildings used to be. His eyes fixed on the village, but he did not see it as his feet carried him through the ruins. Grass had started to come up where he never thought he'd see life rise again, and it gave him mixed feelings to see nature already claiming what once was his home.

His voice was hollow as he spoke to no one in particular. "This was the stables, and there was the inn. That was the granary and bakery; you could smell the bread baking across the area." He walked as if in a trance, detached and refusing to think. Distantly, he heard the sound of someone walking toward him but refused to turn around to look because he was unsure what expression his face would hold. *Dark Army soldiers accompanied me here, perhaps some of the very ones who had been the cause of this. What would the villagers think of me?*

Mykel stopped beside him, standing a small distance away, showing respect and space for him, or perhaps he was preparing in case Apollo swung upon him. *I would have punched him had we visited months ago, blaming him for all of this.* Apollo glanced back to see if the soldiers were around him, and to his surprise, the soldiers stayed outside the village, tending their horses and *kelvorvik* in the road or standing guard. A few looked at the ruins with sad faces, some shaking their heads. Three were talking, pointing at the field beside the ruins where flowers grew in dotted rows between new growth of plants. *Did Mykel tell them to stay out of the village?*

Mykel's voice made him turn back, blinking dumbly for a moment. It sounded like he'd been trying to say Apollo's name a few times. "Apollo, my *balutrae*, do you need a drink of water?" Apollo looked at him, both surprised and glad that he did not ask a stupid question like *are you well?* He took the waterskin Mykel held out in offering and drank, closing his eyes for a long moment before handing it back silently, nodding his thanks. Mykel replaced it onto his hip under his cloak, which he'd pulled over his shoulders as if perhaps he were cold.

Apollo began walking again, in case Mykel wanted to start talking, walking a large berth around the village square, once which had been filled with laughter and children, then filled with their bodies in that heap so long ago. *How long has it been?* He glanced back and noticed Mykel followed him, staying in Apollo's footsteps like a silent shadow.

Apollo walked to the other end of the village where the Aldarwood stood, its white bark scarred on one side with black where the fire had started to grow up its side before Clep had thrown water on it, dousing it in an attempt to save the sacred tree. He bent, picking up a broken and burned piece of wood about six inches long and carved in the shape of a man. Brushing it off with his hand, he could now see the large crack had almost bisected the figurine, going from the bottom of the male's leg to the top of his shoulder, and the cord that had gone through the top of the rays of light carved to stand behind him had either broken or burned off. *Did it crack due to the fall or the fire?*

"What is it?" Mykel stepped beside him, seeing what had caught Apollo's attention.

"It's the Father."

Mykel blinked at him. "I do not understand."

How could you, you're Shadon, Apollo mentally snapped, but then he pushed the thought away. He'd not understood anything of Shadon before and had asked questions of Mykel and *balvash* Inara, who both still explained what must have felt like the simplest things a Shadon child would know. "The Light has six aspects: Grandfather, Grandmother, Sister, Brother, Mother, and Father," he said, gesturing to the figurine in his hand. He held it out for Mykel to take, which he did carefully, looking it over slowly. Apollo gestured to the other figurines hanging from the branches of the Aldarwood by cords, each depicting a person standing in front of carved rays of light. "The Grandfather governs over craftsmanship and leadership. The Grandmother looks over children and wisdom. She is who many mothers pray to ease childbirth and to make sure their children grow strong and healthy. The Sister watches over our livestock and animals, while the Brother watches our harvest and ensures our food stores don't rot. The Mother is responsible for nurturing and wellness so people don't become ill."

Mykel's voice held a curious tone. "What was the Father in charge of?"

Apollo swallowed hard. "Protection, guidance." *Was that why we weren't protected because his effigy had fallen to the ground and cracked? Had we offended the Light somehow, and the Aldarwood tried to warn us with his fall, and no one cared to replace it?*

A movement made Apollo come out of his spiraling thoughts, and he blinked at Mykel, who was now kneeling, doing something under his cloak, his hands unseen. When he stood again, he held out a leather cord in his bare hand, his glove in his other hand, and the Father's effigy. Apollo blinked at him dumbly; perhaps he was more shocked than he knew.

"For the Father, so you can hang it once more. It seems the cord had broken, which made it fall from its branch."

Apollo slowly nodded and began running the lace through the hole at the top of the figurine, the two ends of the cord loose so he could tie it. Mykel moved his hand, shadows lifting Apollo off the ground so he could hang the effigy back onto the tree. Once Apollo tied the cord around the branch and tugged a few times on the knot to ensure it would not come undone, Mykel lowered him again to the ground.

"You didn't have to do that."

"I know."

They were silent for a long moment before Apollo looked back at the Aldarwood. "People all over Cetra would travel here sometimes to ask for the Light's blessing. Each human village has an altar or area for their effigies, but not every village has an Aldarwood. They are pretty rare, from what Nan told us growing up. They always grow in good soil and always near a water source."

"I've seen many places that have good soil and are near water, like Stormhold, but I've never seen an Aldarwood until Woodsong, and now."

"Aldarwoods have no seeds that we know of, so we can't replant or farm them, which makes them rare. We don't know why they grow where they do. Woodsong has the largest Aldarwood I know of and is the only one in the immediate area." Apollo turned and looked at him, puzzled. "How can you be so welcoming of something that is not your religion? The Aldarwood is of the Light, not the *Kolosae-ro'jo'aritas*. It's the very opposite of Shadows. I thought you would have tried to cut it down."

Mykel's lip twitched slightly."Years ago, a Lordson of a *Hesta* burned an Aldarwood on his property. It had caused an illness that left his entire *Hesta* and the surrounding village so ill they almost died out. Rumors say that your Light protects them from being cut or burned." He looked back at the Aldarwood, as if studying it. "You are right; it is not my religion, nor one of *ro'belvash*, who live by their *Balsesha*'s will. But it is important to Cetra's people and you, so it is important to me."

Apollo nodded, unsure what to say to that.

"The Light does not demand its followers slay *ro'*Shadon and *ro'belvash* does it?"

That's a strange question. "No."

"The Light does not demand human sacrifice or immoral things of its followers, does it?"

"Of course not."

"The Light wishes the people who follow it to be good, just, and kind towards another. Your aspects seem to stand for such things. Am I incorrect?"

"No, Lordson, you are right."

"If a religion wishes to help you become a better person, as mine does for my people, why would I wish to destroy something that helps the people of Cetra? Shouldn't I learn more about it to learn more about the people I help lead?"

Apollo wasn't sure what to say about that, agreeing with most of Mykel's points, but was genuinely surprised. He finally nodded. "I agree that knowing about each other since our people live together is good."

Mykel nodded, looking over the great tree. "I would never cut them down, especially now knowing more about them. I also do not want to injure the relationship with Cetra's people more than it already is. Respecting their religion, though I do not follow it, seems a good first step to regaining their loyalty."

Apollo shrugged. "I don't know about the rest of the territory; I have never traveled outside of Andears much."

Mykel looked to him. "I understand that; this is the furthest south I have ever been. Would you show me around and tell me what Andears was before this tragedy? I wish to remember it as you once did, with stories of what it was and perhaps what we can rebuild it to be again."

Apollo looked at him, shocked. "You want to rebuild? Here? Why? You can't use the burned wood; the people are... gone. You can't just rebuild and erase what happened here in hopes the people will forget and like you better." A thread of anger warmed his voice.

Mykel put his glove back on his bare hand and set it on Apollo's shoulder. "People come to the Aldarwood to receive their blessings of the Light. Having a new place to rest after a long journey will be welcomed. I suggest we build a place for the travelers to the Aldarwood to have a place to rest and be safe, much like Andears was before."

They walked silently from the Aldarwood, each in their thoughts. "How do you move on after this? How do you make a new place where there was a pile of bodies there," he said, pointing to where the village square once stood, "and animals were slaughtered there, and there in the field, the villagers are all buried because there wasn't enough room in the graveyard on the hill." He rounded on Mykel, his voice shaking with emotion. "You can't just build over it and pretend that nothing ever happened! Because it did! I was there, and it happened, and I can't just cover it up!" Hot tears ran down his cheeks, and he brushed them away with his arm, his breath ragged.

Mykel was looking at him, but it was not pity on his face, but understanding. He waited silently, only opening his mouth to speak once

Apollo finally took a calmer breath. "Assassins slew my Hasta'kan's first Lady and second Lordson in Nar'Shada. She was in a marked *Hasta'kan* carriage; he was riding a horse beside it with our soldiers. One of the soldiers, being human, fled the scene to ride to Stormhold to tell my brak'ha what happened, unable to speak or go through the shadows to do so."

Apollo listened quietly. Mykel's tone never changed as if repeating a story he'd been told a dozen times. "My *brak'ha* went through the shadows to the scene with a dozen soldiers. His first wife died in his arms, and Senka rushed to find her brother and discovered that he was already dead, having fought the assassins but had perished due to his wounds."

"I knew they had died, but I didn't know the story behind it. Did they ever find who did it?"

Mykel gave a slight nod, though Apollo wasn't sure if it was acknowledging his words or answering his question. "My *brak'ha* created a monument to sit along the side of the road as a marker, honoring those lives lost, both of the family and those who died trying to protect them. I do not mean for Andears to be rebuilt and erased from anyone's mind; I want to honor them and their sacrifice."

Apollo's eyes narrowed. "Sacrifice? They were murdered, not sacrificed!"

Mykel held up a hand and waved off the angry tone. "Has their deaths not meant anything? Their deaths, though tragically taken, have given rise to something much greater, which would not have even existed if not for them."

"What do you mean? Of course, their deaths meant something!"

"Their deaths gave birth to you, the true you, Apollo. Your heart was forged in the fires of anger and sorrow, both from your parents' deaths and now from Andears. Your Light chose *you* to replace the Father onto the Aldarwood, to bring protection back to it and this place. It chose to spare you from those who slew your brethren and brought you to Woodsong so you may teach me and help me become a better Shadon, *balutrae*, and man, and I believe I am wiser through knowing you."

Apollo blinked at Mykel at that, unsure of what to say.

"I do not want to build over Andears and erase the tragedy; I want to honor it, to have something beautiful come from the ashes. I want to show the people that *Hasta'kan ik'Blagdon* is not what they are used to, and we will be better than those before us. I do this, Apollo, not for your peace of mind," he said, gesturing out to the field of flowery grave plots, "but for theirs." Mykel turned and walked back toward the waiting soldiers, letting Apollo have time to think and mourn.

MYKEL

Seeing the truth of what happened to the village of Andears was an experience that he'd never thought he would see with his own eyes. He'd never been in a duel, but he'd often gone with his *brak'ha* to his duels, acting as his second who negotiated with the opponent's second on location, time, and place. He had thought that until he had duels of his own, watching his *brak'ha*'s opponents fall would be the closest he would ever be to death.

Mykel looked out at the graves, the only proof that the women, men, and children who once lived in Andears existed. How Apollo managed to bury them all by hand baffled his mind. *It is no wonder Apollo was so angry before, with no way to grieve appropriately. I hope that this trip helps more than it hurts him.* Mykel stared at the burned ruins of buildings until he was sure that this warning of what not to become would be seared into his mind forever.

Feeling like someone was watching him, he turned and saw *sri'balvash* Desira giving him serious eye contact. He nodded to acknowledge her, and she walked across the ground, ash coming up with each step of her black boots. "*Sri'balvash* Desira, you have something for me?"

"During the interrogations on who attacked Ratsbayne, the *belvash* also used the opportunity to find those who were here during the attack on your *balutrae*'s village."

Mykel looked at her slowly. "Are you saying you can tell which men were here when this happened?"

"Yes, those who attacked this village are among those who are here with us. After all, you allowed me to write and post the list of soldiers you wished to accompany you."

Mykel blinked in surprise at her. "You acted upon your own accord, changing the subject of interrogation and writing on my behalf?"

Sri'balvash Desira looked at him flatly. "I am *sri'balvash*; the *belvash* follow my orders. You could have me reported to the *Belvash'ix* for this removed from your *Hasta'kan*'s service. However, I did this to ensure those enemies of you and your *balutrae* cannot backstab either of you." She stepped forward, slipping him a rolled strip of parchment, small enough to be concealed in one hand. "We have been watching the soldiers since the interrogation. We agree the soldiers we name on this strip of parchment are guilty of this slaughter. But the only way to be more certain of those soldiers here is to have them before a Truthspeaker."

Mykel frowned, taking the parchment in his hand but not his eyes off the *sri'balvash*. *What angle do you play, doing this without my consent?* He wished his *Hasta'kan'ix* were there to guide and tell him what to do. *Would sesha even aid me on this, or would she play with whatever the belvash schemed now?*

Sri'balvash Desira looked from him to the graves, and Mykel noticed her eyes had unshed tears, but when she turned to look at him, they were gone. *I've been so used to seeing them as assassins, spies, and ways to get information that I'd forgotten that belvash are beings of feelings and emotions. Of course, they would wish to find whoever murdered innocent women and children. If I am not careful, my perceived assassins and evil deeds will blind me to the real ones.*

"I deeply appreciate the initiative you and your *belvash* have acted upon, and *Hon-Hasta'kan ik'Blagdon* will not forget this." He had no worries about speaking on behalf of his *Hasta'kan*; he was sure Liegelord Blagdon would agree with his words, and the *belvash* may be more willing to use their abilities to discover plots against them before they happened. *Perhaps this is why the Kolotor'ix keeps sri'belvash near him.*

"The *ro'belvash* appreciate that, Lordson *ik'Hasta'kan ik'Blagdon*." *Sri'balvash* Desira said and walked back toward the other *belvash*. Mykel opened the parchment under his cloak, using shadows to read the names of ten soldiers who accompanied Mykel and Apollo. *So many,* he remarked silently, keeping the frown from his face. He watched as the five *belvash* conversed with their hands, using a sign language he did not know. *I wonder what they are speaking about. Are they in agreement with what is about to happen, or are they judging me for making a foolish choice? What will they ask of me in the future in exchange for this precious information?*

Mykel looked at the ruins of Andears, taking a moment to himself, letting out a breath that shook with nervousness. His eyes fell upon the Aldarwood, blackened with burns on one side of its white wood, the cracked Father hanging from one of the branches, one of his bootlaces holding it high with the rest of the effigies of the Light. He closed his eyes and said a prayer, not to the Light, but to the *Kolosae-ro'ja'aritas* for the wisdom of words, the strength to do what he needed to do to restore the wound and honor of his *balutrae,* and ensure that this would never happen again in a territory of *Hasta'kan ik'Blagdon.*

He'd never done this before, and although his *Hasta'kan'ix* would have done this differently in front of the entire territory, he did not feel that it would help Apollo gain closure. He pushed his cloak back over his shoulders to his back, straightening his shoulders and adjusting his black leather armor and sword on his hip before turning around. He glanced at the *belvash,* noting their eyes were all on him silently. *Sri'balvash* Desira gave the barest of nods to him, and he swallowed hard, taking a breath before raising his voice with authority as his fist closed around the parchment in his hand. "*Shadon ik'Hon-Hasta'kan ik'Blagdon,* to me."

The two *Kress'ix* and three Shadon soldiers immediately moved through the shadows, appearing before Mykel. Without question, they went to one knee as a unit, their fists on opposite shoulders. "What will you have of me, Lordson *ik'Hasta'kan ik'Blagdon*? Your command is mine to obey," they said in unison in Shadese. It sent chills down Mykel's back, for he'd only heard such words spoken to *Hesta'kan'ix* and the *Kolotor'ix* himself.

Mykel concentrated, using the shadows in the ears of the Shadon to deliver his voice so only the Shadon gathered would hear his command. "I will give you the names of ten men here; read them and wait for my order." Mykel delivered the parchment of names through the shadows to each Shadon, one by one, watching looks of curiousness cross their faces as they read them. Once they had all read and nodded in acknowledgment, Mykel shadowed the parchment back to his hand and tucked it away in his pocket. "Deliver to me these men unarmed, after which you will stand ready behind them for more orders." Mykel cleared his throat slightly, looking at the curious Apollo and the *belvash* watching with much attention and anticipation. "Rise and do your Lordson's bidding."

The Shadon bowed their heads in acknowledgment and, for a moment, stood facing him, *kriss'ix* Lukras' lips moving quietly, not no sound coming out. Mykel had a moment to wonder if they were refusing his order when three things happened at once; there were shouts of surprise as shadows suddenly wrapped around ten soldiers; they appeared in a line a short distance in front of Mykel, a *belvash* was wrapped in shadows to appear standing beside of Apollo, four of the Shadon appearing behind the condemned men. *Kriss'ix* Lukras and *sri'balvash* Desira both appeared on either side of Mykel, hands on their weapons in warning.

Immediately, the confused and surprised soldiers on the road went for their swords, thinking they were under attack. "Sheathe your weapons," *kriss'ix* Lukras ordered the men, his voice carrying through shadows.

Mykel stepped forward, feeling the tension and confusion rise. "*Hon-Hasta'kan ik'Blagdon* stands before you to accuse those standing here of burning and murdering the village of Andears. The *belvash* interrogations earlier this week have questioned your innocence. I am your *korrati*, and I order you to speak the truth fully and completely, for your lives depend upon it. You have one chance to clear your conscience and announce your guilt before myself and your Aldarwood, and it may save your lives," he added. Now that he understood more of the significance of the white tree, he felt that its influence could be used to loosen the human soldier's tongues and reveal the truth. "Speak falsehood before us at your peril."

He walked to stand in front of the first soldier, Eratas, who struggled as he was being held tightly with shadows by the Shadon standing behind the accused soldiers. *Sri'balvash* Desira and *kriss'ix* Lukras stepped up with him in symbols of unity, support, and protection for their *korrati*. Mykel looked up at the taller and older-looking soldier, frowning. "You should have known better, Eratas. You are of the highest rank and eldest of those in this line. You stand accused. How do you answer?"

"They attacked us, and no one should ever attack the Dark Army and get away with it. Ligelord Blagdon wouldn't allow any of his soldiers to be attacked."

Mykel nodded. "Liegelord Blagdon would have ordered the hand or even the death of whoever killed *kriss'ix* Rigalo-*kyr*. At most, anyone who picked up a weapon against his soldiers would have a hand removed. But explain to me, what did the women, the children do to you? The babes? How did they attack you?"

"I will not explain my actions to you, *korrati*."

"Do you feel remorse?" The question seemed to catch Eratas by surprise, and it surprised Mykel himself as it fell from his lips. Ro'Shadon did not bother themselves with remorse, but he blamed his *balutrae*'s influence upon him. *Would I have asked that had Apollo not been here watching?*

Eratas took a moment to think about it. "You were not there, and you do not know what it is like to be in the middle of chaos, not knowing who was attacking or how many, and only had moments to decide what to do. They gave us no other option, *korrati*."

Mykel turned and walked to the next soldier, asking the same question, giving each a chance to explain their actions. Three agreed with Eratas, echoing his words, while three stated they were following orders. Two stood in sullen silence, refusing to answer, while one spat at him angrily, and Mykel had to stop the *kriss'ix* from backhanding him. After questioning them, he stepped away, turning his back to the accused, and spoke low to the two with him privately, seeking their more experienced counsel.

"Remorse or not, this cannot stand. It will set a precedence, *korrati*," *kriss'ix* Lukras said, using shadows to speak to Mykel's and *sri'balvash* Desira's ears.

"They are nervous, but they are guilty, Lordson. While some deaths can happen in the blink of an eye during the chaos, an entire village cannot. The number of dead is impossible for they not to have hunted down those who escaped, or else there would have been more survivors besides your *balutrae*." The seasoned *kriss'ix* nodded, agreeing. *If anyone knew better, it would be they, both experienced in combat, having served during the Scourge Wars. I wish my brak'ha were here for his advice, but kriss'ix Lukras is one of our most trusted and loyal.* He glanced over his shoulders at the accused soldiers. *I had thought they were trustworthy as well. Perhaps I must be more on my guard and look for betrayal everywhere.*

"I concur with the assessments, both of them," Mykel said after a long moment of thought and sighed heavily, his hand playing along the pommel of his sword. When he realized he was bothered enough to fidget, he forced his hands to be folded before him, determined not to let them betray his nervousness.

Kriss'ix Lukras looked at him. "All due respect, Lordson, but you do not need to do this yourself. You only need to say the command."

"No," Mykel said after a long moment, almost giving in to the suggestion, "I am *korrati*, and I must do this." *One who is strong enough to pass judgment must also be strong enough to pass sentence,* his *brak'ha* once said. He'd never fully understood what it meant until now. When the *kriss'ix* bowed his head to him, Mykel breathed relief and slowly turned back around.

The other soldiers on the road had gathered together, talking low, but had stopped talking when he'd turned, so now all eyes were watching him. The four Shadon soldiers stayed between them and the gathered soldiers to keep the accused from running, and to defend Mykel in case the soldiers rushed forward to attack him. It should have made him feel better, but it made him more nervous, knowing that the protection may be necessary. *Many of the soldiers are friends of those who are accused. There is a chance that this could result in more bloodshed than is necessary.*

He glanced at Apollo, who now had two *balvash* beside him as protection, the other two standing off to the other side of the square, eyes never stopping in watching everyone there as if they'd be asked to report upon this later. *They probably will be,* Mykel realized. *I wonder what Brak'ha and Sesha will think when they hear of this.*

He took a breath, using shadows to make his voice heard by everyone there so there was no misinterpreting his words. "I, Lordson *ik'Hon-Hasta'kan ik'Blagdon*, suggest a sentence of those before me to be given death in answer to their crimes against the people and village of Andears." There were shouts and arguments immediately at this, but Mykel ignored them.

He instead looked at Apollo, standing pale beside the two *belvash* guarding him. "Apollo, as the last survivor, witness to the destruction, burier of the dead, and protector of the Aldarwood and village of Andears, I offer their final sentence to you, my *balutrae*, to accept and have it be done, or deny, and give these accused their lives back. What say you?"

APOLLO

The whispering gave way to silence as the soldiers slowly looked at him, at each other, and at the ten men accused of murder. He shifted uncomfortably under the weight of everyone's gaze, never anticipating anything like this happening. When the *belvash* had first moved to stand beside him, he wondered if he had done something wrong and insulted Mykel somehow. *They are here to protect me in case the soldiers act against me at the proclamation of Mykel's accusation. I thought the idea of balutrae was that no one would attack me, but I suppose it could be forgotten in the rush of anger.* Apollo knew all about rage and the mind-blindness it sometimes brought upon him. But the thought that the punishment would be his to decide shocked him. He was glad his armor was not metal, or it would betray the fact that he was shaking slightly.

He looked to Mykel, then at the Aldarwood standing on the other side of the village square, framing the Lordson slightly. He closed his eyes and prayed to the Light for guidance. *I wanted for so long to kill those responsible for the massacre at Andears, but this is different than what I had envisioned.* He glanced at the field of graves that Clep had dug by hand long ago. *Were their spirits at ease?* Apollo could feel them, watching him, waiting. *I could put those souls to rest, but what would happen to those I condemn? Would their ghosts still haunt me in my waking hours and my dreams?*

Belvash Alandra gently cleared her throat beside him, reminding him that Lordson Mykel and everyone there were waiting for him to decide the men's fates. *Why is this so hard when this is all I have wanted for so long?*

Apollo walked along the edge of the village square to the Aldarwood and knelt before it, bowing his head, praying for guidance and someone else to decide because he was unsure what to do. The Aldarwood was silent, the only sound being the wood creaking gently as the wind blew through the blue-green leaves.

Mykel's voice was gentle in his ear. "There is a difference, my *balutrae*, between vengeance and justice." Apollo thought about that. Putting these men to death would not be vengeance now, as he'd wanted for so long, but a justice long denied to those who had called Andears home. As he realized that, Apollo felt as if a weight had lifted off him, and he realized that during the time he'd been in Woodsong, he'd gone from wanting vengeance to justice. A leaf fell from the Aldarwood, brushing his cheek to rest against his sword hilt on his hip. He wiped it away and stood slowly, walking toward Mykel.

The accused are standing where they had piled the villagers on that night, the stone walk in the village square still stained with their blood. Did Mykel do that on purpose? Apollo looked at the men who stood accused, some looking away, some glaring, one with tears on his cheeks. He looked at Mykel, who watched him patiently. "I wanted to kill these men for so long because I was young and wanted vengeance."

He could see the soldiers relaxing with relief, Eratas glaring at him arrogantly, as if to say *I knew you were too weak to do it.* But Apollo wasn't feeling vulnerable at the moment but tired. He was tired of waiting for justice, being so angry for so long, tired of the fear that someone would attack him just because he was from Andears. He was tired of being away from his brother, of feeling sick to his stomach when he saw fire or smelled burning meat. Only in the past month, he could begin eating around the firepits.

"I do not want vengeance any longer. I want justice done, for the souls of Andears to rest finally, knowing their murderers, their tormentors will be no more."

Mykel raised his voice slightly, sounding surer than Apollo was feeling. "Is that your sentence, my *balutrae*, that those accused shall be no more to walk among this side of Hinestra?"

I wish Clep were here to give me advice, to tell me if what I am doing is right or wrong. He was so much smarter than I when it came to these matters. Would he agree with what I am about to say or be disappointed? Would ma or pa? Are the spirits of Andears watching me with hatred for what I am about to do? Apollo had to try twice before he could get the words out. "I ask the punishment of death for the accused men who are guilty of the slaughter of Andears."

Exclaims from some of the soldiers on the road helped punctuate the growing tension, and the shadon who stood behind the condemned drew their weapons in silent warning as shadows gripped the condemned men and forced them to their knees, their arms still held tight to their sides. The *belvash* looked interested, one drawing her daggers carefully, keeping them by her pants to not call attention to them, another resting her hand on a whip on her belt. The men began pleading for Apollo to change his mind, others calling him a coward and worse. *Kriss'ix* Lukras flicked his wrist, the condemned men's mouths covered with shadows.

"My *balutrae* has spoken. I, Lordson *ik'Hon-Hasta'kan ik'Blagdon*, *korrati* of Woodsong, sentence the accused before me to death. The punishment will be carried out upon the very stones you all had shed the innocent blood to reclaim their color as guilty blood washes it away and eases the pain of their spirits."

Mykel walked to the stand before Eratas and gestured to Apollo. "Your sword is sharp enough to do the deed."

Apollo blinked at him dumbly. "Wait, I have to kill them?" Eratas made a scoffing sound under the shadows that held his mouth closed, and Apollo fought to ignore it.

"Whoever passes sentence should be the one who swings the sword," Mykel said, "for it is heavy duty. It should be you; as the survivor of Andears, you are now its protector." Eratas turned to glare at Apollo, as did a few other soldiers, not just the condemned ones. *I wonder if I will be able to sleep safely tonight.*

Mykel flicked his hand, and shadows bowed Eratas' head to look down at the stones, exposing the back of his neck. "Come, Apollo, as a *balutrae*; this will hardly be the hardest thing you will be asked to do." *By the Light, he's right,* Apollo realized in horror; *eventually, he and I will have a duel, and one of us may have to kill the other.* The idea made his throat tighten.

Kriss'ix Lukras showed him how to stand with his feet apart and adjust how to hold the sword so that the swing would be straight down. *It is harder to swing a sword like this,* Apollo thought, taking a practice swing, the wind of the blade making Eratas' hair move as the blade went past his head. *It is too much like chopping wood, and I hate it for being so similar to something mundane; shouldn't killing a man not feel familiar?* Mykel and the others watched as Apollo finally set his sword on the back of Eratas' neck, feeling the man jump slightly as the steel touched his flesh. The sword shook somewhat, and Apollo was not sure if he was trembling more or if it was the condemned man. *I am not sure if I can do this after all.* He had to step away from the soldiers, taking long breaths that shook, looking out at the field of graves as if willing them to tell him what to do.

I hate this, he decided. *I don't want to have to do this. Can't someone else do this?* His stomach was twisting in his body, his hands were sweating, and his knees were shaking. He looked over at the anger and hatred in the eyes of the condemned, in some of the soldiers who would be traveling back with them after this, sleeping in the same cabin he'd be in later that night. But then he also saw compassion, sorrow, and a few nods of understanding in that same group of soldiers. He looked at the *belvash,* and though their masks helped them betray nothing, one gave him a slight nod. *This is the right thing, isn't it? So why does it feel wrong at the same time?*

Mykel watched him calmly, but Apollo was close enough to Mykel to see the concern in his eyes. *Mykel is a touch pale, too; his hand is fiddling with the pommel of his sword. I am not the only one who is nervous.* It made him feel a touch better, and he prayed again silently before walking back over, and he placed the blade upon the flesh of the soldier's neck once more. It took three times to cut off Eratas' head, his father's sword not making it through the first time, getting stuck in the man's neck bone, forcing Apollo to fight to pull it out to try again, missing the same mark on the second attempt. The still-alive man was screaming through the shadows that held his mouth closed, the sound high-pitched and unearthly like an animal being slaughtered, making Apollo's hair stand on end, his skin covered with gooseflesh-like bumps. The other condemned cried out against the shadows wrapped around their mouths, sobbing and pleading in fear as they struggled against the shadows that held them, listening to the screaming of the dying man, the sickening sound of metal stuck against bone. The air thickened with the stench of bowels and bladders evacuating, copper lingering in the air, and Apollo swallowed hard, fighting not to lose his breakfast.

"You are doing fine, lad," *kriss'ix* Lukras said, "breathe out of your mouth." His gauntleted hands went over Apollo's gently, and the third time, Apollo raised his shaking sword above his head and brought it down. Finally, Eratas' head fell from his shoulders, rolling across the stone to look up at him. The eyes blinked, and the mouth moved wordlessly for long moments before finally stilling, the liquid blood staying inside the headless body even as it collapsed. The world swam suddenly, and *belvash* Alandra went to Apollo and helped him rush away so he could fall to his knees, throwing up violently in the grass beside the ruins of the nearest building.

He could hear more swings of a sword through flesh behind him, punctuated by muffled sounds of the men fighting, crying, pleading, and screaming in fear, slowly drowning away as the heartbeat in his ears grew louder. A wet cloth rested against his forehead, and *belvash* Alandra held out a waterskin to drink from. He took a few small sips, staring off into the distance, trying not to feel the weight of those watching from the road staring at him. *Do they think I am weak for being ill?* He wanted to leave, go to Woodsong, find a place to lie down, and forget the entire ordeal. He would cry, but he wasn't sure he would even be able to.

Glancing over his shoulder, Mykel was being helped to the side of the well by *sri'balvash* Desira, who gave him a waterskin to drink from as he sat. Blood coated Mykel's sword with so much that it looked like the blade was made of it. Blood splattered across his face, and Apollo dared to glance at the condemned soldiers, seeing nine more headless bodies, their blood flowing across the ground like a growing crimson puddle after rainfall, their heads resting in the liquid-like hair-covered islands. The memory of Eratas' head blinking at him made him repeatedly vomit until his entire body ached with the ordeal, and tears ran down his cheeks. He sat fully down in the ash and grass, his legs no longer able to hold him even on his knees. When he finally dared to glance over, *kriss'ix* Lukras was wiping off his bloodied longsword. *Did he have to behead some of the soldiers for Mykel?* It made him feel better that perhaps Mykel could not hack heads off a row of condemned men as if merely chopping logs. *Sri'balvash* Desira was saying something to Mykel that Apollo could not hear, but Mykel shook his head and stood slowly, carefully, as if he were unsure if he could move too much. She moved her hand, and the blood came off the sword, flowing into the ground.

Apollo glanced at his sword, noticing it was bloodless as if nothing had happened and the horrible incident had been a hallucination. However, the dents and imperfections along the sharpened edge of one side of the blade, the side which had hit bone and flesh, told him otherwise. *Balvash* Alandra gave him a single nod as she stood. Glancing at the bodies, he saw their blood flowing freely, soaking the stonework in the remains of the square, but the blood, both old and new, was sinking into the ground via the cracks between the stones, leaving them looking cleaner. *The very rocks which the innocent blood had been shed now will reclaim their color as guilty blood washes it away and eases their pain.* He shakily stood, using his sword to aid him, and shakily went to the Aldarwood to use the time to recollect himself and beg the Light for forgiveness for what he had to do.

After several long moments, Apollo reached where *kriss'ix* Lukras stood, waiting for him. Behind him on the road, Mykel was mounting his *kolvorvik*, who was watching his bloody rider with rapt attention. *It can smell the blood on him,* Apollo thought. *Why didn't the belvash clean the blood off Mykel's face and armor, but just his sword? Do I have blood all over me, too?* He looked down at his armor and saw that he, too, was covered with blood.

"Lordson Mykel is ready to ride back when you are," *kriss'ix* Lukras said, his sword still bare in his hand, "do not worry about the bodies. The Lordson has commanded they are not to be burned nor buried near Andears, but brought back for the *kelvorvik* to eat."

Apollo nodded numbly, and the *kriss'ix* put his hand on his shoulder, a touch of concern in his eyes. "You will need to rest as soon as you get back to Woodsong, and I suggest that you allow the *belvash* to aid you in dreamless sleep tonight, but you may have nightmares about this moment for weeks." *He sounds as if he is speaking from experience.* "Tomorrow, have your sword's blade sharpened. Bone, especially multiple strikes, will cause it to be dull quickly. I will see that Lordson Mykel sharpens his, and I will sharpen my own. My words may not mean much, but you have impressed this day, *balutrae ik'Hasta'kan ik'Blagdon*, and I look forward to watching you grow."

Apollo blinked at the man as he walked to some soldiers, pointing to the bodies and talking. He'd never been addressed as such before by anyone other than Mykel. *Did that mean that the soldiers respected me more for killing unarmed people? Does it change how they feel about me? Does it change how I think of myself?* Some of the soldiers nodded to him in respect, a few wiping their mouths with cloths, looking a touch green as they walked over from the side of the road. *I am not the only one who was ill.*

Sri'balvash Desira spoke low to the Mykel, who nodded and slipped his sword into his sheath after two tries. Mykel silently began walking his mount forward, and everyone else began moving, those soldiers who volunteered to get rid of the bodies staying behind with their mounts. As they passed the field of graves, Apollo thought the flowers growing on them were a little brighter, a little taller. For the first time in a long time, he felt at peace.

It is not what I go to do,
But what I leave behind that scares me the most.

-- Kil'lik'Draven, Bard of the Winds

RATSBAYNE

He wasn't sure what was more surprising, that Eratas and nine other soldiers died due to their actions in Andears or that Apollo had executed them. He went to check on the lad as soon as he heard, finding Apollo asleep, a vial beside his bed, which Ratsbayne picked up and sniffed, finding that it had contained herbs and not alcohol. At least a *belvash* had given him something to take, so he had a dreamless sleep. *Good.*

Setting the vial back down on the table, Ratsbayne quietly took Apollo's armor and his father's sword, heading to the blacksmith. While the blacksmith resharpened and polished the blade, Ratsbayne sat by the fire to clean and polish Apollo's armor, even though there wasn't much blood on it. He assumed that a *belvash* took care of that since it seemed in Woodsong no blood went to waste but was given to the *kelvorvik*, but still, tending the armor made Ratsbayne feel as if he was helping Apollo. *Ah cannot help ya with the upcoming nightmares and waking ghosts, but at least Ah can do this.* He didn't remember if he'd ever killed anyone before, but he knew it was grizzly business, and equipment would suffer if not cared for.

He worked quietly, listening to the soldiers on duty talking quietly among themselves as they recounted what happened in Andears. Ratsbayne had to admit that he was more impressed with both the young commander and Apollo than he had ever been. *The two lads are growing up, and Ah be right about my instincts about Apollo; when he gets older, he will be a force to be reckoned with. Thank the Light he isn't under Kerrik… er… Kerrik'kyr.* He thought about the first time he'd met Apollo in the woods when Apollo tried to fight him unsuccessfully. *Even drunk, Ah could take that lad with one hand tied behind mah back. Now he's cutting the heads off grown men.*

"Never thought the the kid would give a death sentence to anyone, I remember when he couldn't even hold his sword right," a soldier spoke, laughing as he stood beside the armory with his partner on duty.

"He's grown a lot, in fact, I think the only one who has grown more is you, Ratsbayne," his partner quipped, pointing at him as Ratsbayne stood to head to the blacksmith and check on Apollo's sword. The words shocked Ratsbayne, and he wasn't sure what to think, walking past them silently.

"They are right, you know," the mysterious female voice said softly in his head, *"you've grown as well."*

"Bah," Ratsbayne answered as he walked back toward the soldiers' cabin to return Apollo's things. When that was done, he headed back to the stables, stopping to check on the *kelvorvik* and the grey mare before heading to his room to sleep. *It won't be long til the mare be foaling, Ah hope the kelvorvik won't think it be a snack.* He'd have to stay by the stables more instead of walking around the garrison, for if the mare went into labor, he could be there to aid the birth. He'd already set up a stall in the stable with fresh hay and had a stool to sit on when it was time so his legs didn't get tired crouching beside her.

Ratsbayne groaned as he saw a squirrel race along the rooftop of the *kelvorvik* stables. *How long would it be watching and talking to mah?* He walked into his room and shut the door quickly to prevent the creature from darting in after him. After making sure that the window was shut as well, Ratsbayne climbed into his bed and fell asleep.

* * *

The first wave of pain hit him as if someone had suddenly punched him in the stomach, leaving him gasping for air. *What the hells was that?!* Another aching of his stomach made him double, groaning in agony. *What had Ah eaten that made mah stomach twist in knots so? It be like the largest shi--* The last of his thought was cut off as a scream escaped his mouth.

The door swung open, interrupting his thoughts as *korrati* Mykel entered the room, two *belvash* in tow with Ligelord Blagdon. The young commander looked at him with concern as he held a lantern, casting light and shadow around the room as he looked for an assailant. "Ratsbayne, what has happened? We heard screaming. Are you injured?"

"Ah dunno, but when did ya get here, Leig--" he doubled, grabbing his abdomen, groaning greatly.

"Perhaps we did not stop everyone behind the attack; could it be that he is poisoned?" The *korrati*'s tone had a touch of worry in it, and Ratsbayne almost appreciated it.

Balvash Alandra walked over to Ratsbayne, forcing him to sit with a hand on his shoulder, and she closed her eyes, taking a breath. Ratsbayne looked at the floor, trying not to throw up or lose his bowels simultaneously. *Ah dun't know which it would make meh feel better.* "Korrati, Hasta'kan'ix, he has no poisons in his blood, nor is he injured and bleeding anywhere, inside or outside his skin." She stood, and Ratsbayne could almost see almost disappointment in her eyes.

The *korrati* frowned deeply. "I do not understand. What could it be?" *Balvash* Inara walked to Ratsbayne and set her hand on his other shoulder. After a moment, she confirmed what the *balvash* Alandra had said, repeating the diagnosis of the situation.

Blagdon spoke up after a long moment. "I believe I may know what the matter is. But first, *belvash*, please see to the grey mare immediately." The *belvash* glanced at each other and left quickly, heading into the barn proper, leaving the two Shadon with Ratsbayne, who fell over on the bed, curled into a fetal position slightly, crying out as he grabbed his abdomen.

"What the bloody hells be this pain from! Dun't just stand there; help mah!"

Blagdon walked to the side of the bed and pulled out the chair from the desk, sitting, watching him as a cat would a dying mouse, his storm-grey eyes almost gleaming slightly with unsaid satisfaction. *Was this his idea of getting back at mah fer trying ta kill him back at the spar? It be months since then; why would he still be harboring anger fer that?*

A knock at the door made Mykel answer it, and after speaking softly to someone, he closed the door and spoke Shadese. Ratsbayne was in too much pain to even get upset that he didn't understand what was being said. Blagdon nodded, his eyes never leaving Ratsbayne. "Go to the stall and see to things there, Mykel. I will tend to Ratsbayne." *Oh that does not sound good fer meh. Light, what have Ah got mahself into?* Mykel bowed his head and left, the door closing behind him.

Ratsbayne would have asked Blagdon a question, but the pain robbed him of his voice, doubling and writhing slightly.

"It hurts, does it not?" His tone was patient, curious almost.

"What did ya do to mah?" Ratsbayne choked out in between waves of pain.

"I received a missive from *sri'balvash* Desira, saying the grey mare was going to foal this week. I arrived an hour ago to tend to her. But to answer your question, it is not what I did, but what you are. I have tried to find out what I can about you, and finally, I believe I understand. You've done well, hiding among the people, acting the simple drunk, though I do not think you were acting at times. You took your role seriously, and I must commend you, for you have fooled everyone. Well, almost everyone."

What is he talking about? Ah dunno anything about mah past, Ah've never lied about that, so why does he think that Ah did? " Ah dunno what yer talking about. What do ya think Ah be?" Blagdon pulled out something from a pouch on his belt, holding it out to Ratsbayne for him to take. It was an empty bottle with a cork stopper. There was no writing nor label upon it, so he had no idea what it had once held. "Ah dun't understand; what be this?" *Had he poisoned meh, and now held the antidote fer ransom?*

"I found it in the cave north of Thraesh, the village you had said you'd gone to after waking almost three seasons ago. I've been there, trying to find out more about you."

"About mah? Why?" He realized that short sentences seemed to work better than long ones as he tried breathing shallowly as another wave of pain crashed onto him.

Blagdon waited to speak until Ratsbayne was able to listen once more. "You have been the closest being to have killed me in several years, and I do not wish to repeat that mistake." *Ah, so he be still upset about that.* "But now I won't make the same mistake again, as I know what you are."

"So what ya think I be?" He writhed as if something had kicked his ribcage from the inside, and it took him a moment to relearn how to breathe properly once more.

"The grey mare outside giving birth, and you are her Stormrider."

Ratsbayne opened his mouth to ask what that meant when he suddenly felt as if his insides were being stretched and ripped out through his bowels. He screamed in pain, and suddenly, everything went away, leaving him feeling numb and exhausted as the world faded to black.

BLAGDON

Standing before the full-length mirror on the wall, he looked over his leather armor, sighing. A week had passed since Ratsbayne had passed out, suffering from incredible pain in the stables, pain that Blagdon would have previously thought was only experienced by females. To see a male suffer so made him a touch uncomfortable, but it intrigued him as well. His Lordson's future mount was born, walking in the paddock beside his mother, and Ratsbayne was seemingly free of pain once more. It served to prove Blagdon's suspicions.

"Ah heard ya want to see meh?" Ratsbayne said after being allowed into the office. Blagdon gestured to a chair by the desk, pouring a glass of water and setting one before Ratsbayne on the desk.

"I am heading back to Stormhold; I've only been here for the foal's birth and to ensure the garrison knows that *Hon-Hasta'kan ik'Blagdon* supports the decisions made in Andears."

Ratsbayne shrugged. "Ya be a Leigelord, ya got to work from home, not be seeing the sights around the territory."

"The territory of Cetra is my duty to see to," Blagdon answered, taking a sip of water, "and any threats inside or outside of it is mine to see to. Which brings me to the matter at hand: you."

"Ah not be a threat," Ratsbayne answered quickly, as if fearing Blagdon would strike him down there on the spot.

"Are you not? You have said multiple times that you hold no memories of who or what you were before you awoke in the cave near Thraesh. I have traveled there to see what we could find out about you.

We found a vial left inside, holding the remains of a mixture of herbs known to be once used by Ny'fer elves. My poison experts theorize that they were created to put you to sleep, but by whom and for how long, we do not know."

"Ah dun't understand what ya saying," Ratsbayne answered, looking puzzled, "Ah thought that the elves be extinct."

"The elves are not extinct, merely in hiding. My son is courting a Mu'nari elf, the daughter of Li'ana, a former captain in the Byronian Army and friend of the late elven Queen Mari'anath of Meridiah." Blagdon observed him for any reaction to the names that would give Ratsbayne's farce away. *I do not think I could ever escape the shame if this drunkard has been playing us all for fools.*

"That be good fer him," Ratsbayne said, shrugging and sipping his water, "he will give ya grandchildren one day. Ah dun't even know if Ah had a lady mahself."

"Are you so sure about that?"

"Ah'd hope Ah'd remember if Ah had a lady or children. Though Ah was in such bad shape before, maybe it be best Ah didn't."

Blagdon thought about that and had to admit that he agreed with Ratsbayne's sentiment. "No one in Thraesh is your family, nor knew you before you came into their borders."

"Thank the Light," Ratsbayne said, taking a drink of water, "at least Ah dun't have a woman who will be comin' fer meh one day with a fryin' pan for mah head, sayin' Ah left her alone with a lad or lass to raise on her own."

"You say you are not a threat, yet you've thrown a dagger at my head without the slightest of hesitation during a spar, where you've shown the incredible ability for someone who has supposingly never had training fighting before then."

"Ah've been training some now, the commander won't let me not train."

"You acted in muscle memory of some training, and I want to

know by whom and for what reason."

"Ah dun't remember."

"So you've said numerous times." *As well as during various interrogations by balvash Alandra, which included truth-saying oils and potions.* Blagdon changed the subject. "You were in considerable pain days ago, even passing out in your room. I had *belvash* attend you while you were unconscious to ensure you'd live. You had no injuries, no illnesses that would have caused you distress, but still, your body reacted to be in severe pain. Do you know why?"

"Nah, the *belvash* looked meh over and saw no injuries, but Ah be in bedrest fer a week. Ah thank ya fer tending the *kelvorvik* while Ah was made to stay in bed."

"I assure you, I did not do it for you but to ensure my *kelvorvik*, mare, and foal are cared for. If you had died, I would have to send another to tend to them, which means taking them from their duties where they are currently. Ones competent enough around *kelvorvik* to tend to them are hard to find."

"Ya be a hard man ta compliment."

"Compliments are empty words; actions show true intentions," Blagdon replied, "so if you want to impress me, do not waste your words."

"Ah see."

He pulled out a box from one of the many pouches on his hip, the trinkets and emblems of fallen duelists clinking gently as he set the box on the desk. "Do you know what this is?" He opened the box and removed an amulet, letting it swing from his hand as he held it out. The silver amulet had a relief of a griffin flying over hills, with engraved sun's rays behind it. Along the circular frame were carvings in Elvish; though he did not personally read the language, his Lordson's betrothed had been kind enough to translate it. The amulet turned slowly on the chain, the other side showing a crescent moon with a leaping stag underneath it in relief.

"How did ya get mah amulet?" Ratsbayne dug into his tunic, pulled out an identical amulet that hung around his neck and frowned, looking between the two before slipping it away. "That be Apollo's then, and ya need ta give it back. It belonged to his ma."

"Did it now?" *That is a most interesting bit of information*, Blagdon thought quietly, filing it away to ask about later. He held out his gloved left hand, letting the amulet fall into it, careful to keep his hand open and not betray that two fingers were stuffed with cotton. "This is not Apollo's mother's amulet, I assure you. Can you tell me what this beautiful writing around the edges is?" He traced it with his finger gently as if studying the metal, but his eyes were on Ratsbayne.

Ratsbayne didn't look quite at him as if he were listening to something outside the window. "Ah'm not sure Ah can--"

"Does the squirrel tell you you should not translate this for me? *Balvash* Alandra has told me you've spoken of one following you. I thought it was a hallucination from drinking, but there has been no alcohol in Woodsong for quite some time." Blagdon set the amulet down so it faced Ratsbayne, using the movement to lean in ever so slightly, his voice lowering. "Or is there another voice you hear in your head?"

"Voices? No, Ah not be crazy," Ratsbayne said, standing, but the look on his face told Blagdon otherwise. "Ah appreciate the drink and the talk, but Ah need to tend to the foal and the others." He started for the door, and Blagdon let him get his hand on the doorknob before speaking.

"You've heard voices since you've gotten to Woodsong. Perhaps of one who is as frustrated as I am because you don't remember your past. You don't remember who you are because someone gave you that vial of herbs that put you to sleep and robbed you of your memories. You have been drinking to rid yourself of disturbing memories that came as flashes at night, leaving you disoriented and confused." When Ratsbayne didn't react, he continued, knowing he was right. "I know what that amulet around your neck is. I know who and what you truly are, Ratsbayne. That voice in your head is careful not to tell you everything because they fear you will crumble under the truth. I know you are made of stronger things, and I know how to help you. Let me show who you truly are."

Ratsbayne looked over his shoulder at Blagdon. "How do Ah even know if yer telling the truth, that ya aren't making enticing stories based on what Alandra tells ya?" *So he suspects that balvash Alandra reports to me, or is it the voice inside his mind that mistrusts her?*

Blagdon picked up the amulet from the box lid and put it inside, turning the box to show over a dozen of the amulets in a row. "These amulets were given to men and women who served in an airborne mounted cavalry, protecting Meridiah from the skies. They underwent rigorous training, and many who tried to become one of these knights failed. Your amulet is proof that you did not."

"Ah could have just picked it up after finding it, thinking it be nice to wear since Ah didn't have any real possessions when Ah awoke. What makes ya say it be mine?"

How amusing it was that he was stumbling to find logic yet, at the same time, hungry for more information. I wonder what the voice he hears is saying; is it backtracking, coming up with excuses for why it hasn't shared information with him about who he is? "Look at your amulet and tell me the inscription, and I will tell you my reasoning."

Ratsbayne pulled out his amulet and looked at it. "Strength o' the storm, heart o' the griffin." He slipped it away once more. "It be a nice motto, Ah suppose."

Blagdon could almost smile, but instead, he stood, looking at Ratsbayne. "That amulet is engraved in Elvish, a language that few have spoken in the past one hundred and fifty years." Blagdon walked around his desk, going to stand before Ratsbayne. "All Riders were paired with an airborne steed, such as griffins, pegasi--"

"Dragons?"

"No, Dragonriders were considered their own and under no laws of a kingdom except the laws of the dragons, according to the records.

Sigilbearers enchanted the amulets to let the wearer fall slowly if their mounts fell in battle."

"Oh. Well, Ah dun't have a flying mount, so Ah cannot be a knight that flies."

"These knights were bonded with these creatures, so tightly they found feel whatever their steed could, sometimes see through their eyes, or gain abilities similar to them, as well as hear their thoughts." He stopped moving forward, looking at Ratsbayne. "They could even feel their bonded mounts giving birth, sharing her pain."

"How do ya know these things?" Ratsbayne asked after a long moment.

Blagdon made it a point never to lie; many Shadon even wondered if he could. "When I served in the Scourge War, we'd captured as many as we could, and I tried replicating their training and bonding with *kelvorvik*, to make *ro'*Shadon cavalry better."

"Did it work?" Ratsbayne finally seemed interested.

"No, it did not. Some took their own lives, which caused their bonded mount to perish. Others refused to cooperate at first. The things I did learn from those who did finally submit did not work with the *kelvorvik*. Since then, no one has been able to create the bond."

"Then why do ya think that Ah did any of that? Because of some amulet Ah dun't remember getting?" Ratsbayne tried pulling on the doorknob behind his back, but Blagdon held the door closed with shadows. *Some truths you cannot escape, Ratsbayne.*

"The pain you felt the other day was the pain of the mare outside, giving birth to her foal. She felt no pain and made no noise as she foaled, but you cried out and shouted as if your insides were twisting inside you, coming out of places you didn't know existed. You took her pain into yourself to protect her. I've watched how she reacts to you, always watching, holding her head a little higher ever since she'd arrived in Woodsong. She is your bonded mount, and you are her bonded knight. It explains why you were so good in mounted combat sparring."

"Ya said the mounts fly. She ain't got any wings."

"If it weren't for her coloration, I'd guess she was a Windrunner, a creature that can run upon the air like land. They are rare, even in Meridiah, and have a bluish-white coat and blue eyes." The mare was grey with brown eyes, but everything else seemed to fit. Blagdon had extensively researched the creature once encountering it in a tome. If the mare was indeed a windrunner, her foal was half-windrunner, half-*kelvorvik*, which opened possibilities for flying *ro'*Shadon cavalries, as well as securing his *Hasta'kan's* place as *Hon-Hasta'kan'ix*. He'd tried researching ways to enchant an animal to look different and found Sigilbearers of Nature could do so. It did not matter what the mare looked like as long as she and Ratsbayne could bond and were loyal to him.

"Ya sure it ain't the squirrel Ah'm bonded to?"

"I am quite sure, Ratsbayne. Now, we must figure out your name; I refuse to call you this nickname the people of Thraesh granted you. In Stormhold, there is a tome with the descriptions of the Stormrider Knights who had served in the past, and we will go through them and see if you are listed there. Then, you can see the truth for yourself."

"How long ago did you think that Ah was one of these Stormriders? Ah'd never heard of one until now."

"The back of your amulet has the crescent moon and leaping stag, the emblem of the Byronian Kingdom." Ratsbayne looked at the back of his pendant, and Blagdon could see that it was rubbed slightly down, probably from wearing it for so long. "I think that whoever gave you this vial of Ny'fer elf potion adjusted it somehow so you have survived much longer than you were supposed to." Ratsbayne blinked at him, and Blagdon walked back to the desk. "You will no longer be in charge of the *kelvorvik* stables in Woodsong, but will be training with your mount and her foal in Stormhold under my supervision. Pack your belongings; we leave in the morning."

* * *

He stood beside his lordson in watching the main gates of Woodsong Keep, dressed in his leather armor and worn black cloak, gloved hand resting on his rapier as his eyes swept the garrison before him, looking for anything out of sorts. The soldiers had been cleaning for the last week, preparing for the arrival of the newest batch of cavalry-trained men whose job it would be to patrol the roads between the towns in the territory, ensuring the people were safe from bandits and wild animals. His Lordson, Mykel Blagdon, stood beside him, his eyes black with the use of his shadows. "They are arriving," he said, "coming from the woodline now, my Leigelord."

Blagdon nodded. *Ro'*Shadon usually could not travel such distances as the Stormlands to Woodsong via shadow, but there was one Shadon who could traverse it, not through shadows, but darkness, the purest absence of both shadow and light. Doing so meant both places would have to have an area of complete darkness to enter and exit from, but the distance traveled was advantageous, especially in times of war. An advantage of the woods surrounding Woodsong was that the darkness was thicker and almost tangible at night, making traveling with groups of Shadon easier than during the day using mere shadows. He glanced at his Lordson, who blinked as his eyes returned to normal. "Allow them in at your leisure and command, *korrati*."

His lordson straightened and spoke through the shadows to the guards at the gate tower, who blew a horn twice, announcing the arrivals of friendly forces, and the gates pulled open slowly. Three *kelvorvik* with riders walked through the gate, each holding a banner aloft: the black and red emblem of the *ro'*Shadon Empire, the second holding the banner of *Hasta'kan ik'Blagdon,* the emblem of a rearing *kelvorvik's* head in silver on a dark blue field, the third a blue banner which was smaller in size with shadese writing in yellow. The three lead *kelvorvik* stopped, standing side by side, waiting as the rest of the soldiers filed in and pulled their mounts to stop in formation behind them, four abreast. Three rows of Shadon sat on their mounts silently as five rows of soldiers on horseback filed behind them, staying back at least one horse length. The armored middle figure guided their *kelvorvik* forward two paces, putting his right fist before his left shoulder and bowing his head. "Leigelord *Hon-Hasta'kan'ix ik'Blagdon, Korrati* Blagdon of Woodsong garrison; the Blue Company of the Stormland's 24th training regiment await your command." As one, all the soldiers put their fists to their shoulders and bowed their heads. Blagdon nodded once, showing his approval of the display of loyalty and training, and looked to his Lordson.

"Take your mounts to their proper paddocks where they will be tended to, and see *Kriss'ix* Lukras for your cabin and cot assignments. Welcome to Woodsong Garrison, your new home for the foreseeable future." The soldiers began carrying out Mykel's orders while Blagdon headed back to the keep, satisfied that the garrison was in competent hands and would thrive with the leadership he'd placed in charge. As he passed the *kelvorvik* paddock, he heard a familiar accented voice.

"Those mounts ain't all *kelvorvik*; they're smaller, too long in the legs." Ratsbayne walked over from where he was watching the *kelvorvik* paddocks, where the pack gathered, watching the newcomer mounts be walked into the second fenced area. "Why ain't they in the same paddock as the *kelvorvik*?"

Blagdon stopped, watching the two groups of creatures in different paddocks, snorting and stamping their hooves at each other. Even in the torchlight, he could see the difference in the two types of creatures, the newer ones having a more slender build and long legs, their necks thinner than their counterparts in the first paddock. *It is interesting how Ratsbayne can quickly pick up on the differences between the mounts.* "*Kelvorvik* and the other creatures, called *kelvorkav*, are carnivorous and territorial. Differing packs will often clash to gain a single alpha, and I would rather not lose valuable mounts in fights for dominance. Because of this, the mare and her colt were in the stables, safe from conflicts."

"*Kelvorkav*? Ah never heard of 'em."

"*Kelvorvik* are bred for riding into combat. *Kelvorkav* are bred for speed, normally used for delivering messages when *belvash* are unavailable."

"Why when *belvash* aren't available? What do they do with

missives?"

Ratsbayne sounded curious, so he humored the question. *Furthering one's education never hurts someone.* "Some *belvash* can send messages to other *belvash* faster than even the shadows can deliver whispers, though I am not entirely sure how. It is one of the secrets of the Blood Temple, denied to outsiders. Having messengers, both human and *ro'*Shadon, can prove useful. Woodsong can send messages throughout the territory without tiring Shadon soldiers by taxing their uses of shadow or paying *Hasta'kan ik'Branial*, who is in charge of communication throughout our lands."

"Shadon can get tired of using shadows? Ah think Ah'd be doing it all the time."

"Teleporting large amounts is taxing, even if there are multiple Shadon lending power to each other to do so. There are limitations on how far we can go, so we will ride back toward Stormhold to ensure the foal builds up his constitution."

"Ah didn't know that."

"There are many things you do not know, which I plan to correct."

"Have there always been *kelvorvik* and *kelvorkav*?"

Blagdon shook his head. "My grandfather, Addarys, *Hasta'kan'ix ik'Blagdon*, witnessed the creatures in Nar'Shada running free and attempted to tame and breed them over eight hundred years ago. He began creating what the creatures are today with three families of creatures."

"Eight hundred years?! What ya be, half-elf?"

Blagdon gave him a flat look for interrupting. "*Ro'*Shadon live for 400 years or more. The child races, such as dwarves and humans, have short lifespans."

"Here Ah thought Shadon be humans with Sigils, like any other Sigilbearer, just callin' themselves different names."

Blagdon just looked at him. "What exactly do you know about other Sigilbearers, Ratsbayne?"

Ratsbayne looked a touch worried. "Ah heard there were other Sigils; after all, *belvash* got Sigils o' Blood, ya got Sigils o' Shadow, why not others?"

Blagdon was curious now. "What do you mean, why not others?" Ratsbayne had his attention now.

"Ah dreamed o' a girl once; she had a green Sigil of a leaf on her arm. She could make plants grow with a touch of her hand. She made a flower grow once, and then Ah woke up 'cause someone was shouting mah name; ah think it be k*orrati* Kerrik-*kyr*. Ah should go check on the mare and the colt, Ah think." Ratsbayne walked off toward the barn, leaving Blagdon watching him. *That man leaves me with more questions every time I speak with him.*

APOLLO

Apollo went into the soldiers' cabin, sore from the day's training but at least freshly clean from the bath in the bathhouse, where he'd soaked to relax his aching muscles. *When I travel to Silene with Mykel to collect the tax and tributes, I can see him and tell him about what's happened since I came to Woodsong, especially what happened in Andears.* Too much time had passed since he'd last seen his brother, and he was unsure if Clep would even recognize him now; he was taller and more muscular. He also felt different, understanding more than ever, his head often aching with new knowledge.

It had been months since he'd confronted those responsible for the burning and slaughter of Andears, but the incident long haunted his dreams, and he'd wake up in a cold sweat, fearing that the ghosts of the condemned men had returned to haunt him. Sometimes unable to sleep, he took out his frustration upon training dummies and bored soldiers on watch duty who were willing to spar at the late hours.

An unfamiliar large wooden clothing chest occupied the space on the floor at the end of his cot, and curious, he opened it slowly, wondering where his previous clothing chest was where he'd kept his leather training armor. Sitting upon the top was a piece of parchment with the blue and silver wax seal of *Hasta'kan ik'Blagdon*. He slipped a knife under the seal, loosening it gently, not wanting to destroy it.

Balutrae ik'Blagdon:
Accept this gift for the man you are becoming.
It will protect you until the hour of our scrivik ik'balutrae.

Apollo tried to ignore the tightness in his chest as he read the final words. *Mykel is the Lordson of one of the most feared duelists in Meridiah and Nar'Shada, perhaps in all of Andora as well; how could I hope to beat him?* He shook his head, dismissing the thoughts of doubt. He had learned that many *balutrae* did not duel for decades, often using their relationship to protect themselves and push each other to become stronger in areas they were weak. *I hope we do not have to cross swords other than in the sparring circle for many, many years.*

Setting aside the parchment, he reached into the chest and pulled out pieces of plate metal, dark as shadows with rivets of red that reminded him of blood. Crimson and black, the colors of the Dark Army, were once colors Apollo had hated, for it reminded him of the people who took away his home, but now, it symbolized something different. It was wrong of him to lump the Dark Army soldiers as the enemy; for now, he understood that they were humans and Shadon under the armor. *I wonder what Clep would think, seeing me in the same colors as the ones who took away everything from us.* The thought of sending a messenger to Silene with a message for Clep crossed his mind once more, and he shook his head. *Could I explain what happened in the past months in a way that would help him understand? Was there enough parchment in the territory to tell all I have gone through and learned?*

Figuring that it would be better to tell Clep in person, he set aside the armor and looked to see what else it held. The emblem of *Hasta'kan ik'Blagdon* was stamped into a silver buckle of a black leather belt, which had carvings of *kelvorvik* running along it. From it hung a medallion that marked him as a *balutrae*, to let any Shadon know that if they attacked Apollo, they would also face *Hasta'kan ik'Blagdon*. *I can see the advantage of ensuring that all who wished to attack me knew who they were dealing with before they tried, and it is more noticeable than the red marking on the back of my hand.*

After pulling on a fresh set of breeches and tunic, he stood at the end of the cot, looking down at the armor he'd been gifted. He was alone in the cabin; the other soldiers had gone to eat dinner, but not being seen changing that bothered him. He had never had metal armor before; the black leather armor he currently wore was the closest thing he'd ever had to a full suit of protection, but even that was given to him in pieces over the months. *This armor is created to be worn with my leather armor,* he realized as he noticed the fastenings and straps matched the ones on his leather armor. He undid the straps of his armor, replacing the leather pauldrons that he had with the metal ones and attaching the new black fur cloak. He ran his hand over the raised image on the right pauldron, a tree with seven small raised marks connected below different branches, and blinked in surprise, recognizing the design as the one he'd drawn on parchment for the ritual and Mykel now had upon his neck.

An Aldarwood. Did Mykel have this explicitly crafted for me? I thought he had sent extra armor from the armory. He slipped on his leather armor and fastened the cloak over his shoulders, and put on the belt, the *balutrae* medallion hanging from it on one side, a large pouch beside a kidney sheath for his dagger, and a place for his sword's scabbard.

He picked up the sword, looking it over. It was well-used, but the leather grip had been replaced recently, and the blacksmith gave the pommel some attention, removing the dents from the past and making it look better. The blade was constantly polished and sharpened, and the weight was perfect for Apollo to swing with either a wooden or steel shield in the other hand. *How long has it been since I had stopped viewing it as my father's sword and instead calling it my own?*

He reached into the chest, taking out black metal thigh armor, fastening the straps around his legs and over his belt before slipping the new leather boots on, ending higher on his calves than his older ones. He took a few steps to get used to the boots, frowning at the tightness, but then he headed to the nearby bathhouse. Glad that no one was inside, he walked to the far wall and looked at the ground for a long moment before slowly raising his eyes and looking at the figure before him in the mirror, his breath catching slightly.

Gone was the farmboy from Andears, the boy who pretended to sword fight with sticks, ran and hunted in the woods, and waded barefoot through the water in the summer, laughing at the fish swimming between his legs as he tried to catch them. Gone was the boy who toiled in the fields, bringing loads of wheat to the women so they could make bread to sell and survive on. Gone was the coward who ran and hid from soldiers as his village burned and his friends died horribly, the one who left his brother to be safe as he went looking for vengeance.

Here now stood a young man in a black and red mixture of leather and metal, a blending human and *ro'*Shadon worlds instead of the boy caught between them. His hand went to the relief on the pauldron of the Aldarwood, thinking of Mykel's words to him in Andears. *I look like a protector.* He turned this way and that, looking at himself from all angles, adjusting the cloak upon his shoulders, his *balutrae*'s signet on the side of his neck still looking as fresh as the day he'd received it. *I look nothing like I used to, and I cannot say I dislike it. But if I continue to grow, learn, and change, what am I to become?*

* * *

"The armor suits you," Mykel remarked the next day as he watched Apollo going through his sword swings against a soldier, practicing parrying and deflecting an incoming blade. "It will take time to get used to, though, for your leather was lighter than the metal pieces, so you will tire quicker while sparring." The young *korrati* stood outside the sparring pen, his furred cloak around his armor, protecting him from the drizzle.

Apollo ducked under the incoming sword swing, stabbing his sword at his opponent's midsection, but the soldier stepped back, letting the sword pass by harmlessly. He could feel the weight difference in the pauldrons and the cloak, which threw him off slightly and slowed his movements. It did not help that the dirt was slowly becoming mud, and he slipped somewhat with his right foot, causing his opponent to seize the opportunity, putting his sword at Apollo's throat.

"You are getting better," *Kriss'ix* Lukras said, stepping back as he lowered his sword and walked with Apollo to the covered area where they could warm up by the fire and dry their swords before sheathing them.

Apollo nodded, not wanting to argue with the *Kriss'ix*, who, like many Shadon, were not forthcoming with compliments, so for him to give Apollo one meant that he was doing something right. "*Kishtu kavasta kar,*" he replied, though Shadese did not have such a phrase for thanking someone. The *Kriss'ix* seemed to understand his intention and bowed his head, his lip twitching as he walked into the rain to check on his soldiers.

"*Shadese ik'khar kavasha,*" *Korrati* Mykel remarked, shaking off his cloak to get rid of the raindrops gathering in the fur and extending his hands toward the fire. He looked around at the sky, sighing. "You would imagine the rain would bring relief. When does Meridiah get colder and snow? I've read stories about it and have wanted to witness it with my own eyes."

Apollo shrugged. "I don't know. Nan told us that dragons were responsible for changing the seasons. The white dragons would awaken and prepare for their migration, and their yawns would make cold air come from their mountains, making the leaves turn to firey colors. When they migrated south, the snow fell off their wings as they flew overhead, but I've never seen it. It's been summer as long as I can remember."

"In Nar'Shada, we do not have either as well. Between the dragonfire ash in the soil and the volcanic Shadowgulf Mountains surrounding it, the air is much drier than it is here, at least from when I visited it. Perhaps one day you will also visit it with me; it would do you well to see my people's homeland."

"How did Nar'Shada be filled with dragonfire ash? You've mentioned it, but I never asked the story behind it."

"It is a story we are told as children, I forget sometimes you are not familiar with our legends. The great shadow dragon Thraxxis once ruled the dragons in the Dragonlands, overseeing them and the people of Nar'Shada with an iron claw. One day, the other dragons rebelled against him, attacking him while he was flying overhead. The battle that took place overhead was great, their fire scorching the ground and setting fires that spread throughout the land that no water could stop.

We did not have our Sigils then; we were not Shadon and could not outrun the flames. Many thousands of people perished."

"That's awful."

"The dragons distracted Thraxxis, trying to bring him down, and the youngest of them flew overhead and seized his moment, diving down from above and biting behind his head, thrashing as he did so. The two dragons tumbled toward the earth, biting and roaring. The others joined in, ripping Thraxxis' wings so he could not recover and fly away. They say when Thraxxis' body hit the ground, the air came out in waves, putting out the fires and spreading ash throughout the land. The dragons flew off, their foe defeated, and in Thraxxis' dying breaths, he gave his power to any surviving people of Nar'Shada, becoming Sigils on their skin."

"So that is why Nar'Shada means 'from ash?' I honestly thought it was because you were all so pale."

Mykel began laughing. "No, many *ro*'Shadon are pale because the ash still lingers in the air in Nar'Shada and blocks most of the sunlight."

The two laughed, sharing a rare moment before Mykel sobered and cleared his throat. "I will travel around Cetra to the villages to collect our tax and tributes." Apollo blinked in surprise. *Has it already been half a year since I'd arrived in Woodsong?* "You will accompany me. You will be able to help the villagers not be so fearful when they see us, and you're able to defend yourself better."

Apollo thought about the opportunity to see more of the territory and, most of all, to go to Silene and see Clep after so long. His heart sped up at the thought of seeing his younger brother again. "When do we leave?"

RATSBAYNE

The trip toward the Stormlands was long, uneventful, and vaguely reminded Ratsbayne of traveling on the false errand that "Kerrik-kyr" had sent him and his soldiers on before Blagdon had set foot in Woodsong. *At least we don't have kelvorvik coming out of the woods, killing everyone, and Ah dudn't have to walk behind a wagon this time.* He patted the brown mare he'd been given to ride behind the wagon that held feed for the non-flesh-eating mounts, such as the grey mare and her colt, which walked surrounded by the seven *kelvorvik* which Blagdon had brought down with him.

"*Don't look so happy sitting on that mare,*" the voice in his head muttered, sounding slightly put off.

Ratsbayne immediately looked around for the squirrel that had tormented him. *Can Ah not catch a break from the damned creature?* He'd still brought parchments with updates to the fallen oak tree in the woods, where bags of coin still waited for him inside the space between the roots, but he didn't do it as often. He also didn't want to be seen as a traitor or spy, which, if Blagdon thought he was either, Ratsbayne was sure he'd meet a quick death. *Ah'm beginning to like mah life, so Ah dun't want to die just yet.* Still, he'd thought he'd left the squirrel and the mysterious benefactor behind, especially when the last parchment he left said he was leaving Woodsong. *Has the damned creature followed me here, and why? Ah've never done anything to make it think Ah wanted it as a pet.* He was watching the designs of the torchlight's light upon the brown mare underneath him as he fought sleep when he felt the woods open up around them. *Finally, a clearing so we could stop fer the night.*

Ahead of him was a vast expanse of land, acres of fenced-in property as far as he could see. Towers with giant lightstones stood tall, illuminating the grounds with a soft orange light that did not hurt to look at in the darkness, softly highlighting the stone wall that encased the grounds in the middle. At the front of their procession, a Shadon lifted a hunting horn to his lips, blowing two long notes, making many of the horses startle at the sudden tone, including the colt, who tried to bolt, pulling at the rope tied around its neck until and the mare gently nuzzled it to calm it down.

An answering call of two horn blows came through the air, and as they grew closer to the property, the giant wooden gate parted for them.

The gates stood open as a welcoming sign to all who came, soldiers in blue and silver armor going about their business inside the walls. He'd seen garrisons before, but this was much different than the others, with acres of paddocks and grounds for the various creatures to run around safely, each with stables to keep them separate and safe at night.

Griffyns and ravens flew overhead, some with mounts while the others held missives, flying in and out of the grounds regularly. The training grounds were set up with different areas, some for racing lanes, others for courses for mounted swordsmen and archers to try their hands at getting the best scores in their free time.

Tlightstones that illuminated the ground from the top of the watchtowers helped visibility at night, for landing flying creatures in darkness was dangerous for both the mount and rider. Ever since the dwarves had gifted the lightstones, accidents at night had gone down by more than half. High walls around the central part of the garrison were both to protect the soldiers and animals from those who may try to sneak into the grounds, whether with malicious intent or on a dare, which had been known to happen occasionally, especially when there were new soldiers in the Protector's District in Meridiah City. Once, a griffyn had bitten a young soldier's arm so severely that the healers were not sure he'd gain full use of it again.

There was no greater honor than to be here, training with the best of the best, riding the most incredible animals Meridiah had to offer.

As he was led to his room, where other young recruits were getting their beds ready for the following day, he couldn't imagine a grander place and grinned, watching the blue and silver tapestries of a stag leaping under a crescent moon wave gently in the night breeze that came through the window.

"I am home."

"Ratsbayne, stop daydreaming and get dismounted; we want to get all the animals into the stables and our beds before dawn," one of the Shadon snapped at him, startling him out of his thoughts. Ratsbayne looked around, slightly disoriented. He stood beside a stable with orange light cast upon it by the lightstone towers among the stone walls. Black and red banners of the Dark Army stood beside the ones of *Hasta'kan ik'Blagdon*, and the stars above were bright against the sky's darkness, in contrast to the vision he'd just had of beautiful sunny skies. He climbed down and removed the saddle from his mount, setting it onto the fence. He returned to the horse and gave the horse an apple before walking her into the paddock as instructed. A few other horses eyed him, eating hay from bales or turning around in their stalls to go back to sleep. A soldier nodded to him, the light from a lightstone torch glinting off his black and red armor; he settled back into his chair as he kept watch in the stables.

Ratsbayne walked away from the building, looking around. There were other stables, some larger than the others, each with areas for different creatures. *Kelvorvik* walked to greet each other in a fenced paddock away from the horse paddock, nipping at each other's coats and eyeing the newcomers. Signs were posted every few yards along the fence and on the stable's outside wall, with writing in both Common and Shadese, along with a picture of a hand with an X through it painted on the surface. *Caution, predatory creatures.* He noticed a few different stables on this side had those signs and frowned, suddenly deciding what side of the fences he'd rather be on.

"Majestic, aren't they?"

Ratsbayne turned and blinked as a woman in black leathers stood watching, a crimson sash down one arm, marking her as a *Sri'balvash*. Ratsbayne knew they were higher than *balvash* in ranking, though he was unsure what that entailed. *Ah think Ah know about as much as belvash as the Leigelord knows about mah.* Still, he bowed slightly to her. "Good evening, mah lady."

Her eyebrows went up over her leather mask. In the dim lighting of the area, Ratsbayne could see her mask was embossed on both sides, unlike other *belvash*, which only had one side done. The side he could see had the emblem of *Hasta'kan ik'Blagdon*. "How do you know I am a lady? I am *sri'balvash* and not addressed as such by many."

"Ya be a female, ya be a lady," Ratsbayne stated as if it were the most uncomplicated fact in the world, which, to him, it was.

"I cannot argue with that logic," Blagdon's voice came behind him, and the Leigelord went to the *sri'balvash* and took her hand, kissing it as if they were at court instead of surrounded by animal stables. He then looked at Ratsbayne. "This is Lady Narisa *ik'Blagdon*, *Sri'balvash* of the Blood Temple, *korrati* Mykel's mother, and most importantly, my wife."

Oh. Shite.

***

Although he was promised a tour in the morning, Ratsbayne was shown where the bathhouse was so he could get cleaned and turned in for the night. Much to his surprise, the nearby bathhouse was much larger than the one in Woodsong, with ten bathtubs separated by hanging curtains for privacy.

"The water be steaming, but there aren't any fires or stones?" Ratsbayne asked, looking around.

A soldier who was putting on his boots laughed. "They're

enchanted, so the water was always warm."

"How'd that happen? We know Sigilbearers who enchant?"

"Of course not. Stormhold had them already when the *Kolotor'ix* gave it to *Hasta'kan ik'Blagdon*." The soldier shook his head, walking past Ratsbayne as if he'd said something childish. "The only Sigilbearers are those who are Shadon and *belvash*."

Alone in the bathhouse, Ratsbayne stayed long enough that he thought he'd have shriveled fingertips for weeks. Finally, he got out, figuring his muscles had relaxed enough after the several-day ride from Woodsong. Dressing in the clothing he'd brought with him, he headed out of the bathhouse and to the building he'd been told he was assigned to. He heard laughter as he neared the one-story wooden and stone building, and his heart leaped in his chest. *Could it be a tavern? It be ages since Ah'd had a proper drink.* He walked in to see males sitting around a table playing cards, but looking around, he didn't see any bar, shelves of alcohol, or any buxom women. *Krushku.*

"In or out," one of the men said, scratching his beard as he looked over his cards, frowning, "you're letting in the smell of the stables." He glanced at the second male across the table, tossing some coin into the pile on the table and laying down a card.

"Better not be peeking through shadows, Riky," one of the men laughed as he folded his hand.

"Riky knows better than to try cheating in a room of Shadon," one of the males spoke up, his black hair pulled back by a leather cord, leaving his face free of obstruction as he looked over his cards. "Your bed is in the back," he said, glancing at Ratsbayne. He lay down his hand and stood. "Four Dragons, read them and weep, boys." He chuckled at the groaning men around him and headed toward the door opposite the room. "This way."

Ratsbayne followed, noting the main room had the necessities: a table, kitchen, and even some books and a desk looking out at the grounds with a lightstone lamp, journals, parchments, wax sticks, seals, and quills with inkwells waiting for use. "So, is there a tavern here?"

The male looked over his shoulder at him, eyebrow raised. "Do you think it's smart to have stablehands drinking around flesh-eating animals? Don't be foolish; there isn't a tavern here, and we wouldn't be allowed into it if there were. If you want to go drink, you can ride to the capitol on your night off; that way, you can sober up on the ride back to Stormhold." He shook his head, chuckling, walking into the next room, where rows of bunk beds stood on either side with clothing chests between them. He walked with Ratsbayne to the last bed, where he gestured. "This one is yours."

"Thank ye."

The male nodded, his blue eyes overseeing him. "I'm Gideon, in charge of the stablehands; if you need anything, you come to me. If you have a problem with one of the other hands, you come to me. You'll talk it out, or you'll fight it out. We solve issues in-house. You don't want *Hasta'kan'ix* Blagdon solving it for us. We get up at dawn and see to the mounts. Watch what you're doing because if you aren't careful, you will lose a hand, maybe more than that. I've been told you will mainly work with the *kelvorvik*-blood colt and its mother."

"Aye."

"You've got clothing in your chest here, along with boots. They belonged to Mal, but he's no longer here, and you look to be his size."

"What happened to Mal?"

"He got too comfortable and turned his back on a *kelvorkav*. Do you have any questions?"

Ah got tons o' questions, though Ah dunno what to ask first.

"I'll be in the other room." Gideon returned to the common room, leaving Ratsbayne to sit on his bunk and look around. One young man, who seemed younger than Ratsbayne, was on his bed, reading by lightstone, while another shirtless man rubbed balm into his shoulder as he winced slightly; he glanced at Ratsbayne and nodded silently to him in greeting. Across the room was a large window where he could see the paddock for the horses to his left and the meat-eating creatures' paddock to the right. He noticed a space between every paddock's fence, allowing repairs and distance between animals wanting to eat their neighbors. *At least soldiers guard the paddock,* Ratsbayne noticed silently as he watched soldiers patrol quietly on horseback to ensure they could see and resolve any problems before they became more significant.

His clothing chest was filled with simple, better clothing than Ratsbayne had in the past, at least as far as he could remember. He now had various sets made of cotton, linens, and even a collection of wool clothing, and across from his bed hung a mirror with a simple table under it with a wash basin, a pitcher for water, a comb, and a shaving kit with soaps and oils. Between the bathhouse and the upkeep tables in the bunkroom, Ratsbayne was beginning to understand that Blagdon was very proud about appearances and once again wondered if the Leigelord had struck his head when he'd asked for Ratsbayne to be at the grounds.

Ratsbayne lay on the bed and felt his back pop gently as he started to slip his dagger under his pillow, but decided at the last minute to have it on the bedside table instead. *Ah've slept with a blade under mah pillow fer so long, now Ah don't want to. Ah guess Ah dun't want to stab the straw mattress.*

"*Or maybe you feel safe enough you don't need it,*" the voice in his head spoke up softly.

He glanced around for the squirrel, eyeing the dagger on his table. *Ah wonder if Ah could hit it and make it stop following mah. Could Ah get someone to stuff it and send it to Apollo to keep an eye on it fer meh.*

"*You don't mean that,*" the voice chided gently.

"The hells Ah dun't," he muttered as he fell asleep.

APOLLO

Apollo rode his horse beside Mykel's *kolvorvik*, listening to the soldiers beside him ride their mounts, speaking softly amongst themselves. Two soldiers rode ahead, holding high two banners, one of the Dark Army, the other of *Hon-Hasta'kan ik'Blagdon*. A wagon escorted by a dozen Shadon and human soldiers followed, the combination of the wagon wheels creaking and hooves walking on the dirt road, providing a steady tone for the soldiers to sing to as they rode. *It would reduce the number of bandits who may wish to change their minds about attacking us,* Apollo thought with a small smile, imagining masked men who thought about ambushing them and then suddenly deciding against it as they realized the singing travelers were not farmers. He wasn't sure if there were many of them on the roads in the territory, but between Nan's stories and some rumors, he could assume there would be some on at least one of the roads during their trip.

Sri'balvash Desira and a second *balvash* also rode horses among the soldiers. Apollo knew that not all the crimson-clad females shared their identities, choosing to remain part of the faceless crowd, making them more mysterious and intimidating. Nonetheless, Mykel had told him they were there in case any injuries were to occur. When Apollo asked whose injuries they would see first, the villagers or the soldiers, Mykel answered, "Mine."

They rode for four days, camping at night, and Mykel spent most of his time in the *korrati's* tent, going over maps, studying, and conferring with *kriss'ix* Lukras about taxation. Apollo went to take his watch during the night and looked out into the woods, remembering when he was much more foolish and thought he could just sneak up and slit a soldier's throat before killing the rest in the camp. *I was such a fool back then. I wonder what happened to the mare, I hope she found a way to a new home and wasn't eaten by wergs.*

"The first village we will go to is Epine, the furthest in Cetra, then head back towards Woodsong, visiting the closer villages as we go," Mykel said the following day, looking around at the woods as if out for a morning ride instead of on a mission. "They are known for fishing, which makes sense, for they are located on the Blue Rock River. Is there anything I should know about the villages, what to expect, or whom I should speak to first?"

Apollo thought about that. "Most visitors to Andears would either speak to the innkeeper or Elder Noriah." He flinched slightly, remembering the kind old man who tried to reason with the Dark Army soldiers. *After the soldier had hit Elder Noriah, we all attacked, which led to the soldiers retaliating. If we hadn't attacked in defense of Elder Noriah, would the people of Andears still be alive?*

"Apollo. My *balutrae*, look at me."

Apollo blinked, realizing that Mykel had been speaking but hadn't noticed anything the *korrati* said. "Obsessing over the past will not ensure its change. We move forward to affect the future." *He wasn't even looking at me. How did he know my thoughts?* "The Elder in Epine is Arami; we will speak to him first, ensuring a smooth transaction between our people."

Apollo blinked at him in surprise. "I wouldn't think you'd know that."

Mykel shrugged. "I know every *Hasta'kan'ix* and their Lordsons, emblem, colors, and words. I also have to know every member of each *hesta'heh'ix* and *hesta'yo'ix* under *Hasta'kan ik'Blagdon*, not only by name but by sight. Lordsons are next in line to be *hesta'ix*, so I must ensure I know them well. You never know when a Lordson will become *hesta'ix*. Then, of course, I need to know every village in our territory, its Elders, and available resources."

"I'm not sure I'd ever be able to know all of that on top of everything I'm already learning."

"Being a lordson is not easy," Mykel admitted, looking at him, "but I have been training since birth to take over *Hasta'kan ik'Blagdon* when the time comes."

"You're courting the adopted daughter of the *Kolotor'ix* as well. Are you going to become the next *Kolotor'ix*?"

"The process and timing of knowing when a new *Kolotor'ix* steps into power is secret."

"What do you mean? Don't you know when his heir is born?"

"It differs from human and elven royalty, at least for the Mun'ari Clan. They have kings and queens with princes and princesses. We have our *Kolotor'ix*. He is always masked, and we do not know his face underneath, so his heir could step into the role, and we'd never know. The mask slightly obscures his voice as well."

"Why not just check under it with shadows?"

Mykel almost fell off his mount in turning to face Apollo, paling. "I would suggest you not bring up that idea ever again."

Apollo decided it may be safer to change the subject. "So, who is the girl you are courting?"

Mykel took a long moment to recollect himself. "Her name is Mari'aida, and she is a Mun'ari elf." His cheeks reddened slightly, though Apollo was sure he fought it. "They were among the last elven clans in the War of the Turning Leaves. Her mother was a general, a runecarver, a wielder of ancient magick who could carve runes into the world around her and change it depending on her intention. I have been learning about her people's history when I can to become a better husband to her in the future. If one cannot learn their partner's ways, they cannot be a proper partner."

Apollo thought about that and shrugged. "I've never really thought about it; I had a few girls who have kissed me in the past, but nothing ever came from it, at least not in the way of wanting to be married."

"*Ro'*Shadon society is about the *hasta,* and whom you choose to be wed to says a lot about you and the direction your *hasta* will go in. Choosing the wrong partner could be the downfall of your *hasta*, especially if she bears weak lordsons."

"Why is the emphasis on lordsons, and not lords-daughters?"

Mykel wrinkled his nose at the thought. "There isn't a thing called lords-daughters, Apollo. They are simply daughters, and most *hesta* send their eldest daughter to the Temple to be trained as a *balvash*. The *Kolotor'ix* recommends sending at least one daughter there, or risk your *hasta* looking bad for not contributing to society."

"So your sister Senka has also gone to train there," Apollo guessed.

"My half-sister is rare; she is the only known Lady Shadon. They call her *Shokolar Kolotor*, the white shadow. It is unknown why Sigils of Shadow generally appear primarily upon the male population. Even though she went to train as a *balvash*, she could not become one. *Ro'belvash* have Sigils of Blood upon their skin, and she has a Sigil of Shadow already."

"Someone can't have two Sigils?"

"She cannot say if they had tried to give it to her and they failed or if it was refused. The Sigil of Blood is the only Sigil we know of in recent times that is given, and the Sigilbearer is not born with it."

"Nan used to say that dragons gave them to those they felt were worthy of them," Apollo answered, speaking of his mother's mother, who told them nightly stories before bed. Apollo especially loved the ones about knights and princesses. Even though he missed his Nan greatly, he missed her stories the most.

Would I have to one day learn all the things Mykel had to? It wasn't as if I would become a lordson of the Hasta'kan if I ever beat Mykel. However, he wasn't sure and was afraid to ask anyone about it. *Who am I to think I could beat him in our duel? Would asking be arrogant? I don't want Mykel to look down upon me more than he does already. But if I were to beat Mykel,* would the relationship with Hasta'kan ik'Blagdon change? Would the soldiers of Woodsong treat me differently, or would I be attacked in the night like Ratsbayne had been? Would Leigelord Blagdon ask for my head? Apollo was so busy thinking of the whirlwind of thoughts that he almost didn't hear Mykel speak.

"We are here."

* * *

The village Epine was visible from the road, and Apollo could already see the giant wheel turning on the river beside a building, making a soothing sound as they rode closer. Mykel looked back to speak Shadese to *kriss'ix* Lukras, who rode his *kolvorvik* forward to pace with Mykel for a moment before falling back to ride beside the soldiers, repeating Mykel's orders. Apollo did not catch all of it, but he understood that Mykel did not want to frighten the villagers, so half of the soldiers they brought with them would come inside the village while the other half waited on the road with the wagons, just in case. The two groups split easily, and Mykel and Apollo continued toward Epine, riding through the two posts on either side of the forked road that led between the homes.

The villagers stopped what they were doing, looking at them fearfully. A woman grabbed her child, rushing inside a building and slamming the door, while a man glared at them, pausing to sweep the street. *Even the children had stopped playing*, Apollo noticed, and he glanced behind him to see *Sri'balvash* Desira and the soldiers riding closer to him and Mykel. Seeing people look at him with fear and anger unnerved him, and he fought not to squirm in the saddle.

An older man exited a building, stopping in the middle of the road and facing them, leaning on a walking stick. A younger male stepped beside him, gripping a pitchfork as he watched them with suspicious eyes. Apollo looked around worriedly as the bannermen stopped riding, but Mykel rode forward to be in front, finally stopping his *kolvorvik* before the older male. Apollo's mount stopped walking beside the bannermen, and *Sri'balvash* Desira's horse stepped beside his, her hand in a fist before releasing it, and Apollo felt his horse give a slight shudder beneath him as it stamped its feet. *Did she stop my horse from moving forward?*

"I am Mykel *ik'Blagdon* of *Hasta'kan ik'Blag—* "

"We have already gathered your tributes and taxes, we ask you to take them and move on."

Apollo blinked.

Mykel dismounted, standing beside his *kolvorvik* with a sure grip on the reins, staying back enough that the creature could not bite him without turning his head. Even though the Shadon rode and trained with them, they always treated *kelvorvik* as dangerous, never walking in front of them. "You must be Elder Arami."

The older man flinched as if Mykel had said something completely different. Apollo looked around, seeing most of the street empty of people now, many having fled into the safety of their homes. He glimpsed a few faces looking at them from behind curtains, moving them only enough to peek through at them. *Was this how the people of Andears looked to the soldiers who had come every year?*

"I am not here to harm you and yours, Elder Arami. As you can see from your banners flying throughout your village, I am not of *Hasta'kan ik'Remfield*. I am not your old Leigelord's Lordson."

"We don't care," a voice snapped, and Apollo looked around for the source but could not see who was speaking, "Shadon are all the same. You're cruel and always say you aren't like the others, but in the end, you do exactly what you've always done."

"Please, come forth if you wish to converse; I am interested in what you wish to say." Apollo knew Mykel or any other Shadon with them could pull the person to them with shadows, but the fact that they weren't showed how different he was from *Hasta'kan ik'Remhold*. *How do the people not see that? It's obvious to me.*

There was no answer, but Apollo kept looking around anyway,

scanning the rooftops of the buildings, fearing an archer may be ready with a bow, Mykel in their sights. The thought of Mykel falling to the ground with an arrow in his throat made his stomach clench, and he fought not to touch his sword's pommel.

"Please, just leave us in peace," Elder Amari said quietly, "we do not wish for any trouble." He gestured to a small cart, where barrels with fish painted on them sat, covers on them to protect the contents from the elements, alongside what looked like handmade blankets and goods.

Mykel held out the reins to his mount, and a Shadon soldier rode forward to hold them, staying on his mount as Mykel walked to the cart and used his dagger to loosen the cover to a barrel. Apollo could see it was filled with what looked like dried fish, and he blinked in surprise. Mykel opened another, stepping back as water splashed him, full of liquid with shapes swimming within. "There are live fish in here," Mykel looked at the Elder, slight surprise in his voice.

"Yes, Shadon. It is so you can have fresh fish, the biggest ones in the river, as has always been requested."

Apollo wasn't sure what Mykel was thinking, but he saw him shift his weight as if uncomfortable. "You may call me Lordson, *korrati*, or Lordson *ik'Blagdon*. Furthermore, keep the live fish in the river, let them spawn, and create more fish to not deprive your village of its resources. I will accept the dried fish and created goods as tribute." He walked to his *kolvorvik* and mounted, taking the reins from the soldier, who rode to stand beside the others.

"The blankets look beautiful," Apollo said, and Mykel glanced back at him. "please tell the creators we appreciate their hard work." Mykel looked at him for a long time silently before turning his attention back to the Elder.

"My *balutrae* is right; they are pleasing to the eye." Mykel turned his *kolvorvik* and rode out of the village, two soldiers attaching the cart to one of their horses to take to the wagon and unload the tributes. Apollo wondered if the villagers expected the cart back. Knowing Mykel, he'd return it if there was no use for it at Woodsong. *He is different from Lordson Kerrik, who would have taken the live fish, the cart, and whomever he wished as recruits. I wonder what life in Andears would have been like under Hasta'kan ik'Blagdon.* Apollo glanced back at Epine one last time to see a young boy staring them down, a wooden stick held tightly in his hand, reminding him of himself. As they made eye contact, Apollo wondered if the boy's angry eyes would haunt his dreams that night.

* * *

The faces of the past villages had been filled with differing emotions; some proud, some fearful, some angry. Apollo found himself looking over his shoulder for the angry boy from Epine, as if having expected the child to follow them and attack them in the night. *He may have been more of a mirror into my own life. Was I so reckless back then?*

Over the last two weeks, they'd visited four of the villages of the territory, collecting the taxes and tributes due in exchange for the protection of the Leigelord and his soldiers. Each time, Mykel took less than was organized for the soldiers, allowing the villagers to keep what was needed to ensure they would thrive. Apollo had spent the week teaching Mykel how to better communicate with the villagers. They did not have the education of the *ro'*Shadon, and the term *Hon-Hasta'kan ik'Blagdon* did not hold the same importance; they understood the term *Leigelord* better. He also helped Mykel understand that complimenting their hard work and their tributes helped the villagers feel appreciated and valued.

"You are correct; an appreciated and happy people revolt less against their Leigelord," Mykel had relented, leaving Apollo unsure how to answer as Mykel took out a map and began presenting their route for the next morning. With Andears gone, the only two villages left to visit were Silene and Thraesh, but as Thraesh was closer to Woodsong, they headed to the former first.

Apollo had not slept well since they were so close to Silene, for his nerves kept him up, and Mykel noticed when Apollo stumbled out of his tent in the early morning hour. "You look troubled, my *balutrae*, are you still worried about your brother? You will find him soon enough."

"I don't know how he will react when he sees me riding with *Hasta'kan ik'Blagdon*'s emblem on me," Apollo answered, motioning to his *balutrae* medallion on his belt, "or the fact that I will be among Dark Army soldiers. After all, it was they who burned Andears to the ground."

"You avenged them with the guilty party's deaths," Mykel reminded him. Apollo tried not to flinch. The last thing he needed was people thinking he was weaker than they'd thought of him already.

"I wish it could have been done differently."

"My *Brak'ha* wishes his sons and first wife alive, my sister wishes *ro'Shadon* treated her as one of their own, and I am sure your brother wishes you had never left his side," Mykel answered flatly, ignoring Apollo's glare. "We cannot go back and change the past, merely the present and future by our actions. Once singed, the tree will always remember the flames and carry the scars, but it will continue to grow if taken care of. Much like Andears' Aldarwood, is it not?" Mykel gestured to his pauldrons, with their relief of the tree on either side. Apollo couldn't find an argument for the conversation and ate his breakfast quietly, though it did not soothe the knots in his stomach.

The sun had risen to the highest point in the sky when Apollo could finally glimpse the village nestled between farmland fields and new tree growth. The smell of sawdust and bread was welcoming, and he caught himself smiling despite himself. *I will finally see Clep, and he will forgive me for leaving him so long. I can bring him back to Woodsong to live among the civilians there if he wishes; he could make healing salves and never have to worry about his safety again, especially now that I am much better at sword fighting.* The thought lightened his heart so much that he hardly felt any discomfort as they rode the rest of the way and dismounted as soon as he could, tying his horse's reins to the pole outside the stables. He quickly ran toward the inn, forgetting that he was in armor, forgetting he should have waited for his *korrati* to enter first, his thoughts only on seeing his brother again.

The tavern inside looked exactly how Apollo remembered it, and he could not contain his excitement as he quickly tied his mount's reins and hurried across the stone road to the wooden building, muttering his apology as he dodged a woman who carried a basket of goods. The innkeeper's wife looked up as he burst in excitedly, her face trying for a neutral position, but her eyes held worry as she called for her husband. The innkeeper came from a room behind the counter, one hand holding a rag in one hand, still dripping with a bit of water, his face worried, the other on the dagger he wore on his belt. Once he saw Apollo's armor, he immediately took his hand from the weapon. "How may we help you?"

"I'm looking for my brother. Is he here?" The couple looked at each other, confused, and Apollo realized they did not recognize him. "I came here from Andears after it was burned down. I'm Apollo; my brother is Clep. You'd given us rooms upstairs."

Apollo heard the sound of the door opening behind him and glanced over his shoulder to see Mykel and *Sri'balvash* Desira walk inside, looking around. Mykel stepped forward, announcing himself. "I am *Korrati* Mykel, Lordson *ik'Hasta'kan ik'Blagdon*," he said. "We are here for our bi-yearly taxes and tribute collection and to see Apollo's brother. We are not here to harm nor take anything which is not ours to collect already." Apollo was close enough to see the slight look from *Sri'balvash* Desira before she turned, looking at the room around them.

Nonetheless, Apollo saw the two humans relax at his words. The innkeeper's wife immediately poured three drinks and set them on the counter for them, along with a loaf of fresh bread in a basket. "Our apologies, Lordson, we are still learning to trust the Dark Army, especially after..." the woman gestured toward Apollo, unsure how to finish her sentence, at a loss for words.

"It will take a great deal of effort on either side to mend the trust broken between our people, but if you could answer our inquiries of Apollo's brother, it would do much to start in that direction."

"I don't know what to tell you, lad, but your brother is gone."

"I don't understand; what do you mean, he's gone?" Apollo walked to the bar, eyes fixated on the man who, so long ago, gave them a place to stay when they had nowhere else to go. His heart pounded so hard he thought it would break out of his leather armor.

He must have been paler than he thought because the wife spoke up quickly. "He's alive, as far as we know. Please, we did not mean for you to think that he had passed away. We mean, he is no longer here; he left Silene."

"Where did he go?"

"He didn't say," the innkeeper replied, washing a stein with a rag, looking it over to ensure he hadn't missed a spot.

"*Sae-nyr*," *Sri'balvash* Desira spoke up, eyeing a painting on the wall. Apollo knew better than the question her, for all the *belvash* he'd met so far were far too insightful for his taste, but at times, it was helpful.

Before Apollo could speak, Mykel stepped forward, his hand resting on his sword's pommel. "What reason do you have to lie to Apollo about his brother? What makes you choose to deceive my *balutrae*?"

The innkeeper looked at him, confusion in his face. "I don't know what that is." Apollo wasn't used to someone not knowing what a *balutrae* was, for it seemed everyone at Woodsong knew the term and what it meant. *Maybe it isn't as common knowledge as I had thought.*

"It means if you deceive him, you deceive me, the only lordson of your Leigelord Wilihem Blagdon, so choose your next words carefully, sir."

Apollo blinked at Mykel, not expecting him to defend him so fiercely. He turned to the *korrati*, trying to defuse the situation before it got out of hand. He saw first-hand what could transpire when miscommunications took place. "It's okay. We don't need to scare him so badly that he won't tell us."

The innkeeper's wife spoke up, setting plates on the counter for the bread as if offering to soothe the insulted parties with the food. "We feared that the soldiers would come and burn Silene the same way we were told Andears had burned, so a small group of villagers felt it safer to leave, and Clep went with them."

Mykel seemed not impressed with this answer, but the innkeeper spoke up before the *korrati* could speak his mind. "After Apollo had gone missing during the night, Clep was beside himself for days, trying to find him. Talks of fleeing the territory began again, and this time, a group decided to leave, and Clep went with them." Apollo flinched hard. *I'd never stopped to think how Clep would have felt, waking up and finding me gone. I had been so focused on avenging Andears' destruction that I didn't give him a second thought. I'm such a fool.*

Mykel glanced at the *Sri'balvash*, who nodded once, and he looked back to the innkeepers. "Where were they heading?"

"Exonesis Mountain," Apollo spoke up, vaguely remembering the conversations while he was planning to head north to find the Dark Army in his thoughts of revenge, "but I thought that they were frustrated, just saying they were going to travel, not that they'd do it." He looked at Mykel. "Villagers sometimes talked about traveling from Andears, but no one did it because our homes and families were there; why would we ever really leave them?"

"Please do not punish them for leaving, my Lordson; they were fearful of your army's wrath," the innkeeper's wife spoke up softly, her fearful eyes flicking between them.

Mykel took a long moment to speak frustrated Shadese, too fast for Apollo to follow, though he did catch a few words, including the name of the previous *korrati* Lordson Kerrik-*kyr* Remhold, and the word *krushku*. Mykel breathed out and looked at the innkeepers, who looked more fearful at the unknown words. "I will forgive your ignorance this one time, but your current Leigelord, is not the former Leigelord Remhold. I am not *Korrati* Kerrik-*kyr* Remhold. We are of *Hasta'kan ik'Blagdon*, not lesser Shadon. You would do wise to never compare us to them again." He turned and walked out, *Sri'balvash* Desira following quickly, leaving Apollo and the innkeepers glancing at each other in surprise.

***

Apollo sat on a bench outside the inn, watching the soldiers and villagers walk the stone streets of Silene, talking peacefully, children playing and running around, laughing. *The village hasn't changed much since I'd left with only a sword, a mare, and a bag of vials.* He could only imagine how scared and worried Clep had been, waking up to find him gone. *Honestly, leaving was probably the best decision ever because I gained so much more than I ever would have. I've learned how to fight and defend myself, more about the world around me, and better communicate with others through speaking and writing in two languages. I could bring Clep back to Woodsong, and he could also learn; who knows what the belvash could teach him about healing.* He headed to the blacksmith, where Mykel was inspecting a dagger while talking to the blacksmith, a man Apollo didn't recognize. *Perhaps the original blacksmith had left with Clep as well,* Apollo thought, frowning. Glancing around, it was impossible to tell how many people or who had left toward Exonesis Mountain.

"I have to find Clep," he said, walking up to Mykel, "I'm all he has left."

Mykel didn't take his eyes off the dagger as he turned it this way and that in his hand, examining it closely. "Yet, you left him."

"What? This wasn't my fault."

"Is it not? You left him, Apollo, alone and afraid. He'd lost everything: his home, friends, village, parents, everything except you, and you abandoned him."

"Take that back," Apollo demanded, stepping closer to Mykel, hands curling into fists. Out of the corner of his eye, *Sri'balvash* Desira put a hand on her sword, and further behind her, *Kriss'ix* Lukras was walking in their direction as if sensing the growing tension.

"Why should I? It is the truth. When have I ever lied to you, my *balutrae*?" He turned, the dagger still loose in his hand, looking Apollo in the eyes. "You are angry more at yourself than anyone else, and I am a convenient target. You are not a child ruled by his emotions anymore. Feel the anger; harness it, let it go, and do it quickly." He demanded, eyes never left Apollo's. "Or is our *scrivik* to take place now? You will never find your brother if you are dead." His tone wasn't threatening, never raised more than a speaking level, but was flat, as if Mykel were commenting about the dagger in his hand. The *sri'balvash* behind him watched quietly, and the poor blacksmith looked afraid of what was about to happen.

Mykel's seemingly not caring about the conversation irked Apollo, but not enough to push for the duel between them, so he closed his eyes and removed his hand from the pommel of his sword, not realizing that he'd gripped it in his anger. "You are correct."

"Good. When we return to Woodsong, we will prepare." Mykel then returned to the blacksmith and began speaking with him again as if nothing had happened.

RATSBAYNE

He awoke to the sun shining through the window, and birds chirping happily outside. His room looked the same as he'd left it the previous night, and he walked to the mirror to ensure that his hair was brushed back. Sir Roddrick always hated it when his hair got in his face, saying it was distracting in combat and could cost him at the wrong moment.

His armor gleamed silver and blue with golden accents along the rivets, the tunic a dark blue. He headed down the hall and outside to the stables, greeting armored soldiers as they passed. A tall man in full armor stood petting his mount, a halberd leaning against the fence beside him.

"Good morning, Sir Roddrick," he said, looking at the man whose bushy beard twitched slightly as he smiled. "Ya be ready fer some sparring today? Brenhaul's lookin' fer some o' yer blood on her blade," he said, laughing.

"Yes Sir, Ah am!"

The man set a hand on his shoulder, looking down at him fondly." Good lad, get Slipstream, and we'll get started."

Tapping on his foot made Ratsbayne open his eyes, blinking. *Where am Ah?* He sat up, looking around the room, in a slight panic, seeing someone at the end of the bed looking at him. It took him a moment to realize it was Gideon. "Leigelord Blagdon awaits you in the manor; he says the cotton or linen clothing will suffice." Gideon then turned and walked off without waiting for a reply. *Ah'm not sure if that* be practical or rude.

The grounds be much more extensive in the daylight, Ratsbayne decided almost immediately as he stepped outside. There were trees in some of the pastures and between some of the buildings in the central area of Stormland, but most of them were in an orchard off to the side, filled with the smell of apple trees. *They are probably fer the horses.* The orchard, Ratsbayne noticed as he walked toward the main building, which was undoubtedly the manor of Stormhold, was full of trees larger than any apple trees he'd seen in the village of Thraesh or even Woodsong. "Ah wonder what they feed 'em."

"We use the bodies of those men who disobey or disappoint," Blagdon's voice came from behind him. "Legend has it that the first *Kolotor'ix*'s mother was one of the greatest herbalists in Nar'Shada and could make the plants grow in the harshest ash soil. She shared the secrets of creating rich fertilizer from the bodies of our foes." *Ah dun't know if he be joking or not and Ah think Ah be too afraid to ask.* "I assume you had a good rest."

"Ah did, thank ya."

"You will address me as Leigelord Blagdon, *Hasta'kan'ix*, *Hasta'kan'ix ik'Blagdon*, *Hon-Hasta'kan ik'Blagdon*, or simply Sir. I have endured much to obtain such titles and deserve the respect afforded me."

"Ah. then thank ya, sir."

"*Ro'*Shadon do not have use for 'thank you' so you will not hear me nor other Shadon say it." He began walking toward the manor, not looking back, as if expecting Ratsbayne to follow, which he did.

"Ya kind dun't have a lot of words like Common, ya get right to the point, it seems."

"We have our share of words, but I do not see the need to waste them. The conversation is like dueling, best done quickly and to the point. If you want someone to be poetic, speak to Lady Blagdon." He walked up the manor's steps, nodding to those who saluted or greeted him as they passed. *The estate be not quite Ah had expected, smaller and not as grand like Ah'd expected for a Leigelord.* Blagdon had stopped walking, looking at Ratsbayne. "What is it?"

"Ah expected..." he began, but wasn't sure how to finish the sentence. He'd seen the Shadon fight and didn't want to insult him.

"More? A castle, perhaps?" Blagdon finished for him. "Stormhold was a garrison for soldiers to live and train with their mounts. It's located outside the capital city, far enough away to ensure fewer distractions for those within the walls. Stormhold has the most land of any of the *Hasta'kan*'s keeps but has the smallest manor, but I find it fitting, for I am usually not inside it as it is." He began walking, forcing Ratsbayne to hurry up the stairs to keep up.

"Soldiers, ya said," Ratsbayne said, thinking about their previous conversation as they walked into the manor. He blinked dumbly, forgetting what he was saying, seeing the polished stone floors and walls. Along the foyer were alcoves with statues of soldiers and portraits of different animals between them. *Funny, none o' them seem to be man-eating horses with red eyes, but griffins, leonixes, pegasi, and windrunners.* He walked from piece to piece slowly, looking up at the armored men and women's likenesses captured in stone, seeing no two were alike, just like no two animal portraits were alike. *Elves, dwarves, humans, there are only a half dozen here, but how many more throughout the manor?*

"The statues here are those who were the founders of the groups of soldiers here," Blagdon spoke softly, "responsible for bringing different races to cooperate with one goal: to care and protect the people. It is they who had Stormhold and the Stormlands built."

"The Stormlands?" Ratsbayne looked at him.

"The training grounds, so named due to the sounds of combat training. At night in the capitol, it can be similar to the sounds of distant thunder, depending on the wind." He walked down the hall and into the central part of the manor, which opened to a large room with multiple wing entrances and a grand staircase. The ceiling was painted with a scene of a sunny sky above with animals and riders flying overhead, and the staircase's railing ended with wooden horses in rearing positions. The piece that dominated the room, however, was the stained glass window on the opposite side of the room over the staircase, with the sun shining behind a griffin flying over hills, with writing around the oval edges. "Strength o' the storm, heart o' the griffin," Ratsbayne read aloud, his voice a touch distant in awe of the beauty around him. He absently touched the amulet under his tunic.

Blagdon watched him take the room in quietly, hands behind his back. "Welcome to Stormhold, the home and training grounds of the Stormriders."

* * *

Ratsbayne was given the tour of the manor and left to his own devices to explore it on his own, except the west wing, which was Blagdon's residence, which he expressly forbade him from entering. *A bit excessive*, Ratsbayne thought as he saw guards at the doors, but then again, a few months ago, he would have tried to get into the forbidden areas to spite the Leigelord. *Ah'd like to think that Ah be grown and know better now than to cheat certain death.*

Most interesting to him was on the third floor, directly above the foyer, the largest area of the manor. It was an expansive study, with the east wing attached to it being dedicated to shelves of books that reached from floor to ceiling amongst various display cases. While exploring on his own, Ratsbayne had found himself inside the room and hours later, still looking at the numerous items, ranging from armor sets to weaponry. The main window looked out the front of the manor and could see over the wall, past fields, and in the distance, catch a glimpse of a city with a tower and palace that stood tall above its own walled boundary.

He'd been standing in front of it for so long that he didn't hear someone enter behind him until the sound of a tray on a table startled him. "Beautiful, isn't it," Blagdon remarked, going to the window to stand behind him, "That is Meridiah City, home of the *Kolotor'ix* and the

Southern Blood Temple, where *belvash* are given assignments and heal those who seek their aid. Not many from south of Woodsong has ever lain eyes upon the city." Something about the black and red banners hanging along the off-white palace walls seemed wrong to Ratsbayne, who finally had to look away from the window. Blagdon gestured to the tray of cooked meat, potato, and cooked greens on the long table that dominated the room. "You have not eaten, so I brought you food at my wife's behest. She knows I have gotten lost here on more than one occasion."

"The number of scrolls and tomes ya have be incredible," Ratsbayne had to admit, "Where did ya get them?"

"Many of them were already here when I acquired Stormhold, but some of them I have written myself while attempting to learn what I could about the Stormriders. As I have said, I have been trying to replicate what they have done with their mounts for decades. The legends of their bonds with their animals are quite fascinating to read; riders who can know their mounts so well that they act as one, and in many cases, the rider would gain abilities such as eagle-vision or growing gryffin-claws, which is usually used while in combat. One such story tells of a human named Alcion, a Stormrider who gained wings similar to his pegasus Naphiria. Could you imagine what a rider with a bond to a *kolvorvik* would gain?"

Probably a more prominent taste fer meat, Ratsbayne thought but kept quiet as Blagdon continued. "Unfortunately, many Stormriders either refused to give their secrets up or perished in the Scourge War, which led to many acquisitions to my collection." He gestured to the collection of weaponry along one shelf, housed in a glass case with blue silk behind it, which made the metals stand out even more. A few sets of armor stood on stands, each holding light blue and silver motifs along the tunics or cloaks, some with embroidered moons or leaping stags. Each piece had been cleaned and polished, and Ratsbayne wondered if they'd also been sharpened.

"Did you kill any of them?"

"Those who challenged me to duels lost, but I gave them the rare chance to yield. I imprisoned those who did until they were ready to cooperate for their mounts and knowledge. Even with their cooperation, I still have yet to be able to replicate their relationship with their mounts. I beat those who did not yield into submission when I could."

"And those ya couldn't?"

Blagdon did not answer, instead going to a pedestal and gesturing to the thick book. "This is one of the rarest books of my collection, a record of every Stormrider who has come to pass. It was inherited with the manor. The last entries are from the Byronian Kingdom before the *Kolotor'ix* came into power in Meridiah. After you eat, feel free to look through it, but I ask you to be careful with it; it is one of a kind. Since you do not remember your name, you could create your name from the ones here to aid you in creating your new life."

"Mah new life? What do ya mean?"

"You are no longer the drunkard Ratsbayne; the name ill-suits you. You will not be a stablemaster, either, but you will be trained as a knight, a Stormrider."

"But Ah not be--" he started, but Blagdon interrupted him.

"You felt the grey mare give birth, you hear a voice in your head that it is hers. You've been drawn to her since you've seen her. You two have a connection, and I will not waste this opportunity to have the first Stormrider under my *Hasta'kan*." He walked toward the door. "Use these examples to create a new name and embrace your new life." He closed the door behind him, leaving Ratsbayne blinking.

***

After he ate, Ratsbayne went to the large book and began flipping through it aimlessly, muttering to himself. *Pick a new name. How am Ah to do that when there are hundreds of names to choose from?* The book had a page for each Stormrider, with their name, weapon, mount, and achievements. Some of the entries turned out to be interesting to read, while others made him laugh.

Sir Alistar Bargrove

Human Stomrider, born in the Hroxian Era, under King Harold Hroxia of Eta.

    Ratsbayne wrinkled his nose as he turned the page. "Ah dun't think there is a place named Eta that exists."

Mount: pegasus named Ebony, with black wings and a grey mane and tail.

Weapon: longsword known as Silviax.

Most noted for the Battle of Redstrom Bay, where five hundred Hroxian men stormed the beaches to rescue Princess Maddie Hroxian from the Ny'fer Elven Clan. Convinced the leaders of both armies to stand down and deliver the princess safely back to her palace.

Died at the age of 140 from a fall from his mount during a thunderstorm. It was discovered his amulet's chain had broken and was found on the ground beside him. The Bargrove Woods outside of Eta is named in his honor.

    Hmm. Well, Ah ain't good with words, so rescuing people with diplomacy be not what Ah be good at. He turned the page to see a portrait drawing of the man, who looked slightly uncomfortable. *Ah would be too, if Ah had a stick up my backside.*

"Stormrider mounts and riders work together to aid each other where the other one is weaker," the voice said in his head.

Ratsbayne ignored it and flipped the pages aimlessly, landing on another random entry.

Sir Roddrick Pallum

Stormrider Makir Dwarf, born of the Byronian Era, under King Byron and Queen Mari'anath of Meridiah.

Mount: Gryffin named Blacktalon.

Weapon: halberd named Brenhaul." *That sounds familiar.*

Most noted for training recruits to the Stormriders at Stormhold in his later years and creating their weapons with the aid of other Makir Dwarves.

Died at the age of 137 after defending Princess Alar'ina, eldest daughter of King Byron and Queen Mari'anath, from a coup.

Ah'm beginning to think that Stormriders dun't have happy endings often, Ratsbayne thought as he turned the page. A full-page drawing of a man in armor and a bushy beard looked back at him, laughter in his eyes as if he'd heard a joke while the portrait was being drawn. The facing page held a drawing of his mount and a sketch of his halberd. *Ah've seen that weapon before in the display case and in mah dream.*

He turned the pages, reading names absently, before finding an interesting name. "Ah, here we go."

Sir Siral Karog

Stormrider human, born of the Byronian Era, under King Byron and Queen Mari'anath of Meridiah.

Mount: windrunner named Slipstream.

Weapon: longsword named Brightstar." *Eh, decent as far as names went, but the weapon name definitely could use improvement.*

Most noted for acting as Queensguard for Queen Mari'anath and the Princesses Alar'ina, Ker'risa, and Sar'iah. Presumed to have died during the coup.

Well, that be depressing, he thought as he went to close the book, *Ah'm not sure Ah want to have a name by some poor sap who died horribly.* A chittering made him look up in time to see a squirrel sitting on the table, eating the last of his bread on the plate.

"Oh no, ye dun't!" Ratsbayne scrambled up from his chair, chasing the squirrel, which led him in all around the room before slipping out the door and down the hall. "Ye damned squirrel, Ah'll get ye yet!" Swearing, Ratsbayne walked back into the study and back to the book, going to close it and focus on eating his lunch. *Ah'm no closer to finding a good name than Ah was when Ah started reading it.* He reached for the book and froze. Staring back at him from the page was a portrait of himself.

BLAGDON

He stood outside near the *kelvorkav* pasture, watching them race across the grass, nipping and snorting at each other, when he heard Ratsbayne shouting his name angrily. Looking through the shadows, he saw the man storming out from the keep, eyes blazing. Stablehands immediately began heading inside their stables for a safe place to watch. Blagdon reached up and calmly undid the fastening on his cloak, removing it and setting it onto the fence before him, his leather jerkin covering his tunic.

"Oi! Blagdon! What the hells are ya playing at?"

Blagdon could almost hear the collective gasp of those watching, and the *kelvorvik* and *kelvorkav* looked up from where they walked around their paddocks, ears forward and red eyes fixated upon them. Ruin snorted, stamping as he walked toward the fence, and Blagdon patted his neck. Blagdon had not yet turned to see the angry male, instead speaking to no one in particular, his voice never raising or changing in tone. "Get him a sword." *He will learn respect one way or another, even if I have to beat it into him.*

There was movement as the nearest soldier stepped forward, but Gideon pushed past him, taking off his sword and offering it to Ratsbayne hilt-first, giving the man serious eye contact. When Ratsbayne took it, Gideon backed off but remained closer than the other soldiers. *Of course, he would stay close enough to defend me, even unarmed. He would face an entire legion of ro'Shadon if they stood between me and he.*

Blagdon finally turned, one wrist holding the other in front of his belt, passively watching Ratsbayne gripping the borrowed sword, glaring at him. "Do you have something on your mind that you wish to discuss, Ratsbayne?"

"What did ya do? What the hells did ya were doing, putting some drawing of meh in that book, as if it were meh, some Stormrider! Ah won't play yer games!"

Blagdon spoke quietly in Common to not spook Ratsbayne further, shadows carrying his voice so he did not need to raise his tone. "No one else is to interfere." He saw Gideon react to the order, but the man nodded and stepped back.

"Take out yer sword, sir," Ratsbayne demanded through gritted teeth, coming closer.

"No."

Ratsbayne stepped in front of him, sword pointing at Blagdon's throat, the blade shaking but not piercing flesh. The anger and confusion on his face were raw, authentic, and a tear slipped down Ratsbayne's cheek as he seemed to fight with himself, his sword arm trembling as the blade barely kissed the Shadon's bare throat. "Take out yer damned sword, Leigelord, and fight meh!"

Blagdon kept his eyes on the furious younger man. "I will not."

Ratsbayne's face contorted with emotion, a second hand going to the sword's hilt to aid it in shoving it through the front of Blagdon's neck and out the other side. Gideon started toward Ratsbayne, and as soon as Blagdon's eyes flicked to Gideon, the man stopped and took a step back.

Blagdon had to speak carefully not to be cut by the blade. "You won't strike me down, and you won't harm me. Your sense of honor, your sense of purpose, and your training as a Stormrider will not allow you to harm an unarmed man, no matter your emotional state. You know that image in the book is you, and you are at a loss for answers. We can solve this mystery together, Ratsbayne, we can--"

"THATS NOT MAH NAME!" Ratsbayne shouted, cringing at his tone, and he lowered his voice as if fearing it alone would shove the blade through the other man's flesh. "That not be mah name, is it?"

Movement caught Blagdon's eye as the grey mare lept over the paddock's fence and slowly approached them from the side as if not to spook the armed man. She slowly placed her muzzle against Ratsbayne's arm, breathing out gently. After a long moment, Ratsbayne lowered the sword, letting it fall to the ground before collapsing to his knees, his face looking at the dirt, breathing heavily.

Gideon rushed forward to retrieve the sword, but Blagdon held up a hand to stop him, instead looking down at the man before him. "The flashes of memories, the nightmares that never made sense, they've never spoken to you in a way you'd understand. You've buried it so deeply that you've denied everything about yourself, and now you are breaking through the surface for the first time. Do not balk from this moment; do not shirk from it. This will make or break you, and you will not allow it to break you!" His voice finally warmed with threads of anger. "Stand up and face this! Get up, Ratsbayne!"

"That is not--" the man started to say, but Blagdon would not let him finish his sentence.

"Then get up and tell me who you are! Don't just sit in the dirt and pout like a child! WHO ARE YOU?"

The man angrily shoved himself up, holding his amulet tightly in his shaking fist. "I am Sir Siral Karog, Stormrider human, loyal to King Byron and Queen Mari'anath, rider to the windrunner Slipstream, weilder of Brightstar." *His eyes are clearer than I'd ever seen, and his voice is finally full of conviction.*

The grey mare whinnied, and Blagdon felt the tingles of magick in the air as a faint smoke flowed from the Stormrider amulet to the creature. The grey in her mane and coat faded, turning lighter in color until her coat was white and gleamed with bluish highlights, her mane a mixture of whites, greys, and blues. Her eyes were now the color of Meridian skies, and she snorted, nodding her head rapidly, tail swishing in excitement. *A windrunner in disguise has given birth to a kolvorvik- windrunner colt. This is a most pleasing situation indeed. However, there is now the problem of a man claiming loyalty to a royal family that died over a hundred and fifty years ago.*

The Stormrider seemed less enthused. "Well, Ah'll be damned."

End of Book 1

Printed in the USA
CPSIA information can be obtained
at www.ICGtesting.com
CBHW030858210424
7119CB00010B/184